THE ISLAND OF HAWAI'I

Hāwī

Pololū

Honoka'a

KOHALA

Kawaihae
Hāpuna
Puakō
MAUNA LANI

WAIPI'O
VALLEY

Waimea

Waikoloa
Village

HĀMĀKUA

MAUNA
KEA

N

HUALĀLAI

Kailua-Kona
Airport

Hilo

HILO

Kailua

KONA

Kealakekua
Bay

MAUNA LOA

KĪLAUEA

PUNA

KA'Ū

Pacific Ocean

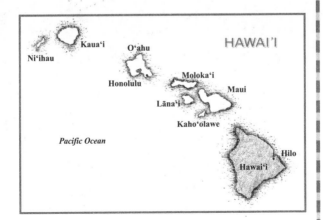

HAWAI'I

Kaua'i

O'ahu

Ni'ihau

Honolulu

Moloka'i

Maui

Lāna'i

Kaho'olawe

Pacific Ocean

Hilo

Hawai'i

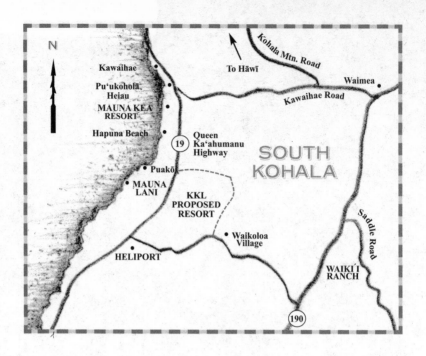

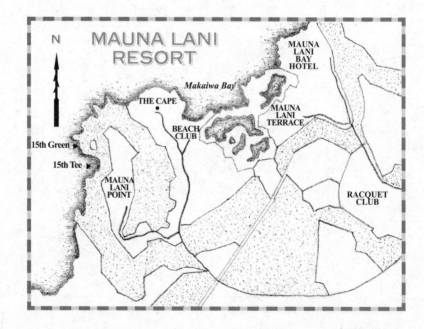

BONES
OF
HILO

BONES
OF
HILO
A NOVEL

Eric Redman

CROOKED
LANE

NEW YORK

Copyright © 2023 by Eric Redman

All rights reserved.

Published in the United States by Crooked Lane Books, an imprint of The Quick Brown Fox & Company LLC.

Crooked Lane Books and its logo are trademarks of The Quick Brown Fox & Company LLC.

Library of Congress Catalog-in-Publication data available upon request.

ISBN (trade paperback): 978-1-63910-214-3
ISBN (hardcover): 978-1-64385-702-2
ISBN (ebook): 978-1-64385-703-9

Cover design by Patrick Sullivan

Printed in the United States.

www.crookedlanebooks.com

Crooked Lane Books
34 West 27th St., 10th Floor
New York, NY 10001

Trade Paperback Edition: January 2023
First Edition: June 2021

10 9 8 7 6 5 4 3 2 1

For Heather, our children, and our
Big Island ʻohana,
including Carolyn, Kuʻulei, Haia, Grace, and Kawika
whose names—
but nothing else, other than a tattoo—
I've borrowed for this tale

Hawaiian Pronunciation

The few Hawaiian words that appear in this book should be understandable from the context. For pronunciation it helps to know that Hawaiian words end in vowels and are accented on the next to last syllable (except for certain compound or merged words). So *haole, heiau,* and *ihe* become "HOW-lay," "HAY-ow," and "EE-hay"—or nearly so. In Hawaiian, *e* is almost always pronounced "ay" as in *lay.*

Kawika, a Hawaiian transliteration of David, is pronounced "kuh-VEE-kuh." This reflects the foregoing rules, plus that *w* is pronounced "v" after *a* and that the 12-letter Hawaiian alphabet does not include *d*, for which *k* is substituted.

The ʻ*okina*, an inverted comma, is considered the 13th letter of the Hawaiian alphabet and signifies a glottal stop before a vowel (pronounced as in "uh-oh"). The *kahakō*, or macron, signifies that the vowel sound is prolonged rather than short.

Some characters in this book, and the author, use the term *Hawaiʻi* and other words with the ʻokina and kahakō. Others generally just say "Hawaii" without the glottal stop and pronounce other words without the ʻokina or kahakō. This is commonplace in Hawaiʻi—and nothing to feel embarrassed about.

Apart from these matters of pronunciation, little else in this book should be relied on as factually or historically accurate. This is a work of fiction, for which facts and history simply provide points of departure before imagination and invention take over.

PART ONE

SHARK CLIFF
AND SOUTH KOHALA
2002

The end of that wind,
The end of this wind,
Join and cause a whirlwind.
>   —Fragment of a chant from E. Smith, C. Handy,
>   K. P. Emory, E. H. Bryan, P. H. Buck, et al., *Ancient*
>   *Hawaiian Civilization* (1933)

1

Waipi'o and South Kohala

Detective Kawika Wong landed by boat and spent the day with Hilo Major Crimes picking body parts off the rocky beach and cliff face far below the Waipi'o Lookout. Kawika's boss, Captain Terry Tanaka, and Kawika's older colleague Detective Sammy Kā'ai seemed almost unperturbed, as if picking up body parts were somehow routine. But Kawika wasn't feeling well.

Maybe it was the sharks. Not just the thought of sharks—the imagined vision of them tearing the broken victims—but actually seeing the sharks, a whole school of them lolling sluggishly at the surface just outside the surf line, rousing themselves at the sound of the police boat like cats at the clink of a bowl. Kawika, repulsed, had struck at one with the body retrieval hook. Then they'd scattered.

Maybe it was the boat itself, unsettled on the sea, unsettling Kawika's stomach as he tried to watch the waves and the beach and the looming cliff face all at once, his eye not able to avoid—his eye in fact searching for—the bits of human flesh scattered here and there on waves and beach and cliff alike.

Or maybe it was imagining the fall, Kawika's sense of what it must be like to be thrown from a cliff, to plummet a thousand feet through darkness, accelerating, the wind tearing unheard screams from the throat—those tumbling last seconds, all too easily imported into Kawika's dreams.

Whatever it was, the next morning it woke Kawika before first light and sent him hurtling to the bathroom, uncertain at first whether to sit on the toilet or kneel before it. He stayed there a long time. Kawika lived alone. His girlfriend, Carolyn, hadn't joined him this night, so Kawika had no bedmate to disturb by bolting from bed. But neither had he a bedmate to calm him, to banish those sharks.

Later, as the sun rose and faced Hilo, Kawika sat with his cup of coffee and faced it back. He rubbed the night's poor sleep from his eyes and tried to settle himself. He often did this before work, especially these past few months, ever since the silent skies right after 9/11 had left every Islander with a sudden sense of Hawai'i's isolation and vulnerability.

When the phone rang, Kawika was shaving, leaning forward at the bathroom sink of his small rental house and thinking about those tiger sharks just outside the surf line, waiting at the foot of the cliff. He welcomed the interruption. Grabbing a towel, he wiped shaving cream from his face and picked up the phone.

"Pack your toothbrush," said Captain Tanaka. "You're headed to South Kohala. Woman found a dead guy at the Mauna Lani resort this morning. Someone killed him on a golf course with an old Hawaiian spear, ancient maybe. The division chief in Waimea asked for you by name. They want a 'real Hawaiian' to take the lead, he said, because of that old spear and some other evidence, cultural stuff. And someone from over here, objective, because of some local controversy there, something about Native Hawaiians and developers."

"A real Hawaiian?" Kawika replied. "That's a bit of a stretch, Terry. You know what happened in Seattle, that time the chief thought I was Chinese American. It's risky, picking people by their names."

"I know," Tanaka said, "but he wants you over there, and you're smart. You'll figure it out. So I gotta pull you off the Shark Cliff case."

"After one day, boss? I was just getting my stomach back."

Tanaka arranged the Major Crimes helicopter to fly Kawika to the scene. As the chopper rose over the saddle between Mauna Kea and Mauna Loa, the great volcanoes of the Big Island, and as the leafy rainforest and tree ferns gave way to the dry expanse of barren Kohala, Kawika thought, *It began as a simple homicide investigation—or so he imagined.* Kawika read murder mysteries. He always had. During a case he'd often wonder how a mystery writer might present it, how a fictional detective might approach it, what the book's first line might be.

He reached the Mauna Lani just after eight AM, landing on a fairway by the ocean. A Waimea cop lifted the yellow tape, and Kawika ducked under it. He crossed the lawn to an elevated oceanside tee box built of lava rock and resembling an ancient Hawaiian heiau, or temple. Kawika climbed the steps, then stopped. The victim—a middle-aged haole, or white person—well-dressed but barefoot, lay in a pool of bloody grass. Kawika saw the thin wooden stake protruding from the dead man's chest. A Hawaiian spear, all right.

Kawika could guess what someone intended him to see: an ancient human sacrifice.

"Any of you know him?" Kawika asked the Waimea cops. All four shook their heads. With a nod, he turned the crime scene back to them. Before squatting down to watch their work more closely, he flipped open his cell phone and called Tanaka.

Two hours later, evidence gathered and body removed, Kawika stood alone on the championship tee box. It provided a breathtaking view of the sea beyond the Kohala shoreline bound in black lava rock and beyond the vivid green of the golf course. Just below him, spray from the surf added saltiness to the pungent marine air. Play continued on the South Course, with a spare hole at the clubhouse placed into service. The fifteenth hole—the Mauna Lani's signature hole, an over-the-water par 3 featured in all the resort's advertising—remained off limits. Curious golfers, slowing their carts as they detoured around it, could see Kawika on the tee box, looking up and down the coast, then back at the resort, then out to sea.

Turning away from the view, Kawika saw a blonde woman observing him from the lawn outside her condo, separated from him by a gully of jagged lava rock. Probably the woman who'd reported the body. He waved and motioned to indicate he'd take the path to the condos. She answered his wave, then turned to walk inside. Kawika noticed bright sun on well-shaped calves.

A Waimea detective named Tommy, in plainclothes and wearing a University of Hawai'i cap, took Kawika to her door. A tile hung above the bell: "Hawaiian style—Please remove your shoes. Mahalo." Kawika slipped his off. Big and black, they dwarfed a pair of pink sandals set neatly by the mat.

"Patience Quinn," said Tommy. "Crazy name, yeah? She's from San Francisco."

A petite blonde answered the door, and instead of flashing a badge, Kawika handed her his card. "Kawika Wong," she pronounced, hesitantly but correctly.

"Good," he said, and smiled. "Hawaiian's tricky, even for me." He didn't want to mislead her, let her think him more Hawaiian than he really was. With Mainlanders, he knew, race could create discomfort and excessive caution.

Patience Quinn told a simple story. She'd awakened at six, brewed coffee, then taken a cup outdoors. She liked to watch the first rays of sun strike the summit of Haleakalā across the channel on Maui. In the early light she'd noticed an unfamiliar shape on the championship tee box about two hundred feet from her condo. She couldn't quite make it out. Then she'd seen it was a man—a man with something sticking out of him.

She led Kawika onto her lanai so he could stand where she'd stood, see what she'd seen, minus the body and the spear. He took in the scene, then motioned her back inside. A fragrance, faint and pleasant, trailed behind her.

Kawika asked routine questions. No, she hadn't seen anyone else. She hadn't heard any unusual noise, just the crash of breakers and the calls of doves and francolins. No, she wasn't a tourist; she considered herself a kama'aina, or resident. Her parents once owned the condo, but it was hers now; she visited several times a year for extended stays, by herself or with family. On this trip she'd arrived alone. She and her husband had recently separated. No children. She worked for *San Francisco* magazine. She wrote feature stories. She was here to do a possible article on Hawai'i's 9/11 victims, the ones who'd died on Flight 93.

Kawika glanced around the condo, out at the golf course, then back again at Patience Quinn. They were "all of a piece," his mother would say: elegant, well-kept. Patience appeared to be in her twenties still—like him. She couldn't have been married long.

Kawika's phone vibrated. He excused himself and stepped outside, walking back to where Patience Quinn had watched the sunrise touch Haleakalā.

"They ID'd the body," Tanaka told him. "Ralph Fortunato. Big-time real estate developer. Got a wife and kid up in Waimea. You're in charge, so better get up there, yeah?"

Kawika walked back inside. Patience Quinn looked inquisitive.

"The victim's named Ralph Fortunato," he said. "Heard of him?"

"Oh my God!" Her hand leapt to her mouth. She grabbed a chairback to steady herself, and her lightly tanned face became paler instantly. "Oh my God!" she repeated. "He's the one trying to build Kohala Kea Loa!"

Kawika observed her shock; it was real. "A new resort," she explained after a deep breath and a shake of her head. "A huge one. Across the highway, all the way up to Waikoloa Village. KKL, people call it. It's a giant controversy. Oh my God."

Kawika's cell phone vibrated again. "Wong," he answered curtly.

"Aloha, *Little* Wong," the caller said, chuckling. "It's *Big* Wong. You over here? You spend the night? Come for dinner? We talk story?"

Kawika sighed. "Yeah, Pops," he said. "All those things. Call you later." He snapped the phone shut and smiled with embarrassment.

"My dad," he explained. "Lives in Puakō. No one can do anything on the Big Island without him knowing it. Now I gotta go see him."

Patience Quinn smiled slightly, recovering herself. "Sounds like you *should* go see him," she offered. "Maybe he knows who did it."

Kawika noticed her teeth: very even, very white. They went with that lightly tanned and cared-for skin, the fineness of her clothes and facial features. He wasn't used to standing next to women like this one, especially haole women. He wished his plainclothes weren't quite so plain. He thought of Raymond Chandler's ill-dressed detective, Philip Marlowe, in *Farewell, My Lovely*: about as inconspicuous as a tarantula on a slice of angel food cake.

Departing, Kawika turned to look at her once more than necessary. Then he let Tommy the local cop drive him up to Waimea, past the broad lava fields, grown grassy now, where Kamehameha—Hawai'i's last great warrior king—had trained his armies. On the way, Tommy told him more about Ralph Fortunato and KKL, his controversial real estate development.

"You didn't recognize his body, though?" Kawika asked.

"Never seen 'im before," Tommy replied. "But you live here, you know the man, believe me. He's not popular."

Kawika looked away, up the slope of Kohala Mountain, the dormant volcano looming ahead of them, up to the dark green line of ironwood trees on the Kohala Mountain Road, the road to Hāwī. Tommy noticed.

"Heard you were born in Hāwī," Tommy said. "Like Kamehameha, yeah?"

Kawika merely nodded. He was concentrating on an inconvenient sensation: the god of desire, with the tip of his ancient spear, had nicked Kawika's heart.

2

Waimea

"**F**ucking Hawaiians."

The newly widowed Corazon Fortunato spoke contemptuously.

"*Fucking* Hawaiians," she repeated, this time with anger. Sitting across a koa wood coffee table from her, Kawika could guess she was a Filipina. Dark and smooth-skinned, ordinarily she might have seemed beautiful. Today she looked tear streaked and blotchy. A painting of a sunlit sandy beach fringed with palms hung behind her. On the adjacent wall hung color photos of a beaming Ralph Fortunato in head shots with individual suntanned golfers, presumably famous ones; even from a distance, Kawika recognized Tiger Woods.

"*Fucking Hawaiians.*" Kawika could guess what she meant: "*Native Hawaiians, people of Polynesian blood, killed my husband. They did it for a stupid Hawaiian reason. I hate them.*"

"You think Hawaiians did it?" he asked. "Which ones?"

"Those *temple* Hawaiians," she said. "The ones trying to block KKL. The ones who wanted *money.*" She looked ready to spit, right there in her own living room.

"Forgive me," Kawika said. "I'm from Hilo. I heard about Kohala Kea Loa for the first time this morning. I don't know the temple Hawaiians."

Corazon Fortunato sighed, composing herself. "Okay," she said, and began to explain. Kawika took notes: *Kohala Kea Loa—proposed new resort and real estate development. Big one. Thousands of acres. Stretches from Waikoloa Village down to Highway 19. All just a lava field today—vast open wasteland. Desolate, dry, remote. What's planned: a luxury hotel, two golf courses. Shops, health club, tennis courts. Housing, all types: estates, bungalows, townhouses, condos. Hundreds of millions of dollars of investment—more likely a billion. Thousands of jobs.*

"Ralph runs it," she said, not surrendering the present tense. "President of the company. Been working on it for three years, since 1999. Getting the permits, the funding, keeping it on schedule. Everything was going great until they found some ruin. Out in the middle of nowhere."

As she described it, the ruin was just a fallen-down pile of rocks. No one knew about it before. Lava rock on lava rock: not much contrast.

"Guys came from the University," she went on. "They said it was some human sacrifice thing. That's when the temple people got involved. They claim they're Native. They formed this group called HHH. Something-something-Hawai'i. They say the rocks were a temple. They say Kamehameha built it, trying to stop a lava flow."

According to his widow, Fortunato had done everything reasonably possible to accommodate HHH. He offered to pile the lava rocks back up, preserve the site, install interpretive signs, provide public access, handicapped parking—everything. But then, she said, HHH started to play rough.

"They said we couldn't build at all. They said because of the human sacrifice stuff, the entire site was sacred. We couldn't touch it. They said it was kapu."

HHH held protest rallies, she said, outside Fortunato's office at Waikoloa Village, blocking traffic. Shut down the shops, made people mad. Terrible publicity. "The investors, they're Japanese," she said. "They got worried. The politicians and unions got worried. Everyone told Ralph to solve the problem—just fix it."

She paused, glaring at Kawika. He thought, *She just realized I'm a Native Hawaiian.* She lowered her eyes, then continued. "HHH told Ralph, 'Meet us in private.' They wanted money. Of course. That's what they wanted all along, just money. They said, 'It's a temple, you have to make a sacrifice.' They said, 'We can explain it to the gods, we can make them happy.' They laughed about it."

"Did your husband pay?" Kawika asked.

"*Hell*, no," she replied. "It wasn't an official site. It wasn't protected. It was just a pile of rocks, and they didn't even care about it. They were using it for extortion. So Ralph went to the County and got a permit. Then he bulldozed the whole thing."

Kawika blinked. "Bulldozed it?" he repeated.

"Damn right," she snorted. "Told HHH to fuck themselves. He had their extortion thing recorded—had it on tape. He told them, 'Make a fuss, I'm giving it to the press.'"

"So," she concluded, exhaling with a long sigh, "that's why they killed him. Because of that damn pile of rocks."

Kawika felt uncertain what to say. He'd never interviewed a surviving spouse, and Corazon Fortunato's red-hot anger didn't make it easy. He wanted to speed through it, get it over with. He understood the importance of an investigation's first hours, the potential importance of the victim's wife. But he wanted to be out the door and chasing more likely suspects.

"Only a few more questions," he said finally. "Who's the leader of HHH?"

"Peter Pukui," she answered. "Supposedly, anyway. Lives in Kawaihae with his girlfriend, Melanie something. She's the leader as much as he is, I think."

"Do you have the tape?"

"No, Ralph probably kept it at the office."

"Your husband's movements yesterday?"

"Got up, went to work, met with the head of the Japanese investors, came home, went out after dinner. Had another meeting, didn't say where or who with. Never came back."

"The head of the Japanese investors?" Kawika asked.

"Mr. Shimazu," she replied.

"First name?"

"Makoto," she said. "But he does it old style: Shimazu Makoto."

"Mr. Shimazu lives here?"

"No, in Tokyo."

"You know where he's staying?"

"No, but probably at the Mauna Lani."

"Any business partner or close associate of your husband's here in Hawai'i?"

"Just Michael Cushing, his Chief Operating Officer, over at the company office in Waikoloa Village."

"Any enemies you know about?"

"HHH, I told you."

"No one else?"

"No. No one."

"Any—sorry to ask—girlfriend?"

"Jesus," she shouted. "Those Hawaiians did it. Just catch them. *Please.*"

A baby cried from another room. Corazon Fortunato stood up and moved angrily away, toward the child. She didn't look back.

Kawika let himself out. "Let's keep a guard here," he told Tommy. "And have your Waimea guys find this Peter Pukui, the one she said heads up HHH, and his girlfriend, Melanie, down in Kawaihae. See if they can find Makoto Shimazu too. Right away." Tommy nodded and pulled out his phone.

From the steps outside Fortunato's front door, flanked by bright pink bougainvillea, Kawika looked east and south, turning slowly to take in Mauna Kea, Mauna Loa, and Hualālai. Hualālai was partly veiled in volcanic haze, Kīlauea's "vog." But Kawika wasn't thinking about the Big Island's volcanoes. He was puzzling over Kohala Kea Loa, a planned Hawaiian luxury resort bearing three of their names: a resort with no beach.

3

Hilo

Captain Tanaka sat waiting outside the office of his boss, Haia Kalākalani, the Chief of Police for Hawai'i County. He knew the chief would question his having put Kawika in charge of the Fortunato murder case over in South Kohala, mostly because Kawika remained somewhat unproven after his recent short-lived career on the mainland

Kawika had joined the Seattle Police after graduating from college and the police academy. When armed robbers struck the gambling club of a Chinese tong, the Seattle police chief had assigned the rookie, Detective Wong, because she'd assumed he was Chinese American. Kawika solved the robbery, but not discreetly. Police responded with a "zero tolerance policy" on gambling, raided local clubs, and hustled away Chinese American leaders in handcuffs. The Chinese American community erupted—and blamed Kawika. Faced with a fiasco, the Department gulped, retreated, and blamed Kawika too.

The Seattle police chief said "Too bad," when she'd fired him. And Kawika had replied, "I'm Hawaiian. We're used to chiefs sacrificing us."

An impertinent thing to say, but Tanaka respected Kawika for it. Fortunately, Tanaka knew Kawika's father, Jarvis Wong—had met him at a fishing club. For years now, they'd shore-fished as a team, the diminutive Japanese American and the outsized Hawaiian, spending long nights together on beaches and rocks, catching small fish for live bait, then setting their lines for hundred-pound giant trevally, known in Hawai'i as ulua.

"My boy's a cop," Jarvis Wong told Tanaka one night on the beach. "Been on the mainland. Needs a job."

"Send him to me," Tanaka had replied.

That was how Kawika returned to the Big Island, the island of his birth, and took a job at Major Crimes in Hilo. Steamy Hilo: Hilo of the torrential rains, dark-in-a-downpour Hilo. Working-class Hilo: tired Hilo, run-down Hilo. Hilo, until recently Hawai'i's second largest city, but perhaps the city of least appeal to Mainlanders. Tanaka didn't expect Kawika to stay. Hilo was just a place to gain experience, to start over. Tanaka guessed Kawika would make it to Honolulu in a few years. After that, Chief Wong, Mayor Wong, Governor Wong—who could tell? *Iiko, iiko,* Tanaka often told him, a Japanese parent praising a child. The kid was dutiful, exceptionally pleasant, trained in the field and at Tanaka's knee, not just the academy. That would help him in this case. This case might help him in turn.

Kawika's weak point, Tanaka thought, was his distaste for loose ends. He considered every bit of evidence a clue or a deliberate red herring. In real life, Tanaka had told him, the pieces don't fit satisfyingly into a completed puzzle. Every case presents scores of facts and observations that simply elude understanding or explanation. The "strays," as Tanaka called them, just don't matter. What matters is justice, catching the guy who did it, wrapping up and moving on.

These lessons went hard with Kawika, Tanaka knew. A killer Kawika had chased into the Kā'u Forest Reserve, a well-known druggie, had been found unconscious and disarmed, his hands cuffed behind him around a young koa tree. Why? Kawika kept sifting and resifting evidence to answer that nagging question, that *why.* Tanaka understood. In police work, he told Kawika, the fact that something's true is more important than why it's true.

Why someone cuffed the guy to a tree didn't matter, Tanaka had told his young charge. "Maybe another dealer did it. Maybe a jealous husband. Maybe they wanted him to die. Maybe they just wanted you to catch him. Doesn't matter. He was a killer, and you caught him." *Iiko, iiko*: Good boy.

Chief Kalākalani broke Tanaka's reverie, opening his door and inviting Tanaka into his office. Tanaka stood, shook hands, and pulled his mind back to the present.

"You sure Kawika's right for this one?" the chief asked when they'd sat down, just as Tanaka had expected. The chief began chewing a malasada from a box Tanaka had brought for the occasion. "I know he's got balls, that deal down in Kā'u," the chief said. "And I understand why Waimea asked for him. But still."

Tanaka tried not to react defensively. "Well, he didn't just catch that guy in Kā'u, chase him into the forest; he solved the case on his own. Plus that other murder down in Puna, the wife killer. And anyway, I've got everyone else on Shark Cliff. Looks like there might be a meth war going on."

The Shark Cliff case had indeed swallowed up Tanaka's people. It had begun with an intrepid German tourist, a young woman who'd wanted a photograph looking straight down the cliff face at Waipiʻo. She'd secured a safety rope behind her and inched out until her telephoto lens pointed at the beach and breakers a thousand feet below. She saw activity in the surf line: big sharks. She watched through her long lens, realized what they were tearing—a human torso—and called 911. Arriving by boat, Tanaka's team had found the scattered parts of at least three corpses, maybe more. Only one could be identified, a known drug dealer. Evidently someone had been dropping local druggies off the cliff.

Shark Cliff would be tough to solve. The dead druggies provided few clues, and others wouldn't talk. Someone needed to bust some live ones, cuff them, push them toward the cliff edge, terrify them, get some answers. Tanaka had men and women suited to that work. Kawika wasn't one of them. Despite single-handedly catching two killers, the cuffed-to-the-tree guy down in Kāʻu and the wife murderer in Puna, Kawika seemed an innocent, still green and finding his footing, even a bit naive, not yet thirty.

Tanaka knew Kawika wasn't ready to menace a druggie at the top of Shark Cliff. He was still too squeamish and, more important, still too principled about law enforcement; basically a straight arrow. "Mister Clean" Tanaka called him—not entirely a compliment. But none of that necessarily meant Kawika couldn't handle this case. Especially with backing from the Waimea police.

"Yeah, Shark Cliff—I get it," said the portly chief, helping himself to another malasada. "Still, Kawika's not very experienced. And this case could blow up: a dead haole over there with the rich folks. You think he's learned? He stumbled pretty bad, back in Seattle."

"But not really his fault," Tanaka replied. "It was complicated. They thought he was Chinese American, sent him into Chinatown. Anyway, you know I've been training him myself? You've seen his fitness reports?"

"Yeah, I get that part too. Good training on the mainland. Lots of ambition and dedication—plus guts," the chief acknowledged. "Joe College like you and me, so he speaks well."

Tanaka smiled. "And he really likes being a detective. He just wants to solve crimes. It's always, 'Put me in, Coach, put me in!' He works all the time. Hardly goes surfing anymore. Plus he's got brains. Truly. Maybe that's most important. He learns fast."

The police chief chewed his malasada and, mouth full, nodded approvingly. "So you're not concerned? About Kawika and this case, I mean?" he asked when he'd swallowed.

"Of course I am," Tanaka conceded. "An old Hawaiian spear, the victim displayed on that fake heiau—fancy way to kill a guy. Someone sending a message, obviously. Not a very clear one. Maybe the physical evidence will be enough. But maybe Kawika will need to figure out the message."

"Well, Terry," the chief concluded, tearing another malasada in two and preparing to pop half in his mouth. "I trust your judgment. But this one's on you, okay?"

Tanaka understood. One risk was Kawika's rudimentary knowledge of Hawaiian history and culture. Despite having a Hawaiian father and first name, Kawika didn't speak the language, didn't know the songs or symbols. From age eight, when his parents divorced, he had grown up mostly in Seattle, just spending summers with his dad, Jarvis Wong, in Puakō. His mother was haole, his father a quarter Chinese and three-quarters Native Hawaiian at best. With his brownish hair and hazel eyes, Kawika could almost pass for a tourist with a good tan.

Ordinarily, Tanaka thought, *the Hawaiian part might not matter.* Tanaka himself was a third-generation Japanese American. He didn't speak Hawaiian and knew more about Japanese temples than Hawaiian ones, yet he could solve an ordinary Big Island murder. But this case just wasn't ordinary.

Fortunately, Tanaka knew, Kawika had Hawaiian assets, including his father, a lifelong Kohala resident. Jarvis Wong knew Kohala completely: every person, every lava rock, everything Hawaiian. Jarvis could provide a big boost to Kawika—and not for the first time.

Finally, Tanaka reminded himself, there was Kawika's other Hawaiian asset: his girlfriend, Carolyn Ka'aukai, a serious student of Hawaiian history and culture and a doctoral candidate at UH Hilo, even planning to write her PhD dissertation in Hawaiian. Carolyn spoke the language, knew the chants. A heiau, a human sacrifice, an old spear through the heart: Carolyn would help Kawika make sense of it.

4

Waimea

Dr. Terrence Smith strode toward Kawika in aloha scrubs: mint-colored hibiscus blossoms and philodendron leaves against a dark green background. He also wore a matching cap, a bushy red moustache, and a broad smile. Together, the scrubs and moustache gave him a jaunty Christmas color look.

"A-lo-*HA!*" he said, extending his hand. He smelled faintly of chemicals. "You're the great detective, right?"

Dr. Smith, a surgeon and general practitioner, also served as coroner-on-demand—an oddly jocular one on this occasion, Kawika thought. The Kohala Coast didn't possess a morgue and didn't really need one. But sometimes the North Hawai'i Community Hospital in Waimea was pressed into service.

"Got our friend in the other room," Smith said. "No write-up yet, of course. But I can show you what ails him."

Smith led Kawika to an operating room—the coldest room Kawika had ever entered in Hawai'i. A sheet covered the corpse. The doctor stripped it back, revealing Ralph Fortunato to the waist. His torso was neatly slit to the neck, the halves pried apart. He didn't resemble a dead person; he resembled a slaughtered hog. Kawika almost gagged.

"Normal forty-six-year-old male," Smith said. "Dead, of course. But otherwise normal. Died around midnight."

Smith lifted a stainless steel pan with a body part in it: Fortunato's heart.

"Here's the problem," Smith said. "The spear went right through it. Auricles, ventricles: everything's destroyed."

"A single blow?" Kawika asked, quickly looking back up at Smith.

"Yup," Smith said. "Just one blow. But a big blow. And I mean big. Smashed his ribs, went clear through his back, right into the turf. Even took a fair-sized divot. Yes sir, done with emphasis."

Smith replaced the pan on a stainless-steel counter and re-covered the corpse. He pointed toward a larger pan. "Stomach," he said. "The last supper. We'll give you a report, tell you what he ate. There's alcohol for sure—lots of it. Not a cautious type, apparently. He was risking a DUI. Lucky for him he never made it back to his car, eh?"

Smith walked across the room, picked up the fatal spear, brought it back to Kawika. Kawika slipped on a pair of gloves and took it. Very black, as he'd noticed at the crime scene. Heavy, carved from hard kauila wood. Six feet long. Three somewhat dull wooden barbs behind the tip. "Those three barbs made the extraction rather difficult," Smith said. "We had to go slow, be careful. He was dead, but we didn't want to hurt him." The spear still showed powder where the Waimea police had dusted it for prints.

"As you probably know—do you?—this one's called an ihe," Smith explained. "A javelin. It's pretty old. Those three barbs should help identify it. Find out who owns it, you'll probably find your killer. Could be a museum piece—probably missing from a collection somewhere. Kamehameha might have used it, training for the Olympics—if he'd lived at the right time, of course."

"Anything else?" Kawika asked coldly; Smith's jocularity, appealing at first, now seemed peculiar. *Is he nervous?* Kawika wondered. *Why?* He handed the spear back to Smith. Ignoring Kawika's change of tone, Smith took a little run with it, did a cross-step, pretended to throw it. Then he put it down, returned to Kawika.

"Odds and ends," the doctor replied. "For example, he was gagged."

Kawika frowned. "Not when we found him."

"Dead men tell no lies," Smith said. "But alive, men sometimes holler. There were fibers in his mouth, and bruises. Also telltale lacerations."

Smith walked to another counter, returning with a pan that contained a piece of twine. "Here's something that'll interest you," he said. "Another bit of Hawaiiana. It's an old cord. The killer used it to tie our friend's hands. I'd say it's made from olonā."

"Olonā?" Kawika asked.

"A type of nettle," Smith said. "Best fiber plant the old Hawaiians had. Never used today. So this strand is old too—another museum piece. Certainly missing from someone's collection."

Smith put down the twine, then walked to the corpse. Reaching under the sheet, he lifted Fortunato's right arm.

"Look at this," he said. "Recognize those marks?"

Kawika looked. "Cuffs," he replied.

"Bingo," said Smith, still holding the wrist toward Kawika. "Handcuffs. Distinctive ones too. The edge of one cuff was damaged. A chisel or something. Find the cuffs, you'll find the killer."

"But the killer tied his hands," Kawika said. "He used the cord."

"Right again," Smith said. "But notice, our boy's got cuff marks only. No marks or fibers from the cord. No signs of ligature, as they say in the literature."

Kawika scratched his head with his gloved hand and felt the odd sensation of latex in his hair.

"Trust me," Smith said. "He died with cuffs on. The cord came later. And by the way"—Smith covered the right arm and uncovered the left, holding the wrist toward Kawika—"his left wrist was cuffed twice. Caught skin both times."

"But where are the cuffs?" Kawika asked.

"With the gag, I'd guess," Smith answered. "A thousand kisses deep."

Kawika shot him a sharp look.

"Sorry," said Smith. "That's from a new Leonard Cohen song. I simply meant the killer probably got rid of the cuffs too." He lifted the bottom of the sheet.

"And the shoes?" Smith continued. "The shoes must be on a different foot. Or feet. Before he died, he was walking barefoot. Feet have loose dirt on 'em. Also sand, bits of cinders, fresh grass stains. Yes, sir, a lucky man: died with his boots off."

"Not exactly in his own bed," Kawika said, increasingly irritated with Smith's joking.

"No," Smith agreed. "Not exactly." He paused and looked hard at Kawika, as if appraising him. "There's one more thing," he added. He handed Kawika a plastic sandwich bag. Kawika lifted it to examine the contents: a sprig of green plant with white flowers. Looking at it told him nothing.

"It's an unusual plant," Smith explained. "It was in his pocket. You recognize it? No. Well, it's mountain naupaka. And it's fresh."

Kawika turned the bag this way and that, as if looking at the plant would reveal the doctor's point.

"As its name implies," Smith went on, "mountain naupaka grows in the mountains. At least in the wild. It wilts pretty fast, and you can't keep it fresh in water. So this piece is less than a day old."

"Which means?"

"Which means," Smith replied, "if this particular naupaka grew in the wild, then yesterday Mohammed went to the mountain—or the mountain came to Mohammed. Unless, as I'd suspect, there's another source."

Kawika frowned again. Smith frowned too. Kawika could see in that disapproving frown that he'd somehow disappointed the doctor. It puzzled him. "Look," he said to Smith. "We're just getting started."

Tommy, the Waimea cop, was waiting at reception when Kawika emerged from the makeshift morgue. "Checked on Peter Pukui, our HHH guy," Tommy said. "No one in Kawaihae has seen him for a few days. Not him, not his girlfriend either. Her full name's Melanie Munu. Apparently she's a real powerhouse."

"What about Shimazu?"

"Checked out of the Mauna Lani Bay Hotel at six this morning. Caught the eight o'clock JAL flight to Tokyo. Hotel staff printed his boarding pass for him. Airline confirms he's on the plane."

"So he left before he knew Fortunato was dead?"

"Yeah," Tommy said. "Unless he killed him."

5

Waikoloa Village

Kawika had never seen anyone as agitated as Michael Cushing. Cushing had good reason to be agitated: someone had just murdered his boss, and Cushing feared he'd be next. Kawika didn't doubt that Cushing's fear was real.

"Those bastards will kill me!" Cushing shouted. Kawika and Tommy turned in place as Cushing, tall and very pale in a starched aloha shirt, circled his wood-paneled KKL Development office at a near run. Kawika couldn't help smiling at this frantic indoor athletic display. He risked a glance at Tommy, who was trying to suppress a smirk.

"Mr. Cushing," said Kawika, hoping to calm him, "no one's going to kill you. We'll have police officers guard your house, even your office and your car if you want. The killer will hide now—or run. If you'll help us, Mr. Cushing, we'll catch him. Or them. Right away."

Cushing slowed to a walk. Finally he sat down and collected himself. On the wall behind him, the future KKL resort, displayed on an acetate overlay, covered a huge aerial photograph of a lava-and-scrub volcanic flank.

Cushing had a lot of information to impart, once he relaxed a bit. Like Corazon Fortunato, he insisted the "temple Hawaiians" must have committed the crime. But Cushing added details. And he knew what HHH stood for.

"Hui Heiau Hawai'i," he said. "The Hawaiian Temple Association, basically. Association, union, popular front—that's the idea."

"You speak Hawaiian?" asked Kawika.

"A little. Not much. Took Hawaiian studies at UH Mānoa. My family—" Cushing stopped abruptly.

"Your family what?" Kawika asked.

"Nothing," replied Cushing. "I was just going to say, I grew up in Hawai'i."

Kawika let it pass. "Tell me about Peter Pukui," he said.

"Scary son of a bitch. Normal size, but mean. Looks more haole than Hawaiian." Cushing's gaze flickered for a moment. Kawika nodded. *It's okay.*

"He lives in Kawaihae," Cushing went on. "Works in the boat harbor. His girlfriend is as political as he is. Melanie Munu. She's not Hawaiian. Maori, I think. She's the organizer for HHH and some other Native groups. The driving force. But Peter's the spokesman—their 'Orator,' they call him."

"How did it start?" Kawika asked. "The dispute with HHH, I mean."

"We found an old structure of lava rock," replied Cushing. "It was partly broken down, probably by cattle. Parker Ranch used to lease this land. It could've been a temple for human sacrifice, a so-called luakini heiau. Ralph hired a team from the University of Hawai'i at Hilo to check it out. I figured they'd say, 'Yeah, maybe it's authentic, but it's no big deal, it's not a major site or anything.'

He went on. "Unfortunately, it turns out Captain Vancouver's men saw a heiau being built along this coast. They even saw the human sacrifices, wrote about it in their journals. Kamehameha built it to stop a lava flow. The lava's 'a'ā here. You know, the rough kind, not pahoehoe, the smooth kind. Doesn't move fast, just sort of rumbles along. But it was headed for Kamehameha's fishponds—probably the ones at the Mauna Lani these days. So he built a heiau on the mountainside, sacrificed some guys."

"This the same heiau?" Kawika asked.

Cushing shrugged. "Who knows? It's a big mountain; no one recorded the spot. But HHH claimed it was the same one. And they could be right."

Cushing stood up, lifted the acetate overlay, traced a lava flow on the aerial photo. "See, a lava flow does split here, just uphill from the heiau. One part goes almost to the highway, then stops. The other part, over here, goes all the way to the ocean. But it misses the fishponds. So this might be Kamehameha's heiau."

And human sacrifice might have worked, Kawika thought. *Not like ritual killings, the sort you find in murder mysteries.*

"Tell me about the extortion attempt," he said.

"Extortion?"

"Mrs. Fortunato said HHH tried to extort money from her husband, or from KKL."

"Corazon told you that? Jesus."

"It didn't happen?"

"I'm not saying that. You have to understand: Ralph could be stupid sometimes. Plus hot-tempered. Sorry, but it's true. He took offense easily. I would never call HHH extortionists—never. Certainly not to their faces. But Ralph did."

"So what actually happened?"

What actually happened, Cushing explained, was that HHH eventually realized Fortunato wasn't going to give them anything. He'd restore the heiau, make it an attraction at the resort, spend some money on a little interpretive center. But he wouldn't offer HHH any cash. He wouldn't pay them to go away.

"Did they demand money?" asked Kawika.

"They *asked* for money. They said they wanted to hire experts to find sacred sites on other property. Ralph called that extortion. But maybe they just wanted a success—declare victory, get some funding, move on. Most Hawaiian cultural groups have serious causes and are completely responsible; HHH probably started out that way too. But Ralph just outraged them—that's the only way to put it. He did it on purpose."

"Well, we can probably find out whether it really was extortion," Kawika said. "Mrs. Fortunato said her husband taped the key meeting."

Cushing grimaced, then shook his head. "That must be what Ralph told her. What he told me was, 'I should have taped that meeting.'"

"Were you with him?"

"At that meeting? No, but I was with him at the next one—*after* he'd bulldozed the site. They were furious. Ralph loved it. He was taunting them. I thought they'd kill us both right on the spot."

"Why'd he bulldoze it?" Kawika asked.

"Why?" Cushing shrugged. "Because he had incredibly bad judgment? Because HHH really pissed him off? I don't know. None of it made sense. We should've given them money and stuck to our plan—rebuilt the heiau, made it a feature of the resort. A nice outcome for all concerned. But now they've killed Ralph and they'll be coming after me."

Kawika started to speak. "I know, I know"—Cushing held up his hand—"you're going to *protect* me. Great. But how about the resort? Can you save it too, Detective?"

"Well," said Kawika, smiling politely, "let's work on saving you first."

More questions: Had Cushing seen Mr. Fortunato the day before? Yes, Cushing said: at work, all day. They'd eaten lunch together. "Right outside— the burrito place. In the afternoon Ralph went somewhere to meet with Makoto—that's Mr. Shimazu. He heads the investor group from Tokyo. Ralph got back around four. We locked up around five fifteen, maybe five thirty."

"Mr. Shimazu seems to have flown home this morning. Was that expected?"

"Yeah," Cushing replied. "He was here for two days, as usual. Just likes to see things, talk to Ralph in person."

"Does he do that a lot?" Kawika asked. "Fly over here for a day or two?"

"Couple of times a year, I guess. We don't see him often."

Kawika switched topics. "Could Mr. Fortunato have gone anywhere else yesterday?" he asked. "To the mountains, say?"

"I don't see how," Cushing replied. "He didn't have time to get up there with Makoto, and otherwise I was with him till we went home."

"Did he have enemies? Apart from HHH, I mean."

"Nothing serious, far as I know. Ralph could be an asshole. But I don't know who'd kill him, other than HHH. Last time I saw them, they were ready to murder him, me, and the horse we rode in on—like I told you."

"Mr. Cushing," Kawika asked, "do you know if Mr. Fortunato might have had a girlfriend? Maybe a boyfriend? Someone besides his wife?"

Cushing didn't respond at once. He regarded Kawika for a moment. Then he glanced at Tommy, who looked quite alert under his baseball cap. Cushing turned again to Kawika, raising his eyebrows slightly: a question. Kawika nodded, intent on the answer.

"Okay," Cushing sighed. "Yes, he had a girlfriend. It's messy; they're both married. But his love life didn't kill him. I don't suppose that's good enough for you?"

"Afraid not," Kawika said, smiling politely again. "No, as you can guess, we'll need to know who she is, talk to her. But we can be discreet."

Cushing sighed, this time more deeply. "It's our receptionist and office manager, Joanie. Joan Malo. She's Hawaiian too. But I'm telling you, she has nothing to do with this. Neither does her husband. He doesn't even know."

"Receptionist?" Kawika asked, looking around the empty office. "She's not here today?"

"No. She left when we got the news. Around ten maybe. Went home. She lives right here in the Village. Here's her number." Cushing wrote it on a Post-it Note and handed it to Kawika. "But remember, her husband doesn't know."

"We'll talk to her alone," Kawika assured him. "Up in Waimea. Right now we'll go find Peter Pukui and Melanie Munu. Meanwhile, you want police protection at the office?"

Cushing shook his head. "No, I don't think so. I'm only here during the day. It's a public place, pretty crowded. A guard would draw attention, hurt the company. But I definitely want protection in Waimea, at the house."

With that, Kawika noticed, Cushing's agitation began to increase again.

6

Waikoloa Village

Cushing locked the KKL office door behind Kawika and Tommy. Now he was alone. He picked up the phone and dialed quickly, pounding his desk and muttering, "Shit shit shit," as he waited for an answer. Finally it came.

"Yeah."

"Rocco, where've you been?" Cushing demanded. "I've been calling all day."

"Hapuna Beach, remember? But I heard the news. Heard the details too."

"You didn't do it, did you?"

"The fuck. How could I? It isn't time yet. You haven't given me the stuff."

"Then get off the island," Cushing said. "We'll talk later."

"Wait a minute. Who did it?"

"I don't know who did it, Rocco! Just get off the island. Now."

"You didn't double-book this, did you? You're not trying to stiff me?"

"No. I told you, I don't know who fucking did it! Someone else killed him—not you, not me—someone else."

"Really? Funny how they knew your exact plan."

7

Waimea to Puakō

"HHH? You're kidding," Tanaka snorted. "You won't see the joke, Kawika. You're not old enough. But HHH was Hubert Horatio Humphrey. The Happy Warrior, people called him. The Happy Warrior instead of Kamehameha, the Rainbow Warrior. These people are clueless. Named themselves for a dead haole politician and probably don't even know it."

With Tommy behind the wheel, driving down the grassy mountainside from Cushing's office, toward the sea and the setting sun, keeping an eye out for the green flash, Kawika heard Tanaka's snort distinctly over the phone, all the way from Hilo. "It stands for Hui Heiau Hawai'i," Kawika explained. He pronounced it in Hawaiian, with "v" for w. "Hawai'i Temple Association, or Group for Hawaiian Temples—something like that."

Tanaka grunted. "Found the guy yet?" he asked, moving on to Peter Pukui.

"No," Kawika said. "Waimea cops have looked. They've turned Kawaihae upside down. No one's seen him. Not his girlfriend either—a Melanie Munu. She's a big part of HHH too, apparently. They haven't come to work, haven't been home. Not for days."

"Catch a plane?"

"Only if they had fake IDs. No record with the airlines. We're talking to the charters and private pilots."

"Probably hiding," Tanaka guessed. "The Big Island's a big island."

"Might've taken a boat," Kawika said. "He works at the harbor. We're checking. Checking on a Mr. Shimazu too. Shimazu Makoto. He leads the Japanese investors. He was here yesterday, but he flew home to Tokyo at eight this morning."

"Conveniently."

"Yeah, we're thinking that too."

"That all you got right now?"

"Just about. Headed for my dad's."

"Well, I've got something for you," Tanaka said. "From the mainland. Fortunato had trouble before he came here. Developing a resort in Washington, up in the mountains. Place called the Methow Valley." Tanaka pronounced it "METH-ow."

"You know it?" Tanaka asked.

"'MET-how,'" Kawika corrected. "Yeah, I know it. I've been there. It's in the North Cascades. When was this?"

"Five years ago—1997. Got himself prosecuted too. And guess why? He desecrated a Native American cultural site."

"Seriously?"

"Seriously," Tanaka assured him. "He found an old shelter in the rocks, right in the middle of a resort he was planning. Ancient wintering spot, apparently. Dated back hundreds of years. Turned out to be important—helped prove some Tribe's land claim or something. Anyway, Fortunato dynamited the sucker. Blasted it sky high. The Feds were all over him for it."

"Did he do time?"

"Nope. Beat the rap—charges dropped at trial. Government couldn't agree with itself apparently. Justice Department called it a crime. Interior Department waffled, said the site wasn't protected, wasn't necessarily sacred anyway. Can't desecrate something that's not sacred, I guess. Anyway, Ralph's company pleaded to false statements. That was it."

"Jesus."

"Yeah, but get this: the resort went under. Down the tube. Development company failed, went bankrupt. Ralph picked up, moved on, moved here. Sayonara. Aloha."

"This is weird," Kawika said. "I can't believe he'd bulldoze the heiau after that."

"History repeats itself," said Tanaka.

"Doesn't make sense."

"It might," Tanaka said. "Maybe he likes killing resorts more than completing them. Found the heiau, saw his chance. Old dog, old trick."

"But why?"

"Don't know," Tanaka replied. "You're the detective."

"Thanks."

"By the way," Tanaka added, "We say 'hui' all the time, but out of curiosity I just double-checked it in the dictionary. 'Group, union, association formed to pursue a common undertaking.'"

"Yeah, that's what I said—could mean association, group."

"Could mean something else, Kawika. How about 'gambling club?' Or 'tong?'"

"Get outta here."

"Just watch your back, that's all I'm saying. You're in Chinatown again."

"The International District, Terry, the International District."

"Whatever. Say hi to your dad for me. And tell him: guys fishing in our spot last night? Caught a hundred-ten-pound ulua."

"Big one," Kawika responded.

"Yeah," said Tanaka. "Big one that forgot to watch its back."

Tommy had overheard most of the conversation. "So," he asked, when Kawika hung up, "Captain Tanaka, he's like your uncle or something? Not like a real boss?"

Kawika laughed. "More like everyone's uncle and everyone's boss," he said. "We don't find the killer fast, you'll see for yourself."

8

Waipiʻo

Kawika wasn't Tanaka's only Hawaiian detective—or his only ambitious one. There was also Sammy Kāʻai. Sammy was older than Kawika, rugged in appearance and much more experienced. He, too, sought Tanaka's favor and resented what he considered Kawika's unearned access to it. Sammy tended to misinterpret facts at the station; he imagined Kawika had received a plum assignment, for example, failing to see that Tanaka wanted his most experienced—and toughest—detectives to focus on Shark Cliff. But Sammy was a superb interpreter of facts in the field.

On the day Kawika flew to South Kohala, Sammy decided to revisit the rocky beach at Shark Cliff and take another look. He wanted the helicopter for transport but arrived at work to find it gone with Kawika. He asked for the police launch, the boat they'd taken the first time, but it was out rescuing a sailboat that had wrecked on Hilo's breakwater in the night. Sammy couldn't even get a four-wheel drive from the motor pool. In the end, he parked a police cruiser at the Waipiʻo Lookout and proceeded on foot—a mile down the steep road to the valley floor, then south along the boulder-strewn shore to the foot of the cliff.

By the time he got there, a light rain had begun to fall. There wasn't any wind. The surf was heavy and loud from big swells. Sammy pulled up his hood and bent his face toward the beach, searching for any evidence—a wristwatch, a wallet, a ring—they might have missed before, preoccupied as they'd been with body parts and flesh.

What caused Sammy to look up was a pebble bouncing off his hood. He felt a *whap*, then saw the pebble skitter among the rocks at his feet. Other pebbles began to bounce nearby. It took Sammy a moment to realize the stones were falling from the cliff. He turned his face skyward, expecting a rockfall and already moving backward, trying to get out of harm's way. What he saw instead was a body falling toward him—a body falling straight down, right next to the vertical cliff face. Sammy froze, his mouth wide in disbelief. A plummeting stone sliced his chin. He dove behind a boulder and missed seeing the body hit the beach, the actual impact, but he heard the sound—a percussive *whoomph* like a muffled explosion.

He didn't hear a scream.

*   *   *

At the hospital in Hilo, Sammy received Tanaka's undivided attention. They spoke while doctors X-rayed and bandaged injuries from his dive behind the boulder, and even while they stitched up his chin.

"Good work," Tanaka said, patting Sammy on an arm wrapped in gauze and Ace bandages. *Good work*, though not *Iiko, iiko.*

Sammy had provided Tanaka something to go on. "Now we know the murders aren't over—they're still happening," he said to Sammy. "The killers can act by day. Whoever this latest guy is, he's a haole, unlike the others. And thanks to you, we know he wasn't conscious when he hit."

"Wasn't conscious the whole way down," Sammy insisted. Sammy had been a paratrooper in the Army. He'd pushed dummies out of planes to test the wind above a drop zone. The victim's fall had been the lifeless fall of a wind dummy. "I think he was dead, Terry."

"Dead or unconscious," Tanaka replied. "It doesn't matter. The others might have been knocked out too. The point is, this guy changes what we thought. He changes the pattern."

"Not necessarily," Sammy observed. "Maybe he isn't part of the pattern."

"Copycat, you're thinking?"

"Maybe," Sammy replied. "Or maybe he's just a stray."

9

Puakō

As a little boy in his father's embrace, Kawika sometimes felt he could drown in flesh. Even now, Jarvis Wong's huge arms engulfed his son. Kawika's cousin, eleven-year-old Kuʻulei, squirmed happily, waiting impatiently for the paternal hug to end. "Kawika, Kawika!" she exclaimed, over and over. She began to jump up and down.

The Wongs had reunited at Jarvis's house in Puakō, the once-sleepy village where Kawika had spent summers as a boy. Back then, Puakō had been home to artists, beach bums smoking pakalolo—pot—and resort workers like his father. Now the money had begun to show up. Puakō was changing.

Kawika scooped up his cousin, nuzzling her with mock ferocity. She screamed in delight. Kuʻulei's mom was Kawika's aunt, his dad's unfortunate younger sister, a stoner down in the jungles of Puna on the windward and wet side of the island. Kuʻulei lived with Jarvis now, attending private school in Waimea. The Mauna Kea Beach Resort, Jarvis's employer, paid part of her fees through its employees' scholarship fund, even though technically as a niece she wasn't eligible.

"You're working *here*?" Kuʻulei asked. "Did something get stolen?"

"Someone got killed," replied Kawika.

"Ooh," Kuʻulei said, turning thoughtful. "A bad person?"

"Bad? I don't know," Kawika replied, thinking, *Desecration, adultery, who knows what else?* "But even bad people shouldn't be killed, should they?"

"Depends on how bad they are," she answered sensibly.

Jarvis cooked a dinner of fresh fish outside on an old grate set on cinderblocks. Standing beside his father, a beer in one hand and his cousin tugging on the other, Kawika felt himself at home, yet growing ever more distant from his boyhood summers. The house still reflected Jarvis perfectly: a tin-roofed shack on stilts to keep the sea out when storms carried surf over the lava rock wall that Jarvis and Kawika had built together years before. A hibiscus border grew through cyclone fencing. The driveway was a patch of reddish earth surrounded by an irregular fringe of mongrel grass. Surfboards and fishing rods rested on rusty brackets on the street-facing wall. Kawika winced at the surfboards. He hadn't surfed on the Kohala coast for a long time. He barely found time to surf near Hilo.

Kawika realized that with South Kohala's skyrocketing real estate prices, even Jarvis would be tempted to sell his place sometime soon. This house would be torn down, sold to a Mainlander with money and an architect, someone who'd have fun designing a vacation dream house for a tiny ocean-front lot.

"Folks here are selling out," Kawika said. "I see a fancy new place every time I come."

"Nice people moving in, though," said Jarvis optimistically. "Lots of activity. Always an interesting place, Puakō."

For twenty years—most of Kawika's life—Jarvis had been head grounds-keeper at the Mauna Kea. Jarvis liked tending his trees and tropical plants, riding the tractor mower over familiar terrain; he was a supervisor who worked with his crew. The Mauna Kea indulged him in this and other ways. Smart management, Kawika always thought.

Dinner proved complicated. Ku'ulei insisted on sitting on Kawika's lap, as if she were five or six again. "We're studying the gods in school," she informed him. "Lono, right now. We're making leis and ti leaf mats. We're going to do an offering—poi and poke and stuff. Then we're going to study Pele."

"What about Kū?" asked Kawika, his mind on a god who demanded human sacrifice. "You gonna make offerings to Kū?"

"Who's Kū?" asked Ku'ulei, turning to Jarvis.

"The god of war," Jarvis told her. "Kūka'ilimoku, but Kū for short."

Facing Kawika again, Jarvis said, "Nowadays they don't study Kū at her age. Kū comes later."

"Lono, Pele, but not Kū," said Kawika, smiling at his cousin. "Just the cuddly gods."

"Pele's not cuddly," Jarvis admonished.

After Ku'ulei had been tucked in, the men sat facing the sea in plastic lawn chairs, resting their feet on the low lava rock wall. When Jarvis asked about the case, Kawika told him what he knew, but didn't mention KKL's receptionist Joan Malo, Fortunato's married lover. *Kohala's a big district but a small place,* Kawika reasoned.

Listening, Jarvis grunted from time to time, then asked more questions. "I can tell you one or two things," he finally offered. "Might help a bit."

Kawika nodded. "Please," he said.

"Okay. Then first, your Mr. Fortunato? Lives up there in a Parker Ranch house. Works hard at fitting in. Wants people to think he's a nice guy. But there's something funny about that resort. The money's from Japan, right? So where's the resident Japanese guy? And where's the money actually going? You should check."

"The Japanese guy's not resident," said Kawika. "Just seems to fly in and out."

"Huh. Usually these Japanese developers, they've got someone here to keep an eye on things." Jarvis shrugged, then continued. "Well, anyway, next, your Peter Pukui? An angry young man. He's in his forties now, I guess. Drug user, like his daddy. Daddy wrecked his car on Highway 19, the Queen K nowadays, got himself killed. Peter's mom, she's a haole and a drunk. Wrecked a few cars herself. Now she's in an old folks' home."

"Think he'd kill Fortunato?"

"Like I said, he's angry and a druggie. Could kill someone, yeah?"

"Yeah, and he's disappeared. Looks bad."

Peter Pukui had wanted something to believe in, Jarvis emphasized— something to make him more *Hawaiian*—so he'd seized on the heiau. "He grew up here," Jarvis continued. "We've got some big heiau. Then Fortunato finds another one up at KKL. So Peter starts his own movement. They meet below Puʻukoholā, down where the old Hawaiians sacrificed guys to the sharks. You know that leaning stone, the big pōhaku, where the priests watched the sharks feed? That's where Peter's group meets."

Jarvis moved to face his son. "You've gotta understand," he said. "Peter's group, they've got an agenda. They're not into hula or old ways of catching fish. They're not like other Native groups, trying to preserve some of the culture. No, they want to bring back the old religion."

Kawika knew this part of his Hawaiian history: haoles stole the Kingdom, but the Hawaiians themselves overthrew their old religion seventy-five years earlier, right after Kamehameha died and before any missionaries reached the islands. Kaʻahumanu, the king's most forceful widow, and his son the new king took the lead. "And God bless 'em," said Jarvis. "Because the way the old Hawaiians worshipped, they were a bloodthirsty bunch. And Peter's group, they want to be born-again Hawaiians. They're in love with the old ways. It's magic to them. Power. Mana.

"I hope Peter didn't do this," Jarvis added. "I hope it was some jealous husband"—*So he knows,* Kawika thought—"or some Japanese investor. Or folks at the Mauna Lani? They hate Kohala Kea Loa. Folks at Waikoloa Village feel the same. They don't want the traffic, don't want the people, don't want their views messed up. So maybe you wanna check some of those folks too, yeah?"

"Geez, Dad," replied Kawika. "Think someone from the Mauna Lani would sacrifice a guy on the championship tee box of their signature hole? Doesn't sound like folks at the Mauna Lani."

"What folks you know at the Mauna Lani?"

"Well, just the woman who found the body. Interviewed her today."

"Tourist?"

"Part tourist, part kamaʻaina. She owns a condo at the Mauna Lani Point. Patience Quinn."

Jarvis let out a whoop. "Patience Quinn? From San Francisco?"

"You know her?"

"I know the whole family. They used to stay at the Mauna Kea. Big-money folks, but friendly, lots of aloha. They still golf on our course. Patience Quinn—I don't believe it. You two played together at the beach when you were kids."

"Really? I don't remember. You seen her since she was a girl?"

"Sure," Jarvis answered. "Once a year at least. She's a magazine writer, yeah? Did a big story some years back about the fight over the Hapuna Prince Hotel, getting that thing built. Sent me a copy—*New York Times,* that one. My, my. Little Impy Quinn found the body, eh?"

"Impy?"

"Lots of energy," Jarvis explained. "Couldn't sit still. Her mom said, 'Should've named her *Im*patience.' They called her Impy for short. She had attention issues, they said. I called her Flea, though. She'd hang on me like Kuʻulei hangs on you. I'd pretend to scratch at her. I'd shout, 'A flea! A flea! Gotta scratch this darn flea!' She'd laugh so hard, she'd finally fall off." Jarvis chuckled. "She grew up, she married a doctor, like her daddy," he said. "Nice young fellow."

"They're separated now, apparently," Kawika told him.

"Sorry to hear it." Jarvis frowned. "Well, if you see her again, say hello for me."

"I might see her in the morning," Kawika said, and heard the too-casual note in his own voice. "That reminds me," he added quickly, "Terry said to tell you, some guys fishing in your spot last night? Caught a hundred-ten-pound ulua."

Jarvis waited a moment, then spoke.

"How's Carolyn?" he asked.

10

The Mauna Lani

"**D**o you prefer Impy or Flea?"

Patience Quinn looked astonished, then embarrassed. "Oh my gosh," she exclaimed. "Detective Wong; Jarvis Wong. I didn't put it together. You said you were from *Hilo*—"

"Don't we look alike, Dad and me?" he teased.

"Not *much* alike," she replied, and laughed. "He's the biggest man I've ever seen."

Kawika laughed. "Can we take a walk?" he asked. She nodded, stepped outside, and slipped her sandals on. Kawika turned to Tommy. "Mind picking me up in an hour? At the hotel?"

Tommy blinked. "Yes, *boss*," he replied, and turned back.

Kawika and Patience set out toward the Mauna Lani Bay Hotel. With their first steps, they left behind the elevated tee box on which Ralph Fortunato had died the day before. Groundskeepers were busy replacing sod the blood had soaked.

Their route took them along well-maintained walls of greenish fishponds spared from ancient lava flows. They found some shade on a small beach and sat down. Kawika again noticed her well-defined muscles, this time of her neck and arms. *She's incredibly fit*, he realized. She slipped off her sandals, dug her toes in the sand. Kawika kept his shoes on. He wore a soft green and blue aloha shirt, nicer than the one he'd worn the day before, thanks to a few things he kept at his dad's.

Jarvis had told Kawika a bit about Patience. Now she asked about him. His parents had met at Hapuna Beach, he told her. "Dad had the day off; Mom had come from the mainland to work at an observatory." Kawika had been born a year later. "Mom raised me in Seattle after the divorce," he said. "I spent summers here. Dad says you and I played together when we were little."

"I don't remember that, but I sure remember Jarvis from back then," she said, laughing. "He'd take me out in the waves. I'd hold tight around his neck; I couldn't get my legs around his back." Her parents had met Jarvis on the Mauna Kea golf course, she said. "Daddy lost his tee shot in the sun," she explained. "When he got to the green, Jarvis was standing there laughing. Daddy had hit a hole in one—his first and last. I don't know, maybe Jarvis gave it a nudge. Anyway, Jarvis handed Daddy a beer from his cooler. I think later they went out and got drunk. They still make a point of seeing each other whenever Mom and Dad are here."

"Aloha," Kawika said, smiling.

"Aloha," she agreed with a laugh.

"And you've been coming here ever since?"

"Yup," she replied. "My parents love the beach at the Mauna Kea, but Daddy wanted this condo here at the Mauna Lani Point. He loves sitting with a drink, looking out at the ocean and the sunset and the championship tee—" She hesitated for a second, then pressed on. "And that over-the-water par 3. Though he's practically filled the little bay there with his tee shots—plus a five-iron he tossed in there once. The fish must hate him." She chuckled. "Anyway, when I got married, they gave me the condo as a present. I'm there a lot, sometimes for months when I'm writing. But honestly, after the divorce I'll sell it in a minute if I can get a nice place at the Mauna Kea. The beach there—I mean, you know."

That allowed Kawika to turn the conversation to business. "Mauna Kea, Mauna Lani: you know the South Kohala resorts. I don't; Hilo isn't South Kohala. Dad says you wrote about the Hapuna Prince getting built, the fight over it. That's the sort of thing I need to understand. How these resorts get built, how they make money."

"Or lose it," she said. "Some have lost a bundle."

"Losing money—yes. That could be important too."

"Well," she began, "you need to go back a bit." After World War II, she explained, the government made tourism on the Neighbor Islands a priority. They invested in Hilo, building an international airport, a hotel strip. Planners thought visitors to Hawaii wanted nice wet tropical jungles. Lush vegetation. Banyan trees, parrots, rain showers. They figured tourists would never go to Kohala—too hot, too dry, no plants, no water.

"And lava fields," she added. "It's a moonscape here—barren, empty, wide-open spaces. Who'd want to visit?" She laughed again; Kawika had begun to like that laugh a lot. "Hard to believe, isn't it? Nowadays South Kohala's getting crowded. You know what they say? Everyone here has something in common: we all used to go to Maui or Kaua'i."

Things began to change, she continued, one day when the government invited Laurance Rockefeller to the Big Island and placed a helicopter at his disposal. *"Take your time,"* they told him. *"Pick a spot."* He picked his spot, a perfect South Kohala beach. *"I'll build here,"* he said. *"The Mauna Kea."* But on one condition: that he be allowed to build another hotel next door on Hapuna Beach. That way, Patience explained, he'd have the two best beaches in all Hawai'i, and no one on the Big Island could ever compete with him.

"Nasty problem," she said, "because Hapuna's a state park. It was totally pristine back then—not a sign of human development. And it was sacred to the old Hawaiians."

Rockefeller got his way at first, she said. He built the Mauna Kea and made it Hawai'i's premier resort. But he couldn't get anything built at Hapuna. For thirty years, neither could his successors.

"An opposition group formed, called Save Hapuna," Patience said. "Lots of locals joined. Lots of visitors, hippies, Native groups. Even Mauna Kea homeowners. They held concerts, raised money, took the fight to Hilo and Honolulu. In the end they basically lost, because the hotel finally got built eight years ago."

"Sounds like they lost, period," Kawika said.

"Not entirely," she replied. "The hotel's nicer now than when it was first designed—lower, less intrusive. More sensitive, better landscaped. Blends in a bit, don't you think?"

Kawika agreed; he considered the Hapuna Prince quite beautiful. "But how did it get built at all?" he asked. "After thirty years, you'd think developers would give up."

"No one can stop development here," Patience said. "No one. Eventually the forces grow too strong. You've got the developers and their money, the investors. Next you've got the construction unions. Then you've got the locals who aren't rich, aren't retired. They want the jobs. They fight back against groups like Save Hapuna. 'You've got yours,' they say. 'Now you want to stop us getting ours.'"

Kawika sighed.

"And this is Hawai'i, after all," she added. "Government here is, well, *weak* in some ways. Subject to pressure, easily persuaded, let's say. So it's majority rule, or money talks. Either way, development can't be stopped."

"Depressing," he said.

She shrugged. "It's just a fact," she said. "If you promise jobs for the locals and spread money around, well, eventually you'll get your permits."

"So what are the economics of these resorts?" he asked. "How does a developer plan to make money?"

"Well, the hotel is just a centerpiece, a loss leader," she explained. "The money's in real estate. Attract people with a great hotel and beach, let them play a few rounds on a seaside course, get them hooked on the climate and beauty and aloha spirit. Then sell them a house or condo on the golf course or along the beach."

Kawika thought for a moment. "You said Rockefeller got the two best beaches—no one could compete with him. But now South Kohala's got the Mauna Lani, the Orchid, the Hilton at Waikoloa."

"Even Rockefeller couldn't foresee everything," she responded. "Turns out this lava rock is basically just glass. It's sharp—it'll cut your foot. But bulldozers can crush it, grade it, create a new resort anywhere. You can dig a trench in it too, so you can lay a water line—even from the wet side of the island, since it's so dry over here. And you can build a beach or lagoon. Bring sand in by barge. The Mauna Kea and the Prince still have the best beaches. But they can't monopolize them—partly because of public access but mostly because Hapuna's a state park. We have a snorkel beach here at the Mauna Lani. But for surf we get in our cars and drive to Hapuna."

"That doesn't explain KKL, up on a mountain," Kawika said. "Fortunato could build a hotel and golf course, I suppose, but how would he attract people without a beach? What would he put in his ads? A picture of Hapuna? Tell 'em, *'You can drive there in half an hour?'*"

Patience nodded. "Here's what he'd say: *'In Hawai'i, there's public access to every beach.'* He'd also say—you guessed it—*'You can drive to Hapuna in minutes.'* He'd probably say, *'Locals prefer living up on the mountain; not as hot, you've got a great view'*—all that. But what he'd emphasize most of all: *'You can afford it up here.'* He'd make a virtue of necessity and sell real estate at prices way below the Mauna Kea or Mauna Lani. Lower prestige, but lower price points. South Kohala on a budget."

He paused to consider what she'd told him.

"Kawika," she said gently, "KKL's business plan doesn't really matter, does it? You just don't want the killers to be the temple people, the Native Hawaiians. You want someone else to have killed him for some other reason."

He almost denied it, but she was partly right. "Look Patience—or Impy or Flea or whatever I should call you—I do hope someone else did it. But there's stuff we don't know yet, and stuff I can't tell you. We have to check all the possibilities. And something connected with KKL—something besides Hawaiians—well, we can't rule it out. But if the Hawaiians did it, we'll get them."

"I'm sure you will," she reassured him. "I just hate to see you make it difficult for yourself. A man those Hawaiians hated destroyed a sacred site. He made them really angry, and he turns up dead as a human sacrifice, stabbed to death with a Hawaiian spear."

"The killer could still be someone else," he noted. "Maybe someone trying to make it look like Hawaiians did it."

"Maybe. But have you heard of Occam's Razor?" He shook his head. "It's a principle of logic, a way of resolving uncertainty. It says if there's more than one possible explanation for something, the correct explanation is usually the simplest one. Or at least it makes sense to investigate the simplest one first."

Kawika rose, brushing sand from his pants. "Well, we are investigating the simplest one," he said. "But others too."

She also rose but stopped him, putting a hand on his bare arm, touching him for the first time, other than to shake his hand.

"Kawika," she said, "I want to ask you something. Are you married?"

"No."

"Engaged?"

"No." That was true, but incomplete. He knew he should say more.

"Well then," she said, taking a deep breath, "this probably sounds a bit impulsive, and I guess it is. But will you come back and see me? For dinner?"

He hesitated, searching her eyes. "Okay," he said cautiously, not sure what she had in mind.

She let the breath go and gave a laugh of relief. "Tonight?" she asked.

Now Kawika felt uneasy. "Sure," he nonetheless replied. They were just family friends, he told himself, just two people getting acquainted—or reacquainted. It might be all she had in mind; it seemed plausible. She must enjoy company sometimes, living alone. He couldn't quite imagine that a rich, beautiful haole from California would have any other interest in a hapa haole cop from Hilo. And yet, though he knew he shouldn't, he still felt what he'd first felt the day before: a twinge of desire.

Walking with her toward the hotel, a little disconcerted, Kawika noticed a sign the resort had placed near some path-side vegetation—a sign explaining shore naupaka, mountain naupaka, and an ancient Hawaiian legend linking the two plants and their half flowers. He paused to read the little sign, and Patience did too.

All of a sudden I'm learning about naupaka, Kawika thought.

The shore naupaka with its white half flower spread out along the path. But Kawika was thinking of mountain naupaka, with its corresponding half flower, a sprig that lay wilting in Waimea's makeshift morgue, protected by the plastic bag in which Dr. Terrence Smith had placed it after withdrawing it with forceps from Fortunato's pocket.

11

Puʻukoholā Heiau

From the Mauna Lani, Highway 19—the Queen Kaʻahumanu, or Queen K—follows the coast north toward Kawaihae, past Kamehameha's grassy training grounds, then turns east to leave the sea and wend its way up the smooth flank of Kohala Mountain. At that turn stands Puʻukoholā Heiau, like a huge brown pyramid with its top cut off, one of largest heiau in Hawaiʻi and certainly the most significant. Kawika knew the tale: Kamehameha sacrificed his cousin Keoua here, having built the heiau for that very purpose, so he could fulfill a priest's prophecy and conquer the island chain. Within four years Kamehameha did indeed conquer all the islands except Kauaʻi, a failure the priest blamed on Keoua's act of self-mutilation, his spoiling the perfection of his own sacrifice—in his desperate attempt to avert it—by cutting off the head of his penis.

Jarvis had told Kawika that it was here, at a leaning stone of the ancient priests below the main heiau, that HHH held its meetings. Kawika wanted to see the spot. So while driving with Tommy to Waimea for his interview of Joan Malo, KKL's receptionist, Kawika suggested stopping at the heiau.

Tommy parked at the interpretive center. A sign explained the site's history but didn't mention human sacrifice, the reason for the heiau's existence. At a spot well below the massive structure, down a narrow asphalt path, part of the leaning stone still stood, a natural obelisk broken into three pieces—from an accident, a sign said enigmatically. Countless feet had worn the earth around the stone into a circle; recent visitors had left offerings wrapped in long green leaves from ti plants. A warm breeze blew off the sea a few yards below. Little waves covered an adjunct to the main temple, a small underwater heiau where sharks once devoured the remains of sacrificed humans while the priests leaned against the stone and watched—another detail the signs omitted. Queen Emma had been born a hundred yards away. The signs did point that out.

Kawika wondered why the National Park Service chose to downplay human sacrifice here. To avoid unsettling tourists and their kids? Or to avoid unsettling Hawaiians?

"Nice spot for a meeting," he said, gazing briefly out at the sea.

"A small meeting," Tommy replied, looking down at the little circle of bare ground. He kicked the ground lightly with his toe. Kawika got the point: Tommy resented Kawika ditching him at the Mauna Lani, treating him like a chauffeur and making him wait with the car. Silently, Kawika resolved to treat him better.

They turned to study the huge heiau up the slope above them. The Park Service had painstakingly restored the walls, striking not just for their size but for their stones. The walls weren't made of local rock. As Kawika knew, the priest had told Kamehameha the temple must be built of stones rounded by the sea. The closest source had been Pololū, on the windward shore of Kohala Mountain. Kamehameha issued commands, and a human chain had soon reached all the way from Pololū, with thousands of men, including the king, in a single line for miles and passing heavy stones from hand to hand. *It must have made an astounding sight,* Kawika thought.

Looking at the temple's stones, those thousands of tons of sea-rounded rocks from Pololū, each having passed through the hands of Kamehameha himself, Kawika had a sudden inspiration—one that would have earned him an *Iiko, iiko* had Tanaka been there instead of Tommy.

"He's at Pololū, I bet," Kawika said aloud. "Peter Pukui. That's where he'd go to hide. It's the nearest good place. Way back in the Pololū Valley. That's where we can catch him."

12

Waimea

"This is gonna be bad," Tommy repeated as he and Kawika, sitting on an old bench in the shade, waited for Joan Malo outside the Waimea Police Station.

"She's just late. It happens in Hawai'i," Kawika said.

"You don't know her husband, Kai. But I do. We paddle together, down in Kawaihae."

"He doesn't have to find out. We'll keep our mouths shut, okay?"

"Kai will find out."

Finally Kawika allowed Tommy the last word: "This is gonna be bad."

Apart from the caps he wore—today his cap read "Kawaihae Service"—Tommy dressed well for a plainclothesman. And Kawaihae Service, an old local gas station, had been out of business for years. *To Tommy I'm an outsider in Kohala,* Kawika thought. *He's letting me know it.*

Joan Malo finally walked up to the police station: a young woman, small, with a strikingly lovely figure. She wore sunglasses and a head scarf with a brown tapa cloth pattern. Her face—what Kawika could see of it—appeared quite beautiful but unnaturally slack, as if she'd just come from the dentist.

She clutched a purse tightly and did not extend her hand to Kawika as he rose from the bench, nor did she acknowledge Tommy. They ushered her inside to a witness room. Kawika sat on the same side of the table and turned his chair to face her.

"Should I call you Joan or Ms. Malo?" Kawika began.

"Ms. Malo. And I'm not talking with him here." She jerked her head toward Tommy. "Everybody knows everybody here. I'll go to Hilo if you want. I'm not talking to the local police."

Kawika looked at Tommy, then nodded. Tommy snorted and gave her an ugly look. He pushed back his chair, scraping it on the floor, stood up, and left. Kawika and Ms. Malo were alone.

"Okay," Kawika said. "Why don't you and I just talk? No recording, no notes. Just talk." He pushed the recorder to the side, out of reach. "Maybe I'll ask you for a statement later, okay? Something short, something we agree on. How would that be?"

She nodded downward, then didn't raise her face.

"Ms. Malo, would you mind taking off your sunglasses?"

She reached up, jerked them off, set them on the table. Kawika waited. She finally lifted her eyes. She looked exhausted, burnt out.

"You want to know if I killed Ralph," she said. "I didn't. I was waiting to meet him that night. He never showed up. I didn't know he'd been killed until the next day."

"Actually, I—"

"And you want to know if my husband killed Ralph," she went on. "He didn't. He was on Moloka'i with his family, got back the next morning. He didn't know about me and Ralph. I just told him an hour ago. Right before I came here."

"You told your husb—"

"I *had* to," she said with a flash of anger. "You left me no choice. Tommy told me when he called: you talked about me and Ralph, right in our office. With Michael Cushing. And with Tommy sitting there the whole time." She motioned toward the door. "Kohala's a small place—not big like Hilo. Tommy and Kai, they paddle together, the same canoe club. I couldn't let my husband hear about my affair from someone else. And if Tommy knows—" A sob caught in her throat.

Kawika, abashed, understood her reasoning at once. "I'm sorry," he said. Still, he didn't think Tommy would have told anyone. But it didn't matter now.

"Look," she replied. "You're from Hilo, you're just doing your job. I'm the one who had an affair. I was stupid. I wasn't thinking. But it's got nothing to do with the murder."

Kawika swallowed, his lips dry. He hadn't been careful enough here in Kohala. He should've called Joan Malo himself, not asked Tommy to do it. Shouldn't have asked Michael Cushing to name Fortunato's lover with Tommy present.

She began to weep softly. He handed her a tissue box, tried some comforting words. She composed herself, sniffled, wiped her nose.

"Thank you," she said.

Her coloring matched that of Kuʻulei and Carolyn: glossy black hair, eyes so dark that iris and pupil merged, skin a smooth and uniform tone of coffee with cream. Yet she also resembled Patience. It was her body, he realized: small, lithe, very fit. It occurred to him she must work out at a gym—and so must Patience. Women with lovers, women without husbands: *What portion of the gym-going population?* he wondered.

"Maybe I should start," she suggested. "Then you can ask me questions."

"Okay. That would be fine."

Ms. Malo explained she'd joined KKL three years earlier, in 1999. For a long time she'd worked for Fortunato "without anything happening," as she put it. Still, she'd begun to admire him and started to fall for him a bit. It was the situation. He was her boss—not especially nice, not especially handsome, although he could be very funny. But she saw him only at work, always in action, always powerful and making things happen. "And I didn't have to wash his underwear," she said. "Isn't that what women say? I didn't have to ask him to take out the garbage."

Kawika nodded sympathetically, hoping to encourage her.

"He started making passes at me," she went on. "Like he was teasing. Usually after a big meeting, when he was all pumped up. At first I treated it like a joke, tried to laugh about it. Then one day I didn't."

Fortunato had keys to empty houses. First he took her to Kohala Ranch, just past Kawaihae, but it made her nervous. "There's a gatehouse," she said. "The guard could see Ralph had someone with him."

So Ralph took her to Waikiʻi Ranch, off the Saddle Road, the winding two-lane back route to Hilo. Waikiʻi Ranch offered seclusion and romance. At the Ranch's high altitude, a tablecloth cloud creeps down the slope each day. By evening, mist shrouds the grassy meadows. Mist and rain—which South Kohala's lower elevations lack almost entirely—make Waikiʻi Ranch lush and green. The parcels were large too, often forty acres. At Waikiʻi Ranch, Joan Malo felt safe.

"I didn't think of myself as a fallen woman," she said. "I'm faithful—by nature, and because I was raised that way." But sleeping with Ralph, relishing the exhilaration and the novelty, she began to love him. She felt she was cheating if she slept with her husband. She also began to see her husband's shortcomings—one after another.

Ralph warned he'd never leave his wife; she accepted that. He said he'd end the affair if she told anyone; she believed him. Still, he was always attentive, never critical, always grateful. "He made me feel good about myself," she said. She was happy when she could be with him, moody when she couldn't. Ralph gave her a company car—a little white BMW convertible. She began to travel to Honolulu or Hilo with him on business. Often Michael Cushing accompanied them, so by day they'd be discreet. But she'd come to Ralph's room by night.

"Then," she said, "two months ago Ralph had to go to Tokyo for his annual meeting with the investors' group. He asked me to go too. Just me, not Michael Cushing. My husband was upset. He didn't suspect anything—he just hates Japanese people, doesn't want me near them."

Kawika thought, *Maybe Kai Malo* did *kill Fortunato. Maybe he wasn't on Moloka'i. Maybe he killed Fortunato because of something to do with Japan, maybe without knowing of Joan's—*

"Ralph made me sleep with Mr. Shimazu," Joan Malo declared flatly.

"Wait—what?" Kawika was caught off guard.

"Mr. Shimazu," she repeated. "The head of the Japanese investors. Ralph made me sleep with him after we got to Tokyo. He let Mr. Shimazu take me away for the weekend. He gave me to Mr. Shimazu, basically."

"But why?" Kawika asked. "Why would you agree to that?"

"Ralph said we were going to lose the company. Mr. Shimazu was going to cut off the money. Ralph would have to leave the Big Island. He said he couldn't bear to lose me. He hated asking me to do it, he said—he was actually in tears, crying. I was comforting him. I was sick to my stomach. But I told him I'd do it. I'd get through it, I said. I'd do it for him."

She paused for another tissue.

"And so I did it," she concluded, so softly Kawika could hardly hear.

For a long moment Kawika could think of nothing to say. Involuntarily, he saw her as Fortunato or Shimazu might have seen her: a highly desirable woman.

"That weekend was horrible," she resumed, as if compelled to fill the silence. "Ralph said I should pretend to like Mr. Shimazu, call him Makoto, be nice to him. But that wasn't what Mr. Shimazu had in mind."

She took a deep breath. "Afterward, we couldn't come back right away. I had bruises and other marks. So Ralph took me to Tahiti, to Moorea. I called Kai, told him that we had to go to Tahiti with the investors to look at another of Mr. Shimazu's resorts. Ralph got us a hut over the water. He took care of me, tried to comfort me. I tried too. I wanted to forget what happened, just go on."

"Did you tell your husband?" Kawika asked. "About what happened in Tokyo, I mean?"

"No. I'll never tell him. I've hurt him enough, telling him about Ralph."

"Well, I understand, but—"

"I already told you," she snapped. "My husband did not kill Ralph. He was on Moloka'i."

"What about Mr. Shimazu? He might have killed Ralph—he was here, right? And then he left."

She shot him a withering look. "No," she said. "Mr. Shimazu wouldn't have any reason to kill Ralph. He was happy after that weekend. Very happy. He told Ralph everything could go on like before. He hugged Ralph, patted him on the back. Said Ralph had to bring me back in three months. He winked at me when he said it."

"Ralph agreed?"

"To Mr. Shimazu's face, yes. But he would never have done it. Never. Ralph said we'd bought ourselves time, we'd think of something."

Kawika wondered if that was right, but with Fortunato dead it didn't matter now. "Did you see Mr. Shimazu when he was here this time?" he asked.

"I always see him when he's here. I'm the receptionist. But he kept it strictly professional. He didn't even wink at me. Anyway, he was preoccupied with KKL stuff. He and Ralph left the office together every time he came by."

"Still, Mr. Shimazu—"

"Let's not kid each other," she interrupted, her voice rising. "You've got a murder to solve. I've got a different problem: I ruined my life. I ruined my husband's life, my children's lives. My problem is private. It's personal. It has nothing to do with the murder, and neither does Mr. Shimazu. We all know who murdered Ralph: Peter Pukui or someone else in HHH. Now let me go home."

"Wait," Kawika said. "I still need to hear about your husband. What does he do, your husband?"

"Works for PCR—Polynesian Cultural Resources. He does Hawaiian cultural things at resorts, like build the oven to cook a pig or show tourists the petroglyphs. He does luaus too—plays slack-key guitar. He's gone in the evenings. That's what made it possible, the affair."

"You said you have children?"

"Two keiki. Girl and a boy. My mom looks after them. In Waikoloa Village, right near us."

"Forgive me," Kawika said, "but—"

"I already explained," she cut in. "I *worked* with Ralph. I saw him as powerful—smart, successful. In Hawai'i, we're taught to admire warrior kings. Well, he was a warrior king. I got to see him in combat. Being with him made me feel—what? Valuable, I guess. Fit for a warrior king. My husband isn't a warrior. He's not a king. He's a nice Hawaiian man—happy, a good husband, a good father. He's just not going anywhere. After we had the kids, it seemed like a dead end, like I'd die without having lived. I wanted to live. Now I just hope he'll still have me."

She paused, then asked quietly, "Do you have to interview him?"

"Don't know yet," Kawika replied. "Maybe." It wasn't true; he knew they had to interview her husband. He was just trying to be gentle.

She stood up, looking a bit ill now, and put on her sunglasses before walking a little unsteadily from the room and the building. Kawika followed. She tried to wave him off, walking toward her parked car, but he stayed with her. Her BMW convertible had a KKL logo on the door, a blue oval with three mountains, two of them snow-capped.

Kawika held her door. "You might want someone to help you through this," he said. "Your doctor, your pastor—" But she got in her car, slammed the door, and drove off. Kawika stood and watched her go.

Then, from the edge of his vision, Kawika saw a shape: something black, accelerating. A pickup truck squealed along the pavement, rushing toward Joan Malo in her BMW. With a horrific bang and crush of metal the pickup rammed the BMW hard from behind. The convertible lunged down the street as if launched. It careened wildly, nearly overturning.

Then both vehicles stood still, not moving, silent except for hissing steam. The airbags had inflated, then collapsed. Kawika ran toward the car. Over his shoulder he saw Waimea police streaming from the station, shouting, running in the same direction.

A man with a bloodied face and arms got out of the pickup and staggered forward, leaning, falling back, but then walking forward again, moving toward the BMW, always toward the BMW.

"No!" Kawika yelled. He guessed this must be Kai Malo, Joan's husband, betrayed and enraged. Kawika started running down the street toward the BMW. Running and yelling, running and yelling and *seeing*, Kawika felt nightmares begin searing themselves into his brain.

"Kai, no!" Behind him, Kawika heard Tommy and a chorus of Waimea cops running from the station and yelling, running and yelling. "Kai, no! Kai, no!"

Kai Malo had a gun. He pointed it through Joan's window. Kawika couldn't get there in time to stop him, and didn't carry a gun himself, couldn't shoot him. He saw Joan's husband fire twice, pause, then fire again. Kawika was still running and yelling. Kai Malo turned to him—Kawika looked right into his eyes—and slowly lifted the gun to his own temple. Then he blew his brains out all over the BMW's white fabric top.

13

Waimea

Kawika spent much of his day giving a statement to the Waimea police. The crime had taken place before their eyes; they could handle that part. They just needed to know what Joan Malo had told Kawika, what it meant, how it might explain these shootings. The Waimea police handled the situation professionally. If they resented Kawika, the cop from Hilo, or felt any satisfaction at his distress, they didn't show it.

Afterward Kawika went to the men's room and threw up. Kneeling, he retched for a long time. Finally he got up, washed his hands, splashed water on his face. He tried not to look in the mirror.

By that time, Tommy had apparently left the station; when Kawika asked, no one had seen him. The Waimea police loaned Kawika a car so he could get around. He drove out of sight, pulled over, and flipped open his cell phone. First he called Patience to excuse himself from seeing her that night. He explained the circumstances briefly, to her horror, and suggested meeting the next night. Then he called Carolyn in Hilo to explain why he couldn't get home as early as planned. The Malo killings horrified Carolyn too. He promised to see her soon—probably in two days, he said.

Kawika had arrived simultaneously at two of life's worst places. He felt responsible for the death of another person, and he found himself wanting two women enough to mislead one, by omission, and deceive the other. It wasn't like him to deceive anyone, much less Carolyn. This added to his queasy self-disgust. But he couldn't deal with his love life just now.

He knew he'd blundered. Two people were dead and two children orphaned. The dead woman—her desirability, but particularly her immediacy, his sense that she was still sitting there, still talking, her emotions still showing in her fine-featured face—wouldn't let him go. Nor would the image of that same face, dead, above a torso torn to bloody fragments by three bullets in the white BMW.

His third call was to Terry Tanaka. Kawika described his mistakes unsparingly: he shouldn't have made Cushing name Joan Malo in the presence of Tommy, and he should've called her himself to set up the interview, not left that to Tommy. "I was stupid," Kawika said. "I didn't even mention her to Dad last night, knowing what a small place Kohala is. I should've had more sense with Tommy. I should've told him not to mention her affair."

"Yes," Tanaka said sternly, not sparing him. "But Tommy made a bigger mistake. Her boss had been murdered. That was reason enough to interview her. That's all he needed to tell her. He didn't need to mention her affair."

"He probably just wanted to warn her," Kawika said. "Let her know her secret was out, that Cushing knew."

Kawika could tell Tanaka was trying to reassure him—a bit. "You didn't kill her," Tanaka said. "Now go to your dad's, get some sleep. We'll talk in the morning." All the same, Kawika knew Tanaka was shaken.

Kawika arrived at his dad's after sunset. Jarvis sat in one of the lawn chairs, without a light, waiting. "Rough day," Kawika said. "You heard?"

"Yeah," Jarvis said. "I told you: Fortunato pretended to be nice. But he wasn't."

"He didn't kill anyone."

"You know that for a fact?"

"No," Kawika admitted. "But he didn't kill Joan Malo or Kai Malo."

Jarvis rose and drew his son into his engulfing embrace. "Try to forgive yourself, Kawika," he said. "If you don't, you'll never be able to forgive others."

"No one needs my forgiveness."

"Yes, they do," Jarvis said. "Or they will. Starting with Tommy."

In the morning Kawika felt, if not better, at least resolute. He drove Ku'ulei to school in Waimea, treating her to a ride in the borrowed police car. She wanted him to turn on the siren, but he smiled and declined.

Ku'ulei told him about Lono and about Makahiki, the great god's annual four-month festival. "During Makahiki," she informed him, "fighting and war were kapu. Everyone danced, played games, ate tons of food. It was, like, a holiday. A really long vacation."

"Did kids have homework?"

"No, silly!" she laughed. "No one had homework during Makahiki! Everyone just had a really good time."

Kawika gave his cousin the shaka sign—thumb and pinky extended—as she got out of the car at school. She slammed the car door behind her. He thought of Joan Malo slamming another car door. Kuʻulei beamed at him, then turned to run off, waving happily to friends.

At the Waimea Police Station, work went swiftly. Kawika called Tanaka to agree on what needed to be done, and included the Waimea detectives in the call. They seemed to appreciate that. While a police spokeswoman handled the news media—Waimea was suddenly packed with TV cameras—Kawika and the Waimea detectives devised a plan to find out if Kai Malo had really been on Molokaʻi the night Fortunato died.

Then they discussed how to trace the Fortunato murder weapon, the old wooden spear. A museum piece, Dr. Smith had called it, probably missing from some collection. They agreed Waimea would contact museums and dealers and describe the spear, including its three barbs behind the tip.

"But don't release that detail to the press," Kawika emphasized. "Don't mention anything about the barbs. Or the olonā fiber cord or the mountain naupaka."

Next they considered how to catch Peter Pukui and his girlfriend, Melanie Munu. The local police agreed on Pololū as the place they'd probably hide. The Pololū Valley was relatively near and uninhabited—roadless, overgrown, impenetrable, slicing through sheer rock cliffs. A steep path provided the only access. In Pololū no one could sneak up on Pukui and Munu. The Waimea detectives pointed out another fact: the valley contains Hawaiʻi's most dense concentration of ancient heiau. "And ghosts," a detective added.

But how to catch Pukui and Munu in Pololū? One detective suggested using dogs.

"None on the island," a second pointed out.

"Get 'em from Honolulu in a day," a third noted.

"Let's not use dogs on Peter or Melanie," Kawika said. "At this point they're not even official suspects. He's a Native leader. So's she, apparently. He's got his dignity. She probably does too."

"And those TV crews got cameras," one of the Waimea detectives added.

In the end they decided to block access to Pololū and stop Pukui's allies from supplying him and Munu with food. With a barricade, and with Waimea police officers manning it, HHH would understand the situation. If Pukui and Munu were hiding in Pololū, sooner or later they'd walk out, surrender.

Kawika then called Michael Cushing. Cushing seemed far less agitated about Joan's death than he had about Fortunato's. Joan's killer was known and dead—not a threat to Cushing, unlike Fortunato's. "Domestic violence," Cushing told Kawika. "I'm really sorry for Joan. It's awful. Sickening." But not scary; Cushing again declined protection at work. "I'll be gone anyway," he said. "Have to fly to Tokyo tomorrow, try to save this thing."

"You going to see Shimazu?" Kawika asked.

"Yes, of course. That's the point of my trip."

"Tell him we want to interview him right away—here, if he'll come. And give me his contact information, will you?"

Cushing found Shimazu's phone and fax numbers, and Kawika called Tanaka to pass them on. "I'm guessing our Makoto may not be all that cooperative," Kawika said. "He'll probably try speaking to us in Japanese, if he can get away with it. So you'll handle him better than I can."

"*Iiko, iiko,*" Tanaka responded sarcastically.

Kawika wondered why Tommy hadn't showed up at the station. That was the greatest surprise of the day. So Kawika and another detective, one of Tommy's friends, drove to his house. Tommy sat on his lanai, facing the sun, his bronze face reddened by some other force. *He's been crying,* Kawika realized. A woman stood behind Tommy, one hand on his shoulder, the other arm cradling a small girl dressed in a police costume plus a Supergirl cape. The little girl looked distressed.

Kawika wanted to comfort Tommy—*Dad was right; someone does need my forgiveness*—but he couldn't tactfully say, "I blame myself, not you; I was the one who had you make the call." Kawika knelt, with a hand on Tommy's arm. "Tommy," he said, "it's not our fault. You were right: Kai would have found out anyway. She would have told him no matter what. She knew we'd interview him, and we'd have to ask if he'd killed Fortunato as a jealous husband, check his alibi. You were *right*, Tommy. I was wrong, you were right."

Tommy began to cry again. He put both hands on Kawika's shoulder and clung to him, sobbing in anguish. The little girl began to sob in sympathy with her father. "Come on, Grace," her mother said, comforting her and turning away. "Let's leave Daddy with his friends, the nice policemen. Let's go back inside." Kawika felt himself tearing up along with Grace.

No one spoke for a long time.

"Let's do something good," Kawika finally said, "Let's pull ourselves together, go see Joan's mom, Joan's keiki. C'mon, Tommy. I need to go, and I want you with me. I really do. You're my Waimea guy, Tommy. You're my partner."

The grief counselors the police had sent to the Malos the day before were still there when Kawika and Tommy arrived. So were a half dozen other visitors, all busy cooking, cleaning, doing laundry. *Here's aloha,* Kawika thought. Or would the scene be just the same on the mainland? Not with the smell of Spam frying on the stove, he guessed.

Joan's children looked smaller than he'd expected, and bewildered.

14

The Mauna Lani

Hours later, Kawika sat with Patience, facing the sunset at the Canoe House, the elegant outdoor restaurant she'd picked at the Mauna Lani. It struck him as an incongruous choice for a mainland haole dining with a Hawaiian detective, but he didn't care—not this night. He felt his exhaustion yet felt, too, some foundation of himself, something holding him up. He'd smelled death the day before but had begun—perhaps on Tommy's lanai—to smell life as well. The languid Hawai'i evening began to take effect. A warm wind stirred the palms, and ukulele music drifted in from the hotel nearby.

"How long are you staying, this trip?" he asked.

"Ask me later," she said, grinning, adjusting a plumeria blossom tucked above her ear.

After dinner and a long conversation about Hawai'i, their families, their two backgrounds, and with the torchlight playing across her face and blonde hair, he asked again.

"Later," she laughed.

When the check came and she waved him off it—"I invited you, and I get a discount"—he asked her a third time. This time she didn't laugh.

"Kawika." To his surprise, she took his hands in hers. "Your father is the biggest man I've ever seen—I told you that. But Kawika, you're the most beautiful man I've ever seen."

He started to say something.

"Shh! Let me finish," she said, laughing again. "It was hard enough to start!" She lifted her empty wineglass, tried to sip from it, put it down. "I know you can't stop thinking about your case," she went on. "I don't want you to. I'd even like to help you. But tonight, despite all that, I want to be with you."

Kawika didn't know what to say. He just looked at her.

"Be with you," she repeated. "Make love with you."

Again he started to speak, and again she shushed him, very seriously this time.

"I haven't been with anyone since my husband," she said. "In fact, I wasn't with *him* much the last few years." If she blushed, the available light—from torches, stars, the moon—didn't reveal it. "I want to be with you, Kawika. Tonight."

He stammered, not quite ready for this, though he recognized his lapse, his complicity, the swell of guilt contending halfheartedly with his desire. "Are you sure?" he asked, temporizing. "So soon?" He didn't say, *I can't— you're a potential witness* or *I shouldn't; there's Carolyn.*

"I'm not asking you to marry me," Patience replied. "I'm in Hawai'i, I'm unattached, and I'm with a man who's really beautiful. I feel like we're good friends—family friends. That's enough. Enough for tonight."

Once again he tried to speak. Again she wouldn't let him—not yet.

"I'm not looking for love on the rebound," she assured him. "I'm not looking for love at all yet. I just want to be *close* to someone. Physically close. Someone safe—especially the first time. Can you understand?"

Kawika nodded. He wanted to be close to her too. But he didn't consider it safe. To him it felt like being close to molten lava. In an instant, his image of himself as honorable and decent might be crisped into a cinder.

"The reason I didn't say how long I'm staying," she added, "is that I can leave at any time. I won't hang around your neck, Kawika. There's no obligation."

In the end, the temptation was too great. He yielded to it, knowing he shouldn't, feeling swept away, aware he'd conspired in the sweeping and that he'd feel the consequences later.

Back at her condo, she grabbed a blanket and led him outdoors. "Down there," she said, pointing. "Under that pandanus tree. By the beach." It was a long walk, circuitous to avoid the lava rocks. She stopped him several times to kiss. But toward the end, they walked rapidly, no longer stopping at all.

Kawika helped her spread the blanket on the little lawn he'd first crossed two days earlier, when he'd ducked under the crime scene tape. There in the dark, under a tree, mere yards from where Fortunato had died, they felt hidden from view. On the other side of a low rock wall, big waves crashed, rolling sea-rounded cobbles up and down the steep black beach in a rising and falling murmur.

Still standing, they undressed quickly. Urgency overcame them. Sinking awkwardly down to the blanket, they kissed, fumbling. Patience at once lay back, ready to receive him. Kawika savored a brief moment of anticipation: first contact, flesh in flesh, sinking into a new lover for the first time.

But then from some nearby sound or movement, Kawika sensed the presence of someone else, someone right behind the lava rock wall. He yelled involuntarily and spun to his side, scrambling to his knees.

"Don't mind me, folks," a man said apologetically from the dark. "I'm just here to pick up a cat trap."

Groaning, Kawika rolled onto his back. He reached a hand to Patience, lying there beside him. He heard her exhale sharply, a loud puff. Her head thumped softly back onto the blanket-covered turf. For a moment even the waves fell silent. Then a cat yowled plaintively.

Patience began to laugh and couldn't stop.

Kawika laughed too.

"Let me ask you again," he said. "How long are you staying, this trip?"

15

The Mauna Lani

The cat had to be released. Kawika needed a statement from the trapper, and Kawika was in a hurry. There wasn't time to take the cat to the shelter, and making it wait would have been cruel. So the cat went free, yowling one last time as it raced off into the night.

Kawika peppered the trapper with questions, even as he and Patience struggled into their clothes.

"You trapping feral cats?"

"Yup."

"For whom?"

"Kohala Kats. Local group. We neuter 'em, give 'em shots, then turn 'em loose again, back where we found 'em."

"You trap here often? In this spot?"

"Every night."

"You here three nights ago?"

"Yup."

"See anything unusual?"

"The killing, you mean?" asked the trapper.

"Yeah, the killing."

"Yup, I saw the killing."

"You *saw* it? You're an *eyewitness*?"

"Yup. Guy stuck a spear through another guy? Yup, I saw that."

"*Jesus.* Were you thinking of maybe telling the police?"

"Yup. I was thinking of maybe doing that. Haven't decided yet."

"Well, I'm the police. Detective Wong. I'm in charge of the investigation."

"Wow. So you want me to help you?"

"Of course."

"The way this pretty lady was helping you? Not sure I can."

A little later they all sat on Patience's lanai. She brewed fragrant Kona coffee, and they each had a cup. Then she booted up her laptop. At Kawika's request she began typing an official-sounding statement for the trapper, just a preliminary one in the middle of the night, a document to have before Kawika interviewed him formally at the station in the daytime. Patience cleaned up the cat trapper's answers to Kawika's questions.

My name is Jason Hare. I am fifty-two years old. I have no fixed place of residence, but generally live in or near Kawaihae, Island of Hawaii. My address is P.O. Box 173D, Kawaihae.

"I recognize you!" Patience had exclaimed once they'd stepped into the light. "I see you out on the highway."

"Yup," the trapper said. "That's me, the guy who walks along with no hat, no shirt, just my shorts. I look for scat."

"What?"

"Cat crap. Days, I look for cat crap, try to find the cats. Nights, I trap 'em."

As he continued, Patience typed:

I work as a feline retrieval officer for Kohala Kats. My duties include locating feral cats and trapping them. If a cat is ear-clipped, indicating it has previously been captured and treated, I release it. If not, I take it to the shelter in Kawaihae.

"Why do you trap here?" Kawika asked. "At this part of the Mauna Lani?"

"Shitload of cats here, that's why." He said that for the past month he'd kept a trap near the championship tee box on the fifteenth hole of the South Course at the Mauna Lani, because nearby homeowners had complained about the cats. Patience put that in the statement.

Kawika: "Tell me what happened three nights ago."

Jason Hare's statement continued:

On the night in question, I went to check the trap around midnight. The darkness and my location behind a rock wall apparently hid me from view. I heard someone approaching. A man was talking but I could not make out his words.

I observed two men, one behind the other. I could not see their faces. They were of similar height and build. The man in back sometimes pushed the man in front, who sometimes stumbled. The man in front had his hands bound before him at his waist. His elbows were behind him and a pole was inserted in the space between his elbows and his back, so he could not move his arms.

Kawika: "Why didn't you say something? Shout? You might have saved him."

Jason's statement:

I did not alert the men to my presence because I was unsure what was happening. I realized the situation might involve potential violence, but the men might also be drunk or involved in some dare or party game. I thought that if violence was imminent, by disclosing my presence I might end up becoming a victim myself.

Kawika: "Describe the killing."

The men climbed the steps to the tee. I raised my head to see what was happening. Both men were standing. The man in back withdrew the pole from behind the other man and leaned it against a railing. He unfastened the other man's hands and refastened them again in back. Then he pushed the other man to the ground. From below the tee, I could no longer see the other man.

"So you didn't see the actual killing?" Kawika asked.

"Not exactly," Jason said. "But I did see the blow. It was like someone plunging a harpoon into a whale, like in a movie."

As soon as the other man was lying on the ground, Jason said—and Patience typed—the man who'd pushed him grabbed the pole, raised it above his head, and plunged it straight down with great force. Then the killer bent down and did things Jason couldn't see. "After that he walked toward the golf path. I stayed out of sight. I thought he might kill me too, if he saw me."

Kawika looked at him. "Why didn't you call the police?"

"Well, I didn't want to get involved. How do you think the cops would treat me? I'm the guy who walks along the highway without a shirt. They'd treat me like a bum. They'd probably beat me up."

"Patience, don't add the last part, okay?"

Instead, she typed:

I considered calling the police and was still considering doing so when I met Detective Wong. My reluctance reflected concern for my safety if I were identified as an eyewitness to a killing.

When she'd finished drafting the statement and read it aloud, Patience printed it, and Jason Hare signed it on her teak table. "Thankee kindly, ma'am," he said slyly. "That's a right-purty statement. Sounds just like me." Handing the statement to Kawika, he asked, "Can I go now, Detective? Got lots of traps to check."

"Yes, you're free to go tonight. But this statement is just preliminary. You're an eyewitness. We need to interview you at the station," Kawika said. "Up in Waimea."

"I don't have a car."

"We'll pick you up. You have a phone?"

"No."

"How do we reach you?"

"Just call Kohala Kats, I guess. They always manage to find me."

"Okay," Kawika said, and stood up. "Then stay in touch with them. We'll want to talk with you soon."

The trapper nodded, also stood, picked up his trap, and started to leave. Patience restrained him gently with a hand on his arm.

"Mr. Hare?" she said. "Wait a minute, please." She walked indoors, returning with her checkbook. "I'd like to make a contribution to your organization. To thank you for helping the cats."

"Why, thank *you*, ma'am," the trapper said. "Remember, that's Kohala Kats, two *K*s."

16

The Mauna Lani

The moment Jason Hare departed, Kawika and Patience headed straight for her bedroom. Going back outdoors wasn't even mentioned. Within a minute she was on top of him, rocking back and forth. Within another minute she groaned sharply, convulsed, then began laughing—laughing and laughing as she collapsed against his chest.

"Oops," she said, embarrassed. "I wasn't expecting that quite so soon."

"You—?" Kawika started to ask.

"Uh-huh," she said, nodding her head against his. "Guess I'm *Impy* tonight. Sorry."

Kawika held her and began to laugh too. "God," he said, the two of them chuckling together now. "What a night."

A few minutes later it was Kawika's turn to groan.

"*P*—" he began, then muffled his moan with a pillow.

"*What?*" she laughed, looking up. "What did you call me? '*P?*' That's a new one!"

Now Kawika felt embarrassed. "Sorry," he said. "I was thinking Patience-and-Impy-and-Flea, all confused, and then when I said something aloud, it came out *P*."

"*P*," she said, trying it out. "*P*. I have to tell you, I kind of like it." He hadn't expected they'd be laughing in bed, but they were. They kissed and lay close. She fell asleep, but Kawika stayed awake for some time, listening to the waves, to her breathing, to his own heartbeats. He began to feel troubled. He'd known he would.

When Patience awoke in the night, Kawika was staring at the ceiling fan. "Just thinking," he said, turning to her and kissing the top of her head.

"Are you thinking what I'm thinking?" she asked.

He kissed her lips, smiled. "Depends on what you're thinking."

"I'm thinking Jason Hare lied to us."

"Me too."

"What's your reason?" she asked. "Tell me yours, I'll tell you mine."

"Because," he replied, "if he was scared three days ago and every day since, why wasn't he scared tonight? He didn't ask for protection or even ask to keep his statement confidential."

"You mean, he's still an eyewitness? Someone the killer would try to silence?"

"Exactly," replied Kawika. "He didn't make that story up. Not all of it, at least. It fits with the autopsy; Fortunato's left wrist was cuffed twice, for example. So he saw *something*. And he obviously does trap cats here at night, so he was in a position to see it. Yet he's not afraid of the killer now, if he ever was."

"Well, that fits with what's bothering me. He's unbalanced, Kawika. If you lived in South Kohala, you'd see him out on the highway in the sun, no hat, walking along half naked. His skin looks like leather. He's nuts, Kawika. Or at least a bit loony."

"Okay. And so?"

"Well—don't laugh—maybe he suffers from Lizzie Borden Syndrome. You know, loves animals, incapable of loving people."

"Lizzie Borden, as in 'Lizzie Borden took an ax, gave her mother forty whacks?'"

"Right. She killed her parents, got acquitted, inherited their fortune, then left it to charity to prevent cruelty to animals."

"You think he didn't care, seeing someone murdered?" Kawika asked.

"Worse. He's an eyewitness who's not afraid of the killer—as you say— and he lives in Kawaihae."

"Sort of, if he lives anywhere."

"Well," she said, "Peter Pukui lives in Kawaihae too, right?"

"So?"

"So, I bet Jason Hare belongs to HHH. I bet he's Peter Pukui's accomplice."

Kawika snorted, jostling her with the arm he kept tight about her. "C'mon, Patience," he said dismissively.

"P," she insisted. "I earned that nickname honorably."

"All right, *P*." He laughed and jostled her again, kissed her. "Jason Hare wouldn't belong to HHH. He isn't even Hawaiian."

"*Kawika!*" she said, jabbing him playfully. "You think everyone in HHH has lots of Polynesian blood? Where've you been, Kawika? We've got, what, about two dozen Polynesian Hawaiians on the whole Big Island?"

"More than that; don't exaggerate."

"Okay," she conceded, "maybe three dozen."

"P," he protested.

"Kawika," she insisted, "the old Hawaiians are gone. We're all Hawaiians now—you, me, even Jason Hare. It's not *old* Hawaiians or even just Native Hawaiians who organize things like HHH. It's *Hawaiians,* Kawika. *Hawaiians.*"

"You're a Hawaiian?" he asked skeptically.

"Yes, Kawika," she insisted. "I'm a kama'āina Hawaiian. I just happen to be from San Francisco."

Kawika considered her point of view. She stirred against him. "Well then—aloha," he said, not accepting what she'd said, but kissing her, rolling her slowly onto her back.

"Aloha," she murmured in reply.

"Aloha 'oe," she added somewhat later. Kawika understood what she meant; it wasn't *farewell.* They both smiled.

When Kawika next woke, it was nearly morning. Patience slept soundly. He rose quietly, slipped on his shorts, and crept out to the lanai. Except for the waves, the night remained silent. Kawika started thinking about how to write his first report on the murder of Fortunato.

A mystery writer, Kawika mused, might choose to write:

Wrapped in her Japanese bathrobe, a beautiful young tourist stepped out of her condominium to observe the sunrise, stretched her arms, and then saw on the championship tee, built to resemble an ancient Hawaiian temple, what appeared to be a body, and sticking out of it, a spear.

Or:

Wrapped in her yukata, a beautiful young kama'āina haole stepped out on her lanai to see the sunrise touch the distant summit of Haleakalā, and then saw on the championship tee, built to resemble a heiau, what appeared to be another haole, dead, with an ihe plunged into his chest.

It would depend on what audience the author intended. What audience had the killer intended? Why the ancient spear and the heiau? The olonā-fiber cord? The puzzle fretted him. But at the moment the beautiful haole herself—and his faithlessness to Carolyn, his long-time girlfriend—fretted him more. He'd just been unfaithful for the first time. Before Carolyn he'd hooked up with women in the Hilo dating scene, but nothing serious. The start of his relationship with Carolyn had nearly overlapped with the end of another. But Carolyn had soon become different.

The relationship *was* serious; it had been going on for two years. Carolyn knew Jarvis, and she'd even met Kawika's mother and stepdad. True, she'd declined to move in with him—she wanted to finish her PhD dissertation, not get distracted by domesticity; the PhD was hard enough, and writing it in Hawaiian made it harder. And after her PhD, she was thinking of leaving the Big Island to do land restoration work on the barren island of Kaho'olawe. So their future wasn't clear, and they'd never said in so many words that they were exclusive. But that flimsy fact didn't give Kawika much comfort; exclusivity had certainly been understood.

Making things worse, an eyewitness to the murder, someone indispensable to the investigation, had discovered Kawika and Patience making love—or starting to. Kawika wondered how long his secret could last. He could easily imagine the truth coming out, what the consequences might be. Yet he still had a murder investigation he needed to focus on. He didn't know what—or who—he wanted now, except to find the killer.

He'd been thinking for an hour when, wrapped in her yukata, the beautiful young haole came up behind him—silently, on bare feet—and opened the robe, taking his head in her hands and pressing it against her breasts. He could smell their lovemaking on her skin.

"Come back to bed," she said. "I want to hear you calling me P again."

"P," he protested, gently nuzzling her. "I've really gotta go. I have to get back to Hilo. And I've gotta stop in Waimea on the way."

"C'mon!" she laughed, pulling him from his chair, tugging him toward the bedroom. "Just four minutes!" she insisted. "Four minutes! You can spare four minutes!"

"Four minutes?" he asked incredulously.

"Doctor Ruth says any woman can satisfy a man in three minutes," she said firmly. "And as we've already demonstrated, you can satisfy me in one."

17

Waimea

Only three days had passed since Dr. Terrence Smith, in green aloha scrubs and red moustache, first strode down the shiny, waxed linoleum corridor of North Hawai'i Community Hospital toward Kawika. This time Dr. Smith did not look jaunty.

"You look grim," Kawika said.

"This is grim business," Smith replied.

"Did you know them, the Malos?"

"Everyone knows everyone here."

"So I've heard. Were they friends? Your patients?"

"No."

"So tell me what you found."

"Wanna go inside, take a look?" Smith asked. He lowered his chin and looked steadily at Kawika from above his glasses.

Kawika hesitated.

"Didn't think so," Smith said. "Well, there's no need. It's an old story: boy meets girl, boy wins girl, boy shoots girl three times in the chest."

"Anything unusual in the autopsies?"

"Like what? Kai Malo drunk or drugged up? No. But he didn't shoot her in the face. Couldn't bring himself to do it. Which could indicate he really loved her."

"Nothing else?"

"Yeah, something. I'll write it up. I found lacerations in Joan's rectal tissue. Took some samples, ran some tests. Turns out she'd had forceful anal intercourse. Very recently."

"Forcible?"

"No, forceful. Meaning, no lubrication. Except saliva maybe. Torn tissues. Could have been assault, could have been consensual. No way to tell."

"Consensual? With no lubrication?"

Smith shrugged. "It happens," he said. "Anyway, what we got on the swab was sperm. No lubricants."

"Whose sperm?"

"Good question," Smith said. "We've got tissue here from Fortunato and Kai Malo. We can't run DNA tests here; we have to send things out. Costs a few hundred bucks a pop."

"What can you tell me now? Anything?"

"Yeah, one thing: Fortunato didn't do it."

"How do you know?" As soon as he asked, Kawika wondered if he'd just missed something, but Smith didn't pause.

"Did a biopsy on the lacerated tissue," Smith went on. "Looking for little guys called neutrophils. That's how we date lacerations. Blood starts clotting at once, but tissue doesn't respond to injury in the first twelve hours. Then neutrophils start showing up. After twenty-four hours, the first neutrophils begin to deteriorate.

"We found neutrophils, all right, but no deteriorated ones," Smith continued. "So the tissue was probably torn more than twelve hours but less than twenty-four hours before she died. Almost certainly the day before, not earlier."

"And by then Fortunato was already dead," Kawika said.

"By then I'd already handed you his heart in a pan. What about Kai? He a possibility?"

"Maybe. Could have happened that morning, I guess."

"Well," the doctor continued, "if it happened that same morning, we wouldn't have found neutrophils. And we might have found some semen, not just sperm. But the seminal fluid was already gone—absorbed, eliminated. So maybe the night before? Shall we run Kai's DNA, just to check?"

"Yeah," replied Kawika. "And let's run Ralph's, too, while we're at it. Take the guesswork out of those neutrophils of yours."

"There's no guesswork, Detective. It wasn't Ralph. He didn't do it."

"Maybe, but I have trouble believing it wasn't him."

"I said he didn't do it. I didn't say he wasn't responsible."

"What's that supposed to mean?" Kawika asked, uneasily.

"Put it this way," Smith replied. "Ralph didn't shoot Joan, did he? But you'd agree he was responsible for her death?"

Smith looked straight into Kawika's eyes. A challenge? An invitation? Kawika couldn't tell. "Doctor," Kawika said, trying to assert his authority, "if there's something else you know about Fortunato, I need you to tell me."

"Sometimes I think I don't know shit," Smith said, turning away. He raised his arm to shoulder height, extended his thumb and little finger in the shaka sign, and waggled his hand slowly.

"Hang loose, brah," he said. He walked down the corridor, then through a particular door into a particular room: the room of grim business.

Kawika didn't follow. He didn't want to see Joan Malo again. Not that way.

18

Hilo

Detective Sammy Kāʻai, more experienced than Kawika, was also less squeamish. And Sammy was in charge of the Shark Cliff case. So, soon after his painful visit to the Waipiʻo beach, Sammy struggled out of bed and drove, still heavily bandaged and stiff, straight to the morgue in Hilo.

"We don't take walk-ins," said Dr. Elaine Ko, the medical examiner, looking him over.

"Very funny," said Sammy, showing his badge. "I'm here to see that haole."

"You mean Humpty Dumpty," she said. "The guy we can't put together again. All the king's horses couldn't even scrape him off the rocks."

"But you told Captain Tanaka the guy's got tattoos. Just show me those."

"My pleasure," she replied, leading Sammy into Hilo's room of grim business.

She showed Sammy the corpse's arms. One sported a tattoo of an anchor, the other an ancient Hawaiian fishhook, complete with tattooed fish line. Sammy saw even more.

"You were holding out on us," Sammy said, leaning over the dead flesh.

"What do you mean?" Dr. Ko asked. "I gave you the identifying information."

"What about this?" Sammy asked, pointing to the wrist of one arm, then the wrist of the other. "Someone removed something here, didn't they?"

Frowning, Dr. Ko lifted one of the lifeless limbs. She studied it closely, even using a magnifying glass. Then she studied the other. Finally she looked up at Sammy.

"You're *right*," she said. "Someone removed a pair of handcuffs."

PART TWO

HILO

The bones of Hilo are broken
By the blows of the rain.
   —Nathaniel Emerson, *Unwritten Literature of Hawaii:*
       The Sacred Songs of the Hula (1909)

19

University of Hawai'i at Hilo

"I'm not saying HHH didn't do it," Carolyn emphasized. "I'm just saying whoever did it is culturally illiterate."

"I'm sorry," Kawika said. "I should have let you finish. Try me again."

"Okay," she said, adding a quick smile, turning to meet his gaze. "But let's get a drink first." The day was hot and their clothes stuck to them. Carolyn poured herself chilled guava juice from the University's woodshop cooler. Kawika chose a beer.

Carolyn had paused her sanding of the slender surfboard she'd carved from a single piece of koa wood and been fussing to perfect for months. She'd designed it as an exact replica of the historic surfboard of Princess Victoria Ka'iulani—a very thin board with no fins, the type almost no one could ride anymore, even though in the late nineteenth century the teenaged Ka'iulani had mastered it. Kawika looked at it appreciatively from the workbench where they sat.

"You don't finish that thing, we'll never get to take it out together," Kawika teased. "But you *are* making it a thing of beauty."

"It was beautiful to begin with," Carolyn sighed. "I just copied her design. A hundred years since she died. Maybe I'll have it done for the bicentennial, yeah?"

"Along with your dissertation, right?"

Carolyn poked him but laughed. "She's easier to channel through a piece of koa than she is to write about, that's for sure. At least I've finally finished my research. But writing a dissertation is hard, especially in Hawaiian. We have a lot of words for some things and no words for others."

"At least no one else knows enough Hawaiian to grade it," Kawika quipped.

"Ha-ha. I wish."

She smiled and turned in her seat, and for the second time picked up one of the photographs he'd brought. Gliding a finger across it, she said. "First, this so-called heiau isn't just inauthentic—it isn't a heiau at all. A heiau has straight walls, not curved ones. A heiau's filled with packed soil. This has grass on top. Someone might argue this isn't the heiau, it's the lele, the altar. That would fit with finding the body on it. But the altar would generally be entirely of stone. It would stand on the heiau, surrounded by structures. Here, the tee itself is the only structure, and nothing's standing on it."

"I think it's supposed to *resemble* a heiau," Kawika said. "Not be one, just resemble one."

"The resemblance is pretty faint," Carolyn responded. "To me, it's just a structure on a golf course. It's tasteful, because this is the resort's signature hole, right? But it's just a filled-in retaining wall built with lava rock."

"Okay," he said. "Got it."

"Next," she continued, "it wasn't customary to kill the victim on the altar. The victim was killed somewhere else. In battle, maybe. Remember Kamehameha sacrificing his cousin? They killed him on the beach. Killing wasn't the sacrifice. 'Sacrifice' isn't even the right word. 'Offering' would be better. The victim's body was offered on the altar as food. Kū wanted something to eat. Some priests, the kahuna, believed Kū preferred the body cooked, but he didn't care how the victim died."

"Kū didn't require a spear through the heart?"

"He sure didn't. And that's the last thing. That spear. It's really old, Kawika. It's valuable. I bet you're going to be able to trace it."

"We're trying," he said. "Got calls in to the museums, all the dealers."

"Good," she said. "But that's not the main thing. It's an ihe, Kawika—a javelin. A combat weapon. No kahuna would use it to make an offering. The old Hawaiians kept a pretty strict separation of priests and chiefs. Don't forget, the kahuna worshiped Captain Cook; they thought he was Lono. But the chiefs didn't—they killed him."

"So why did priests make sacrifices to a war god?"

"Well, everyone worked for the king. The priests made offerings to Kū so the chiefs could bring the king a great victory. But the priests did it on their terms."

"And the javelin doesn't fit?"

"None of it fits," she replied. "The victim was murdered on the spot, with a javelin, and the spot itself isn't a temple and it's not an altar. As I said, it's culturally illiterate."

"Thank you," Kawika said. "But still, someone killed this guy with an old Hawaiian spear—a hard weapon to find. The victim was developing a resort, and they killed him in a resort. And they did it on—I don't know, a *spot*—that looks like some sort of ancient Hawaiian *something*. Not an easy place to kill someone. Hard to get to. Hard to get away from. Risky."

"So you're saying . . . ?"

"Someone wanted to make a statement, not just kill him. And not all killers are literate, much less culturally literate. The HHH folks? They're probably not scholars. They're activists."

"Well," said Carolyn, "I'm just saying, if HHH *did* kill him, they're culturally illiterate. And why would they kill him at a resort anyway? Why not kill him at Kawaihae, at the Puʻukoholā Heiau? That would be more authentic. Safer too."

"Carolyn," he replied, "if we'd found him there, right where they hold their meetings, not a mile from Peter Pukui's house, who would we suspect?"

Carolyn thought for a moment. "Let me see if I've got this right," she said. "You think HHH took the trouble to kill Fortunato with a spear, on a golf course, in a resort, so that you *wouldn't* suspect them?"

"Maybe."

"Why wouldn't they just throw him off a cliff?"

Not a bad question, Kawika thought.

20

Hilo

"How you feel depends on what you're thinking."

Kawika's mother had taught him that as a boy. He remembered it on the road downtown after seeing Carolyn at the University. Because Kawika felt maytagged.

Maytagged: dumped hard by a big wave, tumbled helplessly beneath the surface, thrown forward and over and spun sideways, astonished that the tumult isn't temporary, doesn't end, just keeps going. It's like being churned inside a giant machine, a Maytag washer, long enough to think about it, long enough to get scared.

Kawika knew why he felt maytagged: he was thinking about too much at once. About Carolyn, whom he'd just visited but to whom he hadn't confessed—not yet. About Patience; about his night and morning with her; about the mess he'd created. About the murdered Joan Malo. About Fortunato, a murder victim he couldn't help disliking strongly, unprofessional though that might be. About whoever killed the man—Peter Pukui? Someone else?

A few days earlier Kawika's life had felt integrated and unperturbed. Now it felt kaleidoscopic. A young woman's death—not at his hands, but fairly laid at his feet. Another woman in her other woman's bed, a stranger really, a temptation he should've resisted. And because of that, the sudden upheaval of his settled Big Island existence, just when he'd finally fitted in again, at home in his skin and his own land, with his own Hawaiian girlfriend. Now everything seemed spilled, stomach-turning, in full turmoil. Maytagged.

He shook his head, decided to think about something else. He thought about seeing Tanaka and began to feel better.

Tanaka had just returned from the morgue when Kawika reached the station.

"We found cuff marks on the latest Shark Cliff guy," Tanaka said, "but no cuffs." Clapping Kawika on the shoulder, Tanaka changed subjects. "So, ready to talk?"

Kawika wanted to talk about the cuff marks, but Tanaka had already changed focus. "I've had enough Shark Cliff for today," he said. "Let's tackle your new novel, *Murder at the Mauna Lani.*"

They sequestered themselves in a meeting room with a large whiteboard. "Couple of things first," Tanaka said. "Waimea cops called. They found Fortunato's car at the Beach Club at Mauna Lani."

"Interesting," Kawika said. "That's not too far from where he died— a quarter mile at most. Could have walked that distance barefoot. Might explain the grass stains and cinders on his feet."

"Also," Tanaka continued, "one of the FBI guys who investigated Fortunato on the mainland? A guy named Frank Kimaio. He retired here, lives up on Kohala Mountain Road. The agent in Seattle, we were on the phone, I was asking about Fortunato's earlier resort thing in Washington, and he kinda threw that in there."

"Great, let's have Tommy talk to this Mr. Kimaio," Kawika said. "We get done here, we can call Tommy."

"Speaking of calls," Tanaka said, "you got one too. From Patience Quinn."

"Patience Quinn?"

"Yeah," Tanaka said. "Woman who found the body. You interviewed her."

"I haven't forgotten. I'm just surprised she called."

"Said she has new information, thought it would interest you. About a couple who lives at the Mauna Lani. At the Cape. *Really* rich, right?"

"Yeah. A couple, she said? I wonder what she's got?"

"Don't know. We'll call her later, okay?"

"I'll do it," Kawika said.

"We can do it together," Tanaka said. "Right after we call Tommy."

Tanaka walked to the whiteboard. "Let's get to work," he said. Uncapping a marker, he began to write a timeline. He started with a dot he marked *Death.*

"We know Fortunato died around midnight, because . . . ?"

"Dr. Smith's best guess." Kawika replied. "There's also Jason Hare, the eyewitness. He's not telling the whole truth, but what he says about the killing itself checks out. Like, he says the killer uncuffed Fortunato and recuffed him behind his back. That fits. Dr. Smith says Fortunato's left wrist was cuffed twice."

"Ms. Quinn spotted the body at . . . ?" Tanaka continued.

"Around six AM," Kawika said. "Maybe six fifteen."

"And Fortunato left home . . . ?"

"About seven PM the night before. Left work around five fifteen, apparently. Went home and ate, then went out, according to his wife."

By dinner time, working together, they'd filled the whiteboard with the timeline. Then they called out for pizza, sat down, and looked at what they'd written. The first entry went back three years: *F arrives Hawai'i 1999.* The last entry was *Today.* The dozens of entries in between included:

Heiau discovered
Heiau bulldozed
Angry mtg w/HHH
Peter Pukui & Melanie Munu last seen
Shimazu departs
Kai Malo returns from Molokai (?)
Joan Milo assault? (Tanaka added *"Stray?"*)
Kai kills Joan & self

Kawika felt profoundly tired, and it showed. "Let's take a break," Tanaka said. "Make our calls. Pizza comes, we'll pick up again. Long night ahead of us."

Long night ahead of us. Not a bad title for a murder mystery, Kawika thought. He stretched, working to fight off the long night behind him. The night of Jason Hare and Patience, a night he hadn't slept much.

They went to Tanaka's office and called Tommy. Tanaka put him on the speaker.

"Need you to pick a guy's brain," Kawika said. "Retired FBI. Lives on Kohala Mountain Road. He investigated Fortunato on the mainland. He might be able to help us. What's his name again, Terry?"

"Frank Kimaio," Tanaka said.

"Kimaio?" Tommy asked. "Hawaiian? Could it be Kīmai'o? You know, with a little stop? Don't want to make a mistake when I go see him."

"No," Tanaka replied. "It's just a mainland name, I think."

"Find out what he knows," Kawika added. "What they found in their investigation. I'll follow up with him if you get anything interesting."

"Right," Tommy said.

"And there's a guy over there named Jason Hare. He's an eyewitness." Kawika told Tommy what Hare had reported, and promised to fax his statement. "We'll want to interview him again at Waimea as soon as I'm back there." Kawika knew it had to be done, but he was worried. What if Hare talked about how they'd met?

Tanaka said they should call Patience next.

"Here? On the speaker?"

"Yeah, why not?"

"Okay." Kawika dialed her number.

"Hello?" she answered.

"Hello, Ms. Quinn?" Kawika said, as formally as possible. "It's Detective Wong. I'm here with Captain Tanaka. We've got you on speaker."

"Oh. Hello, Detective. Hello, Captain." *Whew,* Kawika thought.

"Aloha," Tanaka said.

"Captain Tanaka says you called. About a couple at the Cape?"

"Yes," Patience said. "I thought you should hear this. The Murphys, from California. Both doctors, retired here maybe five years ago. Well, this morning everyone was talking about them. Seems Fortunato visited them at home the night he died. The Murphys told people about it the next day, down at the Beach Club. Apparently they really hated him. Turns out they're suing KKL, trying to block construction. Something about defective legal title—title to the land."

"Defective title?" Kawika asked.

"That's what the Murphys told people. They were explaining why Fortunato came to see them. They figured he wanted to settle the lawsuit. But when he got there, he apparently threatened them. So they kicked him out. And then he got murdered not too far away."

"Thank you, Ms. Quinn," Kawika said, making notes. "We'll definitely talk with them."

"There's more," she said. "The Murphys have been buying up property at the Mauna Lani. They're speculating in real estate. That's what people say, anyway. And KKL would harm their property values."

"Where are the Murphys now?" Tanaka asked.

"They're gone. They left this morning."

"You sure?"

"Yes," she replied. "I talked to them as they were leaving. After I heard about them at the Beach Club, I walked past their place on the way to my condo. And there they were, scurrying around, closing up the house. I said, 'Pretty shocking about Ralph Fortunato, isn't it? Everyone's talking about it.' Dr. Murphy, the husband, just scowled at me—and the other Dr. Murphy, his wife, she scowled at me too. Then he said, 'Someone was going to kill the son of a bitch sooner or later,' and went back around the house. Right after that an airport shuttle pulled up, and away they went."

"Well," Kawika said. "Thank you again, Ms. Quinn. This is very helpful."

"Wait a minute," she said. "Let me finish."

"Go ahead, Ms. Quinn." Tanaka waggled an admonitory finger at Kawika.

"I think Fortunato walked to their house from the Beach Club," she said. "There's a path—remember, Detective Wong? That's how we walked to the hotel. In the other direction, of course. The Murphys' is right near the Club, the third house. I think Fortunato parked at the Club and walked to their house that way."

"Sounds logical," Kawika said.

"The same walk I took today," she continued. "And after they left, I even went up to the Murphys' house."

"The gate was open?"

"No, I just stepped over it. It's not high. And I found a slipper at the door. You know, a sandal. A man's Teva."

"Just one Teva?"

"Yes. Just one."

"Did you leave it undisturbed?" Kawika asked.

"No," she said. "I didn't have my phone, I couldn't call the police. So I took it, just to be sure you'd have it as evidence. Fortunato was barefoot, right? I worried the Murphys might remember his Tevas and get someone to get rid of them. Or it. There's only one."

"Yes, but . . ." Kawika began.

"I thought you might *want* it, Detective Wong," she said. "Couldn't Fortunato's wife identify it? If it's his, then don't you see? It means he never got back to his car. It means he parked first and then something happened at the Murphys'. Something that prevented him putting his sandals on. And if it's his, maybe the Murphys just overlooked it in their rush to leave."

"Normally we ask folks not to disturb potential evidence," Kawika responded. He looked at Tanaka and thought, *She really is impatient.*

"I know, but I figured you'd want me to preserve it. The Murphys might destroy it. Now it's safe. I can always testify about how I got it, can't I? Explain why I took it?"

For a long moment, no one spoke.

"Did I make a mistake?" she asked. "If I made a mistake, I'm very sorry."

"No, no," Tanaka reassured her. "You didn't make a mistake, Ms. Quinn. You did fine. Thank you. We'll show it to Mrs. Fortunato, just as you suggest. It might even have Fortunato's DNA. We'll have the Waimea police pick it up."

"Whew," Patience said. "I'm glad I did the right thing. You had me worried, Detective Wong."

"Keep it safe," Tanaka added.

"Keep *yourself* safe," Kawika insisted. "Don't tell anyone you have it. No one. Don't go near the Murphys' again. Promise you'll be careful, P. No more sleuthing around, okay?"

"Okay."

"Promise?"

"I promise."

Tanaka regarded Kawika closely as he hung up.

"P?" Tanaka inquired.

"Pizza," his assistant announced from the doorway.

21

Café Pesto

"You and Terry reach any conclusions last night?"

Kawika had joined Carolyn for dinner at Café Pesto, her favorite, on Kamehameha Avenue facing Hilo Bay. Evidently she wanted to keep discussing his case—a relief for Kawika, compared with any more romantic topic.

"We made some progress," Kawika said.

"So, tell me."

"Well, you know Terry: start with what's true. Someone wanted to send a message. That's true. We don't know the intended audience. But someone took a lot of trouble to kill this guy in a conspicuous manner."

"So if HHH killed him, that's why they didn't throw him off a cliff?" Carolyn asked. "Because they wanted it to be conspicuous?"

"Well, right now, throwing people off a cliff is pretty conspicuous too."

"Shark Cliff, you mean. What do you think is going on there, anyway?"

"There, I'd guess someone's sending a message to drug dealers, and the message is pretty simple: you're next. So that killer is probably some rival dealer or maybe a vigilante."

"Or a cop," Carolyn added. "Maybe a vigilante cop."

"A cop?"

"Yeah, you know—some guy who doesn't have time for niceties. Decides to make himself judge and jury. Executioner too."

Kawika smiled. "I'll tell you a secret," he said. "If you catch a drug dealer, you can convict him. You cuff the guy, you can send him away."

"But that's all you can do," she insisted. "You can't kill him. No death penalty. So if you cuff the guy, you can send him to jail. Or you can throw him off a cliff."

"Funny you should say that," Kawika said. "Terry says one victim actually had been cuffed."

"Ha!" She beamed with triumph. "Can you trace the handcuffs?"

"Don't have 'em. Killer took 'em, before he gave the guy the push."

"Well, start questioning cops—that's my advice," said Carolyn, disappointed. "So what do you guys think is true back at the Mauna Lani?"

"We know it took a lot of planning," Kawika resumed. "Special site, the old spear, and—once again—handcuffs. Probably a vigilante cop, right?" He smiled at her.

"Right. Probably the same cop, Kawika." She returned the smile. "Keep going."

"Okay, there's also the olonā cord, another deliberate clue of some sort. You tell me—you're the expert."

"Makes me think someone's trying to frame HHH."

"Possibly," he allowed. "Plus there's the mountain naupaka in Fortunato's pocket. We don't think he spent time in the mountains before he died."

"You can grow it," Carolyn suggested. "Not hard, I bet. Maybe he just happened to have some in his pocket."

"We also know he visited a couple named Murphy the night he died," Kawika continued, "and we believe he was snatched at their house. One of his sandals turned up outside their door. His widow identified it to the Waimea cops today."

"One of his sandals? A slippa?"

"Well, a Teva."

"What about the other one?"

"Slipper Dog strikes again?" Kawika suggested, invoking Hawai'i's most common explanation for a shoe or sandal or flip-flop missing at the door. "I don't know. But I think that's what Terry would call a 'stray.'"

"Maybe. Or maybe the slippa you found is planted evidence."

Kawika cocked his head at her. "Ever heard of Occam's Razor?" he asked.

"The principle of logic, you mean? If you can explain something in more than one way, go for the simplest way first?"

"Jesus," he said. "Is there anything you *don't* know?"

"Hey, I am getting a *doctorate*, after all," she replied. "So is the simplest explanation that someone wanted to frame somebody?"

"Possibly," Kawika replied. "Not necessarily."

"You think the simplest explanation is that someone snatched this guy off a lanai? Knew he'd be at a house near the fake heiau, had the spear and the cord and the cuffs ready, then walked him barefoot—how far?"

"Quarter mile, more or less," Kawika answered.

"Walked him barefoot a quarter mile across the lava and then killed him?"

"Not across the lava. There's a path. It's mostly paved."

"No lava at all?"

"Some pretty sharp cinders," Kawika admitted. "The last bit is grass. Autopsy found cinders and grass stains on his feet."

"Cinders and grass stains—that sounds like something true. The rest sounds like speculation, Kawika."

"There's more," he said. "This Murphy couple hated the man. They're suing to stop his resort. They knew he'd come see them that night; they had time to prepare. And then they blew town. Never talked to the police. The Waimea cops think the simplest explanation is that they killed him and tried to make it look like Hawaiians did it."

"Which could explain . . ." she began.

". . . the cultural illiteracy of it all," he added, and she laughed.

"You're one hell of a detective," she said teasingly. Smiling, she let down her hair and shook it out. "Does this couple grow naupaka at their place?"

Kawika smiled again. "We'll ask. Terry called 'em in California today, told 'em to get back here—not now, but *right* now. Wikiwiki."

"Wikiwiki's for tourists, Kawika. Say 'āwīwī—if you want to be culturally literate." She laughed and gave him a small poke.

Not ready to stop talking, they ordered dessert and coffee.

"Fortunato had enemies," Kawika continued. "The Murphys hated him, Peter Pukui and HHH hated him. Maybe his Japanese investors hated him— we think they were pretty concerned, at least. He may have been a fraudster."

Kawika told her about Fortunato on the mainland. "The Feds charged him for desecrating the Indian site. A retired FBI agent who investigated him, a guy named Frank Kimaio, lives in Waimea now."

"Kimaio?" she asked. "Hawaiian?"

"No, mainland haole, it seems. My Waimea cop partner talked to him today. This Agent Kimaio says the Feds were actually trying to nail Fortunato for real estate fraud. They just used the desecration stuff to put pressure on him."

"What happened?"

"Prosecution fell apart. Have to talk to Kimaio myself, get more details. But Fortunato's development went bankrupt. Had a close shave on the mainland, came here, started over. Somehow he convinced the Japanese to back him. There's definitely something fishy about it."

"Fishy how?"

"I don't know yet. But the Japanese are unhappy. I'm guessing he was ripping them off somehow. You know what Dad said about Fortunato? *He pretends to be nice, but he's not.*' New enemies popping up all the time. But still."

"What?"

"Like you said before, why wouldn't they just throw him off a cliff?"

Carolyn paused for a moment. "Maybe framing HHH was what they wanted," she replied.

"That actually looks like a reasonable guess right now," he said gently.

Pleased with that possibility, Carolyn nodded. "This has been fascinating," she said, pushing back from the table. "Thank you for letting me in on it. Seriously."

"Not at all," he said. "Thank you for helping. Terry said you could, and he was right."

"It's your biggest case yet, right?" Carolyn turned to face him directly. "Well, let's go take your mind off it. My place—it's closer."

"Also cleaner," he added. *And there's no danger of Patience calling me there.*

She held his arm as they walked, her body warm and coconut fragrant beside him. His feet carried him toward a familiar destination. Perhaps nothing had really changed—nothing important anyway. Maybe the thing with Patience had just been an accident, an aberration. The thought made him swell with hope: *Maybe the god of love allows us a grace period for mistakes and indecision.*

Carolyn, however, apparently couldn't stop thinking about the case.

"It looks bad for Peter Pukui because he ran away, right?"

"No one's seen him or his girlfriend since before the murder. She belongs to HHH too. Although she's Maori, apparently. Melanie Munu."

"Oh, shit," Carolyn said.

"What? Is she bad?"

"Not bad as in 'criminal' or 'violent.' Bad as in 'political.' She's with S&R, Kawika—Sovereignty & Reparations, the Native group. She's one of the founders. It's not like other cultural groups. Not at all."

"They're radicals?"

"Very radical," Carolyn said. "Not so much their goals. It's their methods, Kawika. They're always outraged, always going for publicity. Damn. If Melanie is part of this, you're gonna be in Chinatown all over again."

"This is one mean tong we're talking about? Is that it?"

"Truly, Kawika. One very mean tong. *Shit.*"

22

Hilo

In the room at the station with the big whiteboard, Carolyn, Kawika, and Tanaka held copies of a press release Sovereignty & Reparations had issued that morning.

"We original Hawaiians may or may not still exist," Carolyn said. "Either way, we're incredibly angry. But nothing justifies this. Nothing." She picked up the press release and began reading it again.

Sovereignty & Reparations Condemns
Racist Probe of Big Island Native Rights Group,
Demands Investigation by Native Authorities

Sovereignty & Reparations (S&R), Hawaiʻi's most active Native rights organization, today condemned a racist Hilo police investigation—led by Captain Teruo Tanaka and Detective Wong, without any Native Hawaiian supervision or participation—that unjustly seeks to blame Big Island activist and heiau preservation leader Peter Pukui for the alleged "homicide" of Ralph Fortunato, a colonialist real estate developer whose pillaging of sacred Hawaiian religious sites and denial of traditional hoaʻāina rights to ahupuaʻa tenants Pukui has courageously organized Hawaiians throughout Kohala to resist.

"*Alleged* homicide," Tanaka said. "How can they say that?"

"Maybe we're looking at it wrong," Kawika replied in disgust. "Maybe Fortunato planted the spear, cuffed his hands behind his back, got a running start and threw himself on it, then flopped over with it stuck in his chest."

"Doesn't explain the divot," said Tanaka.

"*Guys,*" Carolyn admonished. "Cut it out. You're missing what's going on. They're trying to make you targets. Racial targets. Both of you. Notice they use your full name, Terry, because it's Japanese. Kawika they just call 'Detective Wong.'"

"We noticed," Tanaka assured her.

"And what's this about Fortunato denying hoaʻāina rights to ahupuaʻa tenants?" she asked. "You ever hear that before?"

"Don't even know what that is," Kawika answered. "Do you, Terry?"

Carolyn rolled her eyes. "Guys, you've really got to get ready for this meeting," she said.

"This is why we need you here," Kawika said.

Carolyn sighed, then leaned forward, arms on the table. Native Hawaiians whose families once lived in a particular subdistrict, or ahupuaʻa, she explained, still retain rights to use the land, or ʻāina. "They can take plants and animals," she said, "or use the land for cultural or religious purposes. That's what S&R is talking about. The courts have upheld those rights, and in a Big Island real estate case too. So S&R is saying there's more here than just a bulldozed heiau."

S&R demands that County authorities immediately remove the Tanaka-Wong cabal and empower a team of Native Hawaiians to investigate the case, including Tanaka's and Wong's baseless persecution of Peter Pukui.

"Detective Wong has a miserable record of racial insensitivity," declared S&R spokesperson Mele Kawena Smith. "He washed up in Hilo after being fired in Seattle, where he badly bungled a routine robbery investigation in that city's International District and grossly offended ethnic minorities, precipitating a notorious civic crisis."

"Detective Wong has no business leading a homicide investigation anywhere," Mele Kawena Smith insisted. "Much less should he lead an investigation among indigenous Hawaiian peoples."

Mele Kawena Smith pointed out that two Hawaiian residents of Waikoloa Village, Kai Malo and Joan Malo, have already died violently in the course of Detective Wong's investigation. "These unnecessary deaths are squarely on Detective Wong's head. He's responsible. His crude blunders with ethnic Hawaiians can only compound this tragedy over and over until he is removed."

"Notice they never call her 'Ms. Smith,'" Carolyn said. "They gotta get her Hawaiian names in there every time. I bet she was born 'Mary Devine,' not 'Mele Kawena.'"

Kawika shook his head and smiled appreciatively. "The 'International District' instead of 'Chinatown,'" he said. "These guys are the first ones to get that right."

"They couldn't call you a racist in Chinatown. Not someone named Wong."

"Didn't slow folks down in Seattle," Kawika said.

After decades of tireless work on behalf of disadvantaged Hawaiians, Peter Pukui, who is descended from ancient lines of Hawaiian royalty and priests, last year organized Hui Heiau Hawai'i (HHH), a grassroots association devoted to preservation of sacred Hawaiian temples and other religious sites. HHH immediately gained immense popularity and support among Native Hawaiians of all islands.

"Carolyn actually is descended from Hawaiian royalty," Kawika told Tanaka.

"Yeah," Carolyn said dismissively. "Like one part in sixty-four, one part in a hundred twenty-eight or two fifty-six. Something like that. But descendants of royalty take this professional Hawaiian stuff seriously. They think they're the ones who've lost the most."

Fortunato illegally destroyed one of Hawai'i's most important cultural treasures, a heiau built by Kamehameha the Great in the path of a lava flow, where offerings were made to Pele, Goddess of Fire, to save ancient fishponds on which the common people depended for sustenance. Pele spared the ponds, which foreign developers have now expropriated to serve as quaint attractions for pampered rich tourists at an ultra-luxurious South Kohala resort.

"Fortunato's proposed Kohala Kea Loa resort is a monstrosity," S&R's Mele Kawena Smith stated. "It desecrates Native lands and cultural resources. It violates the rights of ahupua'a tenants. The developers do not even have valid title to the land. If someone did resist Fortunato in self-defense of Native rights and culture, then that person deserves our understanding and sympathy, at the very least."

"Self-defense?" Tanaka asked. "We meet with these people, they're going to tell us someone killed Fortunato in self-defense?"

"I doubt it," Carolyn said. "That's for public consumption—*alleged* homicide, remember? They claim self-defense includes protecting Hawaiian culture against racism, colonialism—all that—and that it's okay to 'self-defend' against the 'dominant culture.' But I don't think any of them would actually kill someone. Anyway, don't forget this other thing: '*The developers do not even have valid title to the land.*' Is that something specific, you think? Or just the notion that no foreigners can legitimately hold title to land in Hawai'i?"

Kawika shrugged. "Don't know for sure," he said. "But that Murphy couple I told you about last night? The ones from California? That's why they're suing KKL, we heard." He didn't say more or look at Tanaka. He didn't want to invite mention of Patience Quinn right now.

"Carolyn, you can see Kawika's right—we really do need you for this meeting," Tanaka said.

"But I'm so close to these folks," Carolyn complained, "even though I'm mad at them for this." She waved the press release. "Otherwise, I'm pretty much one of them, really. I'd definitely be okay with Hawaiian sovereignty. It's just too late."

Tanaka's assistant, interrupting, poked her head through the doorway. "They're here," she said.

"Show them in," Tanaka told her cheerfully. "Tell 'em the Tanaka-Wong cabal will see them now."

The S&R delegation consisted of five people. Awkward moments passed while extra chairs were brought in. No one shook hands. Then Tanaka began.

"I'm Captain Teruo Tanaka. This is Detective Kawika Wong. And this is Carolyn Ka'aukai, an expert in Hawaiian history and culture who is assisting us in this investigation."

Two S&R representatives nodded. Three did not. All appeared surprised by Carolyn's presence.

"I agreed to meet for three reasons," Tanaka continued. "First, you asked. That's all you needed to do. Second, you're going to apologize to Detective Wong. You don't need to apologize to me. I've been treated worse by tougher folks than you."

The S&R representatives glared.

"Third, our team has work to do. We're conducting a murder investigation. We don't judge the victim. We don't judge the killer—we just catch him. We believe you have relevant information. We do not request—we *require*—that you provide that information. If you withhold evidence or conceal a fugitive, you will face harsh penalties. Trust me on that."

Then Tanaka added more gently, "You wish to help Peter Pukui. So do we."

Looks of disbelief—fading to cynicism—appeared on all five S&R faces.

"Mr. Pukui is not currently a suspect," Tanaka explained. "He is a person of interest. You can help him by persuading him to come forward. If he's innocent, we'll establish that quickly. If he does not come forward, we will hunt him down. When we hunt people down, innocent or guilty, sometimes they get hurt. That is not something any of us wish for Mr. Pukui. Consider this carefully as you introduce yourselves and apologize to Detective Wong. Then we can begin."

A tall and rather gaunt woman, wearing some sort of ocher cloth wrap, spoke first. "I am Mele Kawena Smith," she said. "I'm S&R's orator. This is our attorney, Mr. Ted Pohano. Ted will speak for us today. And these are three of our members who are here as observers. Keoni Ana, Mataio Kēkuanāoʻa, and Iona Piʻikoi."

Carolyn looked startled. "I'm sorry," she said. "What are those names again?"

"Keoni Ana, Mataio Kēkuanāoʻa, and Iona Piʻikoi."

Carolyn wrote on a yellow pad, then showed it to Kawika and Tanaka, as if helping them understand the spelling. But what she'd written was "FAKE NAMES."

Ted Pohano, the lawyer, looked prosperous and formal in glasses and a business suit. Nothing about his features suggested he was Hawaiian. He cleared his throat and smiled. "Detective Wong," he began, "please accept our apology for anything in our press release that may offend you. And please do not take it personally. We meant nothing personal—the press release is purely political. We hope you understand."

The lawyer waited for Kawika's reaction. So did Tanaka and Carolyn. The silence lengthened uncomfortably. Finally Tanaka broke it. "Perhaps you could explain."

"Certainly," Pohano replied. "Our organization's objectives are real. We demand that Hawaiʻi be restored to its status as a sovereign nation—allied with but independent of the United States—and we demand reparations for Hawaiian people. We're serious. However, we're also realists. We can't achieve success overnight. We have to raise consciousness first. The press release is a consciousness-raising tool. It has nothing to do with Detective Wong personally, or with our purpose here today. To reach Native Hawaiians—also haoles and others—we need publicity. Sadly, too, we have to compete with other Hawaiian cultural groups for members and funds—make a splash sometimes. So again, we meant nothing personal. It was, as I said, purely political."

What happened next caught Kawika by surprise. Something seismic, some column of molten lava surging upward, shook Carolyn. Pele seized her, then erupted furiously.

"*Nothing personal?*" she shouted. "Are you *crazy*? You make Kawika the target of the worst kind of racial hatred, and it's nothing personal? What if some whacked-out kanaka takes a shot at him? Would a bullet in Kawika be purely political, you think?"

She was standing now, leaning angrily across the table at Pohano, supporting herself on her hands, with fingers spread, as if she were about to launch herself at his throat. Kawika and Tanaka each leapt up and grabbed one of her arms.

"Let's take a break," Tanaka suggested. "Will you excuse us?" He led Carolyn and Kawika out the door and down the hall.

Five minutes later the police team returned, with Carolyn somewhat subdued but still looking angry.

"Ms. Kaʻaukai is a Native Hawaiian," Kawika said, when everyone sat down again. "She's not a police professional, but she is descended from Hawaiian royalty. I'm a Hawaiian too. We understand our history—Carolyn in particular understands it—and we know the injustices Hawaiians have suffered. We can sympathize with some of your political views, but—obviously—not with your press release. I've heard your apology. Now let's move on."

"Thank you," Pohano said. "We agree. Let's move on."

Turning to the three S&R representatives who hadn't spoken, Kawika asked, "Which one of you is Keoni Ana?" They looked at one another in confusion, then at Mele Kawena Smith and their lawyer.

"What is this, Detective?" Pohano demanded. "These individuals are here as observers, not participants."

"But their names aren't real," Carolyn said. "They're names of historic figures, people who've been dead a hundred years. We know who they are: the Hawaiians who helped draw up the Great Māhele, the division of the lands back in 1848."

The visitors looked surprised. "Captain Tanaka and I are just policemen," Kawika explained, "but as I said, Ms. Kaʻaukai is an expert in Hawaiian history."

Pohano smiled. "Let me explain," he said, recovering smoothly. "Our members face intimidation, reprisals. We try to protect them. Where, as here, their real names don't matter, we may substitute names of other Hawaiians—ancestors, if you will. Members of our ʻohana, our extended family."

The police team sat silently, waiting.

"We picked these names for a reason," Pohano added. "Ms. Kaʻaukai put her finger on it: the Māhele. We're here to talk about the Great Māhele. It matters to your investigation."

Carolyn smiled—or perhaps grimaced—in vindication.

"We're going to talk about the Māhele?" she repeated, just to make sure.

"Among other things," said Pohano. He cleared his throat and set a legal pad on the table. "Here's what we came to tell you," he began, glancing at his notes. "We don't know where to find Peter Pukui. We reject any notion that he's a fugitive from justice. However, we're prepared to try to find him. We think that will take about a week."

Pohano paused and looked up at Kawika, who snorted in disgust.

"A week?" he said. "Let me guess: you have suggestions to help us pass the time."

"Exactly," Pohano replied. "We have information—new leads to investigate. It's in our interest that you catch the killer and bring him to justice. We don't want Mr. Pukui blamed for a crime he didn't commit."

"So you agree there's been a crime—not just an alleged crime?" Kawika asked.

"Of course," Pohano acknowledged, refusing to be baited. "But we're not shedding tears for Mr. Fortunato. He broke the law in at least three respects. Any of those could provide a motive for murder. You're focused just on destruction of the heiau—and on the wrong part of that. The heiau's destruction was illegal—"

"Although he did have a permit," Kawika interrupted.

"He did. But he got the permit by bribing a public official here in Hilo. After the University team confirmed the heiau's authenticity, Mr. Fortunato decided to challenge that conclusion. He hired a contract archeology firm to write a second report, one that would support his permit. The public official accepted that second report and granted the permit."

"And the bribe?" Kawika asked.

"The official who granted the permit is a secret partner in the firm that wrote the second report. He recommended his own firm to Mr. Fortunato, who promised to pay the firm an unusually large sum. But once Mr. Fortunato had his permit, he refused to pay them. He was, after all, a crook."

"You think he was killed for double-crossing this guy?"

"It's possible," said Pohano. "The guy's a very tough local. Bingo Palapala—great name, probably not the one he was born with. He's got a racket going. It includes some supposedly respectable PhD bone-diggers—people with a lot to lose. They must've hated being double-crossed. Also, Mr. Fortunato probably threatened to expose them when they demanded payment, wouldn't you guess?"

Kawika and Tanaka exchanged glances. "You're talking a major public corruption case," Tanaka said. "If this is true."

"I know you're skeptical. But you *should* be skeptical about someone getting permits to bulldoze a heiau. I mean, c'mon. Kamehameha built it. Without bribes, no one's going to let you bulldoze it. You agree, Ms. Ka'aukai?"

"I'd have to see the consultants' report," she replied. "I doubt they said, 'Here's a heiau built by Kamehameha the Great; it has no significance, so go ahead and bulldoze it.'"

"Fair enough," said Pohano. "Read the two reports, compare them. Decide for yourselves. But remember, the private one was procured by fraud. The University's wasn't."

"That's one crime out of three," Kawika noted. "What's next?"

"Next," Pohano went on, "we've got the denial of rights to ahupua'a tenants. The law is arcane, but perhaps Ms. Ka'aukai explained it?" Kawika nodded. "Good. Well, the tenants wanted to hunt wild pigs and goats. Mr. Fortunato said the tenants weren't legitimate—that they couldn't trace their rights back. And Mr. Fortunato claimed they'd have no right to hunt the pigs and goats anyway, because the pigs and goats aren't indigenous. They're descended from ones Captain Vancouver gave Kamehameha. Finally, Mr. Fortunato claimed that even legitimate tenants couldn't hunt with rifles or bows, because they aren't traditional. He said they'd have to use old Hawaiian spears—javelins."

The unspoken suggestion hung in the air: *someone did use a javelin.*

"The dispute grew heated," Pohano added. "But of course it isn't really about hunting."

"Because no one would want to play golf or buy a home in the middle of a bunch of hunters?" Carolyn suggested.

"Exactly, Ms. Ka'aukai. The resort can't sell much real estate or get financed if the hunting rights are established."

"Who are these hunters?" Kawika asked.

"We don't know them all," Pohano said. "They formed a group in Waimea. It includes some Waimea police officers."

You live here, you know the man." Tommy's words came unbidden to Kawika's thoughts.

Pohano continued, "By the way, I also represent Peter Pukui's group on destruction of the heiau. We're challenging the permit. Not for bribery—we couldn't touch that without betraying our sources, putting them in danger. No, strictly on procedural grounds: lack of notice, defects in the record, arbitrary and capricious action—that sort of thing."

Pohano must have seen the suspicion in Kawika's eyes. He quickly added, "You wonder why we'd challenge the permit after the heiau's already destroyed?"

"No," said Kawika. "I'm wondering who pays you. And I'm wondering what any of this has to do with the Māhele—with Fortunato's title to the land."

"I'm coming to that," replied Pohano. "I'm paid by other clients, ones who care about title to the land. A couple from California named Murphy. Perhaps you've heard of them?"

Kawika and Tanaka stared at Pohano, then at one another. Meanwhile Carolyn wrote herself a note: *Destroy Heiau = Federal crime?*

"The Murphys are bankrolling other people's lawsuits?" Kawika finally asked, turning to Pohano again. "I thought they were suing Fortunato themselves."

"They are," replied Pohano. "Their suit will show that KKL lacks title to the land. The defect goes back to the Great Māhele. The Māhele allocated the land to a chief named Kuʻumoku. But the chief's heirs didn't live on it—it was mostly hard lava—and someone else eventually claimed it. That family kept handing it down and finally sold it without ever gaining title. And eventually someone else, a Thomas Gray over in South Kohala, sold it to Mr. Fortunato."

"Didn't anyone try to clear title in court?" Tanaka asked.

Pohano smiled. "In fact," he said, "the original seller tried that, but without giving proper notice to Kuʻumoku's heirs. He knew who some were. But he never served them with papers. He just published a notice in the newspaper, and that's not good enough. So it's a showstopper. Without valid title Mr. Fortunato's company can't sell real estate. They can't finance the development."

"They could pay the heirs to settle the lawsuit, couldn't they?" Tanaka asked. "It doesn't sound like Fortunato broke any law. He sounds like the victim: paid good money but didn't get good title."

"Ah, but he did break the law," Pohano replied. "The law against fraud. He knew the title was bad when he bought the land. And—here's the fraud—he even promised to pay someone to expose that fact, on command, the moment he gave the order."

"Why would he do that?"

"Mr. Fortunato was a crook. He had some crooked scheme in mind."

"How do you know this even happened?"

"Because the woman he promised to pay if she exposed the bad title almost became my client. I'm not going to name her. The important point is that Mr. Fortunato was going to pay her to expose his defective title. Which means he was defrauding someone else, probably his investors. And *that* provides a motive for murder."

Kawika immediately became suspicious. "Were you in on this scam?" he asked.

"Absolutely not!" Pohano insisted. "She didn't tell me about her deal with Mr. Fortunato. She just said she was an heir of Chief Ku'umoku and wanted to sue to invalidate KKL's title. I knew her from HHH, Peter Pukui's group. I trusted her. I thought it was all legit."

"How'd you learn it wasn't?"

"Well, as I've told you, I was preparing the Murphys' suit. We'd already found an heir of Chief Ku'umoku, a guy from Honolulu who'd be our lead plaintiff. We didn't need any more Ku'umoku heirs for the suit, but I told this woman she could become a co-plaintiff if she wanted, and the Murphys would pay for it. But I didn't hear from her again—until Mr. Fortunato was killed, that is. Then she came back. She was afraid she'd be a suspect."

"Why would we suspect her?" Kawika asked. "We didn't know anything about this."

"Mr. Fortunato had assaulted her, days before he died. She got treatment at the hospital. She thought the doctor would report it."

No one spoke for a moment. "Apparently the doctor didn't," Tanaka said, clearing his throat. "You're going to have to tell us more, Mr. Pohano."

Pohano paused to pour water from a pitcher on the table. His hand shook; everyone could see. "After our first meeting," Pohano began, "this woman apparently went straight to Mr. Fortunato and told him I already represented someone who would expose his faulty title. So her doing so would be redundant. Mr. Fortunato told her the deal was off, in that event. He refused to pay her—sort of a pattern with him. Anyway, there was an altercation. In Mr. Fortunato's motor vehicle."

"That's how she got injured?" Kawika asked.

"Yes. Mr. Fortunato stopped the car—this was on the Queen K—and pulled her out. He struck her several times, causing facial injuries. Another motorist pulled over and took her to get medical attention. Mr. Fortunato jumped back in his car and drove off."

"So someone knew Fortunato had beaten her," said Kawika. "That's why she figured she'd be a suspect in his murder?"

"Exactly," Pohano said. "But, uh, she would not have killed Mr. Fortunato. Believe me. She was in a relationship with him—a physical relationship."

"Yeah, getting beaten," Tanaka said. "Pretty physical."

"No," said Pohano. "You know what I mean. They'd conspired together and somehow they'd become close."

Poor Joan, thought Kawika. *Poor Corazon. Ralph was cheating on them both.* Uncomfortably, he remembered that he'd become something of a cheater himself.

"The names," Tanaka prompted. "We need the names."

"Well, the motorist was a doctor who took her to the hospital in Waimea," Pohano responded.

"And—let's see—the doctor just happened to have medical privileges there," Kawika said. "Dr. Terrence Smith."

Pohano seemed surprised. "How did you know?" he asked.

"A wild guess."

"She asked him not to report it." Pohano repeated. "She was afraid."

"And the woman's name? You can tell us now."

Suddenly Carolyn interrupted. "Wait a minute," she said. "I bet I know. It's Melanie, isn't it? Melanie Munu."

Pohano, startled, turned to Mele Kawena Smith.

"C'mon," Carolyn insisted. "You told us you knew her from Peter Pukui's group. That kinda narrows the field, Counselor. It's not a group with a lot of women. Plus Melanie's one of your founders here too, right? An old bud of Mele Kawena? What could *possibly* be the reason you didn't mention that just now?"

Mele Kawena Smith glared.

"Melanie Munu is Peter Pukui's girlfriend," Carolyn said distinctly, looking directly at her.

"Sort of," admitted Mele Kawena Smith.

"Ah!" exclaimed Carolyn. "The orator speaks!"

"Wait a minute," Kawika said. "I thought Melanie Munu was Maori. She's Hawaiian, descended from a chief?"

"Hawaiian enough," replied Pohano.

Carolyn pushed back from the table in disgust. "You guys don't need me anymore," she said to Tanaka. "I'm outta here."

23

Hilo

Carolyn's abrupt departure left a sudden void, an awkward silence. Without words spoken, it seemed the meeting had come to an end. Without ceremony and with jaws set, the S&R delegation silently followed Carolyn out the door. Tanaka and Kawika watched them go, but didn't linger. They went to check their messages. Kawika had one from Patience and one from Tommy.

"Detective Wong," the voicemail from Patience began, "I saw something today I thought you might want to know about. I went to Waikoloa Village for groceries, and as I parked, a car with the KKL logo pulled in beside me. A tall white guy in an aloha shirt got out and took a piece of office equipment from the trunk. I thought it was a printer. Then he went up to the KKL office, above the shops, two steps at a time, in a hurry. I thought about following him, telling him I'm a journalist, asking him questions, but I've promised not to sleuth. So I went into the Village Market, and as I was handling a Maui sweet onion, the outer skin—you know, the papery part—fell to pieces, just disintegrated in my hand. And then I realized: that wasn't a printer the KKL guy had—it was a *shredder*. Anyway, like I said, I thought you'd want to know. That's all. Okay, goodbye now."

Michael Cushing with a shredder? *Why?* Kawika wondered.

Tommy's voice message asked Kawika to give him a call. "Hey, man," Tommy said when Kawika reached him. "Just want to update you on tracing the ihe. We've checked with museums and dealers throughout the state, but nobody's missing theirs. I thought we were close at Kohala Historical—after all, it's the museum closest to the crime scene. But we struck out there too."

"What happened?" Kawika asked.

"The assistant curator, a woman named Kiku Takahashi, looked at the photos of the murder weapon, and she oohed and ahhed over it. Said it's really old and valuable, definitely dates from Kamehameha's time. She said the museum has one that's really similar. So she took me to the display case to see it, but it wasn't there."

"Where is it then?"

"A little card in the case says it's on loan to the Bishop Museum in Honolulu. She hadn't known that. But she says it can't be ours anyway."

"Why?"

"Theirs has a different number of barbs. She showed me a picture. They don't have one with three barbs, like the murder weapon, and all the other museums and dealers, if they do have any three-barbed ones, they've still got those. No one is missing any. They all checked."

"Hmm. So, close but no cigar with Kohala Historical?"

"Right. But she did make a good suggestion. She said we should check with private collectors too, not just dealers and museums."

"Okay, how are we going to do that?"

"I don't know," Tommy replied. "But we'll figure it out."

A few moments later, just as Tommy said goodbye, Tanaka walked into Kawika's office, smiling but shaking his head. "Got a call back from our friend Shimazu-san," Tanaka said. "He left me a nice long voice message. I thought my Japanese was pretty good. Not good enough, it seems. I'll have to call him back, test his English. Why do I suspect his English language skills will disappear suddenly?"

"Well, he does seem skilled in sudden disappearance," Kawika replied.

24

Hilo

Kawika awoke feeling cheerful and knowing why: S&R hadn't proven so scary after all. He rolled over and found Carolyn awake, lying on her stomach, her face resting on her smooth brown hands. She was gazing into the distance—although the distance was limited to palm fronds rattling against her louvered window—and looking past him with a countenance so profoundly sad that his spirits sagged.

He summoned his mother's wisdom: *"How she feels depends on what she's thinking."*

"What are you thinking, Carolyn? You look so sad."

She blinked, re-focused, forced a small smile, reached out and stroked his hair. "I love you so much," she said. Looked into directly, her eyes seemed even sadder.

"That makes you sad?" Despite his sudden unease, he tried to tease her into a laugh.

"No, loving you doesn't make me sad—usually." She smiled again, a little less wanly. "But that wasn't what I was thinking. Not just that, anyway."

"Then tell me," he said. He wondered if she'd say, *"I was thinking Peter Pukui did it."* That might explain her sadness. But crime was his preoccupation, not hers. They'd met randomly during his first week in Hilo, when he'd found and returned her snatched purse. Even then she didn't care much about the theft. What intrigued her was a Hawaiian guy moving from Seattle to the Big Island instead of in the opposite direction—and to Hilo, even. Plus those hazel eyes and that smile and everything that went with them. She'd wanted to learn more.

"Well," she began, "First I was thinking about Hawai'i. About what's been lost—everything, really. Everything's lost. I wondered if Kamehameha should have killed the haoles instead of relying on them and their guns. He probably couldn't have conquered the other islands. He didn't need the haoles for anything else, really. But that could've been okay, each island with its own royalty."

Kawika started to speak, but she spoke for him. "Then I realized, of course, the haoles could have found another chief on another island, or he could have found them. They would have armed that chief, who would've achieved the same result. And the haoles would still have come."

"So Hawai'i had no escape? That's what's making you sad?"

"No escape from haoles," she replied. "Of course that makes me sad. But what's the point? We're practically all hapa now; even you and me, hapa haole. And nothing could have been done about it. Not really."

"No," he agreed.

"Still, the haoles could have done a better job here. Everything else aside, still, all this development—all this tourism, real estate, resorts, shopping centers—it's all gone too far, Kawika. Way, way too far. It doesn't have any *boundaries*. None. It's pushing us into the sea."

She got up, pulled on a short robe, gathered and pinned her shining hair. Her movements briefly exposed her leg tattoo, the dark black ala niho running from ankle to hip, the tale of her life in permanent ink, from her ancestry all the way to her future, the ala niho ending in symbols for land, 'āina, and restoration. Kawika loved that black tattoo. He considered it part of her beauty, both visually and symbolically. He could have gotten one himself. But after his night with Patience, an ala niho stood on the other side of a Hawaiian cultural chasm he didn't know how to cross now, didn't know if he was worthy to cross.

"It's not just the environment that's been destroyed," Carolyn continued. "Not just the scenery, the native species—even the native people. It's the way people *act* that's wrong now. Development—all the money, the greed, the corruption, all the reaction and the radicals on power trips—it's ruined the society, Kawika. Turned everyone into phonies and crooks and sluts and scumbags."

"I can see how all that might make you sad," Kawika said, forcing a small laugh. "The end of Hawaiian civilization. That's a lot."

"But for me, it was just the *beginning*," she said, laughing at herself a little now too. "Because then I started thinking about your work. You and your work, really."

"Me and my work?"

"Crooks and scumbags are who you spend your days with, Kawika. And you're going to do it for the rest of your life."

"Whoa," Kawika protested. "Someday I'm going to retire."

She smiled but didn't slow down. "For the rest of your *working* life, okay? And that's a long time. Unless you get killed."

"Uh . . . did you dream about a whacked-out kanaka taking a shot at me?"

She nodded solemnly. No trace of a smile now. "Yes, but I've thought about that before. You're a cop, you take risks. I just never thought about the scumbag part—not until yesterday with S&R."

"*I'm* not a scumbag," he said, worried that a one-night stand in South Kohala might have just made him one. "And I don't spend *all* my time with scumbags. C'mon, Terry's not a scumbag."

"No, but Terry has his Japanese roots and culture to anchor him or hold him up—otherwise he might be a scumbag too. You're not Japanese, Kawika. What's a lifetime of this work going to do to you? A *professional* lifetime, I mean."

She paused, looking at him mournfully. He couldn't say what he knew she needed to hear: *You anchor me; you hold me up.* A few days earlier it would have been easy.

"Lie down with dogs, get up with fleas—that what you mean?" he tried. "Tanaka's got flea powder and I don't?"

"Something like that," she said, turning away.

"Wow, babe. That's heavy-duty stuff. On top of civilization coming to an end." He was still trying to jolly her out of it, and not succeeding. He put his arms around her, but she drew away gently, wrapping herself in her own arms.

"That's not all, Kawika. Thinking about your work got me thinking about my work."

"And?"

"Kawika," she pleaded. Her eyes brimmed. "You have no idea how much I just want to get my degree, switch to forestry, get over there to Kahoʻolawe, start planting trees. Can you even imagine how much I want that, Kawika? I need an escape from the scumbags. There's some sort of purity in planting things. Restoring something, saving something."

"I know, I know. I understand. I support you—you know that."

"You *don't* understand," she insisted. "I don't want to be alone, Kawika. And there isn't any police work on Kahoʻolawe. There aren't any *people* on Kahoʻolawe."

"Hey, there's bomb disposal work," he joked. The island had long been a Navy bombing range. That's why it needed restoration—and why restoration would be difficult.

In frustration, she hit him on the arm—not hard, but not in jest either: *Take me seriously.*

"Okay," he said, deciding to spin out a future they hadn't discussed, and now might never discuss. "We've got options. We can live on Maui or O'ahu. You have to commute to Kaho'olawe anyway—there's no housing out there."

"There will be housing. There'll be a workforce."

"So you could stay out there on weeknights only, right?"

"We'd be apart all week."

"Not on weekends, though."

"Kawika. Two days out of seven? Three nights?" Kawika had never considered what portion of a week a couple should spend together. Apparently Carolyn had.

"Okay. Second option, then. You work there for a year or two. Earn your stripes. We have weekends, vacations, breaks. Then you take your experience and your credentials and get some big forestry job back here."

"Oh, God, Kawika, you really *don't* understand. The Big Island, O'ahu, Maui, Kaua'i—I'd be living with all these scumbags again."

As she'd poured out her heart, he'd tried using logic's leaky ladle to refill it. It wasn't working. He changed his approach.

"Third option: I become the constable of Kaho'olawe," he joked. "Maintain order among restoration workers and bomb squads. Keep an eye on saloons and whorehouses. That sort of thing."

She was beyond soothing by jokes. But at least she let him hold her. He thought of her Hawaiian-ness, its depth and ingrained nature. Once again he sensed his love of it in her—and his love of her for it. It had never become ingrained in him. Neither Hawai'i nor the mainland ever had, he realized. And that helped explain the upending of what had seemed, until a few days ago, his settled existence.

By ancestry and blood, Carolyn was no more Hawaiian than he. He knew her name Ka'aukai survived only because her Portuguese grandfather, a fisherman, assumed it from his half-Hawaiian wife when he learned it meant "man of the sea." But Carolyn was somehow Hawaiian, and despite this morning's emotions, at peace with being Hawaiian, in a way and with a completeness that Kawika never quite could be.

"Carolyn." He spoke softly. "Babe. There isn't even a restoration program on Kahoʻolawe yet. We've got time to work this out. We don't have to solve it this morning, do we?"

Tearfully, she shook her head. "No," she admitted. "No, we don't. You're right."

"Then come back to bed," he said, leading her toward it.

He made love to her, not believing it would fix anything—much less everything—but feeling stupid that he couldn't think of anything else to fix things. He felt responsible for her sadness. Somehow, he sensed, it all related to Patience, not his work—to his guilt, his confusion, to the hundred ways one's doubts betray themselves to a lover even when the existence of another lover remains a secret.

Carolyn fell back asleep. He held her, thinking of Kahoʻolawe, the pummeled isle. He'd often seen it on flights to Honolulu, looking like nothing but dirt, without a green thing on it. He remembered Kuʻulei saying the ancient Hawaiians used the channel between Kahoʻolawe and Maui to align their canoes for the voyage to Tahiti. He felt like paddling to Tahiti, taking Carolyn on the long voyage. But when he suggested it—he must have dozed off too, and dreamt—she murmured that Tahiti, too, was ruined.

When next he woke, Carolyn was pummeling him again, playfully this time, her eyes bright with blinked-back tears.

"Constable of Kahoʻolawe," she laughed. "You don't find me some breakfast ʻāwīwī, I'm gonna lock you up with your own keys and have the Navy drop one great big bomb on you."

25

Hilo

"**M**urder. In general, you shouldn't generalize about it," Tanaka began. Kawika waited to see if Tanaka would smile. They were both a bit rattled. Safe now, seated in the room with the big whiteboard, they'd had to push through a knot of noisy demonstrators to get in the building. They hadn't expected that. They'd thought the news media would scoff at S&R's press release. Carolyn had said she wasn't so sure. Still, no demonstrators recognized them. None knew what they looked like.

"But," Tanaka added, "in this case, some generalizations are worth considering. One: The victim generally knows his killer. Fortunato knew his killer, right? He wasn't just in the wrong place at the wrong time."

"Right."

"Two: Generally the killer hates the victim. The feeling is white-hot, at least for that moment. Extremely personal."

"Well, not if it's a contract killing, right? Maybe the Japanese had him hit. Shimazu, that bunch."

Tanaka nodded, then moved on. "Drug killings aren't personal either," he said. "Just business. Generally."

"Generally. But you don't see this as a drug killing, do you?" Kawika asked. Tanaka shook his head.

"No, that's Shark Cliff," Tanaka said. "Enough murders there for the druggies. They're having a war, I think."

"That reminds me," Kawika said. "I need to ask you about those handcuffs."

"Later, okay? We're getting somewhere here." Tanaka moved to the whiteboard. "Who really hated Fortunato?"

Kawika started counting. "Pukui, of course. And not just for the heiau, right? Probably for Melanie too." Tanaka wrote *2x* after *Pukui*.

"Sex, betrayal—lots of white-hot hatred there," Tanaka observed. "Causes a bunch of murders. Including one of yours, right?"

Kawika lurched slightly in his chair. "What?" he asked.

"The one you solved in Puna," Tanaka said. "That stoner who killed his wife. He thought she'd cheated on him, right?"

"Oh. Yeah." Kawika remembered. *"You cheat, you die,"* the stoner had said.

"So, for sex-and-betrayal suspects, besides Pukui we've got . . . ?"

"Joan Malo, I suppose."

Tanaka frowned. "I suppose," he agreed. "Throws her life away to be with the guy, and he abuses her in every way. Even cheats on her with Melanie Munu."

"I doubt she knew it," Kawika said. "When I interviewed her, she was depressed, not angry. She'd made a bad mistake and it was eating at her. If she'd killed someone, she would've acted differently."

"I believe you. Still, you can't cross her off the list." Tanaka wrote *Joan Malo*.

"Cross her off the list." Tanaka's matter-of-fact words stung; Joan was dead and Kawika still felt responsible. "Can't cross Kai Malo off either," Tanaka added. "Not yet, anyway." *Kai Malo* joined *Joan*.

"Then there's Melanie Munu," Tanaka continued. "Sleeping with Fortunato, cheating on Peter. Running some big risks. Fortunato said he'd pay her to claim she's an heir of Ku'umoku and challenge his legal title in court, part of some fraud of his. But then he calls off the deal, beats her up. Hell hath no fury, and all that." Kawika noticed Tanaka always said *sleeping with*, never *fucking*.

"She's someone Fortunato might meet at night," Kawika agreed. "She could blackmail him. She could make it look like Hawaiians killed him too."

"Right," Tanaka said. He wrote *Melanie* on the board.

"Of course, Melanie may not fit," Kawika said. "Or Joan, for that matter. Jason Hare said the killer was a man. And Dr. Smith said it was a heck of a powerful blow."

Tanaka didn't reply. He waited, smiling at Kawika enigmatically.

"Ah," said Kawika. "I get it. You're remembering we can't trust Jason Hare or Dr. Smith—not entirely, anyway. And even though Joan was small, she was strong. Melanie could be a power lifter for all we know, right?"

"Right. Very good. *Iiko, iiko.*"

Kawika frowned at a new thought. "Then should we at least consider Corazon Fortunato?"

"Probably," Tanaka agreed. "But we both hear a little voice saying, 'It's not her.' Those little voices are worth listening to."

"Generally?" Kawika asked.

"Generally," Tanaka agreed with a laugh.

Kawika got up and walked, like Tanaka, to the window, trying to see if the demonstrators had dispersed. Evidently they'd left. *Whew,* Kawika thought.

"Corazon's small," Kawika said. "Not dainty, just small. Could she strike that blow? And did she know where her husband was going that night? Plus, she's got a baby."

"So the logistics seem tough?" Tanaka asked.

"Yeah, but would she kill him anyway? She and the baby might be better off with Fortunato alive and earning money, even if she divorced him. And she was angry when I talked with her. Practically ballistic about Peter Pukui and HHH. Though I suppose she could be a great actress."

"But guilty people can't act," Tanaka said.

"Generally?" asked Kawika, following his boss and resuming a seat.

"Generally." Tanaka smiled. "You know all this."

Kawika did know it. An innocent person doesn't have to act. A guilty person does. A guilty person has to imagine how an innocent person would act, what an innocent person would say.

"There's always—okay, *generally*—some telltale hesitation," added Kawika, ever the good protégé. "The guilty person has to think up the script before acting it out, right?"

"Right," replied Tanaka. "There's that little hitch or delay when you talk with them. You can't use it to prove guilt, but you can spot it."

"Corazon didn't seem to be acting, though," Kawika said. "But we'll question her some more, check those logistics." He wrote himself another note. "Who's next?"

"The Murphys, our California doctor couple," said Tanaka. "You make them for the murder?"

"Hard to say. Haven't met 'em yet. But it looks bad for them. They were in a legal battle with the guy. He went to their house, never got his Tevas back on. And then the Murphys took off. They must've been the last people to see him alive."

"Except for the killer and Jason Hare."

"Yeah, but the Murphys and Hare could be the killers," Kawika said. "That's what the Waimea cops think. Or the Murphys might've bought off Hare to silence him—maybe by giving a lot of money to Kohala Kats." Kawika knew Hare accepted donations; he'd taken Patience's check.

"The Waimea cops probably want the killers to be haoles," replied Tanaka. "Shimazu would do too—he's not Hawaiian."

"Maybe, but they might be right," Kawika said. "Even if the Murphys didn't kill Fortunato, they might have set him up for the Hawaiians. They're working pretty closely with Hawaiians on those Pohano lawsuits."

"Well, question them," Tanaka said. "As soon as they get back. Do it at their house. Make them walk you through their meeting with Fortunato. See if you can trip 'em up. See what you can learn."

"Okay," said Kawika. "But you really don't make the Murphys for this, do you?"

"Just a hunch," Tanaka replied. "To me, they don't seem like guilty people trying to act innocent."

Kawika laughed. "You mean, guilty people trying to act innocent wouldn't take off, they'd stay put?"

"Not bad," Tanaka said, "But there's a simpler explanation."

"Uh-oh," said Kawika. "Time for Occam's Razor?"

"What?" Tanaka wrote *Murphys* on the board.

"Nothing," Kawika replied. "What's the simpler explanation?"

"The simpler explanation is they had no reason to kill Fortunato. They were going to beat him in court. He didn't have good legal title. That's what they convinced themselves, anyway."

"So you figure they'd be smug—cocky, arrogant, something like that— but not white-hot with hatred?" Kawika asked.

"Yeah. They might enjoy humiliating him—and I bet that's what they did. But why kill him?"

Kawika paused to think. "Same goes for the hunters? The tenants? Still, we should question them. Especially if Fortunato taunted them about using spears."

"Absolutely," replied Tanaka. "Have Tommy do that. So, who's that leave us?"

"Bingo Palapala, the guy who gave the bulldozing permit," said Kawika. "Him and his firm, after Fortunato stiffed the firm—and probably threatened them."

"Agreed." Tanaka went back to the whiteboard. "I could see them doing it—and just the way it was done." *Hunters,* he wrote. *Bingo & firm.* "Who else?"

"Shimazu?" suggested Kawika. "Fortunato was up to something. The Japanese would have been the marks, right?"

"Had to be, I guess." Tanaka added *Shimazu* to the list. "Shimazu had the opportunity, if he had a motive. Besides interviewing him, we'll have to see the company books, do some forensic accounting."

"I'm sure we can do that," Kawika said, making another note.

"Not sure anyone Japanese would've killed him with a spear, though. And how would Shimazu have gotten it?"

"We may know more when we know where the spear came from. We're still working on that."

"Good. Okay, who's next?"

"Mainland guys," Kawika offered. "Someone connected with Fortunato back in Washington where he blew up the Indian site. And we know the Feds were after him for fraud there. So the mainland guys could've had more than one motive."

Tanaka scratched his head. "Same problem as with the Japanese. Why would mainland guys use an old Hawaiian spear and cord? Or have him hit that way? I can see them killing him. But with all that Hawaiian stuff?"

"I don't know. But I gotta follow up anyway with Frank Kimaio, the FBI guy. I'll do a deep dive with him—check the mainland angles, find out if Fortunato made enemies back there. Anything Tommy doesn't get from him."

"Good." *Mainland guys,* wrote Tanaka. "Anyone else?"

"Who're we missing?"

"Michael Cushing?" Tanaka suggested. "Sometimes the number-two guy offs the number one."

Kawika smiled and shook his head. "Talk about someone who didn't have to act innocent," he told Tanaka. "You should've seen him with Tommy and me that day, Terry. The guy was scared he'd be next—scared shitless." Tanaka frowned—at the word *shitless,* Kawika realized. "Sorry, Terry," he said. "How about 'The guy was quaking in his slippas?'"

Tanaka smiled and moved on. "Well, what about Ms. Quinn?" he asked. The woman who found the body."

That startled Kawika. He tried to imagine Patience as a diabolical killer, someone whose every action since he'd met her could suggest a guilty person trying to act innocent. Someone who was toying with the police, with him.

It seemed crazy. Could it fit? He had to think for a moment. Finally he said, "Everyone else has some kind of motive. What would her motive be?"

Tanaka smiled. "Good," he said. *"Iiko, iiko.* Still, does she have an alibi?"

"Probably the same alibi everyone has for a murder at midnight," Kawika replied. "Asleep in bed."

"Then see if she *might* have had a motive," Tanaka suggested. "She's a writer. Who knows? Maybe she wants to write real-life murder mysteries, has to start out with real murders."

"Ah, Terry, c'mon. She wasn't acting when I told her the victim was Fortunato. She was really shocked, almost fell over. Not scared, like Cushing, but genuinely shocked."

Tanaka shrugged and smiled slightly. "I've gotta go work on Shark Cliff," he said. "And by the way, there's nothing on the dead haole yet, the handcuffed guy. Nothing about the cuffs either. They didn't leave distinctive marks, not like those on Fortunato."

"Hmm. Maybe no connection," Kawika said. "Well, go ahead then. I've got this under control, I think. This helped a lot."

"You feeling confident?" Tanaka inquired.

"Yeah," Kawika answered. *"Generally."*

Tanaka laughed, seemingly proud of the protégé who'd become his colleague. *"Iiko, iiko,"* he said, for the third and final time.

26

Hilo

"You know Fortunato's been murdered?" Kawika looked across the desk at Bingo Palapala, the county official who'd granted the bulldozing permit.

"Yeah. I heard."

"You hear how he died?"

"Yeah."

"Pretty bad, eh?"

"We all gotta die."

"It's possible he died because of the permit you granted. I want to know why you gave it to him."

"He brought us the right report. No reason not to give him the permit."

"You give lots of permits to bulldoze old heiau? Ones built by Kamehameha?"

"Have you read the report?"

"No."

"Didn't think so." Bingo Palapala vanished. When he returned, he slapped a half-inch-thick document on the desk. "Here," he said.

"What's it say?"

"Read it yourself."

"How about a quick summary?"

"Okay, mister. First, this wasn't a heiau."

"What? Not a heiau?"

"It was probably just a boundary marker."

"Boundary marker for what?"

"For an old land division, an ahupua'a. Maybe a boundary marker, or maybe an ahu, an altar where people put their tax money. Doesn't matter.

It wasn't significant and it was already destroyed. Nothing but a pile of rocks."

"Wait a minute," Kawika said. "The University team said it was a heiau Kamehameha built for Pele, to stop a lava flow. Vancouver's men saw the human sacrifices. They wrote about it in their journals."

"Mister, you and the University don't know shit," Bingo Palapala said. "No one made human sacrifices to Pele. They made them to Kū. Kū was the god of war, see? Pele was the goddess of fire. So stick with washing people's shirts, Mr. *Wong*. Now get out of here."

"Not so fast." Kawika brushed off the racist slur; with Wong as a surname, he'd heard it before.

"Yes, mister—so fast. Go read the report. KKL's on lava from Mauna Loa. Mauna Loa never threatened any Kohala fishponds in Kamehameha's time. That came later—forty years later. Kamehameha was dead. Guess what died with Kamehameha, mister? The old religion. Heiaus. Human sacrifice. Got the picture now?"

"You're saying the English never saw a lava flow that threatened his fishponds?"

"Maybe the English saw a lava flow; who gives a shit? It would've been the 1801 lava flow. That one came from Hualalai, not Mauna Loa, and it hit the ocean in Kona, not Kohala. You've seen it yourself, mister. The airport's built on it."

"So you're saying . . . ?"

"Whatever the English saw, it had zilch to do with this broken-down piece of shit on KKL's land. There was nothing to save and no reason to save it. Now get the fuck out of here."

Kawika got the fuck out of there. The menace from Palapala clung to him like sulfurous steam from a fumarole. He went to his office, adrenaline pumping, skimmed the report, and called Tanaka in the field.

"Terry, the County guy's scary. But he's got some cover. The private archeology report says whatever Fortunato bulldozed wasn't even a heiau. It might've just been an old boundary marker."

"You're kidding. Not a heiau?"

"Nope, if that report's right. I've got an idea, though. Remember after S&R yesterday, Carolyn said destroying an archaeological site could be a federal crime? Maybe it's not a heiau, but even an ancient boundary marker is still an archeological site."

"Not a crime if he had permits."

"Yeah, but what if he got the permits by fraud, like S&R says? Then there could be a federal investigation, right?"

"Where you going with this?" Tanaka asked. "We've got our own investigation."

"The Feds have better tools."

"Which tools?"

"Plus the Feds investigated this before, when Fortunato blew up that Indian site," Kawika went on. "So I'm thinking when I see Frank Kimaio, our retired FBI guy up on Kohala Mountain, I'll pick his brain about how the FBI ran their investigation, what exactly they did. Maybe they can learn things we can't."

"Which tools?" Tanaka repeated.

"Well, wiretaps for a start."

"Just a start, Kawika?"

"Yeah, Terry. And the Feds can use a grand jury too."

He hung up, thinking about the pile of rocks, the bulldozer, and what Patience had said about South Kohala lava being as brittle as glass. He remembered, too, what Carolyn had said: *"All this development, it doesn't have any boundaries"*. And apparently one less boundary marker as well.

After work, still juggling two women uneasily in his mind, Kawika called Patience to tell her he'd return to South Kohala in a day or two. Then he joined Carolyn for dinner again at Café Pesto on Hilo's waterfront. As they arrived the sagging black sky finally ruptured. The clouds disgorged themselves and rain fell hard, hard enough to break the bones of Hilo. Kawika and Carolyn watched from the café window, transfixed. However familiar, the sight always filled him with awe. But this time what struck him was the contrast with South Kohala, where what falls hard is sun, and it falls on flesh.

27

Hilo

Kawika spent the night at his own house, alone, and slept deeply. Rested and energized the next morning—and trying to tell himself the prospect of seeing Patience had nothing to do with it—Kawika went to work early and made calls to South Kohala, preparing for his visit. He called Tommy first.

"So, Tommy," he said, "you know some guys there in Waimea, want to hunt on KKL land?"

"Yeah," said Tommy. "They call themselves tenants—hoaʻāina tenants. Hawaiian word. 'Traditional land rights,' I guess you'd say."

"Any of 'em Waimea police?"

"A few."

"You?"

"No way."

"You hunt, don't you?" Kawika asked.

"Yeah, but I hunt for meat. I've got a family and a freezer to fill. I don't hunt for money."

"So you *do* know these guys."

"I see what you're saying. Should have thought of it myself. Okay, I'll check 'em out. Anything else? Need a car?"

"No, but I do need Frank Kimaio's number, if it's handy."

"No problem: 555-8998."

"Easy to remember," Kawika commented.

"That's what Terry said too," Tommy replied.

Next Kawika called Kohala Kats. A woman answered, "Aloha. Kohala Kats."

"Aloha. This is Detective Kawika Wong calling from Hilo."

"Right. Nice try."

"Excuse me?" Kawika said.

"Right, you're Detective Wong—and I'm Queen Emma."

"Actually, I am Detective Wong. Who are you, when you're not Queen Emma?"

The line was silent for a moment.

"I'm sorry," the woman said at last. "I'm Malia Evans. I was just reading about you in the paper. I can't believe it's you calling."

"Yesterday's paper," Kawika said. "Old news, eh?"

"Today's paper, over here," she replied. "Might be yesterday's news in Hilo. We're on island time here."

"Well," Kawika said, "don't believe everything you read in the paper."

"I don't believe *anything* I read in the paper. And you didn't shoot that couple up in Waimea, did you? I bet someone else did that."

"Correct," he replied. "Look, Ms. Evans, I'm trying to reach Jason Hare. He works for you, right?"

"No."

"Doesn't he work for Kohala Kats?"

"Oh, he did for years, but not much this year. Did a little work at the Mauna Kea a while back—just a couple of mornings. Hasn't been around since."

"The Mauna Lani, you mean." *And she must mean nights, not mornings,* he thought.

"No, the Mauna Kea. Not the Mauna Lani."

"You're sure?"

"I'm sure."

"But he brought you a check from the Mauna Lani—from Patience Quinn?"

"Nope," said Malia Evans with a laugh. "That came in the mail, plain envelope, address on the check. I'm just writing her a thank-you. Jason Hare brings me a check, I'd remember it—let me tell you. I will say, the man absolutely loves cats—almost a fanatic—and he's very gentle with them. So I'm quite fond of him, really. But I don't think he's ever had two nickels to rub together."

"Any idea how I can find him, then?"

"Simple. Just drive Highway 19—the Queen K nowadays. Silly, isn't it, naming highways for Kamehameha's wives? Good thing we've got a lot of 'em. Anyway, Jason's out there all the time. Can't miss him. Guy in a loincloth— or just a Speedo, some days—walking along with a tall staff like some lost prophet, and brown as a coconut."

"Yeah, I've heard that. A colorful guy, it seems. Though he was a bit better dressed, the night I met him. And by the way, since you're in Kawaihae, do you know Peter Pukui, by chance?"

"Not by chance—by rescuing his cats. He's a total cat abuser. The worst. We've been rescuing Peter's cats for years—Jason Hare helped us with that in the past. Jason even reported Peter to Animal Welfare. Newspaper says you're persecuting Peter. Go ahead and persecute him, I say. But no one's seen him lately. Not his girlfriend either. Melanie Munu. Sometimes she hangs out with him, feeds his cats. But lately we've been going over there and feeding them ourselves. She's not around, and neither is Peter. I've half a mind to rescue this bunch of cats too."

Kawika called Dr. Terrence Smith next. His assistant explained it was Dr. Smith's day off. "You could try him at the museum," she offered. "North Kohala Historical. He volunteers there on his days off."

"Thanks. If I don't reach him, have him call me, okay?"

"Okay, I will. And you be careful now, yeah? We've all seen the paper. We're worried about you."

Next, Kawika dialed Frank Kimaio, the retired FBI agent.

"Detective Wong?" Kimaio answered on the third ring, without saying hello.

"Mr. Kimaio?" Kawika asked, a bit puzzled. "Did Tommy tell you I'd be calling?"

"He did."

"Well, then . . . I'd really like to pick your brain about Ralph Fortunato. I understand you headed the mainland investigation."

"Not exactly headed. But I did work on it, the investigation of Fortunato's resort."

"Right. Well, I'm coming to South Kohala today. Could I meet you on the way, take you to lunch?"

Kimaio took a moment to reply. "Look, Detective," he said, "you're sort of conspicuous today—the newspaper over here, you know. Me, I'm retired FBI. I moved here to be inconspicuous. Sent a lot of guys to prison. I don't want to have to start watching my back."

"Oh," Kawika said. "Of course. I understand. Should have thought of that. I haven't actually seen the paper over there, just yesterday's Hilo paper."

"Was it bad in Hilo?"

"Bad enough."

"Well, I've got an idea," Kimaio said. "You driving over the Saddle Road?"

"Yup."

"Your car unmarked?"

"Yup. It's mine. I had a cop car from Waimea, but I turned it in."

"Good. Then let's meet on the mountain. There's a good spot on your route, nice place for a visit. Park at the trailhead near the power line right of way. You know it?"

"I've seen it, I think."

"Good. Park there, take the old cattle trail over the lava. After a while, you'll come to a kipuka. I'll meet you there."

"A kipuka?"

"Yeah, a little island of native forest. The lava just split and flowed around it. Very beautiful. One of my favorite places. Lots of native species. No tourists. No locals anyway. I'll bring something for lunch. Around eleven, say? Can't leave it too late—clouds roll in around one. Easy to get lost in the fog, coming back over the lava."

Kawika was happy to meet out of the public eye; he'd begun to feel apprehensive about the newspaper the Kohala folks seemed to be reading. His next call, with Michael Cushing, heightened his unease.

"I'm happy to see you, Detective," Cushing began, "but not at the office, okay? You're the wrong kind of celebrity these days. People see you coming in, we'd have an angry crowd in no time. How about my house, tomorrow night?"

Kawika had been thinking *tonight*. He'd planned to see Kimaio and Cushing, spend the night with Patience—any resolve he'd had not to see her had weakened the nearer South Kohala became—then the next morning interview the Murphys, who'd returned from California at Tanaka's insistence. After that he'd head back to Hilo. If he had to wait and see Cushing the second evening, he'd end up spending an extra night in South Kohala.

"Would tonight work for you?" Kawika asked, fighting the temptation of that extra night.

"Sorry, no," Cushing replied. "Gotta get financial reports to Japan by tomorrow morning."

"Okay," said Kawika. *It's out of my hands,* he thought.

He next reached the lawyer Ted Pohano in Kailua. "I want to meet the Murphys tomorrow at their house," Kawika said. "You're welcome to join, of course."

"No can do, I'm afraid," said Pohano. "I've got them meeting a criminal lawyer in Honolulu tomorrow."

"You're not a criminal lawyer?"

"Not really. They're going to need the very best, don't you think?"

"That's a tricky question for someone who's not a criminal lawyer."

"I try. How about the day after tomorrow?"

"If that's the best you can do." *I'll be spending the night now anyway.*

"Eight o'clock?" Pohano suggested.

Kawika considered how his morning might unfold at the Mauna Lani. "Nine o'clock," he replied. "Nine's better for me."

"Okay," said Pohano. "Nine it is. The criminal lawyer, the Murphys, and us."

"Now, about your press release," Kawika said. "Seems it did a little damage."

"Yeah, sorry about that. The paper over here—someone was confused, I guess."

"What exactly does it say?" Kawika asked.

"You haven't seen it? No one's read it to you?"

"Not yet."

"Oh. Well, ah, some readers might make the mistake of thinking you shot the Malos."

"What?"

"Yeah. Sorry. The reporter kinda muddied it up. She wrote you're *responsible* for the deaths—because of your investigation, you know. And she linked that with your blaming Peter Pukui for Fortunato. Got some stuff in there about Melanie Munu too. So she sorta suggested you've declared open season on Hawaiians. That sort of thing."

"Jesus Christ."

"Like I said: sorry. The article was just sloppy. We could clarify things in another press release, though—hail new developments, new suspects, and so on. *Are* there new developments?"

"You'd know before I do, with all your inside sources."

"Yeah, I hear you met Bingo Palapala. Piece of work, that guy. What'd I tell ya?"

"We were discussing your next press release, I believe."

"Right. Okay, how about this? We say S&R met with police and offered to assist your investigation on lines of inquiry other than Peter Pukui. And we're pleased the police—led by you, Detective *Kawika* Wong—have yielded to public indignation and accepted our offer. We'd also clarify that you didn't shoot the Malos, of course."

"Of course," Kawika replied.

"We could issue it right away. Or maybe we should wait till after you've met with the Murphys?"

"Very clever. Now you do sound like a criminal lawyer: a lawyer who's a criminal." Kawika hung up and called Patience at her condo.

"How are you doing?" she asked.

"I'll be better when I see you. Can't see you in public, apparently." That was a relief, actually; less risk of love affairs colliding.

"Public isn't what I had in mind," she teased. "Went shopping, got everything we need. But by the way, as I was driving up to the Village, I saw something kind of strange. You know how people over here write graffiti on the roadside, using white pieces of coral?"

"Yup, sure do. Bleached coral on lava—blackboard of the gods."

"Okay. Last time I saw some graffiti that said 'KW' and 'HI.'"

"Initials, right?" he said. "Boyfriend and girlfriend?"

"That's what I thought. But yesterday I noticed someone's taken away the 'HI.' The 'KW' is still there. But after a colon it says aloha in block capitals: 'A-L-O-H-A.' What do you make of that?"

"I don't know," replied Kawika.

"Well, I've been thinking," she said. "Could be a coincidence. But maybe someone's trying to communicate with you."

"Two possible explanations? What if we apply Occam's Razor, P?"

She laughed. "Probably just coincidence, you think?"

"Probably," he agreed. "I mean, if someone's using graffiti to communicate with me, how am I supposed to communicate back?"

PART THREE

KOHALA AND HILO

Fallen is the Chief; overthrown is the kingdom,
Gasping in death, scattered in flight;
An overthrow throughout the land;—
                    —Fragment of the epic poem "Haui ka Lani,"
          from E. Smith et al., *Ancient Hawaiian Civilization* (1933)

28

At the Kīpuka

The lava Kawika crossed to the kīpuka consisted mostly of 'a'ā, broken and jumbled and sharp enough to cut shoe leather. At intervals he encountered expanses of smooth pahoehoe, once-molten rock now cooled and weathered. In the 'a'ā, the old cattle trail was a path of crushed cinders. On the pahoehoe—flat and hard and colored like a rain cloud—the trail became indistinct, sometimes visible where hooves had chipped a rocky edge, sometimes marked by small stone cairns.

Kawika knew this vast stone plain was considered beautiful. Still, crossing it made him uncomfortable. Here, where human hands had built nothing—nothing but the cairns—human hands had defiled nothing, but neither were they present to comfort or reassure. Kawika trekked on, small meat on a hot rock, and—thanks to what he'd heard of the local newspaper—feeling it.

Frank Kimaio waited at the lip of the kīpuka. Relieved, Kawika followed him down into the forest, an island of vegetation in a sea of stone. They sat in the shade of native trees, an overstory of koa and others. Kimaio shushed Kawika so they could hear the hidden songbirds.

"You know about the avian malaria, right?" Kimaio asked. "Wiped out the native birds except at altitudes too high for the mosquito, like this place. That's why we hear the birds. Honeycreepers, probably."

"Can't see 'em, though."

"No." Kimaio laughed. "They survive by keeping out of sight. Like most things Hawaiian, yeah?" Kimaio's voice had acquired a Hawaiian lilt. He looked older than Kawika expected, still fit but sinewy and almost gaunt. His aged appearance reminded Kawika of Jarvis's often-stated belief: *"If you retire, you die."*

Kimaio opened a backpack full of convenience-store sandwiches, chips, soft drinks. "No tablecloth," Kimaio joked. "But I got paper napkins. And lots of lunch."

They ate, and Kawika felt reassured in Kimaio's company, even though Kimaio claimed he couldn't help much. "I don't know about Ralph in Hawaii," he said. "I'm an expert on Ralph in Washington, up to a point."

"Okay," said Kawika. "That's what I'd really like to know about."

"Then I'll start with Fortunato 101," Kimaio began. "Italian name, obviously. Great-grandpa came from Italy, caught gold fever, went to Alaska. Didn't find gold but found a Native woman—Athabascan, not an Aleut. Ralph made a point of that."

"Fortunato was part Native American?"

"Part Native Alaskan, yeah. One-eighth. It's nothing, except it mattered later."

"If it mattered later, it's not nothing," Kawika observed.

"Good point," Kimaio admitted. "Okay, so bride and groom moved down to Washington, homesteaded in the San Juan Islands."

"I know the place. I grew up in Seattle mostly."

"Well, good. So you can imagine the isolation of those islands back then. Great-grandpa and his Native bride probably wanted isolation, an interracial marriage in those days. Ralph's granddad was born there. Roman Fortunato. Roman fought in World War I, survived, got back to the islands, and became a crook."

"What kind of crook?"

"Small-time. Smuggling during Prohibition, rum-running from Canada. Small boats, fast boats at night—no lights. That sort of thing. But he killed a man once."

"Killed a man?"

"Yeah. Guy called him a half-breed. Roman would have hanged, but an appeals court reduced the murder conviction to involuntary manslaughter. Racial insults are 'fighting words,' the court said. Use racial insults, people will fight back. Still, Roman did time. He got out, Prohibition was over, so he made money grading roads, public contract things. Probably padded and fiddled every contract he ever had. That's what Ralph learned, growing up."

"Fortunato grew up with his grandfather?"

"Pretty much. Seems Ralph's daddy couldn't stand Roman. Got married, had a kid, then he and his wife split for the mainland—Tacoma, I think. The kid was Ralph, who got left behind with grandpa. So Fortunato was raised by a crook with a bad temper."

"And inherited that somehow?" Kawika asked. Kimaio smiled, then shrugged.

"Okay, fast forward," Kimaio went on. "Ralph's working with his grand-dad, only now he's doing construction: foundations, driveways, docks, putting in septic tanks. Yuppies are beginning to come to the San Juans, building summer homes. Ralph makes money off 'em. Sells some land, pours some concrete."

"I'm starting to see where this is going," Kawika said.

"I'm sure you are," said Kimaio. "Ralph learned the game, but the San Juans—that's small-stakes poker. No big real estate developments, just one house at a time. So when granddad dies, in the 1980s, Ralph moves to the Methow Valley. You know the Methow?"

"I visited a few times, like most Seattle folks."

"Okay. So Ralph leaves the islands, takes a boat to the mainland, and then it's Highway 20 all the way."

Highway 20 to the Methow, Highway 19 to the Mauna Lani, Kawika thought. *North Cascades to the Queen K.*

"If you've been to the Methow, you probably know about the ski resort that never got built?"

"Heard about it," Kawika replied. "Big controversy, yeah?"

"Yup. Well, Ralph gets a job with the ski resort company. They'd been trying for years to get permits, hoped to make it another Sun Valley. They put Ralph in charge of heavy equipment: bulldozers, earth movers. No buildings going up yet; the resort's still on hold. But he's down in the dirt doing infrastructure, running a crew. And he marries a local woman—his first wife. She came from pioneers. Big break for Ralph because now he's a local by marriage. Drinking with the boys, starting to get ideas. Eventually he decides to develop a resort himself. Which is how our paths happen to cross."

"You investigated him for fraud, right? And destruction of the wintering shelter?"

"Right," Kimaio said. "Here's what happened. First, Ralph gets an option on a big spread—Rattlesnake Ranch, about fifteen hundred acres. He doesn't need his own ski area. His idea is to piggyback on the other resort. Folks buy a place at Rattlesnake Ranch, they get wilderness, they get killer mountain and valley views, and they're minutes from the slopes—he hopes."

"Sounds familiar," Kawika said. "At KKL they're minutes from the beach."

Kimaio smiled. "That's our Ralphie. Of course, he changes the name to Fawn Ridge. Cute, eh? There actually is a ridge, and there are deer on it."

"So where's the fraud?" Kawika asked.

"Well, first, Ralph paid a fancy price for the land—to a buddy. Raises eyebrows locally, once folks learn about it. Ralph just explains, hey, money's rolling into the Methow; wait till you see what the Microsoft crowd will pay. That just about killed Methow land sales for a few years, the locals believing Ralph. They put property on the market at ridiculous prices. No one had Ralph's advantage, though. Because secretly, Ralph and his buddy split the proceeds from Ralph paying the inflated price. So right off the bat, Ralph's fleeced his investors—not to mention confusing the locals."

"Ah, that's the fraud," Kawika said.

"That's just part of it," Kimaio continued. "Ralph needs a golf course, even though he doesn't need a ski slope. He plans to sell three hundred condos, plus home sites in five-acre lots. He can't do any of it without water. Which is hard to come by there."

"As I remember that valley's bone dry," Kawika remarked. "The mountains block the rain clouds. Same as South Kohala, right?"

"Right. And with water rights, it's use it or lose it. Gotta maintain continuous usage or your rights lapse. Ralph's buddy could never afford the manpower to irrigate. So he spends years running a scam—this is before Ralph. He keeps irrigation equipment in the fields, puts a little water through the sprinklers now and then. Folks can see he's using water, but it's a trickle compared to what he's recording. He's waiting for someone who wants to buy the land with the water rights. Fortunato comes along, they make a deal, and split the hidden profit."

Kawika shook his head ruefully in admiration of the devious ways of crooks.

"Speaking of water," Kimaio added. He dug in the backpack, came up with bottled water for them both. "Gotta stay hydrated out here."

Kawika took a drink. "How come you couldn't nail him?" he asked.

"Ah, that's where it mattered, Ralph having an Athabascan great-grandmother—though an Aleut would have worked too. One guy in the valley knew what Ralph and his buddy were up to. Guy by the name of Jimmy Jack. An Indian. Married to another Indian—Madeline John."

"Jimmy Jack and Madeline John? Great names for a couple."

"Methow Indians, named for their dads. Jimmy hauled irrigation pipe around Rattlesnake Ranch. He knew the real water usage. Ralph's buddy had to explain the scam to him, since the irrigation pattern made no sense."

"Couldn't Jimmy give you enough to nail them for fraud?" Kawika asked.

"Jimmy *could* but he wouldn't," Kimaio said. "It was a 'White man speak with forked tongue' problem. Jimmy was probably worried about his safety too. But more important to Jimmy was that the government cheated the Methows out of their reservation, back in the day. Gave it to some miners and crammed the Methows onto another Tribe's reservation. So Jimmy hated the government and refused to testify. But at least he did finally spill, once Fortunato dynamited the old wintering shelter. *Then* Jimmy gave us the entire deal—the water rights, the kickback on the purchase price, all that. He said, 'Ralph told me he's got Native blood, but when he blew up the shelter, I knew he's just another lying white man.'"

"But he wouldn't testify?"

"Nope. Wouldn't go that far. We told him we could make him. 'You can make me show up,' he said. 'You can't make me talk.' We begged him to help us put Fortunato in jail. 'Do it yourselves,' he said. And after a while, we realized Jimmy was smart. We needed his testimony for the fraud case, but we didn't need it for destroying a Native American cultural site. That was all public, admitted—right out in the open."

"You couldn't do the fraud case?" Kawika paused in his note taking.

"Nope. No independent records of the water usage. The inflated purchase price got treated as payment for the bogus water rights. Then the buddy *invested*—ha-ha—half the extra amount with Ralph, supposedly as initial capital for Ralph's next project. Who knows? Maybe that launched KKL."

"Makes sense," Kawika said. "Must've needed some money before the Japanese backed him. But couldn't you prosecute him for the dynamiting?"

"Couldn't prove destroying the shelter was a crime," Kimaio said. "Ralph had a report from some fancy consulting firm. Interior Department waffled; wouldn't commission their own report. That fucked us. End of story."

"Destruction of a Native site—so now history's repeating itself," said Kawika. "Besides Jimmy Jack, were there any people—"

Kimaio had started collecting the refuse from their lunch. "Oops," he said. "Almost forgot. Brought you the paper." He handed Kawika a folded newspaper from the knapsack. Kawika unfolded it and found, centered on the front page, his own official police photo—and superimposed over it, the red and white concentric circles of a target, with the bull's eye on his forehead. "WONG TARGET" read the large headline. The photo caption read:

> **Native Group** Sovereignty & Reparations blames Detective Wong of Hilo for shooting deaths of two Native Hawaiians in Waimea, persecution of a third. (Hilo Police Photo)

"Let's save questions for another day," said Kimaio as Kawika sat immobile with the newspaper, stunned. "Got a doctor's appointment, and the fog's coming in." Indeed, beyond the kīpuka the sky had grown gray; light and temperature began to drop as mist spilled in over the edge. A rising wind stirred the tall koa trees. "Give me a head start," Kimaio added. "I'm slowing down, these days."

"We finish this another time?" asked Kawika, struggling to recover his composure, not ready to be alone.

"Sure," Kimaio replied. "I'm around. Not going anywhere. But that's pretty much all I know about Ralph Fortunato. Call me, if you want. You know my number."

Halfway up the little track out of the kīpuka, Kimaio stopped and gave Kawika a crisp salute. "Good luck, Detective," he said, and added, "And you should trace that spear. Seriously. You do that, you find out who owns it, you'll find your killer. Someone will know." Then he vanished into the mist. With dread, Kawika looked down again at the newspaper, at his picture centered in a target.

Kawika dropped to his knees and threw up all over a native shrub.

29

Waikoloa Village

Kawika decided to check on Joan Malo's mother again, and picked up Tommy first. The newspaper had made him suddenly crave some protection—at least some companionship. As they drove, he and Tommy discussed the case. Peter Pukui and Melanie Munu hadn't turned up, and no one had identified the three-barbed murder weapon yet. Dr. Smith had called with DNA results: whoever sodomized Joan Malo, it wasn't her husband or Ralph Fortunato. And Tommy reported that Kai Malo had indeed been on Moloka'i the night Fortunato died.

"Yeah, story checked out. His family held a baby luau for Kai's cousin. Kai played guitar. He was still there when the last plane took off."

Okay, Kawika thought. *Forget Kai.*

But forgetting Kai wasn't easy. Joan's mother lived in a small, well-kept house with so many pictures of Joan and Kai it felt like a shrine. She welcomed the chance to talk. She hadn't seen the paper—she said it distressed her—and didn't recognize Kawika's name. But she recognized Tommy as one of Joan's high school classmates and greeted him fondly. Then in one long monologue, she recounted her daughter's life, which, Kawika realized, was actually what he wanted to hear.

Joan had been born in Hāwī, her mother began. Joan's late father had worked maintenance for sugar companies until the industry failed. Then he moved his family to Waimea and worked for the schools. He earned extra income from the County by traveling around Kohala, affixing little reflective rectangles to highway signs, selectively turning *a, e, i, o,* and *u* into *ā, ē, ī, ō,* and *ū.* "You can still see his work everywhere," his widow said proudly.

Joan had done well in school. Her mother showed Kawika and Tommy report cards and honor roll certificates she'd saved, plus photos of Joan in school pageants, dancing the hula, or playing Pele—and once, an incongruous sylph-like version of the enormous Ka'ahumanu. Her mother had a scrapbook devoted to Joan's other triumphs, first as Miss Kohala, then as Big Island Beauty Queen, finally as second runner-up in the Miss Hawai'i competition in Honolulu. The youthful Joan looked wholesome and desirable in swimsuits and in gowns she'd made herself.

"All the local boys wanted her," Joan's mother said, "but we told her, 'Save yourself for someone better.' She had it all—looks, brains, common sense. Her dad and me told her, 'Go for reception, not housekeeping. You won't meet anyone decent changing sheets.' So she went for reception, and she got it."

Not "Her dad and me told her, 'Go for college,'" Kawika thought.

"The Mauna Lani," her mother said proudly. "That's where she met Kai, when he came to perform. That's where she met Mr. Fortunato too. Great husband and a great job—all from working reception."

Kawika looked at Tommy, who discreetly rolled his eyes. Joan's mother must have been in denial or shock about Joan and Kai, Kawika realized, but she probably never knew about Joan and Fortunato.

"Well, one thing's true," Tommy told Kawika, back in the car. "Joan didn't go with local boys. We were never good enough for her. Or good enough for her mom and dad. That's why I gave Joan that stink eye, up at the station. I was still mad at her."

"Not mad for Kai then?"

"No," Tommy admitted. "Mad for myself. She'd never have me, right? She wouldn't have no local guy before she got married. But after she's married, she cheats with that haole dirtbag." He turned to his window, his face hidden.

Kawika wondered what to say. "Tommy," he began, "I'll tell you something. When I talked with her in Waimea that day, I got sort of envious of her husband too."

Tommy turned to face him. "Huh," Tommy said. He sounded unconvinced.

"And today," Kawika continued, "today, when I saw those pictures, I was so sad for Joan all over again. She was gorgeous. Very beautiful, very smart, very sexy. It's okay, Tommy. We're human. Let's not worry about it. Let's just find whoever killed Ralph."

Tommy nodded. A moment later, lapsing into pidgin, he declared, "So, cool head main ting, right?"

Kawika laughed. "Cool head main ting," he repeated. "I like that. That and stink eye. You got more of that for me?" Tommy laughed too.

Kawika thought about Joan's sun-bleached Honda Civic, slowly rusting in her mother's yard. "She didn't need it," Joan's mother had told them. "Not after she got the BMW." Kawika felt he'd found some missing pieces, understood better the puzzle of Joan's desires, her fall, the lure of a haole lover. He kept it to himself. It wasn't relevant to the case. It would be painful for Tommy to talk about. And Kawika had his own desires to brood over, his own potential fall.

30

Mauna Lani

The night Patience dined with Kawika—the night they'd spent together, the night of Jason Hare—she hadn't known him well. She'd wanted him, certainly, but her impulsiveness worried her a bit. Was she falling into what her Bay Area friends called a "PDFF"—a post-divorce fucking frenzy? She couldn't tell, and she'd been nervous, so she'd chattered a bit during dinner. One thing she'd chattered about was why she preferred Hawai'i to the Caribbean and other places in Polynesia.

"Here," she'd said, "I'm in a tropical paradise, but in the United States. I don't feel like an Ugly American. I don't worry that my pleasure rests on exploiting downtrodden people."

She'd regretted it, of course, as soon as she'd said it. *So foolish,* she'd thought; *so privileged and insensitive.* But Kawika had handled the moment gently.

"Well," he'd said, "it's true the local people—most of them—want you here. And, yes, they're Americans, whether they admit it or not. They want the jobs, as you've said. All the same, they're capable of feeling exploited. Tourism does rest on their labor. Some are angry. Most just feel a bit . . ."

"Resentful?" she'd suggested.

"*Soiled,* I was going to say."

Now, a few days after she'd dragged Kawika back to bed, Patience spent her early morning as she more frequently did. She brewed her Kona coffee, watched the sunrise strike the top of Haleakalā, then went for a jog. She loved the still cool air and the great mountains of her own island backlit against a dawn more pale than blue.

On this morning she noticed something for the first time: two rivers of headlights flowing down the mountain, one from Waikoloa Village and, further north, one from Waimea. For a moment she was puzzled. Why bumper-to-bumper traffic at this time of the near-night, snaking down the lava fields toward the resorts? Then, of course, she knew: the local people were coming to work. All coming to work for her and for tourists. She felt a bit abashed.

After breakfast, Patience got in her car and wound her way up the mountain toward Waikoloa Village. The traffic had vanished; everyone was already at work. Including Kawika, she realized. She couldn't stop thinking about him.

Usually she would have driven straight to the Village Market. Today she decided to poke around a bit, explore the Village itself. She drove along the side streets, observing the housing, the yards, the flowering vegetation. She tried to imagine where Kawika had driven, which house might be Joan Malo's, which belonged to mainland retirees and which to Kawika's local people—the ones who worked at the resorts, who might feel *soiled*.

Returning to the Mauna Lani, Patience met her trainer at the gym, then followed her workout with an outdoor massage. After that, she stopped for coffee and noticed the large number of single parents at the hotel restaurant, adults without wedding rings, alone with children, sitting placidly, their gazes resting on their kids or raised to the horizon. A guide explained to some newly arrived guests, "It's so dry here, there's not a single year-round stream on the entire South Kohala coast."

Patience wondered about a year-round life for herself on the South Kohala coast. Or in Hilo. "Damn," she muttered, with a small laugh. "I really *am* impatient." Impatient for the night ahead.

31

Mauna Lani

Kawika and Patience awoke three times in the night. The first time, they used few words.

"Jesus, Kawika."

"I know. Me too."

The second time, she lay with her cheek on his chest while he nuzzled her hair.

"You're an incredible lover," she said.

"But not very considerate," he replied. "I'm sorry."

"What are you talking about?"

"I realize there's something important happening here, P. With us, I mean. I wasn't expecting this, or anything like it. I know I should focus on it, but I can't. I'm preoccupied with this case." He knew that wasn't strictly true. He was also preoccupied with his personal dilemma.

"It's okay," she murmured, and kissed him. "Be preoccupied. You should be. You've got a murder to solve. But not tonight."

She settled her face on his chest again. He regarded the whiteness of her hand against his belly, the contrast greater in the low light. White hands on dark skin: it might be a novel sight for her—he guessed it probably was—but it wasn't novel for Kawika. A white woman had raised him, and on the mainland he'd had white girlfriends. It wasn't her whiteness that seemed unusual; it was that she wasn't Carolyn. He was accustomed in the night to other hands.

Kawika sighed inwardly. He longed at some level for the familiar—for Carolyn, for his settled existence, for the durable intimacy Carolyn might offer if they could agree on one island or another, and if she didn't need someone more Hawaiian. He also dreaded, at some level, the arduousness of the new—of Patience. But he couldn't avoid seeing that dread for what it was:

insubstantial, flimsy. Nothing—not longing, not dread, not guilt or scruples—could restrain him from exploring Patience, from exploring himself with Patience. For the first time in his life, he felt the power of sexual thrall, and something more, some feeling about himself that went with it, some feeling he really liked.

But in not talking about their situation he wasn't simply avoiding a difficult discussion. He really was preoccupied with the case—and worried.

So the third time, Patience awoke to find Kawika staring intently at the ceiling fan. "Let me guess," she said. "You're thinking about a guy who traps cats."

"Not just that. I'm also thinking about a guy who shreds papers. Assuming that was Michael Cushing you saw with the shredder."

"Well, earlier tonight you said there's some kind of fraud going on," she observed. "Not surprising papers get shredded."

"What's surprising is Michael Cushing shredding them," Kawika said. "Not Fortunato, but Cushing. The fraud was Fortunato's, right? But Cushing must be in on it."

In the morning, she found him sitting on the lanai, watching the sunrise strike the summit of Haleakalā. "Sorry," he said. "No coffee yet. Didn't want to wake you."

As if out of habit—as if two occasions could form a habit—she slipped behind him, opened her yukata, and held his head against the bare skin of her chest. She said softly, "I'm not in love with you, Kawika. Not yet. But I am in major like."

He reached an arm up to her, pulled her closer.

"How can I help you, Major Like?" she asked.

"Make the coffee?" he suggested, laughing.

"Pig," she said, kissing the top of his head. "No more Major Like for you." Then she went to do as he'd asked. He followed her and sat at the kitchen counter.

"Seriously," he said. "Help me figure out Jason Hare." He recounted his conversation with Malia Evans of Kohala Kats.

Patience frowned. "Well, we knew he was lying about something. Guess he was lying about a lot."

"Yeah, but not about everything," Kawika said. "He saw the killing. The details fit. We've known that all along."

"So now we know something else," she said. "He probably wouldn't work with Peter Pukui, right? Because Pukui's a notorious cat abuser. Jason Hare even reported him."

"Right. And Hare's not just a cat lover. According to you—and Malia Evans, I guess—he's right up there with Lizzie Borden."

"Quit teasing," she warned. "This is serious."

"Very serious," he agreed. "Jason Hare witnessed the killing, but he's not afraid of the killer. And that can't be because the killer's Peter Pukui. Jason wouldn't work with Pukui or even protect him."

"Which means . . . ?"

"Which means I must be guilty as charged."

"Guilty of what?"

"Guilty of persecuting Peter Pukui."

32

Waipi'o and Hilo

Sammy Kā'ai and his team of cops were busy terrorizing a druggie atop the cliff at Waipi'o, trying to crack the Shark Cliff case, when a ragged and nearly skeletal Peter Pukui staggered up out of Waipi'o Valley. Startled, the police stared at Pukui, who stared back uncomprehendingly and then crumpled to the ground, muddy and stupefied. Sammy immediately set free the druggie they'd been terrorizing at the cliff top. The druggie ran away quickly, as if he couldn't believe his luck and didn't want to test it further.

Peter, exhausted, started talking to Sammy and wouldn't stop. He explained why he'd gone into hiding. He had drug debts—bad ones. Pukui's words came in a flood. Almost delirious, he kept babbling. Sammy wrapped him in a blanket to keep him from going into shock, gave him a bottled water. Peter seized it greedily.

He'd always been a user, Pukui said after a long drink, showing Sammy the tracks on his arm. Not pakalolo, not meth—heroin. He'd rarely had money, always had trouble paying. And with the heiau thing, plus his girl-friend Melanie sleeping with Fortunato—even though he'd agreed to it, her becoming an extortionist for him, to get him money to pay his debts—he found himself shooting up more and working at the boatyard less.

Peter explained to Sammy, who didn't understand all of it, that once Fortunato agreed to pay Melanie Munu to wave around a page from the Māhele Book and announce herself as Chief Ku'umoku's heir, Pukui had convinced his dealers that big money was on the way. His credit became good again. He'd gotten more drugs; his debts grew.

"Then Fortunato wouldn't pay," Peter said. "Threw Melanie out of his car, beat her up. No money. I was a dead man." He'd fled to the Pololū Valley, he said, because Pololū was the nearest impenetrable place of refuge.

Now, nearly two weeks later, he'd emerged from Waipiʻo, seven treacherously deep valleys and impassably high ridges south of Pololū. It was an extraordinary feat of cross-country travel. Yet Pukui had obviously done it. Sammy could tell, just by looking at his tattered and emaciated condition.

"So you didn't kill Fortunato?" Sammy asked, smiling at his police buddies. "Not like Detective Wong thought?" Sammy didn't really know what Kawika thought, but he'd read the newspapers.

"Kill Fortunato?" Pukui asked, seemingly baffled. "Detective Wong?"

"Forget about Detective Wong," Sammy said. "Fortunato's dead. Did you kill him?"

Pukui just sputtered, shaking his head, looking bewildered beneath the dirt and grizzled beard. "Fortunato's *dead*?" he repeated, with evident disbelief.

"Yeah, Peter," Sammy said, clasping his shoulder. "Mr. Fortunato is very, very dead."

"I, I . . . I don't . . . He was alive when I left. He beat Melanie. He was alive. I swear."

"You willing to take a lie detector test?" Sammy asked.

"About killing Fortunato? Of course, of course. I didn't kill him. I didn't even know he was dead!"

"Calm down," Sammy reassured him. "We believe you. But someone popped him while you've been gone."

"Melanie?"

"No, a man did it," Sammy replied.

"I mean, where's Melanie now? Is she okay? Gotta find her," Pukui said, struggling to stand.

"Okay, Peter," Sammy said. "We'll drive you to Hilo. I gotta take you in anyway. We'll put you in County, you can call a lawyer. He'll help you find your girlfriend."

Sammy tried to notify Kawika. He couldn't reach him, so he left a voice message: "Hey, we got Peter Pukui over here. Taking him to the station. But Kawika, I don't think he's your man."

Within hours, Pukui had passed the polygraph test. Sammy gave him a lawyer's number, and the lawyer arranged bail, receiving the money in cash from three young men in the courthouse parking lot as Sammy watched. Then the lawyer collected Peter Pukui, and the two of them vanished into the night, followed by the three men who'd put up the cash. There was barely enough light for Sammy to read the license plate of the second car. He wrote it down, just in case. Cash money for bail, handed to a lawyer in a parking lot, wasn't all that usual in Sammy's experience.

33

South Kohala

Because Carolyn might try to call, Kawika kept his phone off while he was with Patience. When he drove away in the morning and turned it back on, he found himself far behind.

Listening to the newest message first, he heard, "Okay, Peter made bail, so now he's gone." Kawika flushed; his neck grew hot all at once. He hung up without listening to earlier messages and dialed Terry.

"Not back yet," Tanaka's assistant said. "Maybe still fishing with your dad."

Kawika tried his own assistant next.

"How we feeling today?" she asked. "Like a king or a piglet?"

"What?"

"You got an e-mail from Carolyn. She says she read both reports on the bulldozed heiau. She says the one from the private firm is actually correct, because KKL isn't located on any lava flow the British saw. She says you'll understand. She went to the University to find the author of the first report, and he told her Fortunato paid the University team to say his rocks might be Kamehameha's heiau—*might be*, she put it in caps—but they aren't even a heiau. She says she's disgusted and that she's going home to Maui to stay with her dad and work on her dissertation. She hopes you'll join her there."

"That's everything?"

"No. Like I said, she also calls you her king and her piglet—in Hawaiian, of course. There's a story behind the piglet, am I right?"

"Can't talk about it," Kawika replied, trying to sound normal. She laughed and transferred him to Sammy Kā'ai.

"Peter didn't kill Fortunato," Sammy declared. "Unless the lie detector lies. And believe me, he was in no condition to fool it."

"Okay," said Kawika. "So why was he hiding?"

"He was hiding from his dealers. Turns out he's a junkie. Heroin, not meth. He owed them a lot of money. He thought they'd kill him."

"And now they *won't?*" Kawika asked, barely containing himself. He heard a muttered curse. "We put a tail on him, right?" he continued. "When we let him go?" It took a lot for Kawika to say *we* instead of *you.*

"Um, we didn't do that, actually. He was gonna spend the night at his lawyer's."

I can't believe this, Kawika thought. "Well, where was he going after that?"

"Probably to find his girlfriend," Sammy replied. "Melanie Munu, yeah?"

"Where else, you think?"

Sammy thought a bit. "To meet his dealers?" he ventured. "Make peace, buy some time, score some shit? That what you're thinking?"

"Yeah. I'm also thinking, if Peter thought they'd kill him, these could be the guys you want for Shark Cliff. Another reason to tail him."

"Shit," said Sammy, sounding a bit unnerved. "Shark Cliff. It's possible, I guess. But there's lots of drug gangs."

"Just find him again, okay?" Kawika asked. "Melanie Munu too. Bring 'em in right away, bail or no bail. Please? And don't let 'em go before I get there."

"All right, we'll find him. We know his lawyer, and I've got the license plate of the guys who paid his bail."

"What guys?"

"Three young guys. Almost kids, really. They paid in cash. A bit strange, I thought. I was gonna run the plate today, see what I can learn."

"Christ," Kawika murmured.

"We did try to find you," Sammy said defensively. "We left messages. Couldn't track you down. Looked everywhere."

"Yeah, well," Kawika muttered. "My fault, I guess."

"Hey, these things happen."

Looked everywhere. Kawika knew who to call next.

"Aloha, Jarvis Wong speaking."

"Dad, it's Kawika."

"Kawika. You call the station? They left messages with me yesterday, looking for you."

"Yeah, I guessed that."

"They said you were spending the night in South Kohala."

"Yup."

"They figured you'd be with me and Ku'ulei."

"Yup."

"I was fishing with Terry. Ku'ulei stayed with a friend. I got worried when I heard the messages."

"Sorry. I really am."

"So where *did* you spend the night?"

"Dad," said Kawika, "I need to come talk with you."

"Uh-oh," Jarvis said. "Pilikia, yeah?"

"Yeah, Dad. Pilikia."

Pilikia. Trouble.

34

On the Queen K

Patience had promised she'd stop sleuthing. But she couldn't quite. So after Kawika left that morning, she booted up her computer and began, with a sigh, to endure the Big Island's slow connection speeds.

Initially, the work was tedious—article after article with no new information. Fortunato's photograph, his grinning tanned face, appeared often. She didn't recognize him. She'd seen him only once, from a distance, lying on his back with a spear through his chest.

She found articles on the heiau, HHH, and Fortunato's death, along with one on KKL sponsoring a slack key guitar competition Kai Malo had won. Finally an entry popped up that intrigued her:

Kohala Kea Loa (search): *Obituary* . . . Thomas ("Tom-Tom") Gray . . . fisherman of the Kona Coast . . . sold the land for **Kohala Kea Loa** Resort . . . [Puako Post, Hawaii, 6/30/2000]

Patience clicked on it, waiting—and reverting to Impatience—as the screen slowly filled with text.

OBITUARY

Thomas ("Tom-Tom") Gray, Loved to Fish

PUAKO—Services were held Sunday, June 25, at Hokuloa United Church of Christ for kama'aina Thomas ("Tom-Tom") Gray, 58, a well-known fisherman of the Kona Coast, missing and presumed drowned after his 35-foot sportfisher, the *Mahi Mia*, was found adrift near the Mid-Channel buoy between Maui and Hawai'i on Thursday, May 25.

Gray was born in Hilo on April 8, 1942, the son of William Gray, a Parker Ranch supervisor, and Leslie Mercer Gray, a homemaker. He was educated at Waimea schools and West Point, an appointee of former U.S. Senator Hiram Fong (R–HI). He served in the Mekong Delta of Vietnam as a first lieutenant and won promotion to captain in the U.S. Army. In 1965, he was decorated for bravery in combat. He received the Purple Heart in 1966.

After Vietnam, Gray returned home and started his Puako-based realty firm. In 1999, on behalf of the Gray Family Trust, he sold the land for Kohala Kea Loa to NOH, a Japanese consortium. He retired and realized a lifelong dream by buying the *Mahi Mia*, on which he set forth almost daily from Kawaihae Harbor in pursuit of his own "grander," or thousand-pound marlin.

Gray never caught his "grander," but he came close with a 904-pound monster in December 1999. He was well-known for sharing catches with neighbors in Puakō and Kawaihae. Friends nicknamed him "Tom-Tom" in reference to his frequent boast that he was one-quarter Cherokee.

Authorities believe Gray fell overboard while fighting a fish or attempting to retrieve a fishing rod or other object.

Gray's children, son Kamehameha "Kam" Gray and daughter Emma Gray, returned from the mainland for the service. They remembered their father with stories of warm aloha. Gray's wife, Leilani, preceded him in death in 1988. The family suggests donations to Kohala Kats, a feline rescue organization Thomas Gray founded in 1989.

OMG, Patience thought. *Kohala Kats.* Excited now, she started a new search for "Jason Hare." Only one entry turned up:

Jason Hare (search) . . . George M. Aaron, et al. v. William V. Perry, in his capacity . . . Joseph W. Hamaukala, **Jason Hare**, Edward R. Hart . . . [Honolulu Advertiser, 10/19/95]

Patience waited a long time for the item to open. When it finally appeared, she recognized it as a complaint in an Agent Orange lawsuit filed on behalf of Hawaiian veterans. Patience checked: Jason Hare was a listed plaintiff, but Thomas Gray wasn't. Still, Thomas Gray and Jason Hare were both Vietnam vets. And Kohala Kats also connected them. She knew she'd found something significant.

Patience slipped on her sandals and headed to her car. She wasn't sleuthing, she told herself. She knew Kawika wanted to interview Jason Hare again, so she was just trying to determine Hare's current location. If he happened to be walking along the Queen K, she'd just pass along that fact.

Patience reached the highway and turned north. North proved wrong; she drove to Kawaihae without seeing the half-naked, half-mad Jason Hare. Then she drove almost to Kona Village and Hualālai Resort before turning back. As she slowly lost the expectation of finding Hare, her thoughts began to drift. What was happening to her, this past week or so?

She felt regret over her impending divorce. The weight had rarely lifted until she met Kawika. Her husband had been a young doctor, just starting out, working exhausting hours and needing her home when he was. But after her own long hours at a downtown ad agency, not in the creative part either, just to help him through med school, she couldn't wait to resume the work as a journalist she'd barely begun before. The *New York Times* had published her Hapuna Prince article when she was still in college.

The magazine *San Francisco* re-launched in 1997, and with her *New York Times* credential, she'd been hired on the spot. She was home to begin with, but the editors gave her enticing work further afield—assignments like "figuring out Nevada," as one put it, and "will Wyoming send us wind power—or coal power?" She traveled often, wasn't home as much. And she was too young to consider her situation carefully, *too* impatient, too caught up with getting published and the exhilaration of her new career opportunities. In truth, her husband's whining also put her off. He wanted children but eventually got a lover instead—"someone who's here for me," he'd yelled. Patience didn't really blame him for ending the marriage; she considered that her own fault in large part. But she did blame him for taking a lover first.

Patience understood why she'd gone to bed with Kawika. She'd asked, and he'd accepted. She'd told him why she asked. Most of it, anyway. She'd left out—it seemed too personal, too complicated—her desire for new love-making to think about, something to displace from the surfaces of her body, right away, the lingering stale smoke of sex with her husband. In seven years every cell in one's body is replaced, she'd read. *I couldn't possibly wait,* she thought. *I needed someone to paint over every cell he ever touched.* It was a cleansing for her, not revenge. But she didn't understand why the sex was so good. Nor why—despite every expectation—she'd started to fall in love again, and with such an unlikely person. *He is beautiful,* she told herself. *And fun. Smart, strong, well-spoken, those eyes . . .*

Half consciously, Patience began looking for her turnoff to the Mauna Lani after her unsuccessful scouting mission. But as she approached another turnoff, she saw a nearly naked dark brown haole with a walking staff coming down Waikoloa Road toward the highway. She slowed down so quickly she nearly got rear-ended. It was Jason Hare, no doubt. With his staff and halo of sun-bleached hair, he resembled Christ in a buckskin loincloth, Christ in serious need of a haircut and shampoo.

He was walking past the heliport at the junction of Waikoloa Road and the Queen K, the takeoff spot for volcano tours and other "flightseeing" trips. Patience noticed bright blue helicopters and panel trucks on the tarmac a hundred feet behind him. More blue copters whirled their way in from halfway up the mountain.

Patience faced a small dilemma. If she didn't turn, as a slowing car normally would, and instead regained speed to continue on the Queen K, she'd probably get an irritated honk from the car behind her or otherwise startle Hare, who would almost certainly look up and see her. But if she turned she'd pass very close to him; he might look up anyway. She'd also be headed to Waikoloa Village instead of home. She looked at Jason Hare—striding along purposefully, eyes at his feet, smiling to himself—and made the instant decision to turn, averting her face as she did so.

Then Patience needed to turn around to see which way Hare went when he reached the Queen K. She remembered a pullout where she'd seen the "KW: ALOHA" graffiti; she could make a U-turn there. She sped up. But when she reached the graffiti, she braked hard, pulled onto the shoulder, and stopped abruptly. A cloud of her own dust overtook her.

The graffiti had changed. Now it read:

KW: MC
KKL

Holy shit, she thought, fumbling in her bag for her phone. *Holy shit.* This was completely improbable, ridiculous even, and yet there it was: a graffiti message for Kawika about Michael Cushing and KKL. It had to be. She dialed Kawika's office in Hilo, reached his assistant, and explained—somewhat frantically—that she needed to leave a message for Detective Wong.

Occam's Razor cut differently now. And sharply.

35

Waimea

Before meeting Jarvis to share his pilikia, Kawika first needed to talk with Dr. Terrence Smith. And the hospital wasn't far out of his way.

"This isn't a chat," Smith protested after the first minutes. "It's an interrogation. If I'd known, we could have found a place with better coffee."

Kawika asked why, at their last meeting, Smith had suggested Fortunato was responsible for Joan Malo's death. And why had he treated Melanie Munu's injuries without reporting her beating at Fortunato's hands?

"Same answer in both cases," Smith responded. "Confidentiality of doctor–patient communications. In Joan's case I violated it; I should have said nothing. In Melanie's case I respected it, but maybe I violated the law. I regret that. If harm comes to Melanie, I'll regret it even more."

"Why should harm come to Melanie?" Kawika asked. "Fortunato's dead. Who else would harm her?"

"Tut-tut," Smith replied, wagging his finger. "I should've reported her beating. But I'm not going to report what she said as my patient. She made me promise not to talk. She had her reasons. It's enough to tell you this: Melanie Munu is still in danger."

"Will you help me find her?"

"I don't know where she is. If you do find her, she'll tell you what she told me."

"What if we don't find her? Or find her dead?"

"Then I'd tell you."

Why did Smith believe the confidentiality of doctor–patient communications died with the patient? That wasn't Kawika's understanding. But, as Tanaka had taught him, right now the fact that Smith believed it was more important than why.

"Okay," Kawika said. "Let's go back to Joan Malo's autopsy—what you said about Fortunato's responsibility. What you knew. *Why* you knew."

Smith waved his hand. "That's where I violated Joan's confidences," he said.

"How could you? You told me she wasn't your patient."

"She wasn't. But after she was shot, one of my colleagues came to see me. She'd been his patient, and she'd told him about her affair."

"Wait a minute," Kawika said. "Then if anybody violated doctor–patient confidentiality, it would be your colleague, right? Not you."

Smith frowned, considering the point. "Maybe," he said. "But two doctors conferring doesn't violate patient confidentiality, I think."

"But you weren't conferring about a patient," Kawika responded. "His patient was dead. He was giving you information about a corpse."

"That's one way of looking at it."

Kawika circled back, probing a weak spot. "Doctor, a moment ago you said you'd tell me what Melanie told you, if I found her dead."

"Right. And I would."

"Well, I did find Joan dead."

Smith looked at Kawika steadily. "Very clever, Detective," he said. "Let me think about it for a minute." Smith walked out into the hallway and paced slowly, a hand to his chin. Then he strode back and sat down.

"Okay," he said. "You asked for it. I warn you: it won't help, and it isn't pretty."

"It wasn't pretty seeing her die," Kawika responded.

"No," Smith conceded. "I don't suppose it was." Then he explained. When Joan had confided in her doctor about the affair, he'd urged her to take precautions at least—practice safe sex—but she'd said Fortunato wouldn't agree to it. "She told her doctor, 'It'll be safe anyway because I'm not sleeping with anyone else except my husband. And Ralph's not sleeping with anyone else except his wife.' Her doctor said, 'If he cheats on her, he could cheat on you. And his wife could cheat on him. The point is, you don't know.'"

"Joan wasn't persuaded?" asked Kawika.

"No, it wasn't that," Smith replied. "According to her doctor, she just felt helpless. Helpless to end the affair, helpless to insist on safe sex. Still, she worried for her husband. She didn't want to infect him with anything."

"But she couldn't go home and tell her husband to start using condoms," Kawika ventured. "Not if she wanted to keep the affair secret."

"Right," replied Smith. "Condoms cause questions. That's one reason they aren't used when they should be." He looked at Kawika pointedly, as if accusing him. *But how could he be?* Kawika thought.

"A few months ago," Smith resumed, "Joan and Fortunato traveled to Japan. Afterward, she came to see her doctor. She was worried because on the trip she'd had sex with others, not just Fortunato."

"Others?"

"Some men."

"Some? Not one, not two, but some?"

"Yes. Some men. An indeterminate number."

"All Japanese?"

"With respect, Detective, I believe you're thinking like a man, not like a woman."

Kawika, chastened, nodded glumly to concede the point and gestured for Smith to continue.

"Fortunato's Japanese boss provided entertainment to his guests," Smith went on. "On this occasion the entertainment was Joan. Some of it didn't pose a disease risk—bondage, and so on. But some did. So now she was even more worried about infecting her husband. Her doctor took tests, reassured her as much as he could. Not that it mattered in the end."

Kawika felt queasy. Joan had been vague in describing her weekend with Shimazu. She'd said just enough, no more. Nothing like this.

"That's why I blamed Fortunato," Smith said. "He pimped her out, broke her spirit. She must've confessed something to her husband—you didn't tell me what—and her husband killed her. When I saw you that day I'd just heard all this, just opened her up and taken her apart. I was angry. But I should have kept my mouth shut."

"When she talked to me, it didn't sound like rape," said Kawika. "It seemed she'd just made a bad mistake."

"It didn't start out as rape," Smith replied. "Basically, she consented to be wrecked. A thousand kisses deep."

"What?"

"Sorry. That Leonard Cohen song again. Runs in my head. I only meant, she agreed at the start. Then things, well . . ." Smith's words trailed off.

Something else troubled Kawika. "You didn't know any of this when you performed Fortunato's autopsy," Kawika said.

"The stuff about Joan? No, I didn't. She was still alive."

"And yet you were in a pretty good mood that day. Joking around with me. Not like when you autopsied the Malos—grim business, remember?"

"Well, I already knew Fortunato was a bad guy," Smith explained. "Don't forget, I'd seen him beating Melanie."

"Was that all?" Kawika asked. "Nothing else?"

"Yeah, that was all."

"So was it just happy coincidence, you driving right behind Fortunato's car when he pulled over and started beating her?"

"Yup. Just a coincidence. Wouldn't call it happy."

As they walked to the hospital entrance together, the former FBI agent Frank Kimaio came around the corner. He smiled and raised a hand.

"Hello, Doctor," said Kimaio. "Aloha, Detective." Kimaio shook hands with them both.

"You know each other?" Smith asked.

"I was going to ask you the same question," Kawika replied.

"Frank's a patient," Smith said. Kimaio confirmed this with a nod.

"Well, he's helping me with my investigation," said Kawika.

"Trying anyway," responded Kimaio. "You still going to call me, Detective?"

"Or I just could wait here if your appointment won't take long."

"Sorry," Smith said, motioning Kimaio toward the entrance. "He'll be a while. Go on in, Frank. Things are all set up and they're ready for you. I'll be right there."

"Sure enough," said Kimaio, smiling. "Talk later, Detective."

When Kimaio had left them, Kawika said, "He looks tired."

"It's the chemo," said Smith.

"Chemotherapy? For cancer? What kind of cancer?"

"The kind you get from Agent Orange. Not looking good, I'm afraid."

"Meaning what exactly?"

"Meaning the prognosis isn't good," Smith explained. "You win awhile, and then it's done, your little winning streak. As Leonard Cohen would say."

"So . . . ?"

Smith nodded. "So, soon we'll bid aloha 'oe to Frank, I'm afraid." He smiled sadly, waved the shaka sign, then followed Kimaio inside.

Seems you just bid aloha'oe to patient confidentiality, Kawika thought. *Why? This patient's still alive.*

36

Waimea

Once burned, twice shy: Kawika checked his messages as soon as he left Dr. Smith. Tanaka's came first, reassuring Kawika that he'd had Sammy take charge of the search for Peter Pukui and Melanie Munu. Patience was next, reporting her discoveries: the roadside graffiti, Jason Hare on the highway, the links between Hare and Thomas Gray, the man who'd sold KKL its land.

Kawika listened, then braked hard, pulled over, and called her, his hands shaking.

"Hello?"

"*Patience? P?*" He was practically shouting.

"Kawika. Did you get my—?"

"Yes, I got it; thank you. It's important stuff. But P, *you're not listening.* You can't go searching for Jason Hare. You know he's an accomplice, at least. He could be the killer."

"I know, I know!" she exclaimed. "It explains so much."

"Yes, but he's dangerous. Not harmless. Not eccentric. Dangerous. And he knows how to get to your condo. You've got to stay away from him, P."

"Okay," she said. "I will, I promise."

"You promised last time."

"This is different. I wasn't snooping around the Murphys'—"

"That's not the point. You didn't stay away from him."

"Okay," she repeated. "I get the point. Honest. But Kawika, listen. There's something else. Could someone have killed Thomas Gray? The man who sold KKL its land? Supposedly, he fell off a boat. I saved the obituary for you."

"Thomas Gray fell off a boat? Why would someone kill him?" Kawika asked, surprised.

"I don't know," she admitted. "Maybe because he sold Fortunato the land? And he was tied to Jason Hare somehow—Kohala Kats, and they're both Vietnam vets. Although Thomas Gray didn't join an Agent Orange lawsuit for Hawaii vets, and Jason did. I found it on the internet."

"That lawsuit, can you check another name for me? Frank Kimaio. That's K-I-M-A-I-O."

"Sure, just give me a sec." Kawika heard the click of computer keys, then a beep. After a moment, she said, "Nope, not here. Nothing under Kimaio. Why?"

"Supposedly, he got cancer from Agent Orange. When was the suit filed?"

"It says 1995."

"Ah, he wasn't in Hawaii yet."

"Want me to print out the document?"

"Yes, please. I'll look at it tonight. I'll get to your place as soon as I'm done with Michael Cushing."

"Speaking of Cushing—"

"Right," he said. "The new graffiti message."

"Think it refers to him?" she asked.

"Yup, I do. That 'KKL' at the end pretty well clinches it."

"So someone really is using graffiti to send you messages?"

"Looks that way," he said. He remembered Arthur Conan Doyle's maxim, *"Eliminate all other factors*—in this case, coincidence—*and the one which remains must be the truth."*

"Someone's pointing a finger at Cushing," he said. "So someone wants me to think he's a bad guy."

"But who? Who's doing the graffiti?"

"Where did you see Jason Hare?" he asked. "On the Queen K or walking toward it?"

"Ah, I see what you're saying. He could have done it. He was by the heliport, still on Waikoloa Road. With the graffiti a ways behind him. And sort of a smirky smile on his face. But if he's an accomplice and he wants you to suspect Cushing—?"

"Then Cushing probably didn't do it," Kawika said. "Speaking of people who didn't do it, there's some news. Peter Pukui turned up."

"Alive and well?"

"Not well. Turns out he's a junkie, hiding from his dealers. Heroin. Nothing to do with Fortunato. My pals in Hilo let him go. Now we gotta find him again before the dealers do."

"Whew."

"Whew is right. Anyway, sorry I shouted. I really am grateful for your help."

"But no more of it, right?"

"None that puts you in harm's way. Stick to the internet. It's good you found the Thomas Gray obituary and the Agent Orange lawsuit. I'll look at them tonight."

"Tonight, I might not let you," she teased. "But if you're good—I mean really good—I might let you tomorrow morning."

"Ha!" he replied. "So far, the only things you've let me look at in the morning are the same things you let me look at in the night."

"The ceiling fans?"

"Not the ceiling fans. You know what I mean."

Kawika drove off to meet his dad for lunch—late, but not by island standards. Patience returned to the internet, searching for more on Thomas Gray. All she found were letters to the *Puako Post* responding to the Thomas Gray obituary, arguing over whether he'd claimed to be one-quarter Cherokee or only one-eighth. And whether he'd actually said Cherokee or Sioux or Cheyenne.

37

Puakō

Jarvis Wong served his son a lunch of poke and kalua pork, leftovers from a luau at the Mauna Kea Hotel.

"We're eating up your fringe benefits," Kawika said.

"Sure beats dog, though," said Jarvis. "That's an old Hawaiian dish, you know." Both men looked at Jarvis's dog, pacing impatiently nearby. Jarvis chuckled and threw a piece of pork. The dog snapped it up.

"That reminds me, any slipper dogs at the Mauna Kea?" Kawika still wondered why only one of Fortunato's Tevas had turned up. Had some "slipper dog" taken the other, as so often happens with footwear left at the door in Hawai'i? But what if Carolyn had been right, suggesting the lone Teva might be planted evidence instead?

"No way," Jarvis said. "No dogs on the property."

"How about the Mauna Lani?"

"Even less likely there. Surrounded by lava, more isolated. Slipper dogs, you find 'em in towns mostly, where locals live."

"How about cats?" Kawika asked.

"At the Mauna Kea?" responded Jarvis. "Not lately. Colony cats, we call 'em. A virus wiped 'em out. Happens every ten years or so. They'll come back, but not right away. Why?"

"Just wondered. Someone told me a guy named Jason Hare ran cat traps at the Mauna Kea."

"Jason Hare, the highway guy?"

"Yeah. You know him?"

"Just know he walks along Highway 19. Long hair, no clothes."

"Yeah, that's him," Kawika said. "He also traps cats."

"He ran cat traps at the Mauna Kea? Recently?"

"Not too long ago," replied Kawika. "Maybe just for a few nights."

"No way," Jarvis said. "Trust me. I'd know."

"I'm sure you would."

"That's the pilikia?" Jarvis joked. "You had to wait overnight at the hotel to catch a cat trapper in the morning? Couldn't sleep here?"

Kawika shook his head. "No," he replied. "I couldn't sleep here because some whacked-out kanaka might come looking for me."

"You serious?" Jarvis asked.

"Halfway," Kawika said. "I am a bit scared, Dad."

"Don't be scared over here," Jarvis reassured him. "In Hilo, maybe. But not here. Over here, the boys know you. They know you're Hawaiian."

"Dad," protested Kawika. "Even I don't know I'm Hawaiian."

"Of course you are. You grew up here, went to school here. You've got a Hawaiian name. The paper even spelled it right."

"*Dad*," Kawika objected. "I grew up in Seattle mostly. I didn't go to school here after second grade. Any Tom, Dick, or David can change his name to Kawika."

"Well, over here every Hawaiian knows you're my son."

"*That* might keep me safe," Kawika agreed. "Over here." He put a hand on his father's massive arm. "Unless Carolyn comes here and kills me. That's the other pilikia."

Jarvis frowned. "Son, when you came back from Seattle, that Chinatown thing, didn't you tell me the greatest dangers in life probably aren't physical?"

"Something like that. I was quoting Father Brown—a detective priest, in stories." That triggered something. *What was Father Brown talking about?* Kawika asked himself. *The dangers of high places—dangers greater than falling.*

"Well," Jarvis said, "Carolyn won't kill you. But she might dump you. You ready for that?"

"No."

"You ready to give up the other one?"

"No."

"Ugh," Jarvis grunted. "Pilikia."

"Dad, it's Patience. Patience Quinn."

"Son, I figured that would happen the first time you said her name."

Kawika didn't respond. Just hung his head.

"You look miserable."

"Yeah, I am," he replied. Then he began to talk.

Jarvis listened to what became a waterfall of words. As a boy in shorts, going to school in Waimea, Kawika had been happy to be Hawaiian, he said. Then in Seattle, he became just a kid who looked different, a kid other kids sometimes teased. Most thought it was cool Kawika's dad lived in Hawai'i, and even cooler—*you're so lucky, dude*—that Kawika spent summers there. He grew up, went to college and the academy, joined the Seattle police. There, among his fellow officers, he encountered serious racism for the first time. But it hadn't fazed him. Then he'd gotten fired. He hadn't failed as a detective, but as a *Chinese*—a thing he wasn't, a thing he'd never even thought about, not for a single moment.

"Did you ever consider yourself Chinese, Dad?" Kawika asked. "Because of the name Wong?"

"No," Jarvis said. "Never."

"And you're a quarter Chinese," Kawika pointed out. "I'm only an eighth. How can anyone be considered X or Y or Z when he's only *one-eighth*?"

Jarvis shrugged, seeming to recognize that this wasn't Kawika's real question, the one that needed an answer.

"So I came back," continued Kawika. "To Hilo, thanks to you."

In Hilo, he explained, he'd felt relieved to become Hawaiian again. Even happier, once he met Carolyn, an authentic and serious Hawaiian. Also an authentically good person—generous, lively, intelligent, loving—and beautiful. She was perfect.

"Two years together, and she still seems perfect," Kawika continued. "But there's a sadness in her, Dad. About what's happened to Hawai'i. She needs a real Hawaiian, someone who can share that sense of loss with her. But me, a real Hawaiian? I'm just not, Dad."

Kawika sighed and shook his head. "Then out of the blue, I meet Patience. She's also generous and loving and smart—all that. Beautiful, for sure, and playful; she teases me a lot. She calls herself a kama'aina, but really she's a long-time visitor. Yet here's the thing: my being Hawaiian doesn't matter to her. And when I'm with her it doesn't matter to me either. I really like that. It feels good—like coming home somehow, not having to think all the time about being Hawaiian or hapa, a Mainlander, or anything else."

Worn out, Kawika stopped talking. "So, Dad," he said, "what do you think?"

"Well," Jarvis began sternly, "For starters, I think you can't keep a woman in Hilo and a woman in South Kohala, no matter what. Holding hostages while you make up your mind. It isn't right, and it isn't fair."

Kawika grimaced.

"Plus, you're leading a double life. That's why you're miserable. You know that, right?"

Kawika nodded glumly.

"A person can't live two lives," Jarvis went on, more gently. "You gotta choose *one* life, then live in it—same as you'd live in a house."

"But that's what I don't know, Dad—that life."

Jarvis paused briefly. "Son," he then said, "I can't tell you who you are. Don't worry, you'll figure it out. But I can tell you a few things. Might help."

"Please," Kawika responded.

"Okay, now I don't know Flea well, but I've known her a long time. She's not just a beautiful rich haole—she's got more going for her than that. Still, some haole women do like Hawaiian men because they're Hawaiian. They like the *idea* of a Hawaiian man. Maybe they like the idea more than the man himself. Trust me on this, okay?" Jarvis raised an eyebrow at his son, warding off questions.

"Okay," replied Kawika. He sensed they were on dangerous ground.

"So you might be wrong about Flea," Jarvis said. "Maybe what she likes most about you is the Hawaiian part. Maybe she doesn't realize it. Not yet."

Kawika waited, sensing Jarvis would say more.

"I think," Jarvis continued, "what your mom liked most about me was the Hawaiian part. I think she realized that—in the end, not the beginning."

"Oh," Kawika didn't know what to say.

"Do yourself a favor, son," said Jarvis. "Ask her."

"Who? Mom?"

"Yeah, your mom. Ask her about Carolyn and Flea. She'll give you good advice."

"But Dad," protested Kawika, "Mom's never even met Patience."

"Yes, but your mom *is* Patience. She never could sit still; she couldn't relax. Can Patience?" He sounded sympathetic, almost wistful, leaving Kawika to ponder several mysteries at once.

Kawika knew they'd reached the limits of what they could ask one another, what they could answer, even though Kawika didn't feel much better. And both needed to get back to work.

Jarvis walked Kawika to his car.

"Another house for sale down the road," Kawika said, changing subjects. "Noticed it driving in."

"Your buddy Fortunato's, actually," said Jarvis. "His widow's selling it. Unlucky house. Guy drowned, the one who owned it before. Tom-Tom Gray. Fell off his boat."

"I just heard about that," Kawika said. "Did you know him? Did you think it was an accident, him falling off his boat?"

"Yeah, I knew Tom-Tom. Did someone say it wasn't an accident?"

"No, but he sold Fortunato the land for KKL. And Fortunato was a bad guy, like you told me."

"Huh," Jarvis said. "I did wonder, was it really an accident? I saw Tom-Tom's kids at his service. Kam and Emma. Watched 'em grow up here. Now they live on the mainland. They weren't convinced. Said it didn't seem like something that would happen to Tom-Tom on his own boat. For one thing, they said, he hardly ever took it out alone. I never thought about him and Fortunato, though—that's interesting. Fortunato wouldn't have killed him for the house down the road, though."

"No," Kawika said. "But how about something to do with KKL? Maybe bad title to the land?"

"No idea about that," Jarvis replied. "But after Fortunato bought Tom-Tom's house, he used it himself sometimes, between rentals. He'd bring a woman here. Pretty one, in her thirties or forties maybe. Not Hawaiian, something else: Samoan, Fijian maybe."

"Melanie Munu," said Kawika. "Maori, people say. She's Peter Pukui's girlfriend, supposedly. But apparently she had something going with Fortunato too."

"Don't know," Jarvis said. "Didn't recognize her. She's not local."

Kawika shook his head. "Talk about living a double life," he said, thinking of Joan Malo and Melanie and Corazon. "Or a triple life. You could've told Fortunato a double or triple life would make him miserable."

"Yeah," replied Jarvis. "Maybe it even made him dead."

38

Waikiʻi Ranch

Legs crossed and with a flip-flop dangling from her foot, a relaxed Melanie Munu sat on the lanai of an empty house at Waikiʻi Ranch, slowly smoking a cigarette and waiting patiently for Michael Cushing's man to show up with the cash. She wondered idly if he'd bring it in a big mailing envelope, like FedEx, or a shopping bag. Whatever, she was prepared; she'd brought her own duffel. She'd specified mixed bills, nothing above a twenty. She hadn't considered how large a bundle that might create. But she could hardly accept a check, and with drug wars raging all over the island, she couldn't risk attracting attention with a zillion hundreds. *Okay,* she thought with a smile, *maybe not a zillion. But still, a lot.*

She felt the satisfaction of a harrowing ordeal successfully completed: She'd finally get the money. Peter Pukui needed to stay alive; he was HHH's orator and leading public figure. Plus she truly did care for him. He'd be dead if he couldn't pay his drug debts—maybe even if he couldn't get more drugs, more of that damn H, something she'd never touch herself. To get money, with Peter's drug-driven blessing she'd gone to bed with Fortunato after he refused the HHH demands over the heiau. And even then, Fortunato had demanded more; it wasn't enough just to share his bed. So Melanie had agreed to conspire with him, pretending to be Chief Kuʻumoku's heir—an improbable heir, she'd warned him, since normally she posed as a native from New Zealand.

The whole thing was risky, the idea of Melanie exposing KKL's faulty legal title at Fortunato's command, and the timing had remained fuzzy. Just to be safe, Melanie had taken a hastily provisioned Peter Pukui to the top of Pololū Valley, letting him hide deep in the rugged coastal wilderness until she got a cash advance from Fortunato and paid off Peter's dealers.

Then Fortunato had reneged, dragging her from his car and beating her on the Queen K when she told him someone else was going to sue over KKL's title. And just when she'd decided to extort money from him anyhow—he was married, after all, and using that bad legal title for some sort of fraud—Fortunato had gotten himself killed.

Shocked, it nonetheless took Melanie only a day to realize she could extort the money from Michael Cushing instead. Cushing seemed surprised when she asked to meet for coffee, and stunned when she told him that KKL's title was faulty. Fortunato hadn't let Cushing know everything, she realized. Wisely, she didn't repeat her earlier mistake: She didn't tell Cushing the Murphys and their lawyer Ted Pohano were going to expose KKL's bad title anyway.

"Ralph wanted me to declare myself the chief's heir in court," Melanie had said to Cushing. "But you don't want me to do that, do you?"

"Definitely not," he answered, flushing bright pink.

"Well, I'll just forget my claim in return for what Ralph promised. Same amount, nothing more. But he's dead now, and you're still here."

"Your damned boyfriend, Peter Pukui, killed him," Cushing said, angry now.

"He didn't," she replied.

"Liar. You're a liar."

"Look, if Peter killed him, I'd know," she said calmly. "After all, I was fucking them both, wasn't I?"

"You're *such* a liar," Cushing repeated. "You weren't fucking Ralph and he wasn't fucking you."

"Suit yourself; I'm not proud of it. But hey, let's stay on track here." Melanie started to get tough. "Do we have a deal or not?"

"What if I refuse?" Cushing asked.

"Well," she replied, "in that case I'd have to pursue my claim."

"So basically it's pay you now or pay you later?"

She'd smiled and handed him a card with her phone number. On it she'd also written a dollar amount.

"I need to hear from you in two days. Sorry for the rush." She'd tapped the card and walked out.

Two days later, right on schedule, Cushing had called and said a man would bring her the money in twenty-four hours. Cushing told her to wait at a particular house at Waikiʻi Ranch, one she knew well; she used to meet Ralph there. What a relief to get the money, get this all behind her. Peter had called her from Hilo after his wilderness ordeal, and she gave him the good news. But since she didn't have the money yet, she'd told him to go with his lawyer and keep out of sight.

She'd been waiting only about twenty minutes when a man drove up in an SUV and got out, but not carrying a bag. That confused her.

"Hi," the man said as he approached. "I'm Rocco."

"You're from Michael Cushing?" she asked, stubbing out her cigarette and standing up.

"No, I'm from California," he replied. "So's this," he added, pulling a handgun from his waistband.

"Whoa, wait a minute, Mister," Melanie said, raising both hands to slow him down, to placate him. "I haven't broken into the house. Just came up here to enjoy the view. I'll leave right now."

"No, you won't," said the man who called himself Rocco.

39

South Kohala

Though he sometimes forgot, Kawika tried not to go into a meeting without a specific objective. Kawika's objective for his meeting with Michael Cushing was simple: get the man talking. Here he applied a lesson from Dashiell Hammett's fictional detective Sam Spade. *"Get a man talking,"* Spade observed, *"and maybe you can get somewhere."*

Kawika didn't suspect Cushing of murder—not after interviewing him that first day. Cushing had been terrified of an unknown killer and desperate for Kawika to catch him. Cushing had suspected Peter Pukui, but Kawika no longer did. He half suspected Jason Hare, but half suspicion was as far as he could get. Hare didn't strike him as a killer. An accomplice, maybe. Perpetrators betray themselves, Kawika believed. Hare hadn't done that.

Kawika felt Hare had been clumsy, though. He'd lied in his statement. The graffiti messages seemed clumsier still, assuming they were his, and a stupid idea to begin with. They might have been missed entirely, and the first ones seemed meaningless. The third—"KW: MC KKL"—managed to convey information. But to Kawika, its only practical import seemed to be that he should interview Cushing again—something he'd already arranged. So was "KW: MC KKL" clumsy of Hare too?

Nothing could overcome Kawika's powerful first impression: Cushing didn't know who'd killed Fortunato. *So why,* Kawika thought, *would Hare bother to compose "KW: MC KKL"?* Occam's Razor suggested Hare hoped to misdirect him, to have Kawika suspect Cushing instead of the real killer. But who could know for sure?

Kawika wondered if Fortunato's real estate fraud—not his sex life, not his battles with HHH or others—might have gotten him killed. The exact nature of the fraud eluded Kawika. He had wisps of understanding, nothing more. He felt—and this was his most elegant notion—that if he could get Cushing talking, he might finally comprehend the real estate scam. Then he could winnow through motives and opportunities and come up with possible suspects.

40

South Kohala

Cushing, too, tried never to go into a meeting without a specific objective. Now, alone and pacing around his KKL office, he tried to think what his objective with Kawika should be.

Cushing's ultimate objective—wealth—didn't require rethinking. He'd grown up with tastes dependent on it. His mother's fortune came from two Big Five families, the missionaries' descendants who'd grown rich. But Cushing's father had ruined Cushing's mother and vanished, and the family scandal had mortified Cushing's wife. She now spent little time in Hawai'i, preferring to lose herself in the South Pacific on tours she led for *National Geographic*. Her earnings helped, but Cushing wanted *real* money.

With KKL, he'd thought, he and Fortunato had a very good thing going. Then, inexplicably, Fortunato had begun jeopardizing it all—jeopardizing a billion-dollar project and multimillion-dollar paydays for them both. Why? Cushing had no idea. He tried to restrain Fortunato, cautioning at first, then arguing, finally pleading, but Fortunato had just laughed.

In desperation Cushing hired Rocco, a contract killer from the mainland—but someone else had killed Fortunato first, in precisely the place and manner Cushing had planned. Who had done that, and how? The question nagged Cushing incessantly.

Cushing opened a sliding door, went out onto the office deck, and lit a cigarette. He'd quit smoking a decade earlier. But now he'd started again. He inhaled deeply, looked out at the mist-shrouded Mauna Loa and Hualālai, and tried to think.

After Fortunato's death, Cushing learned—from Melanie Munu, of all people—that the whole development rested precariously on a faulty legal title. The heiau incident and the hunters—KKL could survive those, Cushing figured. But a title problem running all the way back to the Māhele? Fortunato had not only concealed this potential fatal flaw but clearly intended—somehow—to exploit it. It presented a mortal threat to KKL. And Melanie couldn't be trusted to walk away even if he paid her. So Cushing had arranged for Rocco to solve the Melanie problem, and with it, he thought, the Māhele problem. Who else would know or care about a long-dead Hawaiian chief's title to a lava field?

Then Cushing had traveled to Tokyo. There he found Shimazu violently upset by the killings of Ralph and Joan. But Shimazu made clear he wasn't going back to help the Hawaii police.

"I doubt you're a suspect," Cushing had told him, although the thought had occurred to him.

"Not the point," Shimazu had replied. "Got no time for that, with KKL in the spotlight because of these murders." He demanded that Cushing prepare a revised business plan quickly, something Shimazu could use with investors, banks, and regulators. "They're pressuring me," he said. "Hard."

Now, on the night before he was to meet Kawika, Cushing had finally gained access to KKL's real books, the ones Ralph had never showed him. Cushing understood their significance immediately: no way could KKL possibly succeed. Period. Shimazu was wiped out already; he just didn't know it. Ralph had cheated him.

Fortunato had paid too much for the land—far too much, even if he'd gotten valid title. Ralph had wasted—stolen?—far too much as well. He'd grossly inflated income estimates for the hotel and golf courses. And it would be impossible to sell real estate at prices high enough to make a profit, because the prices Ralph had projected for the benefit of the Japanese investors were a joke. Cushing couldn't believe it. Ralph had used real estate at the Mauna Kea, the Mauna Lani, and Hualālai as comparables, for Christ's sake. Hawai'i's top three resorts. *But Kohala Kea Loa won't even have a fucking beach.*

It was time to put KKL into bankruptcy, a victim of Ralph's fraudulence, although only Cushing knew that yet. And with KKL dying, Melanie Munu couldn't extort a cent as the supposed heir to some long-dead Hawaiian chief.

So Cushing could have called off her killing. But he'd already frustrated Rocco once, when someone else had murdered Fortunato. Cushing crushed out his cigarette and lit another. He worried that Rocco had traveled a long way—twice. It might be risky to disappoint him again. Cushing thought about paying Rocco a bigger breakup fee this time—maybe the whole amount? But if the entire fee had to be paid, why not just go ahead with Melanie's killing? Keeping her alive wasn't a priority.

Cushing found it hard to think clearly. He'd been up all night, and the bookkeeping he'd had to unravel, combined with jet lag, the destruction of his financial dreams, and the imminent end of his employment, left him exhausted. So he went to bed. He woke up a bit refreshed and resolved to escape: escape Melanie's killing; Fortunato's killer, whoever that was; Kawika; Shimazu; the whole lot of them.

His objective for the meeting with Kawika, Cushing decided, should just be to talk: talk as long as Kawika let him. Talk and tell him nothing. Let Kawika say good night no wiser than when he'd said hello, and Cushing could get some more sleep. Then he'd be fully rested. Then he'd make a plan. He crushed out his second cigarette, closed up the office, put the top down on his KKL convertible, and headed down the mountain toward the Queen K for the long drive home.

41

Hilo

Sammy Kāʻai devised a sensible plan to discover the identity of the Shark Cliff victim he'd dubbed the Handcuffed Haole, though he still suspected the man was a stray. First, he asked a fellow officer to look through the missing person reports. The Big Island generated a lot of them. Then he had Dr. Ko, the Hilo coroner, provide enhanced images of the dead man's tattoos, the traditional anchor and the ancient aku fishhook with coiled line. Sammy had these printed on scores of flyers. Finally, he picked a small team—just two officers—to canvass the boats and crews in Hilo harbor.

The plan had shortcomings. Sammy knew his pair weren't the most diligent; they were just the officers Hilo's top brass were willing to spare. Maybe they'd get lucky on the first try, or early at least. But Hilo Harbor was jammed with boats—big boats, little boats, fishing boats, tugboats, all kinds of boats. Some were almost always out to sea. Others came to port only at night. And whatever else they did, Sammy's pair of officers didn't work at night. Some boat owners and captains and crew weren't possible to identify, much less find. A lot of them lived in Honolulu or even Alaska.

Sammy had the pair check the Big Island's other major harbor, Honokohau in Kona, a marina that provided all the frustrations of Hilo's, plus a lot more lazy afternoons on the island's dry side for the two officers. Sammy urged them to stick with it. "Sooner or later we'll find someone who knows him," he insisted.

Sammy did not ask them to check the tiny boat harbor in Kawaihae, the one near Puʻukoholā Heiau. The one with only a handful of watercraft, although it did include the racing canoe that Kai Malo and Tommy once paddled together.

42

Waimea

Cushing lived halfway up the slope between Kawaihae and Waimea. From that elevation, you could see twenty miles down the coast and far out to sea. But Cushing's house, curved like a wide-angle lens, faced Kohala Mountain instead. People were meant to enter this house and walk right through it, out the other side and into the view—one of the biggest views on the Big Island. As Kawika drove up, he noticed that the Waimea cop guarding the house had positioned himself to be able to enjoy that view.

Cushing answered the door. "A yellow Mustang convertible?" he said. "Pretty nice cop car."

"It's mine," Kawika said. "Second-hand from Mr. Hertz."

Cushing chuckled and led Kawika inside. "Thanks for meeting me here," he said. "Hope you understand. We've got the place to ourselves. My wife's off leading a tour in Raiatea."

"Good," Kawika said. "Then I don't feel so bad, taking up your evening."

"How about a drink?" Cushing asked. "I know you're on duty, but I make a mean Mai Tai. Personal recipe. Got the ingredients ready and waiting."

"Can't turn that down, I guess." Kawika figured it might help if Cushing had a drink. He resolved just to sip his.

"Look around," Cushing said. "We can talk while I work." A half wall separated kitchen and living room. Kawika turned slowly to regard the décor.

"You've got a Hawaiian museum here," Kawika said appreciatively. "You've even got an old ihe." The four-barbed spear hung over the front door. Kawika walked over to inspect it.

"Correct," said Cushing. "But not the murder weapon, right?" Cushing laughed to signal the small joke.

"Nope," Kawika replied. "We've got that one locked up in the evidence room."

Cushing switched on a blender. When the noise stopped, he said, "My ihe's not just old, it's historic. It's one Kamehameha used in a famous exhibition for Captain Vancouver. Dealer in London got it for me." Cushing retrieved limes and cherries and pineapple from his refrigerator. "There were six to begin with, all thrown at Kamehameha. He caught or deflected or dodged them all. Then he gave them to Vancouver as a present. Vancouver kept one, delivered four to the British Museum, and gave the sixth to one of his fellow officers, Peter Puget."

"Peter Puget, as in Puget Sound?"

"Same one, the guy who raised the British flag on Hawaiian soil. Puget's family kept his ihe for two hundred years. Finally they sold it. I was lucky to get it."

"Amazing," said Kawika, struck by who'd touched this ihe: Kamehameha, Vancouver, Puget. He reached up to touch it himself, running one finger over the four barbs. "Do you know other collectors, folks who might be missing an ihe?"

Cushing laughed. "Sorry, can't help you there. Collectors of Hawaiiana don't hold swap meets. We're rivals, not friends."

Kawika stepped away from the ihe and peered into a display case. "What about this fishhook?" he asked.

"Mother of pearl," Cushing called from the kitchen. "For aku. I don't think mine was ever used, though, judging by the fish line. Doesn't look like it ever got wet. I think the hook was ceremonial."

"The line's made of olonā fiber, right?" Kawika asked.

"I'm impressed," said Cushing, skewering the fruit on a plastic spear. "How do you know about olonā fiber?"

Score one for the Waimea cops, thought Kawika. Just as he'd requested, they'd kept key details out of the papers.

"Strongest fiber the old Hawaiians had, wasn't it?" Kawika replied, avoiding an answer.

"Definitely," said Cushing, completing his work on the drinks. "Hard to find olonā anymore. And who knows the old cordage techniques?" He handed Kawika a drink, clinked glasses, slid open the glass door. They walked out onto the lanai. Cushing set down a wooden bowl of macadamia nuts.

Kawika shook his head in admiration. "Your view is magnificent," he said. He couldn't imagine what such a house must cost. Even now, at dusk, the bare flanks of Kohala Mountain, parched and ocher-toned at their lower elevations, stretched with increasing greenness up to a forest, over which a flat white cloud lay like a cloth. The ironwood trees guarding the road to Hāwī, the Kohala Mountain Road, stood in a dense dark line. In the failing light, Kawika picked out a few dwellings, wondering if one were Frank Kimaio's. A pair of headlights, fused at this distance, slowly wound down the mountain toward Waimea.

The two men sat down and regarded Kohala Mountain in silence—the spectrum of fading colors, the trees lining the road to Hāwī, the tiny comet of the distant headlights. "Nice Mai Tai," Kawika said, sipping his drink. "Strong, though. Whew."

"So, how's the investigation going?" Cushing asked.

"There've been some developments," Kawika replied. "Not allowed to tell you much. But it looks like Peter Pukui didn't do it."

"*What?*" Cushing sputtered and sat up sharply, spilling some of his drink. "How can you say that? If he didn't do it, who did?"

He's not faking it, Kawika thought, noting the sudden flush on Cushing's pale skin.

"We don't know yet. But we're quite sure it wasn't Peter Pukui. I'm not at liberty to tell you why. You understand."

"No, I don't understand. Someone killed Ralph on an imitation heiau with a Hawaiian spear. If not Pukui, then who? Melanie Munu? Someone else in HHH?"

"Possibly. No one's seen Melanie, but the Waimea cops are checking out the rest of them. Still, I don't think so."

"Why not?"

"Again, I'm not free to say much. The killing seems staged to make HHH look responsible. But whoever did it was . . . clumsy, let's say. Culturally illiterate."

Cushing face turned even brighter red. "Culturally illiterate in what way?" he asked. Then, sarcastically, "If you're free to say, that is."

"Well, just taking information that's public, the ancient Hawaiians used javelins for warfare, not human sacrifices," Kawika replied, sounding as if he'd always known this.

Cushing took a deep breath and exhaled heavily. "I would have thought," he said evenly, "that the killer is a modern Hawaiian, not an ancient one."

"Meaning?"

"Meaning, this killing wasn't designed to museum-quality specifications. The killer didn't check with the Polynesian Cultural Center. He just wanted to say, 'Let this be a warning to anyone who would desecrate a Hawaiian cultural site.'"

"Could be," Kawika conceded. "But I doubt it. I think that's what the killer hoped we'd believe. The good news is that you probably have nothing to fear from Pukui or Melanie Munu or anyone else in HHH."

Cushing winced slightly. "So, is there bad news?" he asked.

"Well, we believe Mr. Fortunato's death might be tied to KKL as a business venture. Something to do with the money, where it came from, where it went—that sort of thing. You worked with him, so it's possible that whoever killed him may present a danger to you."

"Jesus. You suspect the Japanese? The investors?" Cushing shook his head, as if trying to comprehend.

Kawika shrugged. "I don't know," he said. "Mr. Shimazu was here personally. But he also could have hired the killer. Anyway, we've got to follow the money. Look at the books, interview Shimazu, and all that. We'd appreciate your help. You told Shimazu we'd like him to come to Hawaii voluntarily? Good. He's being pretty elusive. And you must know the books pretty well; you've been preparing financial stuff for Shimazu, right?"

Cushing nodded slowly but said nothing.

"We can't avoid visiting your office," Kawika continued. "I don't have to go myself, but my colleagues do. Guys in plainclothes. They won't attract attention."

"Of course," Cushing muttered. Then, as if impulsively, "I've got things to tell you, Detective. Quite a few things, in fact."

Just what Kawika had hoped.

"I don't know whether this relates to Ralph's death," Cushing began, "but I'm pretty sure he was defrauding the company. That's what I discovered, when I got to see the real books. And right now I need another drink."

For an hour, Cushing ran Kawika through it: the grossly inflated price Fortunato had paid for the land, the ridiculous revenue projections, the absurd use of the Big Island's best beach resorts as comparables for estimating sales prices of KKL real estate. Cushing explained how Fortunato could freely draw on KKL's available cash. Cushing admitted he still didn't know exactly what Fortunato had been up to, or whether Fortunato colluded with Shimazu. But he'd provided Kawika something new to investigate.

It was late when Kawika rose to go. Cushing, who'd consumed two more drinks, by that time looked a bit disheveled and completely wrung out. As he walked Kawika to the door, he stopped abruptly by the display case, the one with the fishhook and the olonā fiber fish line.

Kawika turned and looked back. Cushing stood immobile, staring into the case as if mesmerized. He shook his head twice and then resumed walking, now with an uneven gait.

"Lost in thought?" Kawika asked sympathetically. He could tell Cushing was drunk.

"Yeah," Cushing answered. "Still trying to figure out Ralph's scheme."

"Me too," Kawika said, cheerfully. He didn't understand the scheme entirely, but he'd made progress. He'd also drunk his whole Mai Tai, a strong one.

Cushing walked toward the door, weaving a bit. Then he stopped suddenly again. His gaze drifted up to the ihe above the door. His eyes opened wide and he staggered back a bit, then looked up at the spear again.

Kawika smiled at Cushing's impaired motion, glad Cushing had drunk too much, enough to lose all caution, enough to divulge what looked like corruption in KKL's finances—a possible motive for someone to murder Fortunato.

Cushing shook his head as if to clear it, but kept looking above the door.

"Admiring your spear?" Kawika asked, also looking up at it. "It's amazing, knowing Kamehameha handled it, maybe just a mile or two from here, yeah?"

Cushing nodded, then turned and followed Kawika to the door. A few moments passed as Kawika sat on the porch and began putting on his shoes. Then Cushing, suddenly becoming animated, said sneeringly, "By the way, Detective, you shouldn't feel bad about killing Joan Malo."

"What?" Kawika looked up sharply. The accusation and Cushing's change of tone—taunting, out of nowhere—startled him.

"You know, making me tell you about her affair while that Waimea detective listened. I tried to warn you. You didn't pick up on it, I guess."

"What are you doing, Mr. Cushing?" Kawika, bristling, stood up to face him.

"You're probably upset with yourself," Cushing continued. "Don't be, that's all I'm saying. Joan was smart and good looking, but she was a slut. Her husband was bound to find out. Good thing it happened when it did. Otherwise, he might have killed me."

"Mr. Cushing—"

"Oh yeah, I fucked her too. Everyone did. Joan loved it. Horny little bitch. Ralph fucked her all the time. He never did kinky stuff with her. But Joan told me that when Ralph took her to Tokyo and gave her to Shimazu—"

"*Mr. Cushing.*" Kawika's angry tone forced Cushing to stop. "You're not a Native Hawaiian, are you?" Kawika asked.

Cushing looked puzzled and shook his head.

"Good," said Kawika. "Wouldn't want to persecute you."

Then he broke Cushing's nose with a right cross, the hardest punch he'd thrown in his life.

43

Waimea

Cushing collapsed on the porch, covering his face with his hands. Blood streamed through his fingers.

"*You son of a bitch!*" he screamed, kicking blindly and pedaling with his feet. "*I'll have you fired for this! I'll sue the shit out of you!*"

The Waimea cop standing guard came running. Kawika sat down on the steps. "Here," Kawika said, pulling a handkerchief from his pocket and pushing it into Cushing's hands. "Here," he repeated. "Use this."

Cushing held the handkerchief to his bloody face. Kawika finished lacing up his shoes.

"What the—?" exclaimed the Waimea cop, nearly breathless. A small sweat towel hung from his pocket. Kawika took it and pressed it into Cushing's hands. He retrieved the bloody handkerchief and held it away from his body.

"Take him to the emergency room," Kawika told the Waimea cop. "Stop the bleeding first, then take him up there. His nose is broken. He needs a doctor."

"What about you?" the Waimea cop asked.

"I'll go ahead," Kawika said. "Make sure they're ready for him. And I'll report this too. You saw what happened?"

"I saw you hit him. I couldn't hear what you were arguing about."

"That's okay. Captain Tanaka will probably want a statement from you."

"*I'll give your fucking Captain Tanaka a fucking statement!*" Cushing bellowed, his face still covered with the towel.

Kawika's meeting was over. Cushing had provoked Kawika into a violent outburst—unprofessional conduct that would get Kawika suspended from the case, Kawika knew, if not thrown off the force. At least he had obtained a sample of Cushing's blood. It could never be used as evidence, the fruit of an illegal search. But it might solve a nagging problem. Cushing's DNA might match that of the sperm Dr. Smith had found in Joan Malo. And that would tell Kawika something he very much wanted to know.

From his car, Kawika called the hospital. Smith was waiting when Kawika arrived. Kawika held out the handkerchief. Smith used tongs to deposit it in a plastic bag.

"I can't believe you've compromised yourself like this," Smith scolded, zipping up the bag. "Professionally, I mean."

"Oh, can't you?" replied Kawika acidly. "We'll have a chat about professional ethics soon, Doctor. If I'm still on the force."

44

Hilo

More pilikia. From the moment Cushing's nose collapsed beneath his fist, Kawika grasped the consequences. He drove through the night to Hilo so he could get Tanaka out of bed and tell him before others did. He asked himself over and over—as he knew Tanaka would—why he'd done it. It began to feel like a stupid mistake.

Did it matter who'd sodomized Joan Malo just before she died? Cushing knew about Joan's ordeal in Japan. Kawika could imagine Cushing forcing that information from her. But with his adrenaline draining away, Kawika could imagine other explanations. Cushing had said, "Joan told me . . ." But Fortunato could have told him. Or Shimazu, on Cushing's recent trip. Which meant Cushing needn't have forced it from Joan. Which meant . . .

It dawned on Kawika—and confused him—that Cushing, even drunk, had somehow guessed Kawika might assault him to defend the honor of Joan Malo. Why had Kawika done it? Had her dignity touched him? Her suffering? Was he avenging her when he hit Cushing, he wondered, trying to assuage his own guilt about her death? He even wondered whether thinking so much about Joan Malo—a conclusively unattainable woman—was some sort of irrational flight from the dilemma of Carolyn and Patience, the two women whose looks were fused in Joan's physical appearance, Hawaiian and petite.

I'm losing it, Kawika thought. *"Cool head main ting,"* he reminded himself. He could have used Tommy beside him in the car.

Kawika felt relieved after calling Patience to explain, for the second time in their still-new relationship, that he wouldn't be able to see her that night. His relief stemmed partly from decisions deferred and partly from her reaction. She sounded worried—not angry, not even disappointed, just worried. *She cares about me,* Kawika thought. *I've got a little time to figure this out.*

A few miles from Tanaka's door, with midnight near, Kawika pulled himself together and found some hard kernel of resolution, determination. The thought of failing—knowing he was close to failing, might have failed already—stung him. *I want to catch this killer,* he decided firmly. *I will catch this killer, if I'm not fired. That's what I need to focus on. Not Joan, not Carolyn, not Patience. The killer.* Being a homicide detective, solving murders, was what mattered most to him, he realized. Maybe it was even his true self.

Tanaka, roused from sleep, listened to Kawika's confession, which was unsparing. But Kawika could see that Tanaka was angry—very angry. Kawika knew Tanaka didn't completely absolve him of Joan Malo's death. He worried that this time Tanaka might conclude he'd erred irredeemably.

But Tanaka didn't act immediately, not in the night. Punishment, he told Kawika, could wait till morning. Instead, having listened long, he offered words Kawika knew were meant to help him.

"I'm not surprised you let yourself be provoked," he said. "You're human. Cushing pushed your buttons. But you haven't asked *why* he provoked you. He isn't a suspect, and he'd just entertained you in his home."

Kawika started to answer.

"Shh," Tanaka admonished him. "Don't answer. Not yet. Get some sleep first, then think about it. It's not a trick question. But I think the answer matters."

"Thank you," replied Kawika as politely as possible. "I was just going to say: you've taught me that what's true is more important than why it's true. What's true is, he did provoke me."

"Ah," said Tanaka. "Hoist with my own petard—isn't that what your fictional detectives would say?"

"Sherlock Holmes maybe. No one more recent."

"Well, Dr. Watson," Tanaka concluded, "in this particular case what's true may *not* be more important than why it's true. But this case is an exception."

45

Hilo

Tanaka took command. He asked Tommy instead of Kawika to question the recently returned Murphy couple. He also asked Tommy to have his Waimea colleagues keep trying to track down Jason Hare, who'd vanished from the shoulder of the Queen K. He pressed Sammy to locate Peter Pukui, whom they'd released, and find Melanie Munu. He placed another call to Shimazu in Japan. And when a call came from Cushing's lawyer—a Waimea lawyer Tanaka didn't know—Tanaka handled it himself.

"My client demands that Detective Wong be suspended and that disciplinary proceedings be instituted to terminate his employment," the lawyer declared. "Further, my client demands that the County initiate prosecution of Detective Wong for criminal assault. Finally, my client demands that the Department not defend Detective Wong or pay his legal fees in the criminal case or in the civil suit my client intends to file against him."

"Is that all?" Tanaka asked.

"My client is a reasonable man," the lawyer said. "He blames Detective Wong, not the Department. Assuming you agree to his demands, my client will not sue you personally as Detective Wong's supervisor, nor file a criminal negligence complaint against the Department or name the Department as a defendant in the civil suit."

"You done?"

"Depending on your response, yes."

"Here's my response," Tanaka said. "Detective Wong will apologize to his colleagues for his loss of self-control. He will do so at a meeting I will call for that purpose. Your client is welcome to attend. Or I can send him a tape. Detective Wong will also be suspended from the case—not from the force.

His suspension will last for five working days. In a murder case, working days include the weekend."

"Five days! You're joking."

"The suspension is not to punish Detective Wong," Tanaka continued. "The suspension is to protect your client. Detective Wong needs to cool off. We don't want him to hurt your client."

"He's already hurt my client."

"I mean *really* hurt your client."

Cushing's lawyer grew incensed. "Captain Tanaka, Detective Wong didn't just hurt my client, he *assaulted* my client. The assault was brutal, and it was completely unprovoked."

"Completely unprovoked?"

"Yes," the lawyer said. "My client merely expressed disagreement with Detective Wong's statement that a Mr. Peter Pukui could be ruled out as a suspect in the Fortunato murder case."

"That's what your client tells you? Well, here's what Detective Wong tells me," replied Tanaka, beginning to lie—he recognized the irony—to protect Mister Clean. "He says your client accused him of covering up for fellow Hawaiians—specifically, for Peter Pukui and his group, HHH. You understand the significance of such an accusation?"

"Of course, but what my client actually—"

"That's not all," said Tanaka, lying some more. "Detective Wong says your client also called him—let me get the exact quote, I've got it right here— a 'typical lazy incompetent kanaka.' And here's another quote: 'a shiftless, good-for-nothing, Hawaiian piece of shit.' You're a lawyer. You understand the significance of *those* words?"

"Captain—"

"Those are *fighting words.*" Tanaka had read the phrase in Kawika's report of his Frank Kimaio interview, done some research. "Fighting words are racial slurs so insulting and provocative that the law considers them an assault. When your client shouted those words, he assaulted Detective Wong. Detective Wong was entitled to defend himself."

"You can't be—"

"It's a matter of degree," Tanaka said. "If I call you a haole, you might not feel insulted. If I call you a *shyster*, you'll take offense. If I call you an *ambulance-chasing* shyster, you'll get angry. And if some Japanese American cop called you a *pinko-gray* ambulance-chasing shyster, which could happen, you might punch him. You see my point?"

"Captain Tanaka, my client did not employ any racial slurs."

"Go ask him. Ask what he really said. Watch his eyes. See if you believe him."

"I believe him already."

"Maybe you shouldn't," Tanaka said. "You know the hardest job of any lawyer is getting the truth from his own client."

"Captain Tanaka, these are scurrilous falsehoods."

"Terrible lies, you mean?"

"Yes, terrible lies. You would not dare assert them in any court of law."

"You don't know me very well," Tanaka responded. "I wouldn't wait to assert them in court. If I hear one more peep out of your client, I'll assert them to Mr. Pukui, his friends at HHH, and the folks over at Sovereignty & Reparations. They're entitled to know what your client says about Native Hawaiians, don't you think? Pukui and HHH—I wouldn't worry about them. They're like a litter of feral kittens. But S&R? You ask me, they're a bunch of tiger sharks. And I know something about tiger sharks."

The line was silent.

"Aloha?" Tanaka asked. "You still there, Counselor?"

"I think I should bid you good day, Captain."

"Okay. But tell your client this: Joan Malo sends him greetings."

Kawika had not misrepresented Cushing's words. He'd repeated them exactly, triggering Tanaka's indignation—and prudery. That's why, in the night, Tanaka had already set his heart against Cushing: *This is a bad man. I won't allow him to destroy Kawika.*

Cushing's insults to Joan Malo made Tanaka choose to communicate—not conceal—his hostility and its source. *To avenge an insult,* Tanaka reasoned, *it isn't enough just to inflict punishment. The wrongdoer must also realize that the punishment is actually vengeance.*

This logic satisfied Tanaka deeply. It also puzzled him a bit. He wasn't sure he'd thought it up. Had he remembered it from somewhere? Read it someplace? It did seem to ring a distant bell.

46

Hilo

Things got worse. Sammy couldn't find Peter Pukui, who hadn't turned up at his house in Kawaihae, nor had Melanie Munu. The lawyer who'd arranged Pukui's bail said he'd taken Pukui to the lawyer's home outside Hilo that first night, settled him outdoors on the covered sleeping porch, found him gone in the morning. Assumed he'd headed home, probably hitchhiking.

Sammy assured Tanaka he'd already run the license plate of the young men who'd brought cash for Pukui's bail. But he hadn't gotten far at the time. The car was registered to a granny down in Pāhoa, a small town in Puna. She'd recently fled the area, destination unknown, for fear of an approaching lava flow, one that actually never got past the village outskirts. No one in her 'ohana knew where to find her, but they knew she had a grand-nephew—Akela, Akoni, or Alika something—who might live in Kea'au or Kurtistown or somewhere like that in Puna, or maybe over in the old sugar town of Pahala.

Anyway, that grand-nephew was a bad kid, people said. Very bad. Sometimes he and his buddies had been seen driving the granny's car in remote areas of Puna, where people tend to remember such things.

Sammy conferred with Tanaka. They didn't have much to go on besides that license plate. They decided to put out an all-points bulletin, an APB for the whole island. Of course, the APB had to be explained to cops all over the County. "So while we're at it," Tanaka told Sammy, "we might as well include Peter Pukui by name in the APB. It's really him, not the car, we're trying to find."

"Melanie too?" Sammy asked.

"Not yet," Tanaka said. "He wasn't with her when last seen."

Word that Pukui was missing spread quickly after that. Tanaka soon received a faxed press release—*Call me,* Ted Pohano had scrawled on the cover sheet.

Native Hawaiians Demand Suspension and Investigation of Detective Wong, Hilo's "Killer Cop"

HILO: Sovereignty & Reparations, Hawaiʻi's foremost Native Rights organization, today demanded the immediate suspension and investigation of Detective K. Wong after Hilo police admitted that Native Hawaiian leader Peter Pukui has not been seen alive since police took him into custody near Waipiʻo as part of a Hawaiian-persecuting investigation led by Detective Wong.

Insisting on anonymity for fear of reprisals from Wong, individuals close to the investigation speculate that Pukui, a descendant of Hawaiian royalty, may well have met death by foul play.

"We fear the worst," said S&R spokesperson and orator Mele Kawena Smith.

"Peter Pukui could be the third Native Hawaiian to die violently in Wong's investigation into the demise of real estate developer Ralph Fortunato," Mele Kawena Smith continued. "That's why Hawaiians all over the state are now calling Detective Wong a 'killer cop.'"

Tanaka read no further. He put down the press release and called Ted Pohano.

"Good afternoon, Captain," said Pohano. "You got our press release okay?"

Tanaka had dialed too quickly; just then an e-mail from Tommy appeared on his computer screen. He took a few seconds to read it.

I met the Murphys at their house. Lawyers wouldn't let them talk. I said RF got snatched from their place, so not talking was a mistake. The Murphys said that's impossible, but I told them we found his Teva at their door.

The Murphys got upset. Lawyers couldn't shut them up. They insist RF put on his Tevas. Mr. M even says he walked RF to the gate.

"You still there, Captain?" asked Pohano.

"Sorry, I got distracted. What's that you said?"

"S&R issued a press release concerning Peter Pukui's disappearance. It's a bit critical of Detective Wong. I wanted to give you advance notice as a courtesy, so I faxed you a copy."

"You faxed me a copy? I haven't seen it," Tanaka lied. It was getting to be a habit—lying to protect Kawika. "Critical of Detective Wong, you say? Why? Detective Wong has never even set eyes on Peter Pukui."

"Yes, but—"

"I can't understand your targeting Kawika. He's a Hawaiian—half Hawaiian by birth."

"Not quite."

"Oh, I'm sorry—he's what, three-eighths? Come on. That's gotta be a lot more than most of your members."

"You're probably right. Still, that's not the—"

"A lot more than you, I bet."

"Yes, I'll concede that."

"Well, if your release is critical of Kawika, I hope you at least included his Hawaiian first name. I'd hate to see you refer to him without that.'"

"As I explained when we met, Captain, our press releases are purely pol—"

"If you'd brought us Peter Pukui when we asked you to, we could've questioned him and ruled him out. That would've helped us focus on the case against your clients."

"Wait a minute—what case? Which clients?"

"The Murphys, of course. That's why I called. I wanted to give you advance notice, as a *courtesy*. I'm having them arrested."

"Arrested? You must be joking. For what?"

"For killing Ralph Fortunato."

"That's absurd! The Murphys didn't kill Fortunato."

"Well, we're like you," Tanaka responded, angry and way out on a limb now. "Sometimes we accuse people of killing other people even when we know they didn't."

"*What?*"

"Don't worry," Tanaka assured him. "It's purely political."

47

Volcanoes National Park

Eleven-year-olds have a lot to say. Kawika had time to listen. He'd decided to start his suspension by taking Ku'ulei on a trip in his convertible. First he drove her to Volcanoes National Park so she could see Pele in action. Then he planned to return to Hilo the next day, so she could see a celebrated hula troupe perform. In the car she talked constantly, sometimes just chattering but other times speaking with utmost seriousness.

"Most boys in my class are named Keanu," she declared at one point.

"Really?" asked Kawika. It wasn't a name he'd heard in his youth.

"Really," she assured him. "The teachers decided to call them Keanu M or Keanu L or Keanu K, depending on their last names. But that didn't work—our class has three Keanu Ks."

Kawika chuckled. "Yeah, we've got a lot of *K*'s in Hawaiian, don't we?"

"Kawika and Ku'ulei," she said brightly.

"Well, yours really is Hawaiian," he said. "Mine's just turned into Hawaiian, from David."

"Who's David?"

"My uncle," Kawika replied. "My mom's brother."

"Keanu Reeves was named for an uncle too," Ku'ulei informed him.

"Hmm. Maybe his uncle's real name was Dean. You know, *K* for *D*."

"Nope," she said, shaking her head. "Keanu means 'cool.' We learned that in Hawaiian class."

"'Cool?'" he asked.

"Yup," she said. "'Cool.' Or maybe 'cold.' *Ke* means 'the,' and *anu* means 'cold.' But I just say 'cool,' because Keanu Reeves *is* cool."

When they reached the town of Volcano, they bought some water. The day was quiet, and with the car top down they heard songbirds—first a few, then dozens. Kawika and Kuʻulei looked this way and that, searching for a flash of bright plumage in the forest canopy. But the songbirds remained hidden, just as they had in the kīpuka.

Soon Kuʻulei was skipping along a trail near Kīlauea's great crater. She tugged Kawika's hand, forcing him to keep up.

"You know what?" she asked. "Madame Pele is really mean."

"Because she destroys things?"

"No, because she destroys people. Turns them into plants."

"Really?"

"Yes," said Kuʻulei, obviously happy to explain. "Once there were two lovers, but Pele was jealous. She wanted the man herself. So she chased the lovers along the shore. She was going to kill the woman. The man told the woman, 'Stay on the beach. I'll climb up in the mountains, and Pele will follow. You run away.'"

"So what happened?"

"Well, Pele caught the man in the mountains, and she was really angry, so she killed him. Then she turned him into a plant—the mountain naupaka."

"She did?"

"Yes," said Kuʻulei sternly. "She did. Then she ran back down the mountain. She caught the woman on the beach and killed her too. She turned the woman into shore naupaka."

"You've seen them, these plants?" he asked.

"Oh yes. They both have little half flowers. You take a flower from one and a flower from the other, put them together, and they make a whole flower."

"Keanu," he joked. He'd already learned that legend from the Mauna Lani's shoreside interpretive sign—though Kuʻulei told the story better.

Kuʻulei punched his arm. "It *is* cool," she insisted. "When you join the flowers, the two lovers are together again."

Kawika was apart from his two lovers. He'd taken Kuʻulei on the trip partly to gain a respite from them both, to think, to get a grip: *"Cool head main ting."* But his cousin's tale of Pele's vengeance unsettled him. So after taking their things to the room at Volcano House, Kawika ditched his cousin briefly in the gift shop and made quick calls, two in succession.

"Just checking in," he said both times, still indecisive, still—he knew—a jerk.

If not worse.

48

Hilo

When Tanaka suspended Kawika, both men took it seriously, but neither of them expected Tanaka to manage the case for long. The baton was never really passed. Tanaka focused on immediate tasks: getting a call with Shimazu nailed down, calling Honolulu for police accountants to review KKL's books, pushing the search for Peter Pukui and Melanie Munu and Jason Hare, and ordering the arrest of the Murphys. He waited a day, then had the Murphys picked up, brought in, and fingerprinted in Hilo.

"Book 'em, Danno," Tanaka told his sergeant, who'd heard this many times before. The Murphys, accompanied by the lawyer Ted Pohano, were not amused.

It took the Murphys a few hours to make bail. Their criminal lawyer flew in from Honolulu. Pohano was still around. Tanaka made sure to show up for their release.

"You're upset," he told them. "Just remember, I could have publicized your arrest, but I didn't. Think about that."

The Murphys and their lawyers didn't speak. They just glowered.

"I come from a family of sugar cane cutters," Tanaka said. "We worked on your plantations. We'd start at one end of the field and cut all the way to the other. The cane's high, it's thick, and there's all kinds of interesting stuff in there: bottles, old tools, maybe even some bones. But when you're cutting cane, you don't stop. Later on, when the work's done and it's quitting time—pau hana, Mr. Pohano—that's when you go back and take a look at what turned up."

Again, no one responded. They didn't seem to understand Tanaka's point.

"Right now, our work is to solve a murder," Tanaka continued. "Not Peter Pukui's—we have no reason to believe Peter is dead"—he nodded sharply toward Pohano—"but Fortunato's."

Ignoring their lawyers, Tanaka looked sternly at the Murphys. "And as for Fortunato, you were the last people to see him alive. You were his enemies. His Teva was found at your door. He never got his sandals back on; his feet had grass stains and cinders. And he was murdered near your house. The next day, you told people he'd threatened you. Then you fled the scene of the crime. Now you're all lawyered up and you refuse to answer questions. That's enough for me—it's not how innocent people act. It's how guilty people act, and right now you're the only people acting that way. That's why I charged you."

Mr. Murphy started to say something, but the Honolulu lawyer grabbed his arm. "All that's purely circumstantial," the lawyer said.

"We've sent lots of killers to prison on circumstantial evidence," Tanaka replied. "Your clients wouldn't be the first." He turned to the Murphys. "Now, it's *possible* you didn't kill Fortunato," Tanaka continued, "and maybe you think the charges won't stick. Fine. But you should try hard to convince us. You know more than you're saying. That makes our job more difficult. You're standing between us and the end of the field, between us and quitting time. Between me and my fishing, more to the point. I don't like it."

The Murphys and their lawyers seemed to start to understand.

"Guess what?" Tanaka continued. "Whether you help us or not, we will get to the end of this case. And when it's pau hana, we'll go back and take a look at those things we turned up in the field."

"What are you suggesting, Captain?" the Honolulu lawyer asked.

"Your clients know," Tanaka replied. "They can tell you about it on the way home. They're trying to corner the market in Mauna Lani real estate."

"Buying real estate's not a crime," the lawyer said.

"Depends on how you go about it, doesn't it? What you disclose, what you don't. Whether there's a conspiracy, an effort to rig the market. How your accounting works, what dummy corporations you set up, what you tell the banks and the tax man. White-collar stuff like that."

"Oh, come on," said the lawyer, feigning disgust.

Tanaka shrugged. "Maybe your clients have nothing to worry about. But just the same, discuss it with them. You've got a long drive ahead of you."

As the Murphys stormed out, Tanaka took Pohano aside. "Look, you phony," Tanaka said, "I checked up on you. Do your clients know you're from Los Angeles, that you changed your name from Pohaus?"

"I'm still Hawaiian," Pohano insisted. "Just born on the mainland."

"Maybe," Tanaka replied. "But know this, Mr. Poor House: if anyone harms a hair on Kawika's head, you and your organization with your hateful press releases are toast. Tell that to Mele Kawena Smith—*and* Keoni Ana."

Tanaka turned and headed to his office. His assistant greeted him with a slip of paper. "Dr. Smith called," she reported. "He said Kawika's voice mailbox is full. I offered to put him into yours, but he asked me just to give you this message: 'The DNA matches, and it belongs to Michael Cushing.' Does that make sense?"

"Yes," Tanaka assured her. "That makes perfect sense. Let Kawika know."

It makes sense, he thought. *But I bet it's still a stray.*

49

Queen Lili'uokalani Gardens, Hilo

When the first bullet whizzed past him, Kawika didn't think, *Someone is shooting at me.* He'd heard no gunshot, just felt a disturbance of the air. The bullet blew through a lava rock wall in the Queen Lili'uokalani Gardens, where Kawika had taken Ku'ulei to sightsee before the hula performance. Kawika heard the noise of the impact—it was very loud—and looked behind him to see a cloud of dusty gray silica mushrooming into the sunlight beside Ku'ulei's head. His first thought was that the wall must be giving way. Instinctively, he looked up, expecting a tree might topple if the retaining wall collapsed. Ku'ulei turned to him, confused, holding a cone of shave ice he'd bought her minutes before.

The second shot ricocheted off the dense basalt of an ancient leaning stone in the Gardens. Kawika heard the bullet's whine and falling pitch as it sped on. Tiny flecks of rock stung his cheek and neck. He smelled something acrid and burning. Carolyn's *whacked-out kanaka* leapt to his mind, speeding his reaction by a fraction of a second. He realized now that someone was shooting at him, and he sensed from what direction. He'd also heard the second shot.

Kawika shoved Ku'ulei down hard, dropping her behind a low lava rock wall and splattering her shave ice, knowing the wall couldn't stop a high-powered bullet but hoping it would hide them. As he tried to cover her, something pushed him hard across his back and upper arm, furrowing his back muscles and his triceps. He felt pressure, not pain. He first knew he'd been shot when, puzzled, he saw warm liquid trickling down his arm. Then the pain began.

Ku'ulei lay pressed to the concrete, her cheek and forearms scraped and beginning to bleed. She was crying, and Kawika's blood was dripping on her. He could smell it now and knew she could too.

"Someone's shooting at us," Kawika whispered. "Don't move, Ku'ulei. Don't move and don't cry." She whimpered but stopped crying at once.

Kawika rolled to his left, still out of sight behind the little wall. He figured the shooter might expect him to peer over the wall but not around the end. He wished he had a gun, but he never carried one, and as he rolled, he realized his right arm wasn't doing well anyway.

He heard a squeal of tires and looked around the wall. A metallic blue panel truck sped away, obscured almost at once by the thickly planted border of the Gardens. The truck had a logo, but Kawika couldn't see it clearly as the vehicle turned and was gone. Something with a helicopter, perhaps? That's all Kawika could later tell Tanaka, who began questioning him while Kawika lay face down on a gurney, the doctors still cleaning out his wounds.

Within an hour the shooting made the news. Within two, Carolyn called Tanaka from Maui, screaming at him—really screaming—to *get Kawika the fuck out of there*. Not just off the island, she yelled; out of the state. Jarvis came for Ku'ulei and kissed his son forcefully on both cheeks. Tommy came from Kohala too, and seeing Kawika's aloha shirt torn and bloody and needed for evidence, Tommy gave Kawika his. "Literally the shirt off your back," Kawika, smiling, said appreciatively. Guarded and bandaged, Kawika was soon aboard a police helicopter bound for Maui. There he shared a brief airport embrace with a frightened Carolyn, surrounded by watchful cops. "You wanted me to join you on Maui," Kawika joked, and she laughed a bit as she sobbed. Then they put him on the nonstop to Seattle.

It all happened so quickly that Kawika couldn't call Patience until he'd landed at SeaTac Airport. He dialed while the plane was still taxiing to the gate. She wept to hear his voice.

50

Hilo

Tanaka took Tommy with him to the station house in Hilo. He'd never been angrier than after Kawika's shooting. But his desire to make a good impression on Tommy—they'd never met in person—restrained him a bit. That saved the job of the woman who answered phones for Major Crimes. Trembling, she awaited Tanaka in tears.

"I just didn't think about it," she confessed, unable to meet his eyes. "A man called, looking for Kawika. I told him Kawika went to the volcanoes with his cousin. Just being friendly, you know? I said Kawika would be back today. For the hālau."

"The hula performance?" Tanaka asked.

She nodded, still sobbing, still not meeting Tanaka's eyes.

"Did you get his name?"

"No. He didn't say. I didn't ask." More tears.

"What did he sound like? A local? Hawaiian? A Mainlander?"

"Not Hawaiian. Haole, I think. I don't know. I just didn't think about it," she repeated, finally looking up at Tanaka. "I'm so sorry."

Tanaka knew he should offer solace. "Well," he said, glancing over at Tommy and trying to soften his look, "we don't know for sure the shooter's the same guy. Probably wasn't, if your guy's not Hawaiian. And Kawika will be okay—just had a close call. But next time don't give out information—take a message. Or put 'em into voicemail."

Tanaka held her shoulder for a moment. She met his eyes with a hopeful look. "Not everyone loves cops," he told her. Then he turned and nodded for Tommy to follow him.

"You think the shooter's Hawaiian, Captain?" Tommy asked when they reached Tanaka's office.

"I think the shooter's some whacked-out local who at least *thinks* he's Hawaiian," Tanaka replied. "Someone S&R stirred up."

"What about Michael Cushing, though, Captain? Bet he's still furious, yeah?"

That forced Tanaka to calm down. Besides Cushing's broken nose, Tanaka had rebuffed Cushing's lawyer roughly. Cushing might indeed be furious—but angry enough to kill someone? "Didn't think of Cushing," Tanaka admitted. "Tell you what: when you drive back, how about stopping in to see him? Don't call first. Surprise him. You've been to his office? You know where he lives?"

"I do. I'll find him, check his alibi."

"Good," Tanaka said. "And I haven't thanked you. For coming over today when Kawika got shot. Giving him your shirt. That meant a lot to Kawika. I could tell."

Tommy left wearing a windbreaker from the Hilo police. Three hours later, he called Tanaka from Waimea. "Bad news, Captain. Cushing has an alibi for the shooting, and witnesses too," he reported. "He was in Kailua. Alibi seems really solid."

"Ugh," Tanaka said in disgust.

"But Captain," Tommy suggested, "just because Cushing wasn't the shooter doesn't mean he wasn't the caller."

51

Hilo

"Yeah, Terry?" Sammy Kāʻai stood in the doorway. Tanaka motioned him in. He'd pulled Sammy off Shark Cliff and the search for Peter Pukui—they had the APB out for that—to help investigate the shooting.

"Where are we on forensics?" Tanaka asked.

"Got four guys on the scene," Sammy replied. "One bullet blew up a retaining wall; it's buried deep. Another glanced off a pōhaku, took a chunk out of it. Bullet probably shattered. One nicked Kawika . . ."

"Nicked?" Tanaka interjected. "I'd say it creased Kawika pretty good."

"Okay," Sammy conceded. "One *wounded* Kawika, then went through a coco palm and toppled that mother. Just cut the tree right in half. So that bullet's out in the bay. Maybe we'll find it, maybe not. We'll dig out the first one for ballistics, though."

"Shell casings?"

"Still looking," Sammy replied. "Haven't found any. But we figured out where the shooter fired from. And something's odd, Terry. You said Kawika saw a blue van peel out of there?"

"Yeah, with a helicopter on the side. Must belong to that flightseeing outfit in South Kohala. Waimea guys are checking. Not all the vans are back for the day yet."

"But Terry, there's no parking space where the shooter was. And how would he know where to park? Exactly where to be? No one knew Kawika would go to the Gardens, did they? At most the caller knew he'd go to the hālau. And the hālau's across town."

Tanaka frowned. "What are you thinking?"

"I'm thinking the shooter spotted Kawika's Mustang and followed it till Kawika parked. Then the shooter shadowed him on foot, stalking him."

"Concealing the gun?

"Yeah, somehow."

"So the shooter must've had a getaway driver, you're thinking?"

"Maybe, maybe not. But I bet the shooter wasn't alone in that van."

52

On the Queen K

Having taken Hawaiian studies in college, Michael Cushing knew that, despite the common misconception, ancient Hawaiians made human sacrifices to other gods, not just Kū. He also knew that in Kailua there are ruins of a heiau for Kanaloa, the god who ruled the ocean, where Hawaiian royalty sacrificed their victims for a special reason: to improve surfing conditions. The bone pits remain, and the site has been preserved as a little park, crowded with tourists.

The man who called in the night told Cushing to meet him at the little park. The call woke Cushing from a troubled sleep. It took him a few moments to orient himself and begin writing down instructions. He was exhausted, not just scared.

"Get this right the first time," the caller warned. Cushing was given no choice. "If you've looked at your old spear or fishhook recently, you already know we can get into your house," the caller pointed out. He told Cushing to leave at a specific time in the morning, well before first light. Cushing was to drive with his convertible top down, despite the cold, so he could be observed and seen to be alone. "Just bundle up," the caller instructed. He told Cushing to drive at the speed limit, precisely fifty-five miles per hour, once he reached Highway 19, the Queen K. "You won't see us," the caller said, "but we'll be watching."

Cushing followed the instructions, like a man driving to his own funeral. It was still dark when he reached the coast, turned south, and began driving sixty miles per hour to the gods knew what. On a straight stretch of empty highway, Cushing heard something louder than the rush of wind past his car: a beating noise, something percussive, something approaching from behind. He looked in his mirrors. Nothing. But the noise grew louder—louder and closer. Cushing turned and looked behind him, overhead.

A helicopter—a small one, though it seemed enormous, flying only thirty feet above the highway—was rapidly overtaking him. The copter displayed no lights. It was a loud black object against a nearly black sky.

Cushing swerved erratically across the highway, his tires squealing. The helicopter crew may not have anticipated this maneuver, because when the helicopter delivered its parcel—a man wrapped tightly from his ankles to his mouth in silvery duct tape, his nostrils flaring and his eyes wide with terror—instead of dropping cleanly into Cushing's back seat, the falling man struck his head on the rim of the passenger compartment, crushing his skull and breaking his neck.

Cushing screamed, braked hard, and swerved off the road, bouncing over rough lava rock until he jolted to a stop, his face whipped by thorny kiawe branches and then punched by his airbag—a blow that broke his nose again. The airbag deflated with a hiss. The tape across Cushing's nose was covered with blood as he turned in horror to look behind him, first at the helicopter—which rose and banked away—and then at the dead man in his back seat, a man he'd never seen in his life.

Later, Cushing told Tanaka that as the helicopter turned away, the first light of morning caught it and it appeared, perhaps, to be blue. Apart from that, Cushing couldn't provide useful information. He had no idea who'd been dropped into his car, or why. He claimed he'd gone for an early morning drive with his convertible top down because he couldn't sleep. He'd needed to think, he said; to clear his head.

"I don't believe you," Tanaka said. "But I'll tell you this: if you didn't need to think before, you do now. That was a crazy Mission Impossible stunt. Don't let it distract you. What matters is this, Mr. Cushing: someone wants you dead."

53

Waimea

Dr. Terrence Smith autopsied the dropped body, but no one could identify it. Smith called him the Duct Tape Mummy—an exaggeration, since nothing was covered below his ankles or above his mouth. Smith guessed the nickname would catch on.

The doctor duly recorded measurements, vital statistics—even the total length of tape in which the dead man had been wrapped. He took photos of the victim's features, his suntan verging on sunburn, and his sun-bleached hair, tattoos, callused hands. He noted the cause of death: a broken neck—cervical fractures and displaced vertebrae—and a skull fracture from a massive blow to the head. *Take your pick*, Smith thought.

The cervical dislocation intrigued Smith particularly. It was as if the man had been efficiently hanged, with the knot against the right side of his neck. Smith had read that during the French Revolution, executioners delighted in displaying a discovery to the crowd. If a just-severed head was held aloft by the hair, the eyes would turn briefly toward someone who shouted the victim's name. Smith wondered if hanged men—men hanged properly, that is, with their necks snapped—also experienced a moment of consciousness after the cervical dislocation. How much had the Duct Tape Mummy known?

As he worked, Smith would hum a bit, then sing a few Leonard Cohen lyrics:

> *And summoned now to deal*
> *With your invincible defeat,*
> *You live your life as if it's real,*
> *A thousand kisses deep.*

Then, unexpectedly, Smith found in the dead man's otherwise empty trouser pockets a sprig of greenery with small white flowers. He recognized the plant: shore naupaka. He whistled in surprise and admiration at the daring of it. *Who do you think you are?* Smith wondered, silently addressing the killer. *The Scarlet Pimpernel?* Maybe, Smith thought, he'd tell the police a bit less in his autopsy report now, rather than more.

Later, with everything neatly put away, Smith turned out the lights, singing softly from the same song:

You lose your grip, And then you slip
Into the Masterpiece.

Smith rolled the Duct Tape Mummy's body into a dark refrigerated body drawer—a crypt, to those in Smith's profession. He had two other crypts available, but Smith chose the same crypt in which Fortunato had once lain, before Smith had cut him up.

PART FOUR

SEATTLE TO THE METHOW VALLEY

"So you find us here, and we find you here. Which is the most surprised, I wonder?"
"There's no telling," said I, keeping as amiable as I could; "nor any telling which objects the most."
—Owen Wister, *The Virginian* (1902)

54

Seattle

Stepping off the Maui flight into the unheated SeaTac Airport jetway, Kawika thought, *The AC's on too high.* Chilly, he entered the terminal, and there stood Lily, his mother, clutching her husband, Pat, and greeting her son with a brave smile and profuse tears.

"Aloha, Sport," said Kawika's stepfather.

For a long time, murmuring reassurances, the three embraced, although lightly. Lily and Pat were careful not to touch Kawika's upper back or right arm. The stream of other passengers split and flowed around them like lava around a kīpuka.

"Don't worry, Mom. I'm fine. Really. It's a scratch."

"Hardly a scratch," said Pat. "You're very lucky."

"Very," Kawika agreed. *Shit, the guy took three shots.*

An hour later, they sipped decaf coffee at the table where Kawika had eaten his cereal as a boy. Lily sometimes wept, and the men put their arms around her. They discussed everything they reasonably could about the shooting and about Kuʻulei's condition—she was okay, no stitches, just scraped up and badly frightened. Then Kawika wanted to turn the conversation away from the narrowness of his survival and Kuʻulei's.

"Remember Father Brown?" Kawika asked Pat, changing the subject.

"Of course," his stepfather replied. They'd read G. K. Chesterton's Father Brown stories aloud together during Kawika's boyhood. A career prosecutor, Pat had enabled Kawika's addiction to murder mysteries from a young age.

"Do you remember Father Brown saying that the greatest dangers in life aren't physical?"

"Father Brown said that?" Pat asked.

"I hope so," Kawika replied. "That's what I keep telling people. Including Dad, it seems."

"Could be, I suppose," said Pat. "But wouldn't Father Brown say something like *'Life's great dangers aren't to the body, but to the soul'*? Only more graceful, I suspect."

"Well, I don't know about my *soul*," Kawika said. "But . . ." Then he explained to them, with hesitation and head shakes and not much elaboration, the dilemma he'd created for himself, his woman problem. "I'm worried—more worried than about getting shot, now I'm here. I've really messed up. And I don't know what to do."

"Oh dear," said Lily, struggling to change her train of thought. "Something went wrong with you and Carolyn?"

"Wrong with me, I guess. I was hoping to talk with you about it—maybe in the morning?"

"Darn," said Pat. "Can't be here in the morning, Sport. Legislature's in session." Pat ran the association of county prosecutors in Washington. He needed to commute to Olympia during the legislative session.

"Actually, it's Mom I need to talk with."

"Your mother?" Pat said with feigned indignation. "What does she know about love that I don't?" Mother and son both looked at him sadly. "Oh," he said. "I get it. She knows about the little brown gal—or the big brown guy—in the little grass shack in *Ha-vai-ee*. Well, yes, she does."

"I'm sorry—"

"It's okay, Sport," Pat assured him, tousling his hair gently. "But, hey, if that's tomorrow's topic with your mom, can you talk about your murder investigation tonight? Just a bit? Give an old prosecutor something to think about in traffic jams on the road to Olympia?"

"Sure," replied Kawika. "But just the Cliff Notes, okay? Still gotta make a lot of calls to Hawaii tonight."

Kawika told a compressed tale. A Big Island real estate developer, Ralph Fortunato, found dead on a golf course with an old Hawaiian spear through his chest. Hands tied with ancient Hawaiian cord. The dead man had angered Native Hawaiians, apparently intentionally. Looked like a Hawaiian group must have done it, but lots of other people hated the dead man too.

"Any eyewitnesses?" Pat asked.

"Yeah, one guy. But—"

"But he lies like an eyewitness, as the Russians say?"

"Exactly."

"And you think?"

"I think he may be an accomplice, but not the killer. It wasn't the Hawaiians—not the organized ones anyway. Whoever did it just wanted us to suspect them."

"That's odd behavior," Pat observed. "If you want to get away with killing someone, the formula is pretty simple. This Hawaiian spear killer didn't follow it."

"What's the formula?" Kawika asked.

"Oh, you know, I'm sure," replied Pat. "First, do the job yourself. Never involve anyone, never tell anyone—then no one can betray you. Second, use a common weapon—a popular gun, say, with widely available ammo, so the cops can't narrow the list of suspects. Nine-millimeter handgun, usually. That's the most common. Then get rid of the weapon. But your killer did the opposite: used an unusual weapon and didn't get rid of it."

"Right—keep going."

"You're not just humoring me?"

"Not at all." But partly he was. Kawika felt guilty about excluding his stepfather from the talk he planned with his mother. He needed to ask her things he couldn't ask in front of Pat—things Jarvis had suggested, things about Hawaiian men and haole women.

"Well, then," Pat continued. "Plan your alibi. The police won't believe it, of course. They don't have to. It just has to be an alibi they can't break. Like, fumble your change and ask an odd question going into a movie theater; the cashier will remember you, and you've got the ticket stub. When the show gets out, have a fender bender in the parking lot—swap insurance cards, maybe even call the cops. If you're lucky, no one can prove you weren't in the theater the whole time."

"Risky. Things could go wrong with that one."

"Okay, but then keep working to come up with a better one. 'Better' meaning less likely to be broken. Any murder with a motive, not a drive-by shooting, the cops will eventually figure out who did it. But with a good enough alibi, they can't send you to jail.

"And that's the last point," Pat emphasized. "If you want to get away with murder, you've got to live the rest of your life with the cops knowing exactly who you are."

"Who you are," Kawika said, "and where you are too. Right?"

"Right. They'll keep tabs on you." Pat stood, squeezing Kawika's good shoulder before heading off to bed and offering a parting thought. "If the cops know who the killer is but just can't prove it, they'll never let an old case become a cold case. Never." Then Pat headed upstairs for the night.

The next day, Pat called Kawika from Olympia. He'd thought of something to add.

"Hey, Sport, remember that Edgar Allan Poe story about the guy who tricks the other guy and walls him up in the catacombs of Venice?"

"'The Barrel of'—something," Kawika replied.

"'The Cask of Amontillado.'"

"That's right. Gave me nightmares as a kid," Kawika said. "Why do you mention it? What's up?"

"Well, I knew the name Fortunato reminded me of something. Took me a long time to remember; it was driving me crazy. Finally I got it. So go get our old book of Poe stories. The blue hardback. It's in the bookcase by the fireplace. Read me the first paragraph of 'The Cask of Amontillado.' I'll wait."

Kawika found the volume and the story. He read the first paragraph aloud to Pat over the phone:

THE thousand injuries of Fortunato I had borne as I best could, but when he ventured upon insult, I vowed revenge. You, who so well know the nature of my soul, will not suppose, however, that I gave utterance to a threat. AT LENGTH I would be avenged; this was a point definitively settled—but the very definitiveness with which it was resolved precluded the idea of risk. I must not only punish, but punish with impunity. A wrong is unredressed when retribution overtakes its redresser. It is equally unredressed when the avenger fails to make himself felt as such to him who has done the wrong.

"Interesting, huh?" Pat asked when Kawika had finished.

"What a spooky coincidence," Kawika agreed. "Of course, it's not a clue."

"Perhaps not," Pat conceded, "if you believe in coincidence."

55

Seattle

Kawika spent a few days in Seattle—long enough to get his stitches checked—and it was there Tanaka called to tell him about the Duct Tape Mummy.

"Dropped right into Cushing's car!" Tanaka still couldn't get over it.

"Sounds impossible," Kawika said doubtfully.

"Yeah, it's crazy. Just the same, someone did it. Sending a message to Cushing—or trying to kill him. Cushing swears he's never seen the dead guy. I asked if he'd take a lie detector test, and he said yes. Very emphatically. And he passed it."

"That naupaka in the guy's pocket—that's not a stray, is it?" Kawika asked.

"No," Tanaka agreed. "Two bodies, two plants, nothing else in the pockets. Can't be a stray. Could be a coincidence."

"How so?"

"Well, the first killer used naupaka to suggest Hawaiians killed Fortunato, right? But we never made that evidence public. If the killer's the same in both cases, that explains it. But if not, the second killer is trying to send a message of his own."

"What message?"

"Could be a red herring: 'The Hawaiians did it.' Or a boast: 'I'm a Hawaiian, and I did it.' Either way, we're meant to suspect a Hawaiian."

"There's a legend about those plants," Kawika said. "Pele killed two lovers, turned them into mountain naupaka and shore naupaka. When you put their flowers together, the lovers are reunited."

"You think Fortunato and the Duct Tape Mummy were lovers?" Tanaka joked. "The Mummy couldn't bear his grief, so he tucked a flower in his jeans, wrapped himself in duct tape, and jumped out of a helicopter? You've been off the case too long, Kawika. But keep thinking."

It's what Kawika was doing. He was thinking about Carolyn and Patience—or Patience and Carolyn, depending on the moment—and about the mess he'd created. But even removed from the case and with Tanaka in charge now, the baton having passed decisively this time, Kawika's thoughts still ran to Fortunato's murder. And in Seattle, what could he do to solve it?

Seattle wasn't a good place to think. There were too many distractions. Lily needed constant reassurance. Pat kept driving up from Olympia to share dinner. Friends from the Seattle Police Department—Kawika still had a few— invited him for lunch or coffee. Everyone in Hawai'i—Patience, Carolyn, Jarvis, even the busy Tanaka—kept calling to check on him.

More important, in Seattle there wasn't a single clue, no evidence, not one line of inquiry for him to follow. With nothing new to pursue, he could think—even obsessively—but not productively. He felt like an electric pump in a well run dry, a pump doing no good, sucking air, getting closer and closer to burning up, shorting out.

He needed water in that well. It didn't take him long to decide where to look: the Methow Valley. He didn't know what he'd find. He regretted not having learned more from Frank Kimaio, the ex-FBI agent. They'd intended to follow up by phone, but Kawika had been distracted. The day Kawika had seen Kimaio last—the day he'd encountered him at Dr. Smith's—was the same day Kawika had broken Cushing's nose and gotten suspended. Then after a day at the volcanoes, he'd promptly been shot.

Technically, Kawika's five-day suspension must have ended, he supposed. But still, he was on medical leave, not on the case. So he wouldn't ask Tanaka's permission to go to the Methow Valley. If he found something, then he could call Tanaka—and after that, if Tanaka allowed him back on the case, he could call Frank Kimaio and try to learn more about Fortunato in Washington.

Meanwhile, Kawika decided, he'd just go recover in the Methow Valley, as any recovering Seattleite might do. And maybe poke around a bit, see the sights, talk with the locals. He'd visit the site of Fawn Ridge, try to meet Jimmy Jack and Madeline John—he loved their names—find Fortunato's first wife, if he could, and anyone else involved in the events Kimaio had described, the people Tanaka had labeled "Mainland guys" on the whiteboard. Maybe he'd be lucky. Maybe he could break the locks on Fortunato's past, search out the secrets of his spear-shredded heart.

56

Winthrop

Kawika drove over the North Cascades Highway, looping up near Canada and dropping down into the Methow Valley from the north. The dramatic mountain passes, high and narrow, might have inspired a line in Owen Wister's *The Virginian*: "Love was snowbound for many weeks." Kawika, though snowbound—or avalanche-maytagged—in matters of love, wound his way down on clear, dry pavement to the imitation Old West town of Winthrop.

He'd chosen Winthrop so he could start with Jimmy Jack, the Methow Indian who'd tantalized and frustrated Frank Kimaio with his knowledge of Fortunato's fraudulent Fawn Ridge activity but who'd refused to testify. Jimmy Jack had a Winthrop phone number. Kawika hadn't wanted to call him in advance; it seemed better to go to Winthrop first, try to arrange a meeting once there, perhaps make Jimmy Jack a little more willing to talk.

Kawika had years ago visited Winthrop, the Western-themed town with its wooden sidewalks and false fronts and cowboy-related images everywhere, a riverfront village set amid grassy meadows and tall ponderosa pines, replete with grazing cattle and scores of lofty Cascade peaks. This time he rented a little cabin at The Virginian, a motel on the bank of the Methow River. While checking in, Kawika asked where to get a good view of the valley.

"Sun Mountain Lodge," said the friendly clerk. "Head for the bar. Go out on the deck. Best view around, anywhere they serve a drink."

Kawika picked up a Methow tourist guide. On the same table, paperback copies of *The Virginian* stood stacked beside a little sign: "Classic Western novel based in part on Methow Valley and the author's visits here in the 1890s.

$7.50. Pay at desk." Kawika almost picked up the book but instead opened the tourist guide, found a map, and noticed an oddity in the sidebar:

> *Fun Fact: First person over the North Cascades Highway on opening day?*
> *Ted Bundy, future infamous serial killer, who was the limo driver for*
> *then-Governor Tom Thorn.*

"Ted Bundy worked for Governor Thorn?" Kawika asked the clerk.

"That's right. Ted had the Guv up at Washington Pass. Tom survived, though!"

Kawika meant to buy a copy of *The Virginian*, but the famous serial killer's odd connection to the governor and the Methow Valley distracted him. He took the map and found his way to the deck of Sun Mountain Lodge, perched on a high hill looking down over the glacier-carved valley and up at the glacier-sharpened peaks. In the warm air, he could smell a fragrant mix of evergreen forests, sage and bitterbrush, haying, and some faint combination of wildlife and cattle, all rising from the valley floor and surrounding hillsides. He ordered a local beer and gazed out across the valley, surveying the smooth and undulating terrain below the mountains. It reminded him of the smooth and undulating curves of the woman he could not decide whether to let himself love.

He saw two horses and riders far below. Cowboys or tourists? Impossible to say. Side by side, far from the ranches on Kohala Mountain's flanks, they left two wakes in the tall grass.

57

Winthrop

When Kawika had confided his romantic dilemma, his mother's frank response surprised him. Now, drinking beer at Sun Mountain Lodge, he recognized she'd given him a lot to think about.

"I didn't stop loving your father," she'd said. "I just couldn't stay in Hawaii. The first two years were heaven. By the last two years, I felt I was swimming in molasses, barely able to move; if I didn't get out, I'd drown. Your dad was the opposite. If he'd left Hawaii he would have wasted away. But in the beginning, I was young, your father was gorgeous, and yes, to be the haole lover of a handsome Hawaiian—that was completely acceptable, yet still exciting, a real turn-on."

"Mom, I—"

"Don't worry, I won't embarrass you. And no, I didn't love him just for that. He's kind and gentle too. Thoughtful, wise, filled with good humor—as you know. Easy to love. But I couldn't sit still in Hawaii. Which is why I'd worry about you and Patience. Could you two be happy in the same place? She sounds like a wonderful young woman—don't get me wrong. I was pretty wonderful too, if I do say so myself. I just wasn't right for Jarvis. Not forever. Too restless for Hawaii, too twitchy."

"But you're not saying, 'Stick to your own kind?'"

"No, of course not. It's more complicated. The divorce didn't involve race; it was personality type. But in the beginning, what was exotic and novel did contribute to desire, and desire led to you. We just couldn't live in the same place. In the end, nothing could disguise that, not even a child."

Kawika's stepfather, Pat, also had advice after Lily had selectively summarized the conversation for him. The next morning, he'd lingered in Seattle to share his own views.

"I don't think race has much to do with this, Sport," he'd said. "Make your choice—flip a coin if you have to—but get out of this two-timing situation. Don't agonize about what would have happened if you'd chosen the other one. You can never know that. If you'd chosen the other one, you might've been hit by a truck on the first day. And for all you know, one or both of these admirable young women is deciding to go her own way right now. Meanwhile, you've got matters of life and death to think about. Focus on those, Sport."

Kawika made up his mind to focus on matters of life and death. "Any cell phone reception here?" he asked the waiter.

"Yes, sir. Here and a few other places in the Valley. Not many, though."

Kawika flipped open his phone. Reception seemed perfect. He dialed Tanaka first. He planned to explain that he'd chosen the Methow Valley to recuperate and then found he couldn't resist a little sleuthing once he'd arrived. He'd worried how Tanaka might react, but he needn't have.

"Glad you called," Tanaka said. "We dug out a bullet—the first shot, from what you described. Went right through that wall and into the dirt. Left a big old trail. Just kept getting bigger and bigger."

"Terry, that's not exactly comforting."

"Sorry. The point is, we got a ballistics report on it. It's a .375 H&H Magnum bullet. Nearly 300 grains, apparently."

"What's that? Never heard of it."

"It's a big slug, Kawika. Used in Africa mostly. Sometimes in Alaska for bears. Not common here. Too big for animals we've got."

"Too big for wild pigs?"

"At 300 grains? Yeah, if you want to eat the pig."

"Do we know the make of the rifle? The model?"

"Nope," said Tanaka. "Presumably a rifle that can handle .375 H&H Magnum ammo."

"Did we find the casings?"

"No. The shooter must have picked them up. But the slug tells us a lot. It's nonstandard, oversized. Maybe handloaded. If we find the gun, we can match it. The ballistics are distinctive."

"Why was the shooter so stupid?" asked Kawika, thinking back to Pat's words on getting away with murder. "He should've used something common, something the locals hunt with, something that uses .30-30 ammo maybe, or .30-06. There must be a lot of those on the island. Or something newer but still common?"

"Maybe he's not stupid," replied Tanaka. "Maybe he wants us to trace the ammo. Maybe it belongs to someone else."

"It's possible, I guess."

"Yeah. Someone tried to frame Peter Pukui for killing Fortunato. Why not frame someone for killing you?"

"Have I mentioned Occam's Razor?" Kawika asked.

"You mentioned it. You didn't explain it."

"Well, let's just say this: the guy's a bad shot; maybe he's also stupid. When I apply Occam's Razor—and even when I don't—I like that explanation best."

"Me too," Tanaka said. "Stupid guys are easier to catch."

"Stupid or not," said Kawika, "catch him anyway."

"We're working on it. Stay in touch."

"I will," Kawika promised. "Right now I've gotta find a man named Jimmy Jack. And a woman named Madeline John."

58

Hilo

"**O**h crap. You say they're .375 H&H Magnum slugs, Captain?"
Tommy was on the phone with Tanaka. "I know a guy who's got a rifle for those," Tommy continued. "He's a Waimea cop, a guy I work with. Bruno Mokuʻele. Lives right here in Waimea."

"Mokuʻele? A Hawaiian?"

"Definitely. He's one of the ahapuaʻa tenants—you know, the hunters? I was checking him out just a few days ago for the Fortunato case, like Kawika asked."

"Hmm," Tanaka said. "You think Bruno might've killed Fortunato? Then figured we're getting too close, once you interviewed him?"

"Could be, I guess. Of course, someone else might have gotten hold of his rifle. So we can't know it's him yet."

"Did he know Kawika was lead detective on the case?" Tanaka asked.

"Well, I mentioned it. But all the Waimea cops know anyway."

"Tommy, I think you'd better pay Bruno another visit," Tanaka said. "Right away. Whether he was the shooter or not, we have to see if the shooter used his rifle."

There was a pause. "Guess I'll grab another detective or two to go with me," Tommy finally said.

"Of course," Tanaka replied, thinking, *Not exactly "Send me in, Coach, send me in." Not like Kawika.*

59

Lahaina and Berkeley

Carolyn had flown home to Maui thoroughly discouraged, and Kawika getting shot made things much worse. She already wondered whether she could find a future with him, this young man she loved. She slowly strolled the beaches of her Maui childhood, deep in thought, deeply breathing the marine air, letting the foamy edges of spent waves cool her feet and wash away her footprints. At the end of each day she devoted extra time to hugging her perplexed father, who really couldn't help her.

The problem, she believed, was incompatibility between Kawika's sensibilities and her own, symbolized by Hilo, his world, filled with rain and spirit-crushing forms of darkness, and Kahoʻolawe, her desired world, beckoning with sunlight and spirit-cleansing work and promise. More than just Kahoʻolawe, the land, ʻāina, and things that spring from the land tugged at her. Hilo—and not only Hilo, but Honolulu and other cities where detectives live and work—repelled her more each day.

She didn't yearn for the past. She yearned for the future, but a future cleansed, a future that skipped the present to sink its roots and find its nourishment in the past. Like Kawika's mother, but for different reasons, in modern Hawaiʻi, in what Hawaiʻi had become, she felt she could no longer breathe. Her spirit struggled for air, even when she lay softly in Kawika's embrace.

She'd read *Ancient Hawaiian Civilization*, the 1933 book written for Native Hawaiian students in the Kamehameha Schools, and she knew what its distinguished authors urged: that she be able to speak the language, chant the glorification chants. That she dance the hula, sing the mele of her ancestors, and perhaps even fashion an exact replica of Princess Victoria Kaʻuilani's surfboard from a single plank of koa. But she couldn't change this: *"Fallen is the Chief, overthrown is the kingdom; an overthrow throughout the land."* For Carolyn, that was real.

* * *

Patience, too, went home after Kawika was shot. For Patience, home was Berkeley. She confided about Kawika to her mother first, including—blushingly—about the sex. Her mother didn't blush and advised Patience simply: "If you want to test your love for this Hawaiian young man, spend time with him on the mainland, away from your little Mauna Lani love nest. Be with him where race can create problems. Then see how you feel."

Her father took Patience aside the next day. "Your mother's keeping your secrets, whatever you told her," he said, "so I'm shooting in the dark here. But you know what a man wants in a woman, Impy? He just wants her to show up and be happy. That's all it takes, my dear. Just show up and be happy."

Since Patience couldn't sit still in Berkeley, she decided to take the advice of both parents. She called Kawika, flew to Seattle and then Wenatchee, rented a car, and drove to Winthrop. It was midnight when she showed up, very happy, and stepped out of her car into the warm pine-scented air. She pressed Kawika's body to hers, far from their little love nest at the Mauna Lani. Yet still, when they were alone in the pitch-dark night—when she couldn't see her skin on his, or his on hers, and when his moans carried no discernibly Hawaiian intonation—she felt that being with him on the mainland was just fine.

PART FIVE

IN THE METHOW VALLEY

For as all men know, he also knew that many things should be done in this world in silence, and that talking about them is a mistake.

—Owen Wister, *The Virginian* (1902)

60

Winthrop

Kawika's day began well. Patience playfully pulled him back to bed, later tracing his stitches gently with her fingertips, and Jimmy Jack agreed to meet for lunch. Jimmy Jack had worked at Rattlesnake Ranch, seen the early days of Fawn Ridge. According to the retired FBI agent Frank Kimaio, Jimmy Jack knew the mainland sins of Ralph Fortunato. But lunch with Jimmy Jack went badly.

"You part Apache, like Ralph?" asked Jimmy Jack, holding Kawika's business card as if it might carry an infectious disease.

"Part Hawaiian. And I thought Ralph was part Athabascan."

"Apache, Athabascan—how about Assiniboine? Just the first part."

"Not a popular man, I guess. Tell me about him."

"So you're part *Hawaiian*?" asked Jimmy Jack, ignoring Kawika's request. "Which part? Your little finger?"

"More than that," Kawika said, trying to treat it lightly.

"Let me guess. You're Hawaiian from the waist up—and Jewish from the waist down."

"I'm Hawaiian on my Dad's side," Kawika said, letting it pass. "He's three-quarters Native Hawaiian."

"Lot of Native Hawaiians named Wong? Or is that Athabascan?"

"Dad's part Chinese too. Chinese American."

"You drink?" asked Jimmy Jack, jerking his head sharply at the waiter, who stepped over to the table.

"A beer would be nice," Kawika said. Jimmy Jack ordered Diet Coke.

"Ralph drank," said Jimmy Jack. "Right at this table. Agent Carlson, he said you shouldn't trust a man who drinks."

"Agent Carlson?" Kawika asked. "I don't know who that is."

"One of the FBI guys who investigated Ralph."

"Oh. I met a different FBI guy who worked on the case."

"Indians, we didn't always have the right to drink," Jimmy Jack said, veering off again. "Not in bars. You know that?"

"No, I never heard that."

"It's true. My daddy, he was the first one legal in our family, when he turned twenty-one. Thanks to Eisenhower. God bless 'im. Ike gave us the right to drink in bars. Only fair, don't you think?"

"Of course."

"Know who got the law passed? National Association of Guys Who Own Bars. White man sold us whiskey illegally for years. Bar guys figured, time to get in on it."

"Huh. I never knew any of that."

The drinks arrived, and they ordered lunch. "You're not buyin' mine," said Jimmy Jack. "Just so you know."

"Okay," said Kawika. "That's fine. But tell me about Ralph Fortunato."

"Tell you what?"

"Anything that might help. As I said on the phone, I'm investigating his murder."

"Murder, you call it."

"What else would you call it? It wasn't suicide, I guarantee you."

"Okay, it wasn't suicide."

"It was homicide. Murder."

"Whatever you say. You're the detective."

"Well, what would *you* say? Maybe I'm not understanding you."

"Hell, I'm no lawyer," replied Jimmy Jack. "Let me put it this way. Ralph's dead, right? Someone did it. But if it weren't for the law, Ralph never would've made it out of this valley alive. No one here would've called it murder."

"Well, that's why I called you," said Kawika, seeing an opening. "I'm trying to learn about Ralph's life here, what he did, what happened."

"And that's what I ain't gonna tell ya. People mess in Ralph's life, they end up dead. I aim to go on livin' a bit. Ain't never got involved in Ralph's shit. Far as I'm concerned, the whole thing's a white man's problem."

"Wait a minute," Kawika objected. "It's true some people in Hawaii ended up dead after Ralph got killed. I almost ended up dead myself. But here?"

"See," said Jimmy Jack, "that shows you ain't done your homework. With what you don't know, you're dangerous."

Kawika was stunned. Yes, he hadn't done enough homework, he realized now. He'd never had a chance to follow up with Frank Kimaio, to progress beyond Fortunato 101, to dig into that category Tanaka had written on the whiteboard, "Mainland guys." Neither he nor his colleagues had used the internet for research on Fawn Ridge matters. But after all, nothing had suggested the need for homework of the sort Jimmy Jack was now suggesting. Fortunato had plenty of Hawaiian enemies, and he'd been murdered in Hawai'i with a distinctly Hawaiian weapon, in a carefully staged Hawaiian killing, perhaps an intended Hawaiian sacrifice.

"Wait—" Kawika began.

"No, I ain't waitin'. You're snoopin' around in Ralph's life. You want to know about Ralph, ask the marshal. You want to know about restorin' land—weed control, native species, that sort of stuff—ask me. That's what I do: land restoration. That's what I know about, what I talk about. Oh, and here's our food."

Kawika considered his options. He decided he wanted to know about land restoration. By the end of lunch he knew a lot, mostly about invasive species. He'd learned the pioneers nearly ruined the land by breaking the sod, and that folks now relied too much on pesticides and too little, Jimmy Jack believed, on biological controls such as beetles and goats. Kawika even took notes, because he finished his food before Jimmy had taken three bites, and it felt awkward just sitting there. Besides, with notes he could always tell Carolyn, who'd probably be fascinated: lessons in comparative land restoration.

After lunch Kawika walked along the Methow River to The Virginian. His interview with Jimmy Jack reminded him of his interview with Bingo Palapala. Kawika had suspected Bingo of wrongdoing and essentially accused him; no surprise Bingo reacted defensively. But Kawika hadn't suggested he suspected Jimmy of anything. So why would Jimmy deflect all discussion of Fortunato—yet discourse happily about noxious weeds? Had anyone actually died here because of Fortunato? Or was Jimmy just inventing an excuse for not talking?

Kawika had almost reached The Virginian when a car horn sounded behind him. He turned and saw Patience driving up in her rental car, smiling happily.

"Hop in," she called as she pulled over. "I'll save you the last hundred feet."

His day brightened. Here in Winthrop at least he wasn't leading a double life, just a life with her. Carolyn and Hawai'i seemed far away. He kissed

Patience when he climbed in the car, and again—several times—when they arrived at The Virginian.

"I found a great place to stay," she said, quite pleased. "The Freestone Inn, up the valley in Mazama. Wait till you see it. It's so romantic. Seriously, Kawika. We'll be happier there. And I've already booked us a suite. We can split the cost."

"Okay," he said, although remaining in Winthrop would've been more convenient.

"Goody," she replied, clapping her hands. "You won't regret it, I promise. And I bet the Freestone has a better internet connection too. I can do some online sleuthing—very safely, I promise—while you go sleuth around in the sagebrush."

"Maybe you should sleuth around the local cemetery," Kawika said. "It seems people may have died here because of Fortunato."

"The local cemetery," she said. "Let me guess. In this fake cowboy town, it's called Boot Hill."

"Boot up and find out," he said.

61

Winthrop

Kawika and Patience drove back down the valley to Winthrop for breakfast. The Freestone Inn would have been simpler, but dinner there the night before had unnerved Kawika a bit. The food was excellent, but he couldn't understand the menu's culinary terminology without help from Patience, and the prices surprised him even though he came from Hawai'i. Patience paid the bill, which made things worse. She'd ordered a nice wine, and Kawika drank several microbrews. As a result, romantic possibilities escaped them that night. In the morning, Patience suggested breakfast in town.

She was gamely picking at her huevos rancheros when a tall and very thin man in a Stetson hat strode by their window, looked them over, and pushed through the saloon-style door. He came straight to their table. He had no spurs on his cowboy boots, Kawika noted. Other than that, he looked like some stereotype from a cowboy Western. Even wore a star on his vest.

"Detective Wong?" he asked. "I'm Marshal Hanson."

"Hello, Marshal," replied Kawika, inviting the marshal to sit down.

"Figured it was him," Hanson said with a smirk, turning to speak to someone at the next table. "Heard he was with a spinner," he half whispered, loud enough to be overheard.

"A spinner?" asked Patience.

"Sorry," the marshal replied. "A small woman, I should've said."

"Small women are called spinners?" Patience looked him questioningly. "I've never heard that."

"Beg your pardon. I shouldn't have said anything, Miss—?"

"This is Patience Quinn," Kawika said. The two shook hands.

"Pleased to meet you, ma'am. You too, Detective." Hanson didn't remove his broad-brimmed hat.

"I'm told you're the man to see with questions about Ralph Fortunato," Kawika began.

"Now there's a coincidence. *I'm* told you're a man with those very questions." Hanson grinned unpleasantly, then called to the waiter. "Hey, Jimbo, how about a cup of joe over here? Joe to go."

Something was wrong. After Jimmy Jack, Kawika wasn't entirely surprised.

"I'm law enforcement, like you," Kawika said. "I'm investigating Mr. Fortunato's murder. You understand."

"Oh, I understand all right. I understand you're about three thousand miles outside your jurisdiction. You're like someone from Quebec here, Detective. We welcome tourists; heck, we depend on them. If you and Miss Quinn are here as tourists, we want you to enjoy yourselves. But if you're here detecting, well, that's not okay with us."

"Why?" asked Kawika evenly.

"*What* I'm telling you is what matters, Detective. The *why* doesn't concern you."

"It does, though—it does concern me. A man's been murdered."

"Not just one man, Detective."

"Meaning what? Others murdered in Hawaii? Or murdered here?"

"Meaning Ralph Fortunato got what was coming to him. Good riddance, folks here will tell you. Whoever killed him—why, he's a hero, as far as we're concerned. Maybe you'll catch the guy, Detective. But not with help from us."

Hanson rose, nodded to Patience, touched his hat. "Pay attention to what I told you, all right? You're up there at the Peach Pit—that's what we locals call the Freestone. You've got yourselves a cozy little room. My suggestion is, put it to good use."

Hanson waved to another diner and walked out, taking his coffee.

"Whew," said Patience. "I don't believe that."

"I believe it," said Kawika. "Let's not talk here. Outdoors."

They paid for breakfast and stepped out onto the wooden sidewalk. Every building boasted an Old West facade. Somehow the Western theme worked; Kawika could imagine a gunfight on Main Street. *Shit,* he thought. *I hope no one tries to shoot me here.* He felt a long way from Hawai'i—a long way even from Seattle—and suddenly a long way from safety. Clearly, people didn't want him here.

"Why are small women called spinners?" asked Patience. But Kawika was looking across the street. He nodded so she'd look too.

On the wooden sidewalk in front of an antiques shop, two women gazed into a cardboard box that one held. Their radiant faces reflected kittens or puppies as plainly as faces can reflect campfires or candlelight. Kawika and Patience crossed the road and looked into the box. It held two kittens—tiny ones.

"Oh my gosh," Patience exclaimed. "They're adorable."

"Yep," one of the women said. "Picked 'em up this mornin'. Momma didn't come back, second mornin' in a row. The others died, so we figured it was time to bring in these two. Hold 'em a minute, will ya?"

The woman handed Patience the box and fished in her bag for keys. She gave a little wave to her friend, who walked off. Then she opened the shop door and ushered them inside.

"Are those milk bottles for them?" Patience asked, looking into the box.

"Yes, ma'am," the woman said. "Wanna try feedin' one?"

"Sure," said Patience. The woman gently lifted one of the mewing kittens and placed it in Patience's hands. Then she held the tiny bottle—meant for eye drops—and squeezed some milk onto the kitten's nose. The kitten licked it greedily. The woman handed the bottle to Patience, who held the kitten easily in her palm.

"Here you go, you sweet little kitty," Patience cooed, "you little ball of fur."

The second kitten mewed piteously from the box. The woman handed it to Kawika along with another bottle. He and Patience stood together, feeding kittens.

In that moment, for the first time, he could truly imagine a life with her. Which meant that—also for the first time—he could imagine letting himself fall in love with her, however improbable the match might seem, to himself and others, and however painful the necessity of confessing his decision to Carolyn, making the inevitable break, explaining to confused and questioning friends. He couldn't decently invoke as an excuse Caroline's desire to go work on Kahoʻolawe or that she might eventually leave him for that. Things weren't that simple, and he knew it. He would just have to tell the truth: "I fell in love with someone else."

The shop owner bustled around, getting ready for business. Her long black hair, beginning to gray, lay straight and heavy down her back, secured by an oval clip of worked silver and turquoise of Native American design.

"Thank you," she said. "Don't have enough volunteers. Gotta do it all myself, some days. Appreciate the help."

"You do this regularly?" Patience asked. "Rescue kittens?"

"Kittens, cats—yeah, that's what we do. Plus I run the shop. These two, we been watchin' the mom and them for days now. Tried to trap her, but the trap's been empty every mornin'."

"You check your traps in the morning?" Kawika asked.

"Yep. Every mornin', rain or shine. 'Course, it don't rain much here."

"I thought people checked cat traps at night," he said.

"Hmm," said the woman. "Never heard of that. Don't seem to make no sense. Your feral cat, it mostly hunts in the evenin' and at first light. Plus, you want the vet to be open when you pick 'em up. That's why we check traps in the mornin'. Leastways that's what we was taught by professionals, over to Spokane."

Kawika and Patience turned to one another. "Jason Hare—" she began but checked herself. Kawika nodded: *That's why I asked.* Kawika remembered Jarvis teasing him too, asking if he'd camped at the Mauna Kea all night to catch a cat trapper in the morning. It hadn't seemed important then.

"What's your group called?" Patience asked.

"We call ourselves Methow Meow," the woman said. "Kinda corny. But folks remember the name. It was either that or Winthrop Whiskers."

"Can I write you a check?" Patience asked. "I'd like to make a small donation." Kawika thought, *She does this every time with cats.*

"Why, thank you," the woman said. "That's very kind. I appreciate it. We'll put the money to good use, I promise ya."

"I'm sure you will," said Patience.

"Here, let me hold the kitten." The woman took it so Patience could open her bag to get her checkbook.

"I'm Patience Quinn, by the way," said Patience. "And this is Kawika Wong."

"Oh," said the woman, startled. The bottle of milk stopped half an inch from the kitten's face. The kitten protested loudly, then stretched to reach it.

"Well, howdy then," the woman said after an awkward moment. "Glad to meet ya, I guess. I'm Madeline John."

62

Mazama

Kawika and Patience didn't consciously obey the marshal, but they did spend the next twenty-four hours at the Freestone. They made love, they worked—he on the phone, she on the internet—and at Kawika's suggestion, they tried the dining room again for dinner, this time with greater success. How you feel depends on what you're thinking, his mom had taught him. Kawika was thinking, *Within these walls I'm safe.*

Kawika's good mood reflected another thought as well: *What a lucky break with Madeline John.* She'd listened respectfully, then in the end promised she'd intercede with her husband, try to get him to give Kawika another chance.

"I'm a Native Hawaiian," Kawika had told her. "Mr. Fortunato destroyed a Native Hawaiian cultural site. It was an ancient boundary marker or an altar; some people thought it was a temple. I know he destroyed a Native American cultural site here too. If you and your husband will just talk to me about that one thing, the wintering shelter, I won't ask about anything else. I promise."

"I'll see what I can do," she'd replied. "But you understand why Jimmy don't wanna talk? It weren't just Mr. Kellogg he thinks Ralph done, but Bill too."

"Mr. Kellogg? Bill? I'm sorry, I—"

"It's all right," she'd said. "Jimmy'll tell ya—or he won't."

When Kawika and Patience left the shop, they'd smiled at one another with satisfaction. "Great move," he'd teased, "writing her a check. If cops had money, we wouldn't have to, you know . . ."

"If you had money," she'd replied, "maybe you wouldn't have to play the race card like you just did." She'd dug her elbow into his ribs. But she'd laughed too.

They headed back to the Freestone so Patience could get on the internet and start searching for the deaths of a Mr. Kellogg and someone local named Bill. Kawika called Tanaka. He intended to pass along the names Madeline John had mentioned and also what she'd said about trapping cats, but Tanaka had more dramatic information.

"We arrested your shooter," Tanaka said. "At least we think he's your shooter, unless someone else got his gun and is trying to frame him. The bullets are his, he owns a rifle for .375 H&H Magnum ammo, and the rifle's missing."

"Oh, thank God," said Kawika. "Who is he?" Patience looked up sharply. Kawika scrawled GOT THE SHOOTER on the Freestone notepad and tossed it to her. She read the note, burst into a grin, and pumped a clenched fist.

"Well, sorry to say, he's a Waimea cop," Tanaka replied. "Bruno Mokuʻele. One of those hunters up at Waimea."

"The ahupuaʻa tenants?"

"Yup."

"Mokuʻele? He's Hawaiian?"

"Yup. But not whacked out, I don't think. A cool customer."

"How'd you catch him?"

"Tommy got him. Your buddy."

"Good old Tommy."

"No kidding. Soon as we told Tommy about the rifle using .375 H&H Magnum cartridges, he said, 'I know who has one.' Tommy and some other detectives went and got Bruno out of bed. The gun case was in his garage, but not the gun. He acted all surprised. Said it was there last time he looked, and so on."

"Does he have an alibi?"

"The usual: off duty, home alone, working in his yard. No one saw him."

"Does the ammo match?"

"Same as the slug. Three-hundred-fifty-grain bullets. Even heavier than we thought. Not handloaded, but specialty items—Woodleighs. We haven't done ballistics yet, but they'll match up."

"Good work, Terry. Thank Tommy for me."

"I will. But here's something important. Guess how Bruno got the rifle and ammo? They were gifts from Ralph Fortunato."

"Fortunato! When? Why?" Kawika sat baffled, but Patience didn't look up. She stared at her computer, wholly absorbed. She typed something, hit a key, and waited.

"Don't know yet," Tanaka said. "Bruno decided to stop talking. Wanted to see a lawyer. That's when we arrested him."

"Is he lying? About Fortunato giving him the gun?"

"Doubt it. That's how Tommy knew about the gun. Bruno showed it to Tommy when he first got it, told him Fortunato gave it to him. We'll try to find out where Fortunato got it. And maybe there's a record of Woodleigh shipping him the ammo."

"Is Bruno someone S&R stirred up?" Kawika asked. "Does he think I'm responsible for the Malos? For Peter Pukui going missing?"

"We don't know. Like I said, he wouldn't talk. But his lawyer doesn't like you."

"Oh no. Don't tell me."

"Yup. Ted Pohano."

"Jeez. Can't we get him disqualified?"

"Maybe. The man's a walking conflict of interest. But we've got a suspect in custody, and that's enough for now. I should have—"

Kawika didn't hear the rest of it. Patience leapt from her chair, grabbed her laptop, and rushed toward Kawika, who was sitting on the bed. She stretched the laptop's phone cord tight but it wasn't long enough. So she held the laptop a few feet from his face. The screen displayed an old article from *Northern Lights*, a newspaper of the Methow Valley. The headline read:

Prosecutor Slain In Wenatchee
Steve Kellogg Led Fawn Ridge Team

63

Mazama

Kawika and Patience both sat stunned. How many bodies, Kawika wondered? It began, he mused, with just one—Fortunato. Just one, that is, assuming no connection to Shark Cliff. The Malos had followed, thanks to Kawika's mistakes but also, as Dr. Smith had insisted, more fundamentally thanks to Fortunato himself. And now there was an even earlier killing, it seemed, one Kawika could easily guess might be connected to Fortunato's much earlier time in the Methow, just as the local paper's headline half hinted.

All of a sudden, "Mainland guys," as Tanaka had labeled them on the whiteboard, seemed more credible to Kawika as suspects. But in that case, why the Hawaiian spear? Why the olonā fiber cord? Why the mountain naupaka?

Kawika and Patience couldn't put work aside, not after what she'd found. Patience—who'd skipped wine at dinner, as Kawika had skipped beer—worked all evening on her internet research, promising to report before they went to bed. While she worked, Kawika called Tanaka to report her astounding discovery. He'd have to call Frank Kimaio next.

"Why are we just learning about this now?" Tanaka sounded exasperated, not just with Kawika but with himself as well. "That FBI guy in Seattle never mentioned this to me. You didn't get it from Frank Kimaio either?"

"No, and that's my fault," Kawika admitted. "We just had a first interview. He gave me the background stuff, called it 'Fortunato 101' and saved the rest for later. He took me through the fraud investigation, the destruction of the wintering shelter, the failure of the prosecution. Then he left for a doctor's appointment. Said we could follow up by phone, and I even ran into him at Dr. Smith's a few days later, but he was just starting a chemo treatment. And that same night I broke Cushing's nose, I got suspended, and then I got shot. So I never had a chance to follow up."

"Well, we sure dropped the ball, you and me both," said Tanaka. "We had 'Mainland guys' on the whiteboard from the start." Kawika expected more blame than that, but all Tanaka added was, "We could have done a Google search, for gosh sakes."

"Doing it now," Kawika said, not mentioning Patience.

"Well, consider yourself back on the case, and call Kimaio," Tanaka instructed. "Better late than never, and all that."

Kawika tried—he remembered Kimaio's phone number with no difficulty—but Kimaio didn't pick up and didn't seem to have an answering machine. "Damn," Kawika said.

Filled with adrenaline—and with Frank Kimaio, Bruno Moku'ele, and the murdered Steve Kellogg tumbling around in his head—Kawika kept trying to reach Kimaio, without success. He finally gave up. He called Tanaka to tell him.

"Okay, it's late where you are," Tanaka said. "I'll call him myself. Meanwhile, I've got an update for you."

Tanaka had finally spoken with Shimazu directly. Unfortunately, Shimazu already had Japanese lawyers and refused to talk. So Tanaka had asked Hawai'i prosecutors for options.

"They say we've got to go to court, get some papers," he told Kawika. "Then we can question him under oath in Japan—eventually. We can't extradite him unless we charge him. That's down the road, to say the least. Right now, we can't question him for weeks—maybe months."

"You make Shimazu for Fortunato, Terry?"

"I didn't at first. Now I wonder. Cushing thinks it might be Shimazu. He's helpful now, worried Shimazu might kill him too. The Duct Tape Mummy really got him thinking. He still claims to know zip about that guy. But he thinks he's figured out the scam Fortunato was running. And he may be right."

"What do you mean?"

"Well, Fortunato was cheating the company, right? Skimming money and keeping KKL going by hyping the financial projections, making KKL look better than it ever could be."

"The luxury resort with no beach."

"Right. But it had to end sometime," Tanaka said. "Now he's studied the real financials, Cushing says the whole thing would have come crashing down, no matter what, if KKL ever got its final permits. Because then KKL would have to go out for construction loans and permanent financing—and the lenders would probably be some sharp Americans with their own due diligence teams. Not sitting in Japan, believing whatever information Fortunato and Shimazu fed them."

"So Fortunato needed to kill the resort?" Kawika asked, recalling Tanaka's comment: *"Old dog, old trick."*

"Actually, he needed a third party to kill it," Tanaka replied. "And at just the right moment, before final permits. That's the point Cushing keeps making."

Tanaka explained what Cushing had told him. Fortunato wouldn't want his hyped financial projections to be what killed the resort. The investors would come after him. So maybe, Cushing reasoned, Fortunato had decided to provoke HHH into challenging the permits. Or let the tenants do it, those hunters. Or find an heir to the old chief to challenge KKL's title in court. Anything to string things out and keep the construction financing stage from being reached.

"It explains a lot," Tanaka told Kawika. "Shimazu might've figured out what Fortunato was up to. So he might've wanted Fortunato dead and for people to think Hawaiians did it. He knew about the HHH guys, Cushing says. Knew they were furious with Fortunato."

When Kawika hung up, the message light glowed red. The Freestone operator said Madeline John had left him a message: *"Meet at shop at nine AM. Come alone."* Hard to interpret that. Kawika hoped it meant good news.

Kawika looked over at Patience. "Ready yet, P?" he asked.

"Almost. This connection is slower than The Virginian's," she confessed, smiling. "I was wrong about that—but you've got to admit, the bed is better." She had pages of handwritten notes beside her computer. A little hourglass, continually draining and refilling with pixels, rotated in the center of her screen.

Kawika decided to call his mother. He assured her he was safe, then asked to speak with his stepfather.

"Pat, do you know the U.S. Attorney for Eastern Washington?"

"Sure. Ernesto Gonzales. Ernesto Che, folks call him. Haven't worked with him myself—he's strictly a Fed, and they keep to themselves. Ernesto's a Bush appointee, new guy in the post. I hear he's good people. Why?"

"An assistant U.S. Attorney, Steven Kellogg—he was murdered."

"Yeah, about five years ago. In Wenatchee, right? No indictments, no convictions. Feds never released names of suspects, of course, and they don't tell us local prosecutors much. Case is still unsolved, I know that much."

"Did you know this Steven Kellogg?"

"No, just knew he'd been killed. But Gonzales must've known him. Ernesto was an Assistant U.S. Attorney in Spokane for dogs' years. Hometown boy. Worked his way to the top."

"Could you call him for me? Let him know I'll be contacting him? I want to pick his brain about the Kellogg case. Might relate to mine."

"Really? Wow, that would be something. I'll call him first thing in the morning."

"Thanks, Pat."

"A pleasure, Sport."

Patience shut down her computer and was ready to tell Kawika what she'd learned.

"Here's the sequence," she began, consulting her notes. "First, Fortunato was developing Fawn Ridge. The plan was to piggyback on the ski resort, but environmental groups challenged the ski resort's water permits and won— unexpectedly, I guess. Right after that, Fortunato blew up the wintering shelter. The government announced an investigation. This Steven Kellogg was lead prosecutor."

"Any mention of FBI agents?"

"No. FBI agents must avoid publicity, I guess. Anyway, Kellogg got the federal grand jury to indict Fortunato for destroying the wintering shelter. Lots of publicity. Then something happened: the government dropped charges against Fortunato. Case got dismissed. His development company pleaded guilty to making false statements, but that was it. Does that make sense?"

Kawika nodded. "It's what the Feds do when they can't nail you for anything else."

"Well," she continued, checking her notes. "Fortunato's company filed for bankruptcy. Then a while later Kellogg got murdered. Fortunato must've been a prime suspect, right? Though probably they had other suspects too; Kellogg had been a prosecutor for a long time. No suspects named in the news coverage."

"No hints from the Feds?" Kawika asked.

"Just cryptic remarks in the paper, like the FBI knows who did it, they're getting the evidence together. No arrests, though. The murder case just sort of petered out, it seems. A few quotes from 'sources close to the investigation.' Like, 'Sometimes you know who's the killer but you can't get the evidence you need.' That sort of thing."

"What evidence was missing, I wonder," Kawika mused.

"I don't know; no indication in the news. One more thing, though. A bunch of Seattle folks bought Fawn Ridge out of bankruptcy. All fifteen hundred acres. They gave it to the Methow Conservancy, the local land trust. The Conservancy preserved most of it as open space. But guess what? The Conservancy gave six hundred forty acres to Jimmy Jack and Madeline John."

"*That's* interesting," Kawika said.

"Oh, and I should've mentioned, along the way Fortunato's wife filed for divorce—Melissa Jane Fortunato, and she took back her maiden name, Melissa Jane Harding. That's almost the only time Fortunato's name turned up in the papers after Fawn Ridge went bankrupt."

Later, in bed, they learned more. She'd been on top of him, rocking, her hands on his chest, when she whispered that she wanted to turn around.

"Oh," he protested weakly. "Don't get up, don't get up."

So she didn't. Instead, she turned, carefully keeping him inside her. She settled down again, this time with her hands on his thighs, and rocked some more. As her excitement grew, she resumed the turn she'd interrupted, this time moving more quickly, with greater confidence, creating the unusual sensation of him twisting inside her, her twisting around him. Moments later, she collapsed against his chest, sweating, his arms embracing her quietly as their hearts raced.

"Now you know what a spinner is," Kawika murmured.

"Now you do too," she murmured in reply.

64

On Fawn Ridge

"You walk good?" Jimmy Jack asked. They'd met at Madeline John's antique shop at nine AM and driven in Jimmy's pickup to the still undeveloped site of Fawn Ridge, the former Rattlesnake Ranch.

Kawika nodded. "Yeah, I walk good."

"Okay," said Jimmy Jack, setting out with long loping strides. They were climbing a grassy hill up to the ridge line. "We'll walk along the ridge to the end of the property," he said. "I'll tell you about the old winterin' shelter. That's it, Hawaii. Nothin' more. You got it?"

"Got it," Kawika replied.

"You know anything about Indian reservations?"

"Not much."

"This land we're on? Part of a reservation once, the Moses Reservation. Named for Chief Moses. He wasn't a Methow. The Methows, we never got a reservation. We got tucked under Moses's wing, like lots of other Tribes. But his reservation was big enough for all of us—ran from Wenatchee up to Canada, and from the Okanogan River to the crest of the Cascades. Methow Valley was right in the middle."

"But there's no reservation here now, right?"

"You see any casinos?"

"No. But I might have missed one."

Jimmy smiled grudgingly.

"Secretary of Interior, way back then, he promised Moses the reservation would last as long as the Cascades. It lasted four years. Last time I looked, the Cascades were still here."

"What happened?"

"First, Uncle Sam took back the whole north end of the reservation. Did it for some miners, up in the mountains. 'Course, the miners went bust, but Uncle Sam never returned that land to Moses. After he lost that chunk, Moses took his people south, waitin' to see what happened next. Big mistake. What happened next was, the white man found gold in the Methow River. Silver too. Not up in the mountains—right in the Methow Valley. Uncle Sam tells Moses, 'You're not livin' on that reservation I gave you, so I'm gonna take it back.' Congress abolishes the entire reservation. Uncle Sam sticks Moses and a bunch of Tribes on the Colville Reservation."

"The Methows too?"

"Methows too. Uncle Sam picks Moses to run the Colville Reservation. Consolation prize. Moses invites his buddy Chief Joseph and the Nez Perce to come live with him. *Really* pisses off the Colvilles. See, the Nez Perce used to kill Colvilles, before the Army run 'em off."

Kawika wouldn't let Chief Joseph distract him. "That's not the end of the story."

"No, it ain't the end of the story. Because the Great White Father, he sets it up so any Indian who don't want to follow Moses to the Colville, well, that Indian can get land from the old Moses Reservation. One square mile. You know how much that is, Hawaii?"

"A square mile? A mile on each side?"

"You're a genius, Hawaii. A square mile is six hundred and forty acres. But almost no one took it."

"Why not?"

"Because the Indian didn't get to choose his own square mile; the white man chose it for him. We still got cliffs around here called Indian Henry's Choice—big old cliffs, filled with rattlers."

They had reached a ridgeline—the ridge of Fawn Ridge. Kawika cast his eyes over the sweeping view as he waited for Jimmy to resume. Looking north, Kawika saw the deep Methow Valley girded with high peaks white with snow and glaciers, running in parallel lines up past the Canadian border. To the west he saw the jagged summits of the Cascade Sawtooth. To the east, high forested hills. To the south, more of the valley, more mountains. A stunning panorama.

"Now about the winterin' shelters," Jimmy continued. "The Methows lived here thousands of years. They hunted and fished, gathered plants and berries. Winters, they just dug in, covered up, waited it out. Took a lotta work—these shelters were big ol' pits with rock walls. The old people, they picked the best sites, where the game wintered too. When they needed fresh meat, they popped their heads out, killed a deer or a moose, dragged it inside.

"Well, about two hundred years ago, the Methows got horses," Jimmy went on. "Soon they couldn't live without 'em. But horses couldn't winter here: too cold, no food. So every winter the Methows just headed south with their horses and fell in with Moses's people. Abandoned the winterin' shelters. Never used 'em again."

"So why would anyone destroy an old shelter if he found one on his land?" Kawika asked. "You'd think Fortunato could've made it a sort of feature of the resort."

"He thought of that. But then he learned somethin'. The Great White Father, he made a special rule for the Methows. A Methow Indian could pick his own square mile, if it had a winterin' shelter on it. The shelter proved his tie to the land through his people, see? And you remember how big a square mile is, Hawaii?"

"Six hundred forty acres, you said."

"Right. And how big was Fawn Ridge?"

"Fifteen hundred acres, wasn't it?"

"Very good, Hawaii," Jimmy replied. "So figure it out. Your Athabascan buddy Ralph stood to lose almost half of Fawn Ridge because of one old shelter."

"Wait—you mean a Methow Indian could still claim that land today?"

"That's one way of lookin' at it. The other way is, the law never allowed a white man to get title to land with a Methow winterin' shelter on it. Any white man on that land, he was a squatter. And your Apache friend, he was fucked, thanks to that shelter. He was developin' a resort, and you can't develop a resort without ownin' the land. You probably know that."

"So I've heard," Kawika said, meeting Jimmy's sidelong glance.

"But Ralph didn't understand," Jimmy resumed. "Not at first. He found the shelter and thought, *'Hey, somethin' to help sell real estate.'* Like *'Now you can winter where the Lost Tribe wintered'*—that sort of thing. So he shot his big mouth off. Shoulda kept quiet, just bulldozed the sucker. Once he learnt how the shelter messed up his title, he bought some dynamite, blew it sky high. *That* got attention. The man always had big plans, yet he never did slow down to think."

Jimmy paused, as if about to add something. But then he said simply, "And that's the last thing I'm sayin' about that Assiniboine. He was a hothead and a dumb fuck."

"He—" Kawika began.

"Yes, *here* we are at the end of the property. Time to turn around."

On the way back, Jimmy talked about the land. "This land, when it was Rattlesnake Ranch, it was a mile wide and better'n two miles long."

"Where's the wintering shelter?"

"You just breathed some of it. Sky high means somethin' when you're dynamitin'. Anyway, the Conservancy, they give me and Madeline some land. Wanted us to have it because of the shelter—also so I'd look after the rest of their land here. They ain't developin' it, they're preservin' it. So I got me a payin' job. I do a bit of irrigation, same as I used to."

"I thought the water rights—"

"The Conservancy ain't greedy. They're just usin' what the ranch used before Ralph. And mostly I'm fightin' weeds without no irrigation. No chemical sprays neither. See, you break the sod out here, you're gonna get weeds. The trick is to keep 'em down with no water. I want to find the best grass for buildin' sod again. Somethin' that don't need nothin' but rainfall and snow. What is that? Blue bunchgrass? Tufted wheatgrass? Don't know yet. But I aim to find out."

Further on, he pointed to a ravine where saplings grew in individual wire cages to protect them from deer. "Plantin' native trees where they grew once," he said. "Got some serviceberry in there too. Good bird habitat."

When he talked about restoring land, Jimmy sounded almost rhapsodic. He explained about vegetative cover: what vegetation different animals favor, the distances from cover they feel safe venturing. He described working with local farmers to intersperse their fields with small groves of trees, lines of shrubs, patches of longer grass—all to provide more cover for native animals.

"You need an assistant?" Kawika asked, jokingly. "Or maybe a business partner?"

"You applyin' for the job?"

"No, but I know a woman who'd love to work with you."

"The woman you're with?"

"Your wife mentioned her?"

"Yeah. Madeline liked her, I guess."

"She liked Madeline too."

"Cats, probably."

"Probably."

"So, that woman or another one?"

"Another one, actually. A Native Hawaiian. She wants to reforest an entire island."

Jimmy turned to Kawika and laughed. "Hell," he said. "That's probably more than fifteen hundred acres. Have her give me a call. We could compare notes." He handed Kawika a simple business card:

Jimmy Jack's
Methow Valley Land Repair
&
Wildlife Restoration

P.O. Box 5454
Winthrop, Washington 98862
(509) 555-5454

Kawika took the card and read it. "I see you matched your box number and your phone number," he said. "That's helpful. Is it easy to arrange?"

"Joe Crane, a guy at the phone company back then, he was helping the Feds with their investigation—he did it for me," Jimmy Jack replied. "Had a friend at the post office too. It's Madeline's birthday: May 4, 1954. That's why I picked them numbers. Easy to remember."

Kawika thought about it: *5454. 5/4/54. May 4, 1954.*

"You have cell phone reception here?" he asked suddenly.

"Not down here, but back on the ridge."

"Excuse me," Kawika said. "I'll be right back." He hiked quickly up to the ridgetop and called Patience at the Freestone.

"P," he said, "Remind me, what date was Steve Kellogg murdered?"

"Let me see," she replied. "Here it is: August 9, 1998."

Kawika stood silently, thinking hard. *August 9, 1998. 8/9/98. 8998. Frank Kimaio's number: 8998.*

"Kawika?" she inquired, breaking his concentration. "I have a question for you. Do you know about Bill Harding?"

"Who's Bill Harding?"

"He was Melissa Harding's brother. Melissa Jane Harding—Fortunato's wife. So Bill Harding was Fortunato's brother-in-law. The guy who sold Rattlesnake Ranch to Fortunato. You won't believe this: *Bill Harding drowned, Kawika.* He went fishing alone, and he fell out of his boat. Does that sound familiar?"

"He drowned?"

"He drowned in that lake right over there," said Jimmy, suddenly pointing over Kawika's shoulder. Startled, Kawika jumped and spun around, dropping his cell phone. Jimmy bent, retrieved the phone, handed it back. He'd walked up right behind Kawika, unseen and unheard.

"Jesus, Jimmy, you scared the shit out of me."

"You said you walk good, Hawaii. But you don't. You walk noisy."

65

On the Road

Kawika guessed Jimmy Jack would call Marshal Hanson and that Hanson would run Kawika right out of town. Which is exactly what Hanson did. By the time Kawika got to the Freestone, the marshal and Patience were sitting in the lobby.

"Your bags are packed, Detective," the marshal said. "Time you hit the road. I warned you, if you poke around about Ralph Fortunato, we really can't have you here. Not right now. Someday we'll welcome you and Ms. Quinn back to the Methow. But that day's not here yet."

Kawika considered what he might say. He decided to say little.

"Okay. Can't blame a lawman for trying, Marshal. But I guess that's it for now. C'mon, P. Let's head down to Wenatchee, get you on a plane."

Hanson smiled tightly and nodded to each of them.

"Oh, one thing," Kawika said, turning at the door. "Okay with you, Marshal, if we take the East Side Road instead of the highway? I'd like Ms. Quinn to see that side of the river."

Hanson smiled. "Take any road you like. Just take it out of town." He tipped his Stetson hat.

Kawika said, "Follow me in your car, P. I'll see you in Wenatchee." He kissed her, then gave her a hug and whispered, "Stick close."

As Kawika expected, Hanson followed them no further than the main intersection in Winthrop, where he watched them turn south. Kawika continued south but passed the turnoff for the East Side Road and stayed on the highway. A mile later he turned onto a dirt road and parked under a big ponderosa, nearly hidden by the lower branches. Patience, confused, stopped her car. He jumped in. "Drive," he said.

She drove, but not without questions.

"I've got to come back," he explained. "The marshal will expect that. He may figure I stashed my car and rode with you, and that I'd come back here by plane. If he does, I'm hoping he'll look for my car along the East Side Road, near the airstrip, not where I just left it."

"Why do you have to come back?"

"I've got to talk with Melissa Harding now that we know about her brother getting killed."

"I can't get over it, Kawika. Fortunato must've murdered his own brother-in-law!"

"Yup, and not just his brother-in-law. Probably Thomas Gray back on the Big Island too, right? Did the newspapers suggest Harding's death might be a homicide? That there was anything suspicious about it?"

"Nope. Not a hint. But the Hawaii papers didn't hint that Thomas Gray's death might be a homicide either. Yet it was, wasn't it?"

"Must have been," Kawika agreed. "Here's where we apply Occam's Razor, right?"

"Right," she said. "It's all so spooky, not just gruesome. I mean, if you didn't know about both deaths, you might never guess either one was a murder."

"Yeah, and if you did you'd never prove it," he said. "For the Hawaii one, Fortunato must've had an accomplice, though—someone who brought him back to shore. They found Gray's boat halfway to Maui. And the accomplice might still be alive; maybe we can find him. But at the lake, Fortunato could have handled it himself. Drown Harding, take the boat to shore, give it a good push back out into the lake."

"Could you prove they were murders now, knowing about both?"

"Maybe," he said. "Especially if we found the accomplice in Hawaii. Two men sell Fortunato land at inflated prices, both end up dead, and both die the same way. If we could prove Fortunato split the overpayment with—"

Kawika's cell phone rang. It was Tanaka. "Got some news," he said. "Kids playing near the Lili'uokalani Gardens found two shell casings for .375 H&H Magnum cartridges."

"What? I thought our forensics guys already searched the whole area?"

"It's embarrassing," Tanaka admitted. "Our guys must've missed 'em. No prints, but the casings do match the cartridges in Bruno's garage. So now the ammo's definite at least."

"No prints on the casings? The shooter wore gloves when he loaded up?"

"Odd, I know. Maybe he wiped 'em, in case they got left behind."

"But why would anyone leave them behind?" Kawika asked. "And where's the third one?"

"Probably still in the chamber when he peeled out of there. The rifle's bolt action."

"But the other two? Careless to leave 'em."

"Maybe he thought one shot would do it, panicked when it didn't."

"Maybe. Or else, like we discussed, someone—"

But Tanaka had other news to impart, and the faltering rural cell signal, going in and out, made it hard to interrupt him. Tanaka said the suddenly cooperative Michael Cushing had offered theories for why Fortunato gave Bruno the gun. Maybe Bruno was Ralph's spy inside the hunters' group. Or maybe the hunters' group was actually Ralph's idea—another way for a third party to stop KKL. Maybe Fortunato gave Bruno the gun so he could pass as a hunter.

"Though it's a heck of a big gun," Tanaka noted.

Kawika switched topics. "Anyone found Peter Pukui yet? Melanie? Jason Hare?"

"Nope. Still looking. No one's seen any of them."

"That's bad."

"Yeah. Peter and Melanie haven't shown up in Kawaihae. And wherever Jason is these days, he's not walking along the Queen K."

"Anything useful from the Murphys then?"

"I hammered them. They're talking with their lawyers now. But there's news on Shimazu. Turns out he's got other South Pacific resorts in development. Probably couldn't let KKL fail; might drag 'em all down. And if he discovered what Ralph was up to, who knows? Cushing says he should have thought of that. Might explain Shimazu acting a little—"

The cell phone connection failed.

"Damn," said Kawika. Patience looked at him, but he was staring straight ahead. *"Damn,"* he repeated.

"What's wrong?" she asked. "The cell—?"

"No, not that. Bruno Moku'ele, the guy they arrested?"

"Yes—the shooter?"

"He wasn't the shooter. Someone's trying to frame him. That's why the shell casings were left behind."

"Wait, who would want to frame him?"

"Whoever tried to shoot me."

She was frightened now, thinking about Kawika's shooter still being out there, still being unknown. "What are you thinking, Kawika?"

"Something I can't tell you."

"Kawika—"

"Honestly, P, I'm thinking something I can't tell you. I'm really sorry. *Damn.*"

Despite her efforts, Kawika fell silent, concentrating with the look he'd had when staring at her ceiling fan, only more intensely. And this time he wouldn't talk.

"You're upset," she said, stating the obvious. "Because someone else, someone other than Bruno, must be your shooter? Someone who's not Hawaiian, you're thinking?"

Kawika grimaced. And for the first time in his relationship with Patience, he didn't even respond. Just nodded and kept staring at the road ahead.

PART SIX

WENATCHEE AND THE METHOW VALLEY

He had been a stanch servant of the law. And now he was invited to defend that which, at first sight, nay, even at second and third sight, must always seem a defiance of law more injurious than crime itself.

—Owen Wister, *The Virginian* (1902)

66

Wenatchee

Kawika sat across the table from United States Attorney Ernesto Gonzales and FBI Special Agent Harold Billings in Wenatchee. The setting—an interrogation room—felt familiar.

Gonzales was speaking. He sounded caring and gentle, like a favorite uncle with a slight Spanish accent. "You have to understand," he said. "Folks in the Methow take the thing personally. They're still grieving for Steve Kellogg, even years later. He grew up there. High school football star, local boy made good. He had a cabin, always got back there for weekends. Always had a project or two for improving life in the valley."

"Sounds like quite a guy," Kawika said.

"That's part of it. But there's another part. You've heard the saying, all politics is local? Well, all crime is local too. Local people really feel it."

"I understand," Kawika said. "Believe me."

"Then you know a murderer is like a terrorist on a local scale. An intimate terrorist, you might say. Imagine how you're going to feel when you hear Osama bin Laden is dead. That's how folks in the Methow felt—heck, it's how folks in the whole Federal law enforcement community felt—when we heard Fortunato was dead. We didn't throw a party or break out the booze. But we felt—what would you say, Harold?—gratified."

Special Agent Billings nodded. "Grimly gratified," he said. "But gratified all the same." Billings looked tall and fit in his short-sleeved shirt, like he belonged in the NFL.

"I get it," Kawika said. "I've learned enough about Fortunato. But still, someone murdered him. I'm thinking it might have been someone from Fortunato's time up in the Methow. Someone avenging Kellogg."

Gonzales shrugged and looked at Agent Billings. Billings shrugged too.

"Could've been, I guess, although Kellogg was killed some years ago," said Billings. "But Fortunato's death—it sounded pretty Hawaiian, at least over here. You could check travel records, I suppose. Big job, though. A lot of folks get out of the Methow in the winter, and then there's Wenatchee, more folks—"

"Anyway, how can we help?" Gonzales asked, moving things along.

"You can tell me what really happened up in the Methow," Kawika replied.

"Sure," replied Gonzales. "Let's start with the basics." He explained there'd been two investigations of Fortunato. One for real estate fraud, with desecrating a Native American heritage site thrown in. Then a second, for murder, after Assistant U.S. Attorney Steve Kellogg had been shot in Wenatchee, with Fortunato as the main suspect. Kellogg had been the prosecutor for the fraud and desecration case, the unsuccessful one that nonetheless led to bankruptcy for Fawn Ridge; he'd definitely incurred Fortunato's wrath. Gonzales himself had led the second case, the Kellogg murder investigation, with Billings as his lead FBI agent.

Gonzales told a familiar story about the first case: Fortunato's suspected real estate fraud, his destruction of the wintering shelter, Jimmy Jack's refusal to testify, and the intense frustration, in the end, of having to drop the charges. One difference: Frank Kimaio had never mentioned the name Steve Kellogg—the murdered federal prosecutor Kimaio had worked with.

Gonzales, on the other hand, didn't mention Bill Harding, the man who'd sold Fortunato the land for Fawn Ridge and then drowned while fishing—Fortunato's brother-in-law.

"Frankly," Gonzales replied when Kawika asked, "no one suspected Harding had been murdered until Kellogg was. We thought Harding just drowned. It was a big setback; we'd subpoenaed Harding to testify to the grand jury in the Fawn Ridge case."

"Forgive me," Kawika said, "but there's something really odd here. When I met Frank Kimaio, he briefed me on Fortunato. He sorta mentioned Harding in passing, but not by name, just called him a buddy who sold Fortunato the land. But he never mentioned Steve Kellogg at all. And he never said you guys suspected Fortunato of murder."

"Probably a simple explanation," Gonzales said. "Frank—and by the way, his name was Frank Carlson before he moved to Hawaii—Frank worked on the Fawn Ridge fraud case and the wintering shelter—the first Fortunato case. Frank was the lead FBI agent, working with Kellogg on those. Then Kellogg got killed. And that was a different case. Agent Billings here was lead agent on the Kellogg murder investigation, working with me."

"Wait a minute," said Kawika. "Frank Kimaio was Frank Carlson before he moved to Hawaii?"

"That's right," Billings said. "Frank always planned to retire in Hawaii—him and his buddy Joe Crane. They flew together in Nam. Joe worked at the phone company here, got a telecom job in Hawaii after that. Frank could've kept working in Hawaii too, but he wanted to retire. I understand he's sick now—right, Ernesto? Dying maybe. Agent Orange, I heard. Anyway, he'd put away a lot of bad guys, so he changed his name. High-profile agents do that sometimes."

"He chose an odd name," Kawika observed. "Hawaiian letters, but not really the right sounds. 'Kuh-MY-oh,' 'Kuh-MAY-oh'? Not a Hawaiian name, it seems."

Gonzales laughed.

"Don't tell that to Frank," Billings said. "You'd hurt his feelings. Frank tried to learn about Hawaii, studied the language a bit. He had more enthusiasm than time."

"Okay," Gonzales continued, "but probably Frank didn't mention the murder because you were investigating Fortunato's real estate scam. That's what Frank worked on here, the real estate scam. In Hawaii you didn't suspect Ralph of murder, did you?"

"Not then. He was the victim."

"Right. And here, of course, he was the suspect. Finally—" Billings looked at Gonzales.

"Finally," Gonzales said, "Frank was Steve Kellogg's head agent. They'd been buddies a long time. That's why we couldn't let Frank participate in the murder investigation. Would've given Fortunato's defense lawyers too much to work with. So I'm not surprised he didn't mention Kellogg. He didn't work on that case, and of course it was all really painful for him. Wouldn't mention it unless you asked. He doesn't know much about the investigation anyway."

"So you two are the experts on Kellogg's murder?"

"Well, more than Frank. Not expert enough to nail Fortunato, unfortunately." Billings shook his head. "Couldn't nail him for fraud, couldn't nail him for murder."

"What kind of gun killed Kellogg?" Kawika asked.

"Nine-millimeter handgun," Billing answered. "Army surplus ammunition. As common a weapon and ammo as the killer could have chosen. We never found the gun."

"Did Fortunato own a nine millimeter?"

"He owned lots of guns," Billings replied. "Kind of a gun nut—or serious collector, depending on your point of view. He never bought from dealers, only at gun shows."

"So we couldn't trace his guns," Gonzales explained.

"Maybe it's different in Hawaii," said Billings. "Over here, a gun bought at a show—you know, a private thing, like a swap meet—there's no permit, no waiting period, no background check. No registration required. Untraceable."

"Still, he needed an alibi," Kawika said.

"Claimed to be in Seattle," replied Gonzales. "He kept a condo there. Fawn Ridge had its corporate offices in Seattle, where most of the investors lived. So he had a legitimate reason for being there. But he had time to drive to Wenatchee and back on the night of the murder."

"You couldn't prove it?"

"Well, he'd set up his alibi in advance," Gonzales said. "Three hours before Kellogg was shot, Fortunato asked his Seattle neighbor there for some laundry soap. And three hours *after* Kellogg was shot, Fortunato answered his Seattle home phone when we called. By the time we got warrants, he'd just happened to have washed his car, the tires—and also underneath. He'd even changed the air filter. We figure he covered himself for the shooting and brought Handi Wipes or something plus a change of clothes. Shot Steve, stripped and wiped down, put everything in plastic bags, dropped 'em at different places."

"And the gun?"

"We checked everywhere between here and Seattle," replied Billings. "Any place he might have thrown it. Big job. We hoped he'd tossed it right away. But he probably kept it till he got to Seattle, dumped it in Lake Washington or Puget Sound. And we couldn't prove he'd ever owned a nine-millimeter handgun anyway."

"You still thought you could nail him?" Kawika asked. "Without the gun?"

"Well, he had means and opportunity, and motive. He really hated Kellogg. He tended to be a hothead—impulsive. So we used a lot of search warrants. Tore his life apart, let's say: the grand jury, his financial records, lots of high-tech lab tests, that sort of thing. His investors knew he was the prime suspect, even though the news media didn't print that. And then—" Gonzales hesitated.

"And then we wiretapped them," Billings said firmly. "Fortunato, his key investors, his wife. All of 'em. Home phones, work phones. Joe Crane, Frank's

Vietnam buddy, ran those taps for us before he moved to Hawaii. We moni-
tored their cell phones too."

"We wanted to see what they'd say to one another," Gonzales said. "We
had maximum pressure on him, and they knew it."

"So what did you get?" Kawika asked.

"No smoking gun—pardon the expression. Fortunato controlled himself
for once. He knew we'd tapped his phones. Still, other Fawn Ridge people
had no doubt he'd done it. Among themselves they'd discuss how he hated
Kellogg. Some had heard Fortunato vow to kill him. But when they'd talk to
Fortunato himself, he'd say, 'You know, I'm not crying about it—Kellogg was
an overzealous prosecutor. But I never would've killed him.' And they'd say,
'Oh, of course not.'"

"Did the wiretaps get you anything at all?"

"Well, one thing," Gonzales replied. "In one call, Fortunato's wife said
he'd flat out threatened to kill her if she cooperated with us."

"Who was she talking to?" Kawika asked.

"J.J."

"J.J.?"

"Jimmy Jack," said Gonzales. "You met him, right?"

"Oh," said Kawika. "Jimmy. Yeah, I met him." *Odd, their knowing that,* he
thought. *And why would she be talking with Jimmy about that?*

"That told us a lot," Billings continued. "We knew we were on the right
track."

"Did Fortunato's wife cooperate?" Kawika asked.

"Nope," replied Billings. "She took that death threat seriously. She knew
Ralph would kill her if she helped us."

"But we may as well tell you: that conversation did help us in another
way," Gonzales added cautiously. "We used it to get a court order letting us
wiretap Fortunato after he moved to Hawaii."

"What?" Kawika said sharply. "You wiretapped Fortunato in Hawaii?"

"Just one year," Gonzales replied. "That's all we were allowed, 1999 to
2000. We hoped he'd slip up and make a mistake once he got there."

"Jesus," Kawika said. "Were you planning to tell us about this?" *You're
like Jason Hare,* he thought. *We have to drag information out of you.*

"Detective," Gonzales replied apologetically, "the judge imposed a specific condition that we could not reveal to non-federal authorities in Hawaii
the existence of the tap or any information obtained from it. Technically, I'm
violating the judge's order right now, although it really doesn't matter at this

point, Fortunato being dead and all." He smiled, then added laughingly, "But just the same, please don't report me."

"As you know, the law won't allow fishing expeditions," Billings added. "The judge said, 'This man Fortunato is a crook, he'll commit crimes wherever he goes, but you're tapping his phone only for the Kellogg murder case. Kellogg's murder isn't within the purview of the Hawaiian authorities. So you can't tell them about any of this.'"

Kawika shook his head.

"I'm sorry, Detective," Gonzales said. "There are lots of restrictions on Federal wiretaps. I hope you understand."

"Sure," Kawika said. "But why don't we ask the judge to modify the order now, in light of new developments. Then you could tell us about the Hawaii wiretaps."

"I'll save you the trouble, Detective." Gonzales looked at him gravely. "We didn't learn anything from the Hawaii wiretaps."

Billings nodded. "That's what brought the Kellogg murder investigation to an end," he said. "We didn't learn shit."

"Not one darned thing," Gonzales emphasized. "Then the wiretaps had to stop, once that year ended. And we never learned anything more about Ralph Fortunato until we heard he'd been killed."

Kawika frowned. Gonzales and Billings exchanged looks; Billings motioned slightly with his head, toward the door.

"Well, I guess that's it," Gonzales said, getting to his feet. "Time for another meeting. Sorry we couldn't be more help. But I doubt you'll find your killer in the Methow, Detective. Or here in Wenatchee, for that matter. And frankly, I hope you never find him—or her. I know you have to try. But don't try *too* hard." He smiled again, making a joke of it.

Kawika still had questions, but as they shook hands, he asked only one. "Mr. Gonzales," he said, "I assume if you'd convicted Fortunato of murdering an Assistant United States Attorney, you would have sought the death penalty?"

"Fuckin' right we would have," replied Gonzales, with unexpected heat. "That puta deserved to die. I'm really glad he's dead."

Kawika felt grimly gratified himself. *Thanks, Ernesto,* he thought. *For a while there I couldn't imagine anyone calling you Ernesto Che.*

67

Winthrop

Kawika found a Cirrus pilot to fly him to the tiny airstrip outside Winthrop. Melissa Jane Harding waited by her car. He'd gotten her number from Directory Assistance and hadn't worried that the operator, probably sitting in Alabama, might tip off Marshal Hanson.

"You're taking a big risk, coming back," Fortunato's ex-wife said. "People don't want you here."

"Gotta pick up my car," Kawika replied, smiling.

"Let's sit in mine," she said. "It'll be dark soon. Then I'll take you to yours."

Melissa Harding tried to persuade Kawika he was making a mistake, not just taking a risk. "I know it's your job to catch Ralph's killer," she said, "but not every murder gets solved. In this case, that might be a blessing."

"Why?" Kawika asked. "Because he was such a bad man?"

"More than that," she said. "For killing my brother, he might have gotten life in prison. But he also killed a federal prosecutor. And for that, he would have been executed anyway—no matter what, and no matter what the governor said, because it's a federal crime with a federal death sentence. The U.S. Attorney made that very clear."

"Generally, though, we don't execute people we haven't convicted," Kawika said. "If he'd been convicted, I'd agree: He'd probably be dead by now. But they never even indicted him."

"That's because I didn't give them the evidence," she said. "I was afraid— a coward, actually. But trust me, Detective, the evidence did exist."

"Then why not give it to them now? Why not give it to me? Ralph can't hurt you."

"Because I want all this to end. I don't want you to catch Ralph's killer. Whoever did it performed a good deed. Terrible, but good. I wish I'd had the courage to do it myself. And that should be the end of the matter."

Kawika sighed. "Well, there's a problem with that," he said. "Whoever killed your ex-husband didn't stop there. He murdered a second man too." Here Kawika was venturing much further than anything the evidence yet supported. But by now he was confident he knew the killer of Fortunato and the Duct Tape Mummy. It was his own shooting that he couldn't figure out—along with what had become of Peter Pukui, Melanie Munu, and Jason Hare, why they'd disappear.

"How do you know those murders are linked?" Melissa Harding asked skeptically. "People get murdered every day."

"Well, there's a Hawaiian legend that links two plants. One is rare, and a sprig of it was found in your ex-husband's pocket. A sprig of the other was found in the second victim's pocket. Otherwise, their pockets were empty."

"Oh," she said. She seemed to understand Occam's Razor intuitively.

"Ms. Harding," asked Kawika, "you think your ex-husband killed both your brother and Steve Kellogg, right?"

"I know it."

"Did you know that Ralph killed someone else too?"

"No—who?"

"A man in Hawaii. A man he bought property from so he could develop a resort. Supposedly his friend. A man named Thomas Gray, who drowned while fishing. Does that sound familiar?"

"Oh God."

"My point is, once people start killing, they often keep killing. We're not just trying to catch a killer. We're trying to stop more killing." *Including mine,* he wanted to add, but it would have invited questions, become a time-wasting digression.

She stared straight ahead, then finally turned to him, eyes brimming.

"Okay," she said. "I'll tell you this much, but no more. Ralph and Bill went fishing the day Bill drowned. Ralph came home early, said he wasn't feeling well, told me Bill stayed out there. Bill's body was found the next day. Ralph made me promise not to tell anyone about the fishing trip. He said it would complicate his life unnecessarily, maybe harm Fawn Ridge."

"So what did you do?"

"Well, for one thing, I stopped sleeping with him," she said. "I didn't trust him anymore. Then he started sleeping with Corazon. Or maybe he was sleeping with her before; I don't know."

"Corazon, his widow?" Kawika asked, surprised. "Corazon was here?"

"She ran the Fawn Ridge office in Mazama."

"But she's Filipina. Isn't she from Hawaii?"

Melissa Harding looked puzzled. "Filipinos live here too," she said. "Ralph took her to Hawaii and married her there. Anyway, after all that—" She wiped her face with her hand, composing herself. "After all that, I knew he'd killed Bill. He'd killed Bill because they'd done something crooked together, something involving Bill selling him Rattlesnake Ranch. He killed Bill just as a precaution, because Bill became a risk once the grand jury investigation of Fawn Ridge started. Nothing more than that."

"I'm sorry," Kawika said, "but I believe you're right. I think he did the same thing in Hawaii, just as a precaution."

She took a deep breath. "He came back to the house sometimes. He didn't have a place for his stuff yet. A few days before Steve Kellogg was murdered, Ralph came and got one of his handguns. He went straight to the shop, where he kept his guns, and left without saying a word—and not carrying a rifle, so it had to be a handgun. Then Kellogg was killed. The next day Ralph came back and said he'd kill me if I talked to the cops. He said I'd never be safe. Told me not to talk about it on the phone. They'd be tapped, he said."

"Well, he was right about that," Kawika said. "Did he admit he'd killed Kellogg?"

"No, but I found out. The FBI talked to me—an Agent Billings. I was too scared to tell them anything. They asked if Ralph owned a nine-millimeter handgun. They'd searched our house and the shop but couldn't find one. I told them I had no idea. But that was a lie."

"He did own a nine-millimeter?"

"He did. He bought it just a few months earlier at a gun show in Monroe. I was with him; one of the last times we were together. He bought ammunition for it too. So the FBI asking about it, that's when I knew for sure. But I kept silent. I was afraid he'd kill me."

And there it was. The last piece Kawika needed. The piece Gonzales and Agent Billings never had. He knew it might not be enough for a jury. But it was enough for him. Now Kawika knew beyond doubt—his own doubt—that Fortunato had killed Kellogg. And that he'd created the motive for his own killing, his own appointment with the Big Island equivalent of Poe's catacombs of Venice.

Melissa Harding had paused and looked away. Kawika regarded her closely.

"Let me ask," he resumed, "did Ralph also—"

"Stop." She turned and held up her hand, fending off further questions. "That's enough; that's all I'm going say. Ralph owned the gun we both know killed Steve Kellogg. Satisfied?"

Kawika started to say something, but she turned the key in the ignition. It had gotten dark. "I'll drive you to your car. We should be able to avoid the marshal now."

There, however, she was wrong. They didn't even make it to the highway. Marshal Hanson came driving in at high speed, bouncing over the gravel potholes and skidding to a dusty stop, blocking their path.

"Uh-oh," she said.

Her concern was misplaced. Smiling in her headlights—this time in an easygoing manner—Hanson strode casually to Kawika's door. Kawika rolled his window down, but only part way.

"Relax, Detective," Hanson said. "I've got good news for you. Your boss called—Captain Tanaka? He's trying to find you. They caught the killer you've been looking for. The guy who iced Ralph."

Melissa looked shocked. "Who is it?"

Hanson smiled broadly. "No one we know, Melissa—no one. Some guy in Hawaii hired a hit man, a contract killer. Captain Tanaka says the hit man confessed. And weirdly enough, it turns out that back in the day, Ralph himself hired that same hit man to kill Steve Kellogg."

Melissa and Kawika sat speechless, astonished.

"There's more, Detective," Hanson added. "The same hit man also tried to kill you."

68

Winthrop

Tanaka spoke with unusual excitement as Kawika and Marshal Hanson listened on the speaker phone in Hanson's storefront office. It was as Hanson had said: Tanaka had arrested Michael Cushing for hiring the contract killer of Fortunato and Melanie Munu—yes, Tanaka said, Melanie was dead—and for the attempted contract killing of Kawika. The Duct Tape Mummy turned out to be a California hit man named Roger Preston, who called himself Rocco.

"Wait," Kawika said. "Back up. How'd this all come together?"

Tanaka laughed—a laugh of relief, it seemed. "A package came to the station yesterday. A lumpy padded envelope addressed to you, Kawika. Mail room guys figured it might be a bomb or anthrax or something, especially with people shooting at you. We evacuated the station while the bomb guys checked it. Turned out to contain a typewritten confession from Rocco—the hit man, the Duct Tape Mummy. The lump was an audio cassette, and the cassette had also been burned onto a CD that was in the envelope. The audio was Rocco reading the confession aloud, sounding very scared."

"Who did he confess to?" Kawika asked.

"I'm coming to that. But first, it turns out Rocco had a room at the King Kam Kourt in Kailua, left the 'Do Not Disturb' sign out. When he didn't return, the manager began slipping notes under the door. This morning the manager finally went in. He found Rocco's ID, some ammo, and guess what? A rifle for .375 H&H Magnum cartridges. Then he called us."

Hanson interrupted. "Excuse me, Captain, but that's an interesting coincidence. Fortunato owned a gun for .375 H&H Magnum ammo. A fancy one, customized. European, I think."

"Perhaps a CZ 550 Safari? From Czechoslovakia?"

"Sounds right. Bolt action, walnut stock?"

"That's what we've got here," Tanaka said. "How'd you know he owned it?"

"He bragged about it," Hanson said. "Got it at a gun show, showed it off. Folks had to tell him, 'That's too big for deer.' That surprised Ralph, I guess. So he said he was going to use it for cougar and bear. Of course, Ralph didn't have any dogs to hunt cougar. Nowadays, you can't use dogs anyhow. Voters passed an initiative against it. But back then—"

Kawika interrupted. He was tired of everyone in the Methow—and Wenatchee—trying to deflect his queries. "Again, Terry, who did he confess to?"

"That's the amazing part," Tanaka said. "You'll see when you read it. We FedExed a copy to your mom's and you'll have it tomorrow."

"Tomorrow?"

Hanson smiled and shrugged apologetically. "Sorry, no fax here."

"Someone snatched Rocco while he was shooting at you—caught him in the act," Tanaka continued on the speaker phone. "We don't know who they are; the confession doesn't say. It just says, 'I'm being forced to confess, but not by cops.' He says he's confessing in order to save his life."

Hanson frowned. "Shit, you're not going be able to use it as evidence then."

"Maybe we can," Tanaka said. "After all, we won't be using it against *him*."

"True," Hanson acknowledged. "He's dead, isn't he."

"We've got the prosecution exception to the dead man's statute if we need to use it against Cushing," said Tanaka. "But I doubt we will. Rocco's confession said we'd find Melanie Munu's body at Waiki'i Ranch. She was there, sadly. That pretty well corroborated the confession. The confession said Cushing paid Rocco to kill her. So we confronted Cushing today. Made sure he had his lawyer present. Told him the Duct Tape Mummy was named Rocco or Roger Preston. You should've seen his face, Kawika! Remember he said he'd never seen the guy in his life? Well, he hadn't. Only knew the man by phone."

"Cushing confessed?"

"No, not yet. But we showed him the Fortunato murder weapon—the spear—and he admitted it was his. His lawyer tried to stop him, but Cushing said the spear was historical, that you knew how to trace it, Kawika. But he says someone stole it from him."

"Wait—" Kawika began.

"Crooks," Hanson interrupted. "Funny, aren't they? The murder weapon always seems to have been stolen from them. But if they're in possession of a stolen wallet or credit card or car stereo, they never stole 'em, always just found 'em in a dumpster."

"We played Rocco's confession to Cushing," Tanaka went on, ignoring Hanson's aside. "He listened to the whole thing. Including about Melanie and about Rocco shooting you with the rifle Cushing stole from Bruno Moku'ele. And after all that, guess what Cushing said? 'But Rocco didn't kill *Fortunato.*' Then his lawyer shut him up."

"Wow," Hanson said. "A negative pregnant with admission! Hardly *ever* see those. One time down in Kittitas County . . ."

"Yeah, that pretty much locks it up," said Tanaka, cutting off Hanson again.

"But wait," Kawika objected, suddenly confused. "Not the Fortunato part. And if Melanie is dead, then where's Peter Pukui?"

"Haven't found Peter yet. It's worrisome. But as for Fortunato, trust me, Kawika. Cushing admits he hired Rocco to kill Fortunato and that the murder weapon is his. And Rocco gives details that aren't public. Wait till you read it, Kawika. It's incredible. Whoever snatched Rocco was a very thorough confession drafter."

"Okay, I'll wait," Kawika replied, still skeptical, and looking over at Marshal Hanson, who was looking intently at Kawika too. "But did you ever reach that guy we were trying to talk to, Terry? You remember his phone number, right?" Kawika guardedly added. "And has anyone found the highway-walking guy?"

"No," Tanaka replied. "But none of that matters now, Kawika. We've got the confession."

"Terry—"

"Go ahead and fly first class to Hilo," Tanaka interrupted, obviously in a hurry. "The Department will spring for it."

Tanaka had to get off the phone—there was work to be done—and Kawika needed to leave for Seattle if he was going to catch a flight the next morning. But Kawika lingered a bit. He gave Hanson an accusatory look.

"Hey, you got your man," said Hanson, fending him off. "Now you and Ms. Quinn are welcome in the Methow. Come back in May; the wildflowers are incredible."

"Before we get to that, Marshal, it seems odd that Terry didn't mention Steve Kellogg just now."

"He already did, when he called me looking for you."

"He told you Fortunato hired this same hit man to kill Kellogg?"

"He did, yeah. It's in the confession, he said."

"Aren't you curious? I mean, why would some abductors, way over there in Hawaii, guys who aren't police, bother to extract that particular confession from this Rocco guy? He'd already confessed to two Hawaii murders, plus the attempt on me. He wouldn't have volunteered anything about an unrelated murder here in Washington."

"Son," replied Hanson, "with respect, I don't need this Rocco or a Hawaiian detective telling me anything about the Kellogg killing. We both know Ralph Fortunato was behind it."

"Yes, I know that now. But why would Rocco's abductors in Hawaii care about that, Marshal?"

"Good question," Hanson replied. "But I've got one of my own. You just learned someone saved your life. Grabbed this fellow Rocco in the act of shooting at you. Isn't that what Captain Tanaka said?"

"That's what he said."

"But you didn't ask Captain Tanaka about it," Hanson pointed out. "Aren't *you* curious?

69

On the North Cascades Highway

The confession confounded him at first, but long before Kawika reached Seattle, he knew it couldn't be entirely true. The notion that Cushing's hired killer had murdered Fortunato was just plain wrong, Kawika was convinced. Cushing's terrified, panicky fear of Fortunato's killer on that first day could not have been faked, nor his reaction when Kawika told him the killer wasn't Peter Pukui. Tanaka hadn't seen Cushing either time. Otherwise he, too, would know that at least part of the confession was simply false.

Tanaka hadn't known who'd abducted Rocco and coerced his confession. Marshal Hanson suggested Kawika seemed incurious about that. Actually, Kawika thought he knew. He simply hadn't wanted to betray his conclusion to Hanson. It was the conclusion that Hanson and everyone else Kawika had met in the Methow Valley and Wenatchee seemed determined to prevent him reaching.

The great relief for Kawika was that Rocco, not Fortunato's killer, had apparently been his shooter. The rifle in Rocco's motel room clinched it. Rocco as his shooter allayed Kawika's deepest fear, the fear that seized him the moment he'd realized his shooter wasn't some angry Hawaiian; the fear that Fortunato's killer intended to kill him too—kill him for getting too close.

Winthrop to Seattle was a four-hour drive. Along the way, where reception permitted, Kawika took advantage of the three-hour time difference with Hawai'i. He called Jarvis and Ku'ulei. Then he called Carolyn at her dad's on Maui. Tanaka had already been in touch with her. Kawika heard her weeping softly, covering the mouthpiece of the phone. He explained he'd been out of communication—basically hiding—until the shooter was caught. Yes, he agreed, it was a relief the shooter turned out not to be an S&R-enraged Hawaiian.

"But, Carolyn, we should have known. Kuʻulei was with me. No Hawaiian would risk killing such an obviously Hawaiian little girl, would he?" This might not be true, but he hoped it might banish one of Carolyn's bad dreams.

As a less fraught diversion, he also told Carolyn about Jimmy Jack. For many minutes he described Jimmy's land restoration work, working from memory as he drove. It did calm her. She even asked questions, took an interest, wanted to know more.

He didn't call Patience; it was too late. He told himself she might still be traveling, or home sleeping in California. But that was just avoidance. In reality, he couldn't share what he now believed about Fortunato's killer. Not until he'd met with Tanaka—who was thoroughly misguided on this point, Kawika felt sure—and even before that, figured out how to handle that knowledge himself. It seemed an intractable problem.

Most of the time there was no cell reception. He drove through the mountains on a clear black night with a nearly full moon. Little other traffic shared the eerie vastness, the uncanniness of the alpine darkness somehow supporting, high above him, huge snowfields and glaciers ghostly white in the moonglow.

In solitude, with the enforced lull, relieved about his shooter, Kawika reflected on how he'd become a detective through the seductions of murder mysteries, stories Pat read him in childhood, and the shared enthusiasm of stepfather and stepson, each hoping to bond with the other. As a result, who were the detectives he knew? Sherlock Holmes, Sam Spade, Father Brown, Lord Peter Wimsey and Harriet Vane, Inspector Morse, Philip Marlowe, Adam Dalgleish, Travis McGee, Hercule Poirot and Miss Marple, Kurt Wallander, Martin Beck, Detective Jim Chee, and so on—the literary detectives of Pat's generation and enthusiasms. None seemed relevant to Kawika in real life. Well, maybe Father Brown. Father Brown always felt uneasy about his soul, never entirely pleased with his own cleverness.

Not entirely pleased with his own cleverness: Kawika knew Tanaka had gotten the main thing wrong, namely, who killed Fortunato. Tanaka's dismissal of inconvenient evidence as strays might be helpful most of the time. But this time? Or maybe Kawika, in his cleverness, was overthinking the situation, hoping to be the one to enlighten Tanaka and earn a satisfying *Iiko, iiko.* Worse yet, maybe Kawika was being disloyal. Tanaka couldn't really have been fooled, could he? He must have some reason for accepting that a hit man killed Fortunato, mustn't he? He and Tanaka needed to talk. And not, Kawika had finally understood, by phone.

Uneasy about his soul. Now that he was heading home, Kawika also tried to focus on his situation with Patience, how to tell Carolyn, all the details and consequences he'd put off in the Methow. He'd escaped to the North Cascades, or been hiding, not communicating anyway, testing the firmness of his choice, trying to delay having to deal with it.

Now, he knew, he couldn't postpone dealing with it for long. But the timing was terrible. He'd just solved the case. He was ready to close the books on it, if he could convince Tanaka that Rocco wasn't Fortunato's killer, and then make the arrest. First things first. He needed to wait at least that long to talk with Carolyn; he needed to temporize a bit longer.

Uneasy about his soul too, for an even more important reason. Even if he convinced Tanaka, was he actually going to arrest the real killer? What would become of him if he did? If he didn't? He couldn't decide as he drove. The intractable problem remained.

Kawika arrived in Seattle bone-tired. He found his mother and Pat waiting up for him as if he were a teenager, greeting him with smiles, embraces, murmurs, the familiar pleasure of their decaf coffee. They'd already spoken with Tanaka. He'd called, thoughtfully, to tell them the details—Cushing's arrest, the winding up of the case—and to assure them Kawika's would-be assassin was dead.

"We got you something to read," Lily said. "The confession will be here in the morning. We didn't want it to be the only thing you had on the plane." She handed Kawika a paperback copy of *The Virginian*. "I wasn't sure if you knew about this," she said. "It's a famous old Western, partly inspired by the Methow Valley. Since you've just been there—"

"Perfect," he said, giving her a kiss. "I saw it over there but missed my chance to buy it."

Kawika stayed up late. He opened *The Virginian* and got far enough to read about the hero, the unnamed Virginian, dutifully and without pleasure lynching two men who'd rustled cattle from Judge Henry, the Virginian's employer, and about Judge Henry's efforts to persuade the Virginian's horrified sweetheart that in the conditions—and traditions—then prevailing in the West, the lynching of bad men was a way of upholding the law, not defying it.

But that was a hundred years ago, Kawika thought. *We're not the Wild West in Hawaii anymore.* It occurred to him, just as he fell asleep, that maybe the Methow Valley still was.

PART SEVEN

THE KAʻŪ FOREST RESERVE

"I think there is something rather dangerous about standing on these high places even to pray," said Father Brown. "Heights were made to be looked at, not to be looked down from."
"Do you mean that one may fall over?" asked Wilfred.
"I mean that one's soul may fall if one's body doesn't," said the other priest.
"I knew a man," he said, "who began by worshipping with others before the altar, but who grew fond of high and lonely places to pray from, corners or niches in the belfry or the spire. And once in one of those dizzy places, where the whole world seemed to turn under him like a wheel, his brain turned also, and he fancied he was God. So that though he was a good man, he committed a great crime."

—G. K. Chesterton, "The Hammer of God," from
The Innocence of Father Brown (1910)

70

From Seattle to Honolulu

The six-hour flight to Honolulu gave Kawika ample time to read and reread the hit man's confession. Each time Kawika did so, the dead killer seemed to tell him more.

Statement of Roger (Rocco) Preston

This statement is intended for Detective Kavika Wong of Hilo.

My name is Roger (Rocco) Preston. I live at 126 Treaty Oak Avenue in St. Helena, California. This statement is true, but I am being forced to make it. My captors are not police. They say they will kill me if they find anything in this statement to be untrue.

Kawika could guess the identities of two of Rocco's captors, although one he'd never met, just knew by name. Perhaps there was a third, if the other two trusted a half-mad highway walker. And might there be a fourth, he wondered—a doctor?

Michael Cushing hired me to kill Ralph Fortunato, Melanie Munu, and Kavika Wong. Fortunato was killed with a Hawaiian spear, which was left with his body. Munu was killed with a baseball bat, which I buried with her. Wong was supposed to be killed with a rifle that Cushing gave me.

Earlier, in 1998, Fortunato hired me to kill Steven Kellogg in Washington. However, I did not kill Kellogg. I believe Fortunato did.

A lot of information there, though some was false. Well, not exactly false, Kawika realized. Fortunato actually had been killed with a Hawaiian spear. But there the confession was deliberately misleading, Kawika knew.

When Cushing first hired me, he said he and Fortunato were having a business dispute. Cushing said I had to make it look like a native Hawaiian group killed Fortunato. He said Fortunato's body should be left on the championship tee box of the 15th hole of the South Course at the Mauna Lani. He said I should drive a Hawaiian spear through Fortunato's chest at that location, put a sacred Hawaiian flower in Fortunato's pocket, and use other Hawaiian artifacts Cushing supplied.

Cushing said he'd give me the spear, the sacred flower, etc., after I got to Hawaii. Each day for several days I drove to Hapuna Beach in a rental car. I left my car keys on the wall of the men's restroom by the parking lot. When I got back from the beach each day, I picked up my keys and drove to my motel in Kailua, where I opened the trunk. The first few days, it was empty. Cushing said I should kill Fortunato on the day after I opened the trunk and found the Hawaiian spear, the sacred flower, etc.

After Fortunato was dead and his body left in the place Cushing wanted, I flew to Honolulu and then to San Francisco on Hawaiian Airlines.

There's the crucial omission, Kawika thought. Right there. Did Rocco ever open his car trunk and find the items Cushing had promised? The confession didn't say so. And if he did, what happened between that moment and when Rocco boarded the plane? The confession was silent on that too.

Kawika could easily imagine the heated negotiations between Rocco and his captors over these paragraphs. A terrified Rocco must have refused to say outright that he'd murdered Fortunato, because his captors had insisted they'd kill him if he lied—and they knew he hadn't murdered Fortunato. So somehow captors and victim had negotiated this not-quite-false but highly misleading compromise language. And it hadn't saved Rocco anyway.

After I returned to California, Cushing had me come back to Hawaii to kill Melanie Munu. He told me Munu was trying to extort money from him.

Cushing did not want Munu's body found. He said I should arrange to meet her at Waiki'i Ranch. I used cash to buy a shovel, a plastic tarp, and a baseball bat in Kailua. I drove to Waiki'i Ranch and stored the bat at the house. I dug a grave beside an animal path about two hundred yards downhill from the house, piled the dirt and sod on the tarp, and left the shovel there.

Cushing called Munu to say I'd bring her the money and told her where to meet me. I got the bat and walked her to the grave at gunpoint,

where I hit her once on the back of the head. It was quieter than shoot-
ing her. Then I buried her and the bat. I dropped the tarp and shovel
in dumpsters in Kailua. I called and left an agreed message for Cush-
ing, who was in Honolulu for his alibi. The message was, "An overthrow
throughout the land."

Poor Melanie, Kawika thought. He could guess what had killed her. She
must've tried the heir-of-Ku'umoku extortion ploy with Cushing after Fortunato was gone, presumably omitting to tell Cushing that the Murphys and
S&R's lawyer Ted Pohano had a real heir who'd challenge the title anyway. It
hadn't worked. Dr. Smith must have guessed something of what she intended;
no wonder he'd told Kawika she was in danger.

Before I left Hawaii again, Cushing called and said he also needed me to
kill Kavika Wong. He said Wong was investigating Fortunato's death and
had information that could link Cushing to the Hawaiian items found on
Fortunato's body.

Each time Kawika read this, he shook his head. He'd missed so much that
evening at Cushing's. Partly it was chance—what if he'd simply said, *The mur-*
der weapon has three barbs, and yours has four? Cushing would have dropped
his blender full of Mai Tais, and events would have taken a wholly different
course.

Yet some of it was Kawika's fault, a failure of alertness even before he'd
sipped a drink. Kawika thought he'd been clever, disguising from Cushing
why he knew about olonā. But he'd failed to put two and two together—or one
piece of olonā fiber with another—as he gazed at the fishing line in Cushing's
display case.

Of course, the confession finally provided Kawika the answer to Tanaka's
question, *"Why did Cushing provoke you?"* He'd wanted to get Kawika fired
immediately. Once arrested, Cushing had admitted that the murder weapon
was his—a three-barbed ihe that should have been hanging above his door.
When he'd walked Kawika to the door and seen the wrong ihe hanging there,
Cushing must've realized in an instant that his own ihe, the one whose leg-
endary history he'd just described to Kawika, had been stolen and used to
kill Fortunato—realized, too, that someone was trying to frame *him*, not just
with the ihe but with Cushing's missing length of olonā fishline. But only
Kawika knew about the London dealer, the man who could link that ihe to
Cushing. If he'd been fired, Kawika now realized, the murder weapon might

never have been traced. Kawika had forgotten all about the London dealer until Cushing's arrest, and until reading the confession Kawika never had any reason to suspect Cushing owned the fatal spear.

I did not want to kill a cop, but Cushing said Wong's boss refused to remove him from the case, leaving him no choice. Cushing also wanted me to use a rifle I'd never seen, one owned by a native Hawaiian. I knew if I didn't cooperate that Cushing could implicate me for the other murders if Wong arrested him, so I went ahead.

Ironic, Kawika thought. If only Tanaka had fired him after he'd broken Cushing's nose—doing what Cushing hoped and what Cushing's lawyer demanded—Kawika would never have found himself in an assassin's gunsights.

Cushing said native Hawaiians were mad at Wong and blamed him for several deaths. Cushing said the native Hawaiian features of Fortunato's death had kept suspicion from him, and the same would be true if Wong was killed with a gun owned by a native Hawaiian.

Cushing gave me the gun and ammo, again by putting them in the trunk of my car. He included a newspaper photo of Wong so I could recognize him. After the shooting I was supposed to leave a message for Cushing, who had gone to Kailua to establish his alibi. The message was "The bones of Hilo are broken." Then I would return the gun to Cushing by leaving it in my car trunk at Hapuna, etc.

Those damn S&R press releases, Kawika thought. *And that damn photo.* True, a Native Hawaiian hadn't shot him after all. But still, there was only one reason for the big front-page headshot.

Cushing told me he called the police station and learned that Wong would return to Hilo from the volcanoes the next day. Cushing said Wong drove a yellow Mustang convertible. He told me the route Wong would probably use. He instructed me to leave the shell casing behind after I shot Wong, so the police could trace it to the gun's native Hawaiian owner.

Kawika bristled every time he thought of someone giving out his itinerary over the phone. Didn't everyone at the station realize S&R was inciting Native Hawaiians against him? And that there must be almost twenty thousand Native Hawaiians on the Big Island for S&R to incite? On the other hand, he did recognize, ruefully, that a bright yellow Mustang convertible might not have been the best automotive choice for a homicide detective.

I spotted Wong's convertible and followed it to a city park. I concealed the rifle in a beach towel. The rifle has a telescopic sight, but I missed him with two shots and only wounded him with the third. I realized the rifle must not be sighted properly and was about to compensate, but Wong ducked behind a wall, and right then my captors abducted me and drove away.

Thank God for small favors, Kawika thought. Either Bruno Moku'ele had never sighted the rifle properly, or Cushing must have bumped the sight while putting the gun in Rocco's trunk—or perhaps Rocco had hit a pothole on the drive from Hapuna. The fact that the rifle wasn't properly sighted was, in this case, definitely more important than why.

Back in 1998, Fortunato called me from Seattle. He said he'd gotten my name at a gun show from a guy whose name I recognized. Fortunato wanted me to kill Steven Kellogg. He said Kellogg had ruined his business.

I did not kill Kellogg, because I was unexpectedly in jail in the summer of 1998. I phoned Fortunato from jail to explain. He was upset, so I suggested he prepare a good alibi and do the job himself. I told him to use a nine-millimeter handgun he said he owned. I told him to break it down afterward and throw away the parts. I warned him the police would not believe his alibi. I said they would wiretap him, so I told him not to call me again.

Kawika imagined that Ernesto Gonzales and Harold Billings, back in Eastern Washington, probably closed the Kellogg murder investigation once they knew Fortunato was dead. But here was evidence that Fortunato had indeed owned the handgun they'd never found, the one whose existence Melissa Jane Harding had confirmed to Kawika after withholding that information from the FBI. How differently things might have turned out if Melissa had told them about that handgun! Fortunato might never have reached Hawai'i, might be in prison even today, appealing a death sentence for murdering a Federal prosecutor.

Here's how Cushing got my name: from Fortunato. I was surprised by that. He said they were having dinner once and ordering bottles of Pres-

ton wine. Fortunato said he knew another Preston in California. Fortu-
nato boasted of our relationship, told Cushing where I lived, and said he'd
once hired me to kill someone who'd ruined his resort development in
Washington. Cushing said Fortunato told him this in order to sound like
a "tough guy."

Well, Kawika thought, *Jimmy Jack got it right: Fortunato was a dumb*
fuck. Although maybe, after multiple bottles of Preston wine, he'd just been a
little too talkative.

71

South Kohala

In Honolulu, Kawika switched his connecting flight to Kailua-Kona instead of Hilo. There was no extra charge. A Post-it Note from Tanaka on Rocco's confession told Kawika to get to the Hilo station before Tanaka's afternoon press conference the next day. Cushing's arrest and the Duct Tape Mummy's confession were hot news, and an official explanation couldn't wait. The police chief would be there in person.

Kawika figured he could fly to Kailua-Kona, do what he had to do, and still reach Hilo in time. From Honolulu, he called Carolyn to say he'd spend the night at his dad's. He had to see Ku'ulei, he explained. He promised he'd see Carolyn for dinner in Hilo the next night, after Tanaka's press conference. She accepted his plans passively, and his heart sank a bit with sadness. But it didn't shake his resolution. He decided to wait a day before returning voice messages from Patience on the mainland; he still had to meet with Tanaka first, decide what to do about the killer.

Next he called and reserved a car at the Kailua-Kona airport. In the end, he'd flown coach to Honolulu, so the Department hadn't had to spring for first class. It could pay for a rental car instead. Kawika drove straight to the King Kam Kourt in Kailua. *"We've got a lot of K's in Hawaiian, don't we, Ku'ulei?"* He made the manager lead the way to Rocco's room.

"The police sealed it," the manager said. "I'm not sure I should let you in."

"I'm Detective Kawika Wong," Kawika repeated, showing his badge. The manager studied the badge, then stood aside.

For the second time in this investigation, Kawika ducked under a yellow crime scene tape. The Waimea and Kona cops had checked every surface for prints, then tossed the room.

"There's nothing they didn't get," the manager said.

Kawika wasn't sure about that. Where was Rocco's handgun? Kawika had a hunch. He entered the bathroom, lifted the lid of the toilet tank, and showed the manager a pistol taped underneath in a Ziploc bag. A smaller bag held some bullets.

"How about this?" Kawika asked. *Disappointing,* he thought. *Our guys missed this, missed those shell casings in Hilo. What else?*

"A handgun." The manager shrugged. He didn't seem impressed, maybe after seeing a big rifle with a telescopic sight in the same room. "What kind?"

"A nine millimeter, probably," Kawika said, replacing the lid. He imagined Melanie Munu confronting the same gun unsheathed. "Don't touch it," he warned, then dialed the police station in Kailua to call it in.

Kawika got back in the car and drove north on Highway 19, the Queen K, all the way to the Mauna Kea. He took the turnoff and parked at the gate house.

"Hey, Johnny," he said. "Can I use your phone?"

"Ain't got your cell, brah?"

"Battery's dead," Kawika said. Johnny seemed surprised but motioned Kawika inside.

Kawika called Tommy on the gate house landline. "Thanks for remembering that rifle, Tommy," he said. "I appreciate it."

"You haven't heard the latest," Tommy said. "You were on the plane. Bruno Moku'ele's talking. Came in this morning. His lawyer convinced him."

"How'd *that* happen?"

"Tanaka showed him Rocco's confession," Tommy replied. "Since Rocco said he shot you and Tanaka had the rifle from Rocco's motel room, Bruno was off the hook on that. But the thing is, Cushing knew where to get that rifle for Rocco. So Tanaka told Bruno he must've been Cushing's accomplice. It was a trick, but it worked. Bruno's lawyer told him he'd better tell the truth."

"And Bruno spilled?" Kawika asked.

"Yup. Turns out Fortunato was paying him. Bruno organized the hunters' group, whipped 'em up to start suing. After Fortunato died, Bruno went to Cushing. He wanted to know what to do next. Showed Cushing the rifle, told him he'd gotten it from Fortunato and had it sitting in his garage except to show folks; sort of proof, I guess, that he and Fortunato really had a deal."

"Wow. Doesn't sound too bright."

"Yeah, well. So what happens to Bruno now, you think? Tanaka wants him thrown off the force."

"Beats getting charged as an accomplice. Or worse."

"No doubt."

"So, Tommy," Kawika said, changing subjects, "remind me—what's Frank Kimaio's address, up there on Kohala Mountain Road?"

"You won't need an address," Tommy said. "You can't miss the house. Little white one that's perched way out there, great big cactus by the gate. You won't believe the view he's got. I didn't want to leave when I interviewed him that time."

"Mahalo, Tommy."

"No problem. Glad you're back. See you at the press conference?"

"Count on it."

Kawika headed north again, then followed Highway 19 as it wound up the slope from Puʻukoholā Heiau, the sacred spot where Peter Pukui and Melanie and HHH had once met to plan campaigns. Halfway up Kohala Mountain he passed the turnoff he'd taken the night he broke Cushing's nose. Further along, the road split. One fork led to Waimea, where Joan Malo had lived an innocent childhood, and where he'd since seen Fortunato laid open on a table and Joan's blood splattered inside a BMW. He took the other fork: the Kohala Mountain Road, the road to Hāwī, the road to his birthplace, and Joan's, and Kamehameha's. Nothing bad had ever happened to Kawika on the road to Hāwī.

Nothing bad happened this time either. He could tell Kimaio's house was probably empty; no car or truck in the driveway. It was an old Parker Ranch line shack, a place for paniolos—cowboys—to hole up for a hot meal or in bad weather and still be able to watch the cattle on the vast grazing area that stretched for miles north and south and down the mountainside below. Some owner before Kimaio had remodeled the place. It looked comfortable, even stylish, and enjoyed one of the most sweeping views of any house in the world.

Kawika knocked at the door, expecting no response and receiving none. A wide deck surrounded the little house on three sides. He walked to the southwest corner, the spot that interested him most. He peered in windows as he passed, feeling entitled—even obligated—to do so. Kimaio had covered them with blinds, but through one small gap Kawika could see a wall almost entirely covered with electronics and blinking lights. Before it stood a table with computer, headphones, an office chair.

Kawika leaned on the corner railing. It was just as he'd imagined. Here one seemed to stand in God's shoes. The volcanoes were all in view: Mauna Kea, Mauna Loa, Hualālai, and over on Maui, Haleakalā. The long coastline was also in view, thirty miles of it, from Kona all the way to Kawaihae. The ocean, corrugated by swells and serrated by winds, lay dappled and shadowed by scattered white clouds so far below him that Kawika looked down on their tops.

Taking his time, using landmarks for reference, Kawika eventually pinpointed in the distance every important location: Waikoloa Village, the land for KKL's planned resort, Fortunato's home outside Waimea, Cushing's home far down the slope, the grassy expanse of Waiki'i Ranch where Rocco had buried Melanie. Kawika could even vaguely see the Mauna Lani's golf courses.

Kimaio had built himself a sturdy observation post like a tiny set of bleachers, something the winds wouldn't move around. It wasn't entirely rudimentary. Kimaio had added padded back supports and arm rests. Kawika climbed up to Kimaio's throne and sat. He wasn't waiting for Kimaio—he figured Kimaio wasn't coming—but for the sunset. He wanted to see more of what Kimaio had seen, feel more of what Kimaio had felt when he was feeling like God.

After sunset, incomparable in its grandeur and celestial scale, Kawika felt he'd gotten what he came for. He walked to his car and drove down to Puakō. He embraced his father and Ku'ulei, compared healed wounds with his cousin, and spent the evening quietly with two people he loved.

In the morning he knew there'd be no point in returning to Kimaio's house. Instead, he drove down the highway to the turnoff for Waikoloa Village. A short distance up the slope he found the roadside graffiti meant just for him. He'd guessed it might be there.

The bleached coral letters stood out against the black lava rock. "KW: KFR." Kawika could guess what "KFR" meant: Ka'ū Forest Reserve. He sighed and dialed the station. Tanaka's assistant took the call.

"Hi," Kawika said. "Do me a favor, would you? Go into my office and pick up this call there." He wasn't sure this was necessary but figured it couldn't hurt. He'd finally understood how to communicate with the graffiti artist who specialized in bleached coral on black lava. Almost nothing about the case, it seemed, could possibly be explained if Kimaio hadn't been listening in on him and others; almost everything could be explained if Kimaio had been. Kimaio's buddy Joe Crane had evidently done a lot more than just get Jimmy Jack a nice phone number and run some wiretaps for the U.S. Attorney back on the mainland.

"Sure, I'll switch this to your office, but why?"

"I'll explain later."

In a few moments, Tanaka's assistant picked up again. "I'm in your office now," she said.

"Thanks. I just wanted to say, I've got to go to Ka'ū." He pronounced it the Hawaiian way, *kah-oo*.

"Now? You're not coming here?"

"I'll get there. But I'll go to Ka'ū first. That's K-A-U."

"I know the spelling, mystery man. See you later."

Kawika checked his watch. It was a long way to Ka'ū, and he'd have to drive fast. Tanaka expected him in Hilo for the press conference, and he could not afford to arrive late. Everything depended on getting to Tanaka first.

72

The Kaʻū Forest Reserve

The Kaʻū Forest Reserve is huge. To say, "Meet me in the Kaʻū Forest Reserve" is like saying "Meet me on the Big Island" unless a specific location is understood. Kawika understood. The location had to be the skinny young koa tree where, not long ago, he'd found unconscious and handcuffed that druggie killer he'd been pursuing, the one Tanaka had used to illustrate that in police work, the fact that something's true is more important than why it's true. "KW: KFR" could have no other meaning for Kawika—a thought that chilled him. In Father Brown's lexicon, Kimaio had been the Invisible Man, Kawika an observed man. For how long?

He drove fast, hiked fast, and reached the tree quickly. Soon, Kimaio stepped out of the shadows, moving silently over ground thick with twigs and fragrant leaves. Kawika realized Jimmy Jack must have taught him that trick, although Kimaio looked so reed thin he might have been weightless. He pointed a handgun at Kawika and dangled a pair of handcuffs.

"Let's put the cuffs in front," Kimaio said. "More comfortable."

"Don't need cuffs. I'm not armed."

"No. But you're young and healthy." Kimaio coughed. "And very dutiful." He threw the cuffs at the base of the tree. Kawika hesitated. "I *will* shoot," Kimaio warned. Kawika walked to the tree, sat with his arms and legs around the narrow trunk, and cuffed his own wrists.

"Okay," Kimaio said. "Who should start?"

"Who has the most to say?" replied Kawika.

"Fair point," said Kimaio, nodding. "Then I'll go first. I wonder what you must think of me."

"That matters to you?"

"Oh yes. And to you, I might add."

Kawika took a deep breath. "I think you're a good man," he said. "A good man who made a bad mistake."

"Not as good a man as you, then?"

"I wouldn't say that," Kawika replied. "That's how I think of myself too."

"Yeah, you're cheating on two women. But you never killed anyone?"

"My mistakes did."

"Nothing premeditated, though?"

"No."

"You know why I did it, right?"

"Yes, I know."

"But you wonder how I justified it?"

"I have to warn you: I'm going to be a tough sell."

Kimaio rubbed his eyes, as if very tired. "Sorry about Rocco shooting you," he said, changing direction. "I couldn't control everything. Despite what you think, we didn't tap every phone on the island."

"Or bug every room?"

"Or bug every room." Kimaio reached into a knapsack. "Water?" he asked. This time Kawika refused, though he was thirsty and even cuffed he could have drunk from the bottle Kimaio offered, the tree was so slender. "We didn't have Rocco's phone," Kimaio continued. "We had Cushing's by then, but he must've used another line the first time he called Rocco about you. Rocco was headed to Hilo when we picked up Cushing calling him again. We had to scramble to get there in time."

You didn't get there in time for the first three shots, Kawika thought.

"That why you didn't save Melanie Munu?" Kawika asked. "Because you couldn't get there in time?"

"Yeah. Like I said, we didn't have every phone on the island. We didn't have Rocco, and we didn't have Melanie. Rocco killed her before we could find him."

Kawika didn't respond.

"Okay," said Kimaio. "You *are* a tough sell. But just to recap: we couldn't control everything, all right?"

If you can't control everything, Kawika thought, *maybe you shouldn't play God.*

"Point number two: I didn't set out to kill Ralph Fortunato. I set out to catch him. I devoted years to that. But I ran out of time. I didn't have long to live. And Ralph didn't either."

Kimaio must have noticed Kawika's questioning look.

"We tapped Ralph's phones," Kimaio explained. "We didn't have Cushing's at first, but he used Ralph's office phone to call Rocco in California. That's when Cushing hired him to kill Ralph."

"You could have reported it," Kawika said. "You heard Cushing hire a hit man."

"Yes, could have saved Ralph from Rocco. But what an unhappy ending—me dead, Ralph alive and free."

"You could have charged Fortunato himself. You had evidence from the tap. Cushing told Rocco that Fortunato bragged about having hired him to kill Steve Kellogg, right?"

"Yeah, but Cushing didn't mention Steve Kellogg when he called Rocco," Kimaio said. "Probably never knew his name. And Rocco didn't kill Kellogg. He was in jail. Finally—"

"Wait—go back. You could've had the FBI bust Rocco back in California, worked your way up from there."

"Let me finish. Finally, as I was about to say, the tap was illegal. We couldn't use anything from it, directly or indirectly. Fruit of the poison tree and all that."

"Because your court order had expired?"

"Only good for one year," Kimaio said. "We tried for an extension. Couldn't get it. This was nearly year four."

"And for the other taps and bugs and cell phone monitoring, you had no court order at all, did you?"

Kimaio smiled. "Let's put it this way," he said. "We were like little boys who went up to the blackboard to spell the word 'banana' and didn't know when to stop."

"You tapped and bugged everyone—spied on all of us—with no authority at all?"

Kimaio shrugged. Kawika couldn't stop himself from shaking his head. He wondered, *If you weren't going to save Fortunato, why didn't you just let Rocco kill him?* But he knew the answer, thanks to Edgar Allan Poe.

"You told Fortunato who you were, before you killed him?"

"He knew me from Fawn Ridge," Kimaio said. "I didn't tell him I was dying. I told him Cushing had hired Rocco to kill him. I said it was more fitting for me to do it."

"You didn't act alone."

"I killed him myself. No one else. I wouldn't have let anyone else."

"But you had help."

"Not in killing him."

"Who's 'we' then? The little boys who went up to the blackboard?"

"You know who 'we' is."

"You, your phone company buddy Joe Crane, and I'm guessing Jason Hare? At least you three."

Kimaio waited, as if to see if Kawika would add more names. But Kawika switched to a different thought.

"Joe Crane ran your wiretaps? Installed your bugs?"

"We flew together in Nam. I joined the FBI. Joe went CIA."

"So later he worked for the phone company? First in Washington, then here?"

"That's how you do wiretaps. A guy works for the phone company."

"But not bugs?"

"No, not bugs or other surveillance. That's dark work."

"Dark work Joe learned in the CIA?"

"Had to learn somewhere," said Kimaio.

"And Jason Hare? Another Vietnam buddy?"

"Nope. Didn't know him there. Recruited him here."

"Based on Agent Orange?"

"Hardly. He was a grunt on the ground, a guy who got sprayed. Joe and I did the spraying, got exposed that way. Joe's okay though."

"You flew together?"

"Yeah, choppers. Most Agent Orange got dropped from planes. Not all."

"Choppers," repeated Kawika. "You boosted the chopper and the van from the heliport, didn't you?"

"Yeah. We had Jason scope out their security. Folks see him walking up and down the road all the time. They don't pay attention to him. He was doing recon."

"He wasn't doing graffiti?"

"Naw," Kimaio gave a small laugh. "Did that myself. It was a long shot. Kinda fun, really. Might not have worked, of course. But we guessed where Ms. Quinn shopped, and so it did."

"What was Hare doing at the Mauna Lani the night I met him? Spying on me?"

"No. He was looking for Fortunato's other Teva. I grabbed Fortunato at the Beach Club after he left the Murphys. Took his sandals to keep him from running. Put 'em in my cargo pants, so we could leave 'em at Murphys' later. I lost one somehow. Sent Jason to look for it the next few nights. In daylight he can't walk around a South Kohala resort—you've seen what the guy looks like. Had him take a cat trap and a cat, in case he got spotted. He never found the other Teva. Just one more thing that went wrong."

"So Dad was right."

"About what?"

"About Slipper Dog. You ought to know."

"I don't know. How would I?"

"Oh, come on."

"We didn't bug your dad's place, Detective. We didn't bug your girlfriends' places or their phones either. Figured they were entitled to some privacy."

"But you did bug my place? Tap my phones? Captain Tanaka's?"

"Well, not your home. Just Tanaka's. He's home more than you are. We did bug the meeting rooms at the station, though," Kimaio added. "We practically tore our hair out, listening to that S&R lawyer. What a bunch of red herrings—bribes, hunters, some old chief."

"Jesus."

"Yeah, well, about Jason Hare: I recruited him here. He knew Thomas Gray."

"So that was the Vietnam connection."

"No, Nam was a coincidence. Thomas Gray started Kohala Kats. Jason worked for them for years before this. He really loves cats, knew Thomas Gray well. I persuaded him Ralph murdered Gray, threw him off his own boat, but that we'd never prove it in court."

"Do you know for a fact Ralph did that?"

"I know it for a moral certainty. Don't you?" Kimaio waited. "Well, don't you? C'mon, Detective—you're the one who told me about Occam's Razor."

"Only because you tapped my phones."

"I'll take that as a yes. Anything more you want to know?"

Kawika's unease spiked sharply. He remembered Sam Spade: *Try to keep your man talking.*

"What about Rocco?" Kawika asked. "Did you think he'd survive that drop?"

Kimaio gave a disgusted laugh, and a spasm of coughing followed. Then he spoke softly. "Rocco was a projectile. I was trying to hit Cushing."

"Why?" Kawika asked. "Couldn't trust the system to deal with him?"

"That wasn't it." Kimaio sounded surprised. "I do trust the system when it works. I just wanted to get away clean. I might have, with Rocco and Cushing both dead. But Cushing's alive; he'll dispute the Fortunato part of Rocco's confession now, just like you plan to. Another thing that went wrong."

"Why the shore naupaka in Rocco's pocket?" Kawika asked, trying to keep the conversation from ending, the gun from being used. "What were you trying to tell us?"

"Wasn't trying to tell you anything. Message wasn't intended for you. Someone else."

"Another blackboard boy? Someone who performs autopsies? A way of tipping him off?"

Kimaio didn't reply, just looked into the forest. They sat again in silence. "More questions?" Kimaio finally asked.

"Yes," Kawika answered. He couldn't avoid it any longer. "Why are you telling me all this? You intend to kill me?"

Kimaio chuckled. "Kill a fellow lawman? No, never. I intend to persuade you. Or rather, give you information to persuade yourself. Information, and time to think about it."

"Persuade myself to do what?"

"To let things be. Your boss has Cushing, he's got Rocco's confession, and he's got lots to corroborate it: Cushing's spear, Melanie's body, the rifle and ammo. He's going to find those distinctive handcuffs at Cushing's house and mountain naupaka growing in Cushing's flowerbed. Captain Tanaka won't want you arresting a retired lawman. Not in these circumstances. Not with Cushing guilty of murder. Surely you must know that."

"But Cushing didn't kill Fortunato. Rocco didn't either."

"Cushing hired Rocco to kill you, though. You were supposed to be 'the bones of Hilo,' remember? He tried to have you shot, whereas—don't forget—I saved your life."

This time Kawika couldn't restrain himself. "You didn't save my life," he protested. "Rocco took three shots at me. You didn't make him miss, did you?"

Kimaio looked puzzled. "No, of course not," he said. "Not in Hilo. I saved your life here, in Kau." He pronounced it "Cow."

"Here?" said Kawika in seeming disbelief, but he knew it must be true.

"Yeah, here," insisted Kimaio. "That killer you found cuffed to this tree? You were chasing him into this forest, and he was lying in wait. He was going to shoot you dead, Detective. I'm the one who cuffed him, took away his gun. You must realize that, since you knew where to find me today."

It was true. Kawika tried to clear his head. "You were grooming me to handle the Fortunato investigation way back then? Before you killed him?"

"Couldn't afford to lose you at that stage."

"And the division chief in Waimea, the one who asked Tanaka to send me to the Mauna Lani in the first place? He was in on all this?"

"No, not all of it. He's a former FBI special agent, like me. A friend of mine, and a friend of Captain Tanaka. I just offered your name as a suggestion to a fellow officer of the law. But enough of that. The point is, you're not going to get to Hilo for Captain Tanaka's press conference. So what are you going to do? Show up later, embarrass him, tell him he's got just one little thing wrong?"

"It's not a little thing. You murdered Fortunato."

"Executed him."

"Lynched him."

"Okay, lynched him. But not unjustly—it was vigilante justice. He knew the custom of the country, as my old friend Marshal Hanson might say. And if you arrest me, I'll make bail and be dead before anyone can try me. Think about it."

"What's there to think about?" Kawika snapped back. "Anyway, you had accomplices—the blackboard boys."

Kimaio took a deep breath. The effort was difficult for him, Kawika could tell. "You're the guy who reads murder mysteries," Kimaio said. "What makes a good murder mystery? The detective has to solve the crime. Okay, you did that. Congratulations. But doesn't the detective have to do more? Doesn't he have to solve himself?"

"What's that supposed to mean?"

"Just this: you're torn between two women—paralyzed. And you can't decide if you're haole or Hawaiian, living that life or this one. If I've heard you correctly."

"You mean *over*heard me correctly."

"Right, overheard you correctly. So those are things you'll try to solve, later today or some other day, now that you've solved the killing. But what you've got to solve right now, this moment, handcuffed to this tree, is whether you're such a straight arrow, so powerless, that all you can do once you've solved the killing is arrest me, arrest us all. Or whether morality is more important."

"Morality? Killing people?"

"Killing killers," Kimaio corrected. "Fortunato and Rocco both. Well, it was justice. You decide what's moral."

"It wasn't moral."

"Not what I meant. The killings were my decision. I meant *you* have to decide what's moral now—whether it's moral to turn me in."

"You and the blackboard boys?" Kawika replied. "You're saying, let you all go? Is that it? That's the moral choice? Because of your idea of justice—vigilante justice?"

Kimaio took another loud raspy breath, then signed deeply. "Detective," he said. "I hope you live a long life. But at the end of it, where I am, you'll find that all you have left—all you've got to cling to—is your image of yourself. My image of myself wouldn't allow Steve Kellogg's death to go unpunished. It's that simple. Now, what's your image of *yourself*? Tanaka calls you Mister Clean. Is that all you are, Mister Clean? A robot? That automatic, that shallow? Here's some advice: Always conduct yourself the way that five years from now you'll wish you'd conducted yourself. Always. Think about that."

"Looks like I've got time to think about it."

"That you do," said Kimaio brightly, checking his watch. "Meanwhile, I've got some questions for you. What tipped you off, exactly?"

"Little things," Kawika replied. "Logical things. Mostly my trip to the mainland. Steve Kellogg's death, because you hadn't mentioned it. Jimmy Jack's business card, his phone number and yours—Joe Crane as the telephone buddy you shared. The Methow Valley filled with blackboard boys—plus two in Wenatchee."

"Well, the plan was premised on you not going to the mainland, and certainly not to the Methow. You were supposed to figure out that the spear and cord and the naupaka were Cushing's, that he grabbed Fortunato at the Murphys' and was trying to frame Peter Pukui. Why weren't you more *culturally literate*?" Kimaio laughed, then coughed again.

The question brought Kawika a realization: *Fortunato died on Kamehameha's spear, yet he died for mainland sins, and a mainland haole killed him. So what did his murder have to do with cultural literacy, with race, with anything Hawaiian at all? The whole thing had been a white man's problem, just as Jimmy Jack had said: a white killer lynched by a white cop.* Kawika wanted to think more about this, but at the moment he couldn't.

"I went to the mainland because someone shot me," he finally responded. "It wasn't planned. Everyone thought a Hawaiian did it, that I wasn't safe here."

"Everyone but you."

"Well, I thought so too—at first. And if I hadn't gone to the mainland, I might never have learned the formula for getting away with murder."

"Ah. You mean do it yourself, don't rely on anyone, use some ordinary weapon, make sure your alibi can't be broken even though it won't be believed—that formula? The one Rocco taught Fortunato? The one Fortunato followed, and I didn't?"

"Yeah, that formula. I realized Fortunato followed it, but in the end, I realized he made a big mistake."

"What mistake?"

"He thought the formula applied even if the person you murder is a federal prosecutor."

"Oh."

"But it doesn't apply if you murder a federal prosecutor, does it?"

"No," replied Kimaio. "No, it doesn't."

"If you murder a federal prosecutor, you end up dead. Right?"

"Right. One way or another, you end up dead."

"Dead in a way that sends a message?" Kawika continued. "Revenge is ours—that sort of thing."

"Right."

"So you needed Fortunato to know who was killing him, and why. And you needed to signal your colleagues back in Washington, in Winthrop and Wenatchee, that the deed was done."

"You *are* culturally literate," Kimaio said. "At least in our culture." He smiled, as if they were good friends sharing a joke.

Kawika didn't smile back. "You needed to get away with it too. Is that why I'm here? So you'll get away with it?"

"Not exactly. It's as I said: you're here so you can make a decision. I'll get away with it no matter what. I'm dying faster than expected." Kimaio looked at his watch again. "I've still got a little time," he said cheerfully. "And you've still got a while to wait."

Kawika shifted position, trying to get more comfortable. "Then what shall we talk about?" he asked. "The Shark Cliff case? That haole who'd been handcuffed?"

"Let's not," Kimaio said. "Different bad guy, that one. Different cuffs too."

They both fell silent. Then Kimaio added briskly, "And before you ask, I have no idea where Peter Pukui is, just so you know."

"I'm surprised. You seem to know everything."

"Sarcasm doesn't become you, Detective," Kimaio said. "And now I need to go lie down for a bit. Happens to me these days. I'll leave you the water," he added, handing Kawika a bottle carefully, at arm's length. This time Kawika took it. He'd be able, barely, to get it to his mouth on it around the slender tree trunk. "Don't worry, Detective—I'll be back before too long; I won't die and abandon you. Meanwhile, there're nothing scary here. No more killers in the Fortunato saga lurking about. You caught the last one."

"Yeah, but not before the last one caught me," said Kawika, giving his cuffed hands a shake.

PART EIGHT

HILO

The Discovery *anchored off Waikiki, and in or near that place three natives were arrested and charged with having had a part in the killing of the English officers. After an extended inquiry, the three accused men were pronounced guilty and were shot to death with a pistol in the hands of a native executioner in a canoe alongside the* Discovery. *Vancouver was fully satisfied of their guilt, but there is much testimony indicating rather conclusively that they were innocent and that the guiltiest person of all, a minor chief, wholly escaped punishment.*
—Ralph S. Kuykendall, *The Hawaiian Kingdom* (1938)

73

Hilo

Terry Tanaka went ahead with his press conference. Kawika's absence irritated him—he assumed Kawika was in bed with Patience Quinn in South Kohala. *Pretty irresponsible,* Tanaka thought, especially since she could've been a witness, if not a suspect. *Anyone but Kawika,* Tanaka thought, *I would've had the guy up on misconduct charges.* But there could be no delay of the press conference. The story was out, the media had assembled. Lights and cameras were already set up. Police Chief Haia Kalākalani was here, hands folded beneath his substantial belly and smiling for the photographers. It remained only for Tanaka to step to the microphone.

Tanaka announced that Michael Cushing had been arrested and charged with the murders of Ralph Fortunato and Melanie Munu and the attempted murder of Detective Kawika Wong. Tanaka explained that Cushing had hired a California contract killer named Roger Preston, or Rocco, for all three crimes, and that Rocco had left a confession, which someone—not the police—had extracted before dropping him, fatally, from a helicopter into Cushing's convertible.

"Has the confession been corroborated?" someone shouted.

"Yes," Tanaka explained, "the confession has been corroborated in key respects. Melanie Munu's body was found where Rocco indicated, along with the baseball bat he'd used to kill her. The rifle and ammunition found in his motel room matched those in Kawika's shooting. Cushing admitted owning the spear that killed Fortunato, and Fortunato's hands had been tied with a piece of ancient fishing line from Cushing's home. This, too, fits Rocco's confession."

"What about motive?" someone called out. Fortunato and Cushing were defrauding their investors, Tanaka responded. They'd had a falling out. Munu was killed to prevent her exposing the fraud. Detective Wong was targeted because Cushing believed Detective Wong had cracked the case and would soon arrest him.

"Had he cracked the case?"

"No," Tanaka answered. "Detective Wong had not solved the crime at the time of his shooting, when he was evacuated to the mainland for his own safety. But he would certainly have cracked the case otherwise."

"Did Rocco's abductors botch a plan to drop him into Cushing's car alive?"

"We don't know," Tanaka said.

"Who were his abductors?" a reporter asked.

"We don't know that either," Tanaka said.

"What's your best guess?"

"We think," Tanaka said, "that Rocco may have been abducted by a particular Hawaiian native group—one I won't name, since we don't know for sure." Tanaka knew the news media would figure it out; they had S&R's press releases.

"Why would they do that?"

"Maybe it was cultural self-defense," Tanaka suggested. "This particular group—sorry, it wouldn't be right to name it—took offense at Cushing trying to frame ethnic Hawaiians for Fortunato's murder. Of course, perhaps the group's motive was different. Some individuals opposing KKL had been getting paid under the table by Fortunato—pretending to fight a developer while secretly conspiring with him in a fraud."

"So could Rocco's death have been a revenge killing?" another reporter called out.

"Sure," said Tanaka. "After all, this particular group, which I'm not naming—well, some members relied on Fortunato for cash. Fortunato's death cut that off. Maybe it made them angry enough to kill the hit man. Who knows? Unless someone talks, we don't have much to go on."

"Is anyone talking?"

"No one from this particular group," Tanaka said. "They refuse to cooperate with the police." Then he added, "To me that means they're lawless."

Tanaka told the assembled reporters nothing about the Methow Valley or anything related to it. Despite requests from the media, he declined to make the text of Rocco's confession public. He told Chief Kalākalani he didn't want the Cushing arrest story complicated by a separate story about a federal prosecutor's murder on the mainland. The Feds had the confession now.

"Let them deal with that part," Tanaka told his boss. "It'll be big news in Washington—both Washingtons, actually."

74

Hilo

So it went. Kawika heard a replay on the radio as he drove through the night, very late, to reach Hilo. For a second time in the case, he got Tanaka out of bed, and for a second time he was worried as he did.

"You're safe," Tanaka said coldly on the doorstep, not even letting Kawika inside. "That's what matters tonight. I don't care about your love life. See me tomorrow."

Kawika hadn't mentioned Kimaio or the Ka'ū Forest Reserve. He hadn't had the chance before Tanaka closed the door. Kawika wasn't sure he would have mentioned them anyway.

By the time Kawika got back in the car, it was far too late to call Carolyn about the missed dinner, much less call Patience, who—despite Tanaka's assumption—was still on the mainland. And circumstances could not be worse. By confirming horrors Kawika might choose never to divulge—and confirming, too, that Kawika's phone calls weren't private—Kimaio had effectively put Kawika's love life out of its misery. He'd have to change his phone number, at least. But even so, Kimaio and Joe Crane would find a way to keep monitoring him. And the things he couldn't divulge would make any normal phone conversation impossible anyway.

Just when I'd finally decided, Kawika thought. "Shit," he said aloud.

75

Hilo and Berkeley

Carolyn worried, of course, when Kawika didn't show up and didn't call. But she realized she also felt relieved. In truth, she'd half-dreaded seeing him; she wasn't ready. The relationship wasn't right, she told herself. She loved him, but she couldn't keep going—didn't want to keep going, didn't think she should. She'd tumbled down a lover's cliff and begun to roll incessantly, sea-rounded, on a stony shore of unforgiving doubts.

* * *

Patience didn't dread hearing from Kawika, but ultimately despaired of it. He didn't return her calls. Something had made him inaccessible. She didn't know what—the distance or the case or their two such different lives. But she suspected the last of these. As for distance, he'd begun withdrawing in the Methow Valley when the distance between them was only from one car seat to another, and he'd suddenly stopped answering her questions. As for the case, well, it had brought them together. If it separated them now, that was a bad sign. After this murder there'd be another and then another. So it had to be their hopelessly different lives, she concluded. Like a stone adze of the ancient Hawaiians, doubt began to thud against the new life she'd been imagining, cutting the lashings, flaking the timbers, reducing it to rubble, chip by chip, chunk by chunk.

76

Hilo

At the station the next morning, Kawika again apologized for missing the press conference. Something personal had come up, Kawika said without further explanation, something he just couldn't talk about. Tanaka waited. Kawika could tell Tanaka still assumed a tryst with Patience had kept him from showing up. He knew his terse apology probably made matters worse. But having thought about it overnight, he realized he had to be very careful with Tanaka right now.

Awkwardly, Kawika began. He wanted to make sure, he said, that Tanaka had considered certain evidence that made Kawika question whether Rocco had killed Fortunato and whether a Hawaiian group—S&R in particular—had killed Rocco.

"What evidence?" Tanaka asked defensively.

"Well, start with the confession. Rocco says he killed Melanie, and he says he tried to kill me. But he never actually says he killed Fortunato."

"He comes close," Tanaka replied. "And it's corroborated. Cushing owned the murder weapon, and Rocco says Cushing told him to use the weapon Cushing gave him."

"But that particular one? It's about the most significant spear in Hawaiian history."

"Yes, but no one in Hawaii would know that. No photos of it, no other identification. Only other person who knew its history, before Cushing told you, was a London antique dealer we'd never think to even look for. Plus, Cushing could always claim the killer stole it—which is what he *does* claim. Same with the cord. And the cord wasn't public information."

"But Terry, the confession doesn't mention the cord at all. I don't think Rocco knew about the cord."

Tanaka ignored him. "The naupaka in Fortunato's pocket," Tanaka continued, "came from a flower bed right next to Cushing's front door. Did you notice that naupaka, after you decked him? No? Well, the naupaka wasn't public information either. We've got Cushing for the Fortunato killing, Kawika. End of story."

"What about the shore naupaka in Rocco's pocket?" Kawika asked. "Doesn't that suggest the same person killed both of them?"

"It's a coincidence, like we already discussed," Tanaka said. "Cushing wanted naupaka in Fortunato's pocket to make it look like Hawaiians did it. Hawaiians put naupaka in Rocco's pocket so we'd *know* they did it."

"But Rocco's confession refers to a 'sacred flower,' Terry. Naupaka's not sacred, is it? I think he was talking about ohia or something."

"Maybe Cushing's culturally illiterate. Carolyn said the killer must be."

"Yet Rocco's statement suggests killing Fortunato and *then* putting his body on the tee box," Kawika responded. "That's not culturally illiterate—it's more authentic than what actually happened."

"Kawika, the cultural aspect of Fortunato's murder was merely simulated—crudely simulated. A haole was killed on a luxury golf course with a spear," Tanaka said. "That's all there was to it."

Kawika tried again. "Okay, then, is S&R culturally illiterate too? So illiterate that suddenly they can't spell?"

"What'd you mean?"

"Rocco's confession spells *Kawika* with a *v*. Consistently. The envelope that arrived here at the station had the same mistake, didn't it?"

"We can check—I don't remember. But I'd say that's a stray, Kawika."

"And his confession never capitalizes 'native' where it uses 'Native Hawaiian.' Does that sound like S&R?"

The expression on Tanaka's face verged on *stink eye*.

Kawika made one final effort. "Let me try one more approach," he offered. "Once Tommy gave me a phone number: 555-8998. 'Easy to remember,' I said. 'That's what Terry thought too,' Tommy said. Why did you think that, Terry? What made it easy to remember?"

Tanaka waved his hand, as if brushing away a fly. "That's Frank Kimaio's number," he said. "It's easy to remember because eight-nine reminds me of August 9."

"And what's special about August 9?"

"Nagasaki. The atom bomb. Hiroshima was August 6, Nagasaki was August 9."

"How about eight-nine-ninety-eight? August 9, 1998, that is?"

"Like I said, Nagasaki. Fifty-third anniversary, I guess."

Kawika clenched his teeth in frustration, but kept trying. "So eight-nine-ninety-eight could be a date? A phone number that would remind you of that date? A number you might get from a buddy who works at the phone company?"

"So what?" Tanaka said. "This has nothing to do with the case, Kawika."

Kawika barely restrained himself. He wanted to scream, *Don't you get it, Terry? Every single clue in Fortunato's murder turned out to be a red herring. We were meant to arrest the wrong guy—and we did.* But Kawika didn't scream. He didn't say anything at all. He was sure Tanaka must understand all this perfectly. Yet for some reason Tanaka had decided to pretend he didn't.

Kawika and his boss spent a long time regarding one another. Finally Kawika spoke. "Why are you doing this, Terry? I'd really like to know."

"What's true is this, Kawika: I'm your superior and I *am* doing this. That's what matters. But as to why—well, whoever killed Fortunato and Rocco killed the right people. Whoever did it probably saved your life. Rocco could have kept shooting, you know; he had plenty more ammo, and that lava wall wouldn't have stopped a pea shooter. Cushing did commit Melanie's murder, using Rocco, and he tried to kill you, so Cushing's not an innocent. And by putting an end to S&R—I think you'll agree I've probably done that—I'm protecting your back, making Hawaii a better place, cutting down a nasty weed so more responsible groups can grow. Is that good enough for you?"

"But Terry," Kawika asked, "have we gone from thinking it's okay if the right guy gets caught to thinking it's okay if the right guy gets killed?"

"Kawika," replied Tanaka evenly, "in this case the right guy *was* caught. You forget—he hired Rocco."

Kawika met Tanaka's gaze. It was softer than a stare but not nearly as paternal as it had been once. "I owe you a lot, Terry," Kawika finally said. "I owe you just about everything. I do appreciate your watching my back, protecting me. Believe me. I really do. Thank you."

Tanaka nodded in acknowledgment, then brushed his palms together quickly, as if ridding them of crumbs. "So, you ready to get back to work?" he asked. Kawika recognized it as a test. A pause followed—but not a long one. Kawika had already made up his mind.

"If you want me to," he replied, trying to sound game. "More than that, I'm even ready to scare a druggie for you out at Shark Cliff."

Tanaka didn't laugh, but he smiled. The smile wasn't warm, yet it was the first smile Kawika had seen from Tanaka in a long time.

"I think you can help," Tanaka said, getting up to leave. "And yes, I want you to."

He didn't add, *Iiko, iiko.*

Epilogue

"I'm a detective and expecting me to run criminals down and then let them go free is like asking a dog to catch a rabbit and let it go. It can be done, all right, and sometimes it is done, but it's not the natural thing."
—Dashiell Hammett, *The Maltese Falcon* (1929)

Michael Cushing pleaded guilty to killing Fortunato. The prosecutors insisted, and they already had him for Melanie's murder and the attempt on Kawika, using Rocco. It wasn't worth the sentencing risk to reject the plea bargain and go to trial, his lawyers told him. He began serving time on Oʻahu, but after threats from Hawaiian inmates, the authorities isolated him and made plans to transfer him to Walla Walla.

Carolyn, too, went to Washington once she received her PhD. She couldn't get to Kahoʻolawe for restoration work—nothing had really started yet—and the rest of Hawaiʻi just depressed her. She met Jimmy Jack in the Methow Valley, having contacted him through Kawika. She took a job with the Bureau of Land Management as a specialist in rangeland management and native species restoration. On weekends she worked with Jimmy and helped him apply for grant money. Together they made advances in biological methods of dry land weed control, discovering, for example, at what growth stage Russian knapweed seems particularly palatable to Angora goats. Madeline John taught Carolyn to ride on a horse named Monte, and sometimes Carolyn helped Madeline trap cats.

Of course, Madeline told her about Patience, but by then it didn't matter. Carolyn had ended her relationship with Kawika, and Kawika had summoned up sufficient character to tell her the truth about his faithlessness, or much of it. "Well," she said, "we were always better friends than lovers," but unlike friends, Carolyn and Kawika didn't stay in touch. She did travel to Washington, DC, each year on behalf of Kahoʻolawe restoration groups, working with Hawai'i's congressional delegation to get more funding. But she didn't go home, not even to Maui.

One day Carolyn and Jimmy rode across Jimmy's property to check the progress of some parasitic Dalmatian toadflax beetle grubs they'd planted as an experiment. Unexpectedly, Jimmy pulled up his Appaloosa and turned to Carolyn, who gently reined Monte to a halt.

"By the way," Jimmy said. "This is where he did it. On this ridge, right here—this spot." He spread his arms, offering the entire view.

"Who?" Carolyn asked. "Did what?"

"Your detective friend. This is where he figured out who killed that scumbag Fortunato. And he figured it out from my phone number—partly anyway." Jimmy shook his head and smiled appreciatively, then leaned out from his horse and spat. "For all the good it did him," he added.

Carolyn felt confused; she'd understood from the official story that Rocco had killed Fortunato, and that Kawika *hadn't* figured it out. Yet here was a spot where Kawika had stood, marked as precisely by Jimmy's spit as if by a stone cairn on the trail to the kīpuka. So Carolyn turned, accepting Jimmy's offer and taking in the entire view, the same panorama of snowbound peaks Kawika must have seen. Jimmy heard Carolyn's sharp intake of breath, as if without warning some god of love had given his deeply buried spear a twist.

Kiku Takahashi, the assistant curator at the Kohala Historical Museum, eventually checked and found that the museum's absent four-barbed ihe had not been loaned to the Bishop Museum. Kawika, meanwhile, grew to suspect that the unidentified spear above Cushing's door might belong to a collection accessible to Dr. Terrence Smith. Kawika waited for a day when Smith was at Kohala Historical as a volunteer, then took the javelin there and handed it to Takahashi in Smith's presence.

"You missing this?" Kawika asked.

"That's it!" she cried. "That's the one! Where did you find it?"

Kawika explained in a few sentences. "Thank you, thank you!" she said. "Oops, I mean mahalo nui."

"Glad to help," Kawika told her. To Smith he said, "Walk me to my car." Smith complied. "If I dusted that spear for prints, I'd find yours, wouldn't I?" Kawika asked. He was still cataloguing the ways this particular blackboard boy had helped his dying patient.

"Detective," Smith replied with a smile, "on the day I first met you, we both already knew not to handle an ihe without gloves."

That taunt reminded Kawika—as if he needed a reminder—that despite struggling with indecision, he'd finally made a decision of great consequence. Stubbornly, he'd stuck with it. He'd let Kimaio go. He could have exposed him, blown the whistle, brought the whole dishonest structure and the blackboard boys tumbling down, whether or not they all got convicted. But he hadn't. He wasn't Mr. Clean this time. He'd learned—perhaps from juggling Carolyn and Patience, or perhaps from Tanaka—to lie by omission. It was not comfortable for him to realize that.

Kawika felt his decision didn't reflect any satisfactory principle; it just seemed to accord with Kimaio's advice: "*Always conduct yourself the way that five years from now you'll wish you'd conducted yourself.*" Still, the decision had a messy habit of sleepwalking. Kawika wasn't sure he'd ever reach the end of its unpleasant consequences.

The worst, of course, was that even though he'd solved the crime—in fact, precisely because of that—he couldn't talk about the solution with anyone. He'd found it on his own, with no tips from informants, apart from Edgar Allan Poe. But Tanaka didn't want to hear Kawika's discoveries. That was clear. Tanaka had resolved the investigation to his own satisfaction, and Kawika knew part of Tanaka's satisfaction lay in punishing those who'd tried to harm Kawika—Michael Cushing and S&R.

All this, especially his indebtedness to Tanaka, silenced Kawika completely. What could he say to Patience, for example, after his day in the Ka'ū Forest Reserve? And after Tanaka had gone public with a story Kawika knew to be false? Nothing, despite having lived almost the entire investigation with her. He couldn't expose Tanaka, nor ask Patience to keep secrets as corrosive to the soul as his. Much less, he thought, could he ask her to do so and still love him. And thus, with Patience as with Tanaka, he recognized—bitterly—that he'd chosen to let intimacy fail him rather than risk a great plunge in reliance on it. Like Fortunato's murder itself, the corner into which Kimaio and Tanaka had painted Kawika had little to do, in the end, with Hawai'i. But it was Kawika's own corner, and if a way out existed, he couldn't find it.

Patience didn't stop visiting the Big Island. She counted herself a kama'āina, after all, and resilient. She reluctantly accepted the official account of Fortunato's murder and never felt sure exactly how the discoveries she and Kawika had made in the Methow Valley actually related to it. She managed to overcome her reporter's urge to investigate further; she couldn't be a character in her own feature story. And she wasn't ready to confront Kawika.

Patience half convinced herself that Kawika had provided just a transitional relationship, that they never could have lasted. Friends told her the same thing. She'd already known, from marriage, that sometimes relationships can get broken in ways that can't be fixed. And this relationship was certainly broken. She did grow more cautious, however, and she did teach herself to sit still. Yet she never stopped wondering.

In time, Patience made love again at the Mauna Lani and even awoke at night to find her lover deep in thought, staring at the ceiling fan. But she never again walked out on her lanai, opened her yukata, and pressed a man's head to her bare breasts. That had been a sacrament, one she felt she'd received, not given. She would recall it in the small hours of the morning, when she held her cup of coffee and lifted her gaze to the sunrise striking the summit of distant Haleakalā. She tried not to look at the elevated tee box a few yards away.

When Patience's father next shook hands with Jarvis Wong, his old friend, he felt overwhelmed with wistfulness, with thoughts of what might have been. That same firm handshake made him dizzy with images of haole flesh joined with Hawaiian, the flesh of his flesh with the flesh of Jarvis's.

Kawika's stepfather Pat also saw things in a wistful way, although none of his flesh was involved. He, too, wondered what might have happened had Patience and Kawika chosen to be together. But he knew it was pointless. "A truck might have hit them the first day," Pat said to Kawika's mother, Lily.

Lily shook her head. "A truck *did* hit Carolyn and Kawika," she insisted. "She's here in Washington now. If they'd stayed together, he'd be home."

"Maybe," Pat allowed, "but a truck might've hit him here too. And anyway, maybe he *is* home."

A truck of sorts did hit Mr. Shimazu. KKL's collapse left him humiliated, not just ruined. His investors provided him a teller's job at one of their retail banks in Tokyo. And they made sure he took it. A teller's job with no chance of promotion.

No truck hit Jarvis. But he did feel bruised, believing Kawika must have failed in some unspoken way. He wanted to embrace his boy again, comfort him, but Kawika stayed resolutely in Hilo. Jarvis felt a bit awkward with his friend Tanaka, and even more awkward when next he encountered Carolyn and, a year later, Patience. Jarvis loved them both, in his avuncular way. He didn't know what to say. Nor did they. They just hugged, each young woman with the massive older man.

The Mauna Lani Resort, after some internal discussion, posted on its website a simple statement that no features of its famous golf courses were intended to suggest Hawaiian cultural sites. At about the same time, Tanaka arrested Bingo Palapala, the official who'd granted the bulldozing permit, on public corruption charges because he'd solicited a bribe from Fortunato for the consulting firm Palapala secretly co-owned. Because of the bribe, Palapala went to jail even though the consulting firm's report itself seemed otherwise legitimate and did prove convincingly that the boundary marker or altar Fortunato destroyed wasn't a heiau.

But once the Fortunato case was closed, and despite his earlier threats, Tanaka never bothered with the Murphys, nor did he expose their lawyer Ted Pohano as Ted Pohaus from LA. He simply despised them.

After waiting a while, just to be safe, the Murphys quietly reached an accommodation with the heirs of Chief Ku'umoku through Pohano. They bought KKL's land out of bankruptcy for a fraction of what Fortunato paid. The Murphys gave the property to a local land trust, and for tax deduction purposes they treated the corruptly inflated purchase price Fortunato had paid as the unassailable measure of the donation's value. Although by now the legacy of fraud clung to the property like a curse, the IRS never looked into that tax deduction.

The hunters group, too, lost interest once KKL was dead. It was rough country, that land, and never had much game to speak of.

Kawika continued to work for Tanaka, but he never had to menace a druggie at Shark Cliff. The great Shark Cliff development was that Sammy Kā'ai managed to solve the case—most of it—and rescue Peter Pukui at the same time, thanks to help from an alert Waimea cop. The night after Tanaka's press conference, the cop stopped a car traveling without lights on the dead end road from Honoka'a to the Waipi'o Lookout. The driver and his two passengers couldn't explain why the fourth man in the car, the terrified one on the floor, eyes wide in the beam of the officer's flashlight, was bound and gagged, with his mouth taped shut for good measure.

The fourth man was Peter Pukui. Fortunately, the Waimea officer had approached the driver's window with his gun drawn; there was no resistance. He ordered the three young men to lie face down on the pavement, disarmed and cuffed them, and radioed for backup.

Sammy Kā'ai got to take the Hilo Major Crimes helicopter this time. Once again, Sammy wrapped Peter Pukui in a blanket to keep him from going into shock. Then Sammy joined the Waimea cop in standing over the prone young men. With police pistols pointed at their nineteen-year-old heads, in quavering voices the three admitted being heroin dealers, Peter Pukui's suppliers and kidnappers, the ones who'd brought cash to Hilo for Peter's bail. Finally, still lying on the road, and even after receiving their Miranda warnings, they also confessed to being the Shark Cliff murderers.

By that point they were all in tears, shaking with sobs. One had urinated all over himself. "The notorious crybaby killers," Sammy said with contempt. "Pathetic."

At the station, where Sammy separated them, the leader of the three turned out to be the bad penny grand-nephew of the granny who'd fled the lava flow threatening Pāhoa. He'd been smart enough to change plates on granny's car, but not lucky enough to get Peter Pukui all the way to Waipiʻo Lookout without being stopped. He admitted they'd been holding Peter captive in Honokaʻa, waiting for Melanie Munu to arrive with money extorted from Michael Cushing. But then they'd watched Tanaka's press conference on television and learned Melanie was dead, her body exhumed at Waikiʻi Ranch. At that point they had decided just to toss Peter off the cliff.

The earlier Shark Cliff victims, the killer said, weren't meth war casualties, just druggies he and his buddies thought knew Peter, and from whom they'd tried to learn his hiding place. They'd finally been told by another druggie—the one Sammy had turned loose when Peter had climbed up out of Waipiʻo Valley—that the Hilo cops had Peter in custody. That's why they showed up in Hilo to assure Peter's release on bail.

Even at the station, though, the three Shark Cliff killers vehemently insisted they knew nothing about the other victim, the one Sammy had dubbed the Handcuffed Haole. To Sammy, the Shark Cliff investigation seemed incomplete as a result.

Eventually, the Handcuffed Haole turned out to be a man named D. K. Parkes, a for-hire boat captain who'd sometimes skippered the *Mahi Mia* for Thomas Gray out of Kawaihae Harbor. Sammy patiently established this, working from the man's anchor and fishhook tattoos and finally showing the flyer around Kawaihae. But that was as far as Sammy could get with the Handcuffed Haole. He'd discovered the man's identity, but not the motive for his killing. No one who knew him thought D. K. Parkes was a druggie.

Kawika, on the other hand, asked Corazon Fortunato about Parkes, once his identity became known and Kawika had a photo of him to show her. She confirmed that her husband had sometimes fished on *Mahi Mia* with Thomas Gray and this Mr. Parkes. Kawika then had no doubt who'd killed Parkes: someone who killed killers. Someone who'd killed Fortunato and the

Duct Tape Mummy. Someone who'd gone to the blackboard to spell the word *banana* and hadn't known when to stop.

So Kawika identified D. K. Parkes as Fortunato's probable accomplice in the Thomas Gray murder—and the third victim of Kimaio's vigilante justice. But Kawika didn't report his discovery officially or tell Sammy. Instead he just told Tanaka quietly, "For Shark Cliff, this D. K. Parkes, the Handcuffed Haole, is a stray—just what Sammy first suspected. He helped murder someone, but that case is unrelated to Shark Cliff. And in that other case, the killer's dead too. Trust me." Tanaka, seemingly incurious, did precisely that, somewhat to Kawika's surprise. It was as if Tanaka already knew.

Soon, Kawika recognized, Tanaka would begin hinting that the time had come for Kawika to advance his career in Honolulu. So Kawika flew to Honolulu for a day, ostensibly to check out a job but really to question Cushing before he was transferred to Walla Walla. "What happened between you and Joan Malo?" he asked. "The night before she died, I mean." With his lawyer present, Cushing was eager to talk. He insisted his story would prove someone else had murdered Fortunato.

"That night, I was completely freaked out," Cushing said. "Someone had just killed Ralph in the exact spot and with the exact type of weapon I'd planned. But it wasn't Rocco, and I still had in storage the ihe I was going to give him; it was an untraceable one. Yet whoever did it stole my ihe, the historic one, to kill Fortunato in order to frame me, and somehow they knew my plan."

"You thought Joan Malo knew your plan?"

"I had no idea," Cushing said. "Maybe she'd somehow overheard me when I called Rocco. Maybe she'd told Shimazu about it in Tokyo, trying to appease him. Maybe it gave Shimazu a bright idea, how he could kill Ralph and not be suspected."

"Did Joan really tell you about Shimazu and his friends? What they'd done?"

"Joan?" Cushing snorted. "No way. Ralph told me. He bragged about it, saying he'd used Joan to buy time with the Japanese. Told me it would let us both get more money out of KKL. That's when I realized he was flying the plane right into the mountain. He had no intention of pulling up in time."

"And so? What happened that night with Joan?"

"That night with Joan, I was scared," Cushing said. "Really, really scared. I figured someone must be on to me. I went completely nuts. I demanded to know what she knew. I threatened her, told her I'd tell Kai about her and Ralph. About Shimazu and his friends. Told her Shimazu gave Ralph copies of the photos."

"Photos?"

"You didn't find them?"

"No," Kawika said. "No, we never found photos. We never knew they existed."

"They existed, all right. Ralph showed them to me. I told Joan I'd seen them."

"So you—?"

"So I . . . I got a little out of control. A lot out of control, actually. I wanted to force her to tell me what she knew. I'd always wanted to, uh, *have* her, I guess. And now I was really angry, really scared—like I said, I just sort of went crazy. And the awful part was this: it turned out Joan didn't know who killed Ralph, or why."

"You're right, she didn't," said Kawika. *But that wasn't the awful part.*

"I still don't know," Cushing said. "Do you?"

"Well, you pleaded to it in court," Kawika replied. "Rocco's confession fingers you directly. You owned the murder weapon. Captain Tanaka says you did it. He's my boss, and the case is closed." *That's what's true,* Kawika thought. *The whys don't matter.*

Flying home to Hilo, Kawika took a window seat so he could gaze down at Kahoʻolawe, an intensely colored long rock with yellow grass set in a white-capped, blue-green sea. Empty, the island seemed lonely and definitely bare—yet perhaps not barren, not forever.

A few months later, Kawika saw a death notice in the paper: Frank Kimaio's. On the printed page, Kimaio's name looked somehow unfamiliar. Kawika had seen it many times on his computer screen and in his reports. He'd never seen it in newspaper type. Kawika opened the Kohala phone directory and looked at Kimaio's name in type again. Still something odd about it. Kawika booted up his office computer and did a search for the name Kimaio. Nothing.

That night, Kawika awoke violently. He was thinking hard. Thinking about his own name: Kawika, a transliteration of David. Thinking about Keanu Reeves being named for Uncle Keanu, about telling Kuʻulei that perhaps the uncle's real name was Dean. And he remembered Carolyn dismissing Mele Kawena Smith: *"I bet she was born 'Mary Devine.'"* Kawika pulled on some clothes, drove to the station, and searched again, this time for Frank Dimaio, not Frank Kimaio.

And there it was on the screen: lots of hits on the name Frank Dimaio. A century earlier, it turned out, Frank Dimaio had been the Pinkerton detective who traveled to Argentina and traced Butch Cassidy and the Sundance Kid to their ranch in remotest Patagonia. By finding them, Dimaio destroyed their refuge, forced them out, and eventually they were hunted down and killed in Bolivia. Dimaio had devoted himself to avenging the lawmen who'd died at their outlaw hands. In transforming himself and choosing a new name, Frank Carlson—despite misspelling "Kawika" when typing Rocco's confession and mispronouncing Ka'ū—hadn't made a Hawaiian linguistic error after all.

Kawika drove home and slept with troubled dreams.

In the wakeful world, the world beyond dreams, the last words very nearly belonged to Leonard Cohen. One night, after he'd finished cleaning up, Dr. Terrence Smith headed for the door of the makeshift mortuary at his hospital. As he reached to turn off the light, he sang softly to himself:

> *And quiet is the thought of you,*
> *The file on you complete,*
> *Except what we forgot to do*
> *A thousand kisses deep. .*

He stopped abruptly, remembering something. He walked back to a cooler where he stored specimens. He rummaged a bit and retrieved a small bag. Crossing the room, he lifted the lid of a container marked "Biohazard— Medical Waste" and dropped the bag inside. Then he switched off the light as he left. The little bag, which he'd tossed in the trash with a satisfying plop, contained two testicles—the last earthly remains of Ralph Fortunato.

In pace requiescat.

That was nearly the end of it, but not quite. *In pace requiescat*—"rest in peace," Poe's final words in "The Cask of Amontillado"—weren't the only valedictory words Kawika pondered that winter. His mother, separated from her son by half an ocean and worried about his well-being, sent him a quotation from her favorite writer, John Fowles. It had always meant a lot to her, she said, and she thought it apt:

> *Life is not a symbol, is not one riddle and one failure to guess it, is not to*
> *inhabit one face alone or to be given up after one losing throw of the dice.*

He thought long about this. As if to confirm its wisdom—another riddle, another opportunity to guess it—the real meaning of *In pace requiescat* finally yielded itself to him. It is not the dead who need a benediction, he realized: they rest in peace no matter what. It is we the living who must find peace. The dead do not demand we make human sacrifices of ourselves. That is their benediction to us.

Eventually, Kawika allowed himself to hear that benediction. Eventually, he let life inhabit new faces and gathered the dice for another throw—and, he promised himself, for another and another, if need be.

So it was that one day Kawika decided to call Tommy—his own Waimea cop, his partner. "Tommy," he said. "I've got an idea. Let's get Terry and my dad to teach us shore fishing. You and I would make a good team, I bet. Not as good as them, maybe. But still, quite a team."

"That would be *great*," Tommy replied. "I'd really like that, Kawika. It would be nice to spend time with your dad. And I haven't seen Captain Tanaka for a long while—not since right after the press conference, when he was here in Waimea having dinner with our division chief and Frank Kimaio."

Enjoyed the read?

We'd love to hear your thoughts!

crookedlanebooks.com/feedback

Acknowledgments

The individuals I have to thank are too numerous to name, but those mentioned here played particularly important roles in helping bring this book to fruition. I thank each of them deeply.

On the Big Island, my cousin by marriage Carolyn Wong, a Native Hawaiian (and mother of the real Kuʻulei) cheerfully helped with matters of Hawaiian language and culture. Gail Mililani Makuakane-Lundin of the University of Hawaiʻi at Hilo reviewed the manuscript from a Native Hawaiian perspective and made helpful suggestions, as did her UH Hilo colleague Todd Shumway. The late Tom Hagen, a one-time activist with Save Hapuna, taught me the history and economics of South Kohala resorts. The Reverend Dr. Teruo Kawata and his wife, Kiku Kawata, then of Volcano, provided comfort and spiritual insight to our family after the 2001 murder of my brother-in-law Tom Wales, the event that prompted this novel. Dr. Cary Waterhouse, a veterinarian, shared information on feline trap-and-neuter efforts in South Kohala. Dr. Terrence Jones of North Hawaiʻi Community Hospital in Waimea, after I'd been maytagged by a wave, attended me with a big smile, an aloha cap, and aloha scrubs. Part of this book was born right then.

In the Methow Valley, my thanks and those of my wife go to Karl and Carol Ege, Dan Dingfield, the late Peter Cipra, and Delene and Bob Monetta, all of whom, in Turgenev's phrase, helped "chain us to the land," very pleasantly; also to the Methow Conservancy, a land trust that not only helps preserve the Methow but also works to sustain its people. These include— aspirationally at least—the few surviving Methows, the Native Americans whom the US Government so long ago removed to the distant Colville Reservation. Ancient wintering shelters are real, but sadly their conferring land rights on the Methow people is imaginary.

Elsewhere on the Mainland:

My lifelong friend Barbara Anderson encouraged, prodded, and poked me into writing this book. I would not have started or finished it without her. I'm immensely grateful.

Frederick C. Allen, author of *A Decent Ordinary Lynching*, a history of the Montana vigilantes, suggested valuable improvements to my manuscript, as did Hoyt Hilsman.

Gary Loomis schooled me in matters of riflery and so much else about the outdoors of the Pacific Northwest and Alaska.

The late Professor Paul A. Freund of Harvard Law School coined the phrase "like a little boy who had the chance to go to the blackboard and spell the word '*banana*' but didn't know when to stop" to describe the Supreme Court under Chief Justice Earl Warren. Blackboards are vanishing, but I thought this playful image should not be lost.

Dr. Pat Jarvis of Seattle taught me a great deal about human relationships and how we think and feel; if there are useful insights in this book, they came from Pat. One character's parting words here, however, were my late father's parting words to me.

My late brother, Michael Redman, a county prosecutor and head of the Washington Association of Prosecuting Attorneys, taught me a lot about how killers get away with murder or don't, as did James Yoshida and Nat Gasperetti, former homicide detectives with the Seattle Police Department.

James and Deborah Fallows are special friends who always give generously of their time to encourage and support my literary efforts, including this time, while writing bestsellers of their own.

My skillful literary agent Anne Depue has shown great patience and good humor; she's been a boon companion on the winding road to publication. My friend and assistant, Terrell Bond, helped me with research and organization throughout.

Karen Schober drew the excellent maps, working from earlier versions by Jane Shasky.

Friends who were kind enough to read earlier versions of the manuscript include Earl Gjelde, Caroline Hagen, Chris Lynn, and Brett Wilcox.

At Crooked Lane Press, my editor, Ben LeRoy, saw the promise of this tale and was indefatigable in his efforts to see that promise realized; his many observations and suggestions vastly improved it, for which I am grateful. Melissa Rechter and Madeline Rathle of Crooked Lane did the work of converting the manuscript into a book and launching it into the world. I thank them both, as well as Jill Pellarin for excellent copyediting.

My wife, Heather Redman, and our three children, Ian, Graham, and Jing, have all been extraordinarily supportive throughout my efforts to bring this tale to the printed page. They deserve special thanks.

To all those named above, and the many more who've helped without recognition, I express my sincere gratitude. If errors remain, they are mine alone.

Kawaihae, Seattle, and Decatur Island 2020